THE
SECRET
HISTORY
OF FANTASY

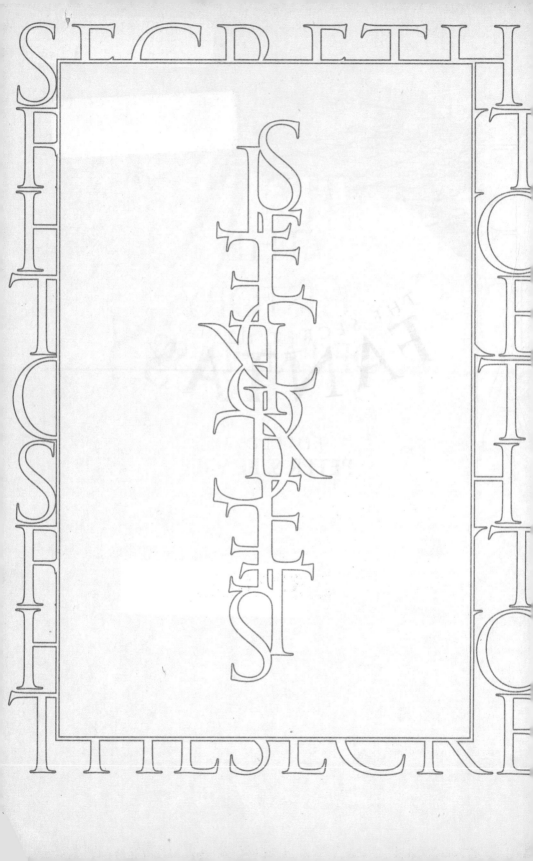

THE SECRET HISTORY OF
FANTASY

EDITED BY
PETER S. BEAGLE

TACHYON

THE SECRET HISTORY OF FANTASY
© 2010 BY PETER S. BEAGLE
INTERIOR DESIGN BY JOHN COULTHART
COVER DESIGN BY ANN MONN

TACHYON PUBLICATIONS
1459 18TH STREET #139
SAN FRANCISCO, CA 94107
(415) 285-5615
WWW.TACHYONPUBLICATIONS.COM
TACHYON@TACHYONPUBLICATIONS.COM

SERIES EDITOR: JACOB WEISMAN

ISBN 13: 978-1-892391-99-5
ISBN 10: 1-892391-99-6

PRINTED IN THE UNITED STATES
OF AMERICA BY WORZALLA
FIRST EDITION: 2010
9 8 7 6 5 4 3 2 1

In memory of Robert Holdstock,
1948–2009

And with gratitude to
Ellen Datlow, John Kessel,
Jill Roberts, Bernie Goodman,
and Jacob Weisman

THE SECRET HISTORY OF FANTASY

INTRODUCTION

PETER S. BEAGLE

I HAVE WRITTEN elsewhere that there was a time when all literature was fantasy. How could it have been otherwise, when a bad corn crop or a sudden epidemic among the new lambs could only have been caused by the anger of some god, or the spiteful sorcery of the people in the next village, eight miles over the hill, who were all demons, as everyone knew? Story then, in every part of the world, was a means of keeping the inhabited dark at bay, and of making some kind of sense out of survival. Even the best and most ambitious of post-Tolkien multi-volume epics inevitably miss that air of great art being first born of terror and ignorance. *Beowulf*, *Gilgamesh*, and the *Popol Vuh* were all created in darkness.

Much of what I glance over in the following pages is covered in greater and more knowledgeable detail further on by David Hartwell. David is a walking history of fantasy in general, and of American and European fantasy publication in particular. If I'm the *Reader's Digest* version, he's the Oxford University Press all by himself, and I'm both proud and grateful to include his contribution in the appendix to this book, along with Ursula K. Le Guin's classic essay "The Critics, the Monsters, and the Fantasists." Together, they make transparent, once and for all, the simple — yet long-disregarded — truth that the best fantasy is as much art as the best of any other form of storytelling. The critical bars on no account need to be lowered.

The segregation of fantasy from actual literature is a comparatively recent business, certainly no older than I am, and I'll be seventy-one in April. Genre fiction, as we understand the term — mystery stories, Gothic horror tales, and romances (Westerns came along a bit later) — appeared as early as the eighteenth century, along with the earliest stories written specifically for children; even so, writers today regarded as classic fantasists, like Lewis Carroll, Kenneth Grahame, Lord Dunsany, James Branch Cabell, Arthur Machen, H. G. Wells, H. Rider Haggard, and William Hope Hodgson, were all recognized as serious mainstream artists in their time. Cabell's novel *Jurgen*, in particular, was the target of a two-year obscenity trial, brought by the New York Society for the Suppression of Vice; it did wonders for sales, and remains his best-known book today.

Later, despite the continued flowering of pulp magazines with titles in the vein of *Thrilling Wonder Stories*, *Astounding*, *Amazing*, *Captain Future*, and *Comet Stories*, such utterly diverse writers as Thorne Smith, Robert Nathan, E. R. Eddison, Clark Ashton Smith, John Collier, Jack Finney, and T. H. White were considered and discussed in major critical venues, like anyone else. In 1954, the *New York Times* devoted the front page of its *Sunday Book Review* to W. H. Auden's laudatory essay on *The Lord of the Rings*; and similar space, in 1958, to White's *The Once and Future King*. As late as the 1960s, my own novels *A Fine & Private Place* and *The Last Unicorn* both received serious individual reviews, just as though they were *real* books, worthy of such attention. I took it for granted then — I wouldn't today.

The above doesn't mean, incidentally, that all of the writers I've mentioned found commercial success, or even made a decent living from their work. When they did strike it rich, it was most often due to a fortunate, usually irreproducible circumstance, as with Cabell's obscenity trial. *The Lord of the Rings*, for instance, was no sort of a bestseller when Houghton Mifflin first published it in this country; nor did it become one for more than ten years. I remember being unable to find it in any bookstore until, in 1958, as a student at the University of Pittsburgh, I ran the books to earth at the Carnegie Library, and disappeared into my dorm room for three days. It was the more affordable paperbacks (first published in the "pirate" edition by Ace Books; then, with Tolkien's formidable sanction, by Ballantine), that set off the great *LOTR* craze, still as yet unmatched, in the long term, even by Harry Potter. We'll consider the full effect of this phenomenon further in a moment.

THE SECRET HISTORY OF FANTASY

My early fascination with fantasy (and my tastes ranged from Cabellian elegance to Robert E. Howard's thud-and-blunder sagas, to Algernon Blackwood's deadpan English manner of showing you cold horror without a vampire or a shoggoth in sight) at least saved me from spending my youth chasing the images of Ernest Hemingway and F. Scott Fitzgerald. It's probably hard today to imagine a time when young male American writers gathered commonly in pubs, university lounges, and party kitchens to debate in all seriousness — I give you my solemn word — whether one ought to shoot lions, run with bulls, or report on wars and revolutions, like Hemingway, or frolic in nightclub fountains, drunk as skunks, like Scott and Zelda. But I'd already discovered Collier and James Stephens in high school, Robert Nathan in college (along with such playwrights as Giraudoux, Anouilh, and Alejandro Casona, whose works were always touched by the fantastic); and I can't remember not knowing the work of Dunsany and White. Neither death in the afternoon nor the beautiful and damned of New York society were my problem.

Robert Nathan, with whom I became friends for the last twenty-odd years of his life, said to me once, "I read Dunsany and Machen when I was young, and I met Cabell once or twice, in the twenties, but I never considered them a literary school or generation of any sort. They didn't especially write alike, didn't meet regularly for lunch — if they have anything in common, I'd say it's that they were a remarkably individual lot who mostly went their own ways." When I asked if he thought of himself as a fantasy writer, he answered, "No — I work around the edges, if you like, but in the end I write what I like to read, like the rest of us. Your boy Bradbury, that windbag Tolkien, *they're* fantasy writers."

Maybe what I'm getting at — and what Robert meant — is that the division between fantasy writers and writers who wrote fantasy wasn't nearly as distinct during most of his publishing career as it has become in recent decades. Kipling wrote fantasy stories; so did Hawthorne, Dickens, and his buddy Wilkie Collins, Conan Doyle, Stevenson, Saki — yet none of them are today thought of as genre fantasists. By contrast, Tad Williams, Patricia McKillip, Guy Gavriel Kay, or Charles de Lint would be forever branded fantasy writers if they devoted the rest of their lives to novels about the emotional travails of aging Congressmen, or footnote-heavy academic studies of the later work of Coventry Patmore. So, for that matter, would I, and I've got a couple of plain historical novels I'm still planning to get to. Well, for Americans, history's largely fantasy anyway, so maybe that's all right.

I personally trace the turning point, the specific moment when commercial fantasy abandoned the realm of literature to the day in 1977 when Judy-Lynn Del Rey, my editor at Ballantine Books, whom I'd known and been fond of since she was Judy-Lynn Benjamin, not all that long out of college, working at *Galaxy* magazine, sent me a massive manuscript of a book called *The Sword of Shannara*, by Terry Brooks, asking for comment and, if I would be so good, a jacket quote. David Hartwell goes into much greater detail concerning the significance of this action: I can only relate my minuscule part in it. After getting no more than a couple of chapters into the manuscript, I called Judy-Lynn in New York, and told her that the book was not only a rip-off of *The Lord of the Rings*, but a tenth-rate rip-off at that, and that she must know it herself. Judy-Lynn loved good writing, and she was no fool.

"Never mind," Judy-Lynn said firmly over the phone. "I know what I'm doing, and Ballantine's going to make a million with this book." (A million dollars was actual money way back then.) "This one's for people who've read the Tolkien books forty times, and can't quite get it up for the forty-first — but they still want the mixture as before. Watch, watch, you'll see. I know what I'm doing."

She did, of course. Judy-Lynn almost always did. My sole contribution was to propose that the novel's gnomes — nasty equivalents of Tolkien's orcs — not be continually identified by the epithet "little yellow men." I have no idea whether or not my suggestion was ever accepted.

The astonishing success of *The Sword of Shannara* meant not only that Ballantine/Del Rey Books would dominate all publishers of fantasy for at least a literary generation, but that the systematic production of what was officially dubbed "sword-and-sorcery" fiction would come to overwhelm the field almost altogether. I can still recall being in Forbidden Planet, the well-known New York City science-fiction bookstore, with my best friend in the late 1980s, peering dazedly down rows of unfamiliar paperbacks, most with mock-Frazetta covers featuring muscular, barechested northern-barbarian types rescuing similarly muscular barechested damsels from assorted monsters, and hearing my friend whisper in utter bewilderment, "Peter, who *are* these people?" I couldn't tell him.

In the wake of the success of *The Lord of the Rings*, and of other fantasy novels (disclosure: these included *The Last Unicorn* and *A Fine & Private Place*), in 1969 Del Rey Books hired Lin Carter as a consultant, to select and present their new "Adult Fantasy" line. I have extremely mixed feelings about this series: not about the books themselves — Carter brought some superb old stylists, from Dunsany, William Morris and Machen, to William Beckford, Ernest Bramah, and George MacDonald, as well as younger writers like Katherine Kurtz and Joy Chant, and overlooked gems like Hope Mirrlees and the great Evangeline Walton, back into the public eye — but about his introductions, and his full-length studies of Tolkien and H. P. Lovecraft. In all of them, he gets so many facts embarrassingly wrong, so many attributions misquoted, that the entire commentary is essentially worthless. Further, although the Adult Fantasy series lasted only five remarkable years, ending in 1974, when Ian and Betty Ballantine sold their company to Random House, Carter's Tolkien-derived theories of secondary worlds created a blueprint for modern fantasy that paved the way for the coming, a few years later, of "Shannara"-esque genre fiction. Overall, his influence on the field has to be regarded as, if not malign… unfortunate.

(And yet, he praised my brilliant, unique, and vastly undervalued old friend, Avram Davidson, at great length — however inaccurately — and he introduced me to the work of John Bellairs, whom I'd never heard of before, and came to know and admire before his death. He did get *some* things right, and I owe him for those.)

But I read a lot less fantasy than I used to in those days. Without wishing to offend, or to name names, Gresham's Law applies in popular art, as in economics: the bad, or the mediocre, drives out the good, if only because there's so much more of it produced that the good goes either unrecognized, unpublished, or — in time — unproduced. I offer the work of Barry Hughart as a perfect example: his three classic novels about Master Li (a sage with "a slight flaw in his character") and his loyal disciple and Watson, Number Ten Ox, appearing in the 1980s, were so completely ignored by his publishers — who never bothered to inform him when the first, *Bridge of Birds*, won the World Fantasy Award in 1985 — that Hughart simply gave up on fiction from that point. Our loss, and a major one.

Yet in an age full of its own fear and ignorance, its own distances and superstitions, the cold and the darkness still generate legendry. Despite the decades-long deluge of imitations of his work that I'm always grateful Tolkien didn't live to see, there are still representatives of an older, eclectic fantasy tradition to be found within reach, and, miraculously, even within print. Leaving the masters of Latin-American "magical realism" out of the discussion, which I do with great reluctance, books like Yann Martel's *Life of Pi*, Robin McKinley's *Beauty*, Susanna Clarke's *Jonathan Strange & Mr Norrell*, Gregory Maguire's *Wicked*, Michael Swanwick's *The Dragons of Babel*, and a growing number of others suggest that inventive, imaginatively written tales that require neither High Elves nor Dark Lords, nor endpaper maps, kings' genealogies, and programmed sequels are thriving elsewhere than the airport bookstore racks. You have only to look.

I am immensely proud and vain of the authors assembled in this anthology, not only for their stories themselves, but for what their presence proves: that Frodo may well live, as the New York subway graffiti of the 1960s defiantly insisted, but that other worlds and quests and heroes do too, and not all of them have a thing to do with Armageddon and magic rings.

ANCESTOR MONEY

MAUREEN F. MCHUGH

IN THE AFTERLIFE, Rachel lived alone. She had a clapboard cabin and a yard full of gray geese which she could feed or not and they would do fine. Purple morning glories grew by the kitchen door. It was always an early summer morning and had been since her death. At first, she had wondered if this were some sort of Catholic afterlife. She neither felt the presence of God nor missed his absence. But in the stasis of this summer morning, it was difficult to wonder or worry, year after year.

The honking geese told her someone was coming. Geese were better than dogs, and maybe meaner. It was Speed. "Rachel?" he called from the fence.

She had barely known Speed in life — he was her husband's uncle and not a person she had liked or approved of. But she had come to enjoy his company when she no longer had to fear sin or bad companions.

"Rachel," he said, "you've got mail. From China."

She came and stood in the doorway, shading her eyes from the day. "What?" she said.

"You've got mail from China," Speed said. He held up an envelope. It was big, made of some stiff red paper, and sealed with a darker red bit of wax.

She had never received mail before. "Where did you get it?" she asked.

"It was in the mailbox at the end of the hollow," Speed said. He said "holler" for "hollow." Speed had a thick brush of wiry black hair that never combed flat without hair grease.

"There's no mailbox there," she said.

"Is now."

"Heavens, Speed. Who put you up to this," she said.

"It's worse 'n that. No one did. Open it up."

She came down and took it from him. There were Chinese letters going up and down on the left side of the envelope. The stamp was as big as the palm of her hand. It was a white crane flying against a gilt background. Her name was right there in the middle in beautiful black ink.

Rachel Ball
b. 1892 d. 1927
Swan Pond Hollow, Kentucky
United States

Speed was about to have apoplexy, so Rachel put off opening it, turning the envelope over a couple of times. The red paper had a watermark in it of twisting Chinese dragons, barely visible. It was an altogether beautiful object.

She opened it with reluctance.

Inside it read:

Honorable Ancestress of Amelia Shaugnessy: an offering of death money and goods has been made to you at Tin Hau Temple in Yau Ma Tei, in Hong Kong. If you would like to claim it, please contact us either by letter or phone. HK8-555-4444.

There were more Chinese letters, probably saying the same thing.

"What is it?" Speed asked.

She showed it to him.

"Ah," he said.

"You know about this?" she asked.

"No," he said, "except that the Chinese do that ancestor worship. Are you going to call?"

She went back inside and he followed her. His boots clumped on the floor. She was barefoot and so made no noise. "You want some coffee?" she asked.

"No," he said. "Are you going to write back?"

"I'm going to call," she said. Alexander Graham Bell had thought that the phone would eventually allow communication with the spirits of the dead and so the link between the dead and phones had been established. Rachel had a cell phone she had never used. She dialed it now, standing in the middle of her clean kitchen, the hem of her skirt damp from the yard and clinging cool around her calves.

The phone rang four times and then a voice said, *"Wei."*

"Hello?" she said.

"Wei," said the voice again. *"Wei?"*

"Hello, do you speak English?" she said.

There was the empty sound of ether in the airwaves. Rachel frowned at Speed.

Then a voice said, "Hello? Yes?"

Rachel thought it was the same voice, accented but clear. It did not sound human, but had a reedy, hollow quality.

"This is Rachel Ball. I got an envelope that said I should call this number about, um," she checked the letter, "death money." Rachel had not been able to read very well in life but it was one of those things that had solved itself in the afterlife.

"Ah. Rachel Ball. A moment…"

"Yes," she said.

"Yes. It is a substantial amount of goods and money. Would you like to claim it?"

"Yes," she said.

"Hold on," said the voice. She couldn't tell if it was male or female.

"What's going on?" Speed asked.

Rachel waved her hand to shush him.

"Honorable Ancestress, your claim has been recorded. You may come at any time within the next ninety days to claim it," said the strange, reedy voice.

"Go there?" she asked.

"Yes," said the voice.

"Can you send it?"

"Alas," said the voice, "we cannot." And the connection was closed.

"Wait," she said. But when she pushed redial, she went directly to voicemail. It was in Chinese.

Speed was watching her, thoughtful. She looked at her bare feet and curled her toes.

"Are you going to go?" Speed asked her.

"I guess," she said. "Do you want to come?"

"I traveled too much in life," he said and that was all. Rachel had never gone more than twenty-five miles from Swan Pond in life and had done less in death. But Speed had been a hobo in the Depression, leaving his wife and kids without a word and traveling the south and the west. Rachel did not understand why Speed was in heaven, or why some people were here and some people weren't, or where the other people were. She had figured her absence of concern was part of being dead.

Rachel had died, probably of complications from meningitis, in 1927, in Swan Pond, Kentucky. She had expected that Robert, her husband, would eventually be reunited with her. But in life, Robert had remarried badly and had seven more children, two of whom died young. She saw Robert now and again and felt nothing but distant affection for him. He had moved on in life, and even in death he was not her Robert anymore.

But now something flickered in her that was a little like discontent. Amelia Shaugnessy was…her granddaughter. Child of her third child and second daughter, Evelyn. Amelia had sent her an offering. Rachel touched her fingers to her lips, thinking. She touched her hair.

What was it she had talked to on the phone? Some kind of Chinese spirit? Not an angel. "I'll tell you about it when I get back," she said.

She did not take anything. She did not even close the door.

"Rachel," Speed said from her door. She stopped with her hand on the gate. "Are you going to wear shoes?" he asked.

"Do you think I need them?" she asked.

He shrugged.

The geese were gathered in a soft gray cluster by the garden at the side of the little clapboard cabin where they had been picking among the tomato plants. All their heads were turned towards her.

THE SECRET HISTORY OF FANTASY

She went out the gate. The road was full of pale dust like talcum powder, already warmed by the sun. It felt so good she was glad that she hadn't worn shoes.

As she walked, she seemed to walk forward in time. She came down and out the hollow, past a white farmhouse with a barn and silo and a radio in the windowsill playing a Reds baseball game against the Padres. A black Rambler was parked in the driveway and laundry hung drying in the breeze, white sheets belling out.

Where the road met the highway was a neat brick ranch house with a paved driveway and a patient German shepherd lying in the shade under a tree. There was a television antenna like a lightning rod. The German shepherd watched her but did not bark.

She waited at the highway and after a few minutes, saw a Greyhound bus coming through the valley, following the Laurel River. She watched it through the curves, listening to the grinding down and back up of its gears. The sign on the front of the bus said Lexington, so that was where she supposed she would go next.

The bus stopped in front of her, sighing, and the door opened.

By the time she got to Lexington, the bus had modernized. It had a bathroom and the windows were tinted smoky colored. Highway 25 had become Interstate 75 and outside the window, they were passing horse farms with white board fence rising and falling across bluegreen fields. High-headed horses with manes like women's hair that shone in the sun.

"Airport, first," the driver called. "Then bus terminal with connections to Cincinnati, New York City and Sausalito, California." She thought he sounded northern.

Rachel stepped down from the bus in front of the terminal. The tarmac was pleasantly warm. As the bus pulled out, the breeze from its passing belled her skirt and tickled the back of her neck. She wondered if perhaps she should have worn a hat.

She wasn't afraid — what could happen to her here? She was dead. The bus had left her off in front of glass doors that opened to some invisible prompt. Across a cool and airy space was a counter for Hong Kong Air, and behind it, a diminutive Chinese woman in a green suit and a tiny green pillbox cap trimmed with gold. Her name tag said "Jade Girl" but her skin was as white as porcelain teeth.

Rachel hesitated for the first time since she had walked away from her own gate. This grandchild of hers who had sent her money, what obligation had she placed on Rachel? For more than seventy years, far longer than she had lived, Rachel had been at peace in her little clapboard house on the creek, up in the hollow. She missed the companionable sound of the geese and the longing was painful in a way she had forgotten. She was so startled by the emotion that she lifted her hand to her silent heart.

"May I help you?" the woman asked.

Wordlessly, Rachel showed her the envelope.

"Mrs. Ball?" the woman behind the counter said. "Your flight is not leaving for a couple of hours. But I have your ticket."

She held out the ticket, a gaudy red plastic thing with golden dragons and black. Rachel took it because it was held out to her. The Chinese woman had beautiful hands, but Rachel had the hands of a woman who gardened — clean but not manicured or soft.

The ticket made something lurch within her and she was afraid. Afraid. She had not been afraid for more than seventy years. And she was barefoot and hadn't brought a hat.

"If you would like to shop while you are waiting," the woman behind the counter said, and gestured with her hand. There were signs above them that said "Terminal A/Gates 1-24A" with an arrow, and "Terminal B/Gates 1-15B." "There are shops along the concourse," the Chinese woman said.

Rachel looked at her ticket. Amidst the Chinese letters it said "Gate 4A." She looked back up at the sign. "Thank you," she said.

The feeling of fear had drained from her like water in sand and she felt herself again. What had that been about, she wondered. She followed the arrows to a brightly lit area full of shops. There was a book shop and a flower shop, a shop with postcards and salt-and-pepper shakers and stuffed animals. It also had sandals, plastic things in bright colors.

Rachel's skirt was pale blue so she picked a pair of blue ones. They weren't regular sandals. The sign said flip-flops and they had a strap sort of business that went between the big toe and second toe that felt odd. But she decided if they bothered her too much, she could always carry them.

She picked a postcard of a beautiful horse and found a pen on the counter. There was no shop girl. She wrote, "Dear Simon, The bus trip was pleasant." That was Speed's actual name. She paused, not sure what else to say. She thought about telling him about the odd sensations she had had at the ticket counter but didn't know how to explain it. So she just wrote, "I will leave for Hong Kong in a few hours. Sincerely, Rachel."

She addressed it to Simon Philpot, Swan Pond Hollow. At the door to the shop there was a mailbox on a post. She put the card in and raised the flag. She thought of him getting the card out of the new mailbox at the end of the hollow and a ghost of the heartsickness stirred in her chest. So she walked away, as she had from her own gate that morning, her new flip-flops snapping a little as she went. Partway down the concourse she thought of something she wanted to add and turned and went back to the mailbox. She was going to write, "I am not sure about this." But the flag was down and when she opened the mailbox, the card was already gone.

There were other people at Gate 4A. One of them was Chinese with a blue face and black around his eyes. His eyes were wide, the whites visible all the way around the very black pupils. He wore strange shoes with upturned toes, red leggings, elaborate red armor and a strange red hat. He was reading a Chinese newspaper.

Rachel sat a couple of rows away from the demon. She fanned herself with the beautiful red envelope, although she wasn't warm. There was a TV and on it a balding man was telling people what they should and should not do. He was some sort of doctor, Dr. Phil. He said oddly rude things and the people sat, hands folded like children, and nodded.

"Collecting ancestor money?" a man asked. He wore a dark suit, white shirt and tie and a fedora. "My son married a Chinese girl and every year I have to make this trip." He smiled.

"You've done this before?" Rachel asked. "Is it safe?"

The man shrugged. "It's different," he said. "I get a new suit. They're great tailors. It's a different afterlife, though. Buddhist and all."

Buddhism. Detachment. And for a moment, it felt as if everything swirled around her, a moment of vertigo. Rachel found herself unwilling to think about Buddhism.

The man was still talking. "You know, I can still feel how strongly my son wants things. The pull of the living and their way of obliging us," he said, and chuckled.

Rachel had not felt much obligation to the living for years. Of her children, all but two were dead. There was almost no one still alive who remembered her. "What about?" She pointed at the demon.

"Don't look at him," the man said, quietly.

Rachel looked down at her lap, at the envelope and the plastic ticket. "I'm not sure I should have come," she said.

"Most people don't," the man said. "What's your seat number?"

Rachel looked at her ticket. Now, in addition to saying "Gate 4A," it also said, "Seat 7a."

"I was hoping we were together," said the man. "But I'm afraid I'm 12D. Aisle seat. I prefer the aisle. 7A. That's a window seat. You'll be able to see the stars."

She could see the stars at home.

"There's the plane," he said.

She could hear the whine of it, shrill, like metal on metal. It was a big passenger 747, red on top and silver underneath, with a long, swirling gold dragon running the length of the plane. She didn't like it.

She stayed with the man with the fedora through boarding. A young man in a golden suit, narrow and perfectly fitted, took their tickets. The young man's name tag said "Golden Boy." His face was as pale as platinum. At the door of the plane, there were two women in those beautiful green suits and little pillbox stewardess hats, both identical to the girl at the counter. Standing, Rachel could see that their skirts fell to their ankles but were slit up one side almost to the knee. Their nametags both said "Jade Girl." On the plane, the man with the fedora pointed out to Rachel where her seat was.

She sat down and looked out the window. In the time they had been waiting for the plane, it had started to get dark, although she could not yet see the first star.

They landed in Hong Kong at dawn, coming in low across the harbor, which was smooth and shined like pewter. They came closer and closer to the water until it seemed they were skimming it and then, suddenly, there was land and runway and the chirp of their wheels touching down.

Rachel's heart gave a painful thump and she said, "Oh," quite involuntarily, and put her hand to her chest. Under her hand she felt her heart lurch again and she gasped, air filling her quiet lungs until they creaked a bit and found elasticity. Her heart beat and filled her with — she did not know at first with what and then she realized it was excitement. Rising excitement and pleasure and fear in an intoxicating mix. Colors were sharp and when one of the Jade Girls cracked the door to the plane, the air had an uncertain tang — sweet and, underneath that, a many-people odor like old socks.

"Welcome to the Fragrant Harbor," the Jade Girls chorused, their voices so similar that they sounded like a single voice. The man with the fedora passed her and looked back over his shoulder and smiled. She followed him down the aisle, realizing only after she stood that the demon was now behind her. The demon smelled like wet charcoal and she could feel the heat of his body as if he were a furnace. She did not look around. Outside, there were steps down to the tarmac and the heat took her breath away, but a fresh wind blew off the water. Rachel skimmed off her flip-flops so they wouldn't trip her up and went down the stairs to China.

A Golden Boy was waiting for her, as a Jade Girl had been waiting for the man with the fedora. "Welcome to San-qing, the Heaven of Highest Purity," he said.

"I am supposed to be in Hong Kong," Rachel said. She dropped her flip-flops and stepped into them.

"This is the afterlife of Hong Kong," he said. "Are you here to stay?"

"No," she said. "I got a letter." She showed him the Chinese envelope.

"Ah," he said. "Tin Hau Temple. Excellent. And congratulations.

Would you like a taxi or would you prefer to take a bus? The fares will be charged against the monies you collect."

"Which would you recommend?" she asked.

"On the bus, people may not speak English," he said. "So you won't know where to get off. And you would have to change to get to Yau Ma Tei. I recommend a taxi."

"All right," she said. People wouldn't speak English? Somehow it had never occurred to her. Maybe she should have seen if someone would come with her. This granddaughter, maybe she had burned ancestor money for Robert as well. Why not? Robert was her grandfather. She didn't know any of them, so why would she favor Rachel? That had been foolish, not checking to see if Robert had wanted to come. He hadn't been on the plane, but maybe he wouldn't come by himself. Maybe he'd gone to find Rachel and she'd already been gone.

She hadn't been lonely before she came here.

The Golden Boy led her through the airport. It was a cavernous space, full of people, all of whom seemed to be shouting. Small women with bowed legs, carrying string bags full of oranges and men squatting along the wall, smoking cigarettes and grinning at her as she passed with the Golden Boy. There were monkeys everywhere, dressed in Chinese gowns and little caps, speaking the same language as the people. Monkeys were behind the counters and monkeys were pushing carts and monkeys were hawking Chinese newspapers. Some of the monkeys were tiny black things with wizened white faces and narrow hands and feet that were as shiny as black patent leather. Some were bigger and waddled, walking on their legs like men. They had stained yellow teeth and fingernails the same color as their hands. They were businesslike. One of the little ones shouted something in Chinese in a curiously human voice as she passed, and then shrieked like an animal, baring its teeth at another monkey. She started.

The Golden Boy smiled, unperturbed.

Out front, he flagged a taxi. The car that pulled up was yellow with a white top and said Toyota and Crown Comfort on the back — it had pulled past them and the Golden Boy grabbed her elbow and hustled her to it. Rachel expected the driver to be a monkey but he was a human.

The Golden Boy leaned into the front seat and shouted at the driver in Chinese. The driver shouted back.

Rachel felt exhausted. She should never have come here. Her poor heart! She would go back home.

The Golden Boy opened the back door and bowed to her and walked away.

"Wait!" she called.

But he was already inside the airport.

The driver said something gruff to her and she jumped into the taxi. It had red velour seats and smelled strongly of cigarette smoke. The driver swung the car out into traffic so sharply that her door banged shut. A big gold plastic bangle with long red tassels swayed below his mirror. He pointed to it and said, "Hong Kong in-sur-ance pol-i-cy," and smiled at her, friendly and pleased at his joke, if it was a joke.

"I've changed my mind," she said. "I want to go back home."

But apparently, "Hong Kong insurance policy" was most, if not all, of his English. He smiled up into his rearview mirror. His teeth were brown and some were missing.

This was not what Rachel thought of as death.

The street was full of cars, bicycles, single-piston two-cycle tractors and palanquins. Her driver swung through and around them. They stopped at an intersection to wait for the light to change. Two men were putting down one of the palanquins. In it was a woman sitting in a chair. The woman put a hand on one of the men's shoulders and stood up carefully. Her gown was a swirl of greenish blues and silvers and golds. Her face was turned away but she was wearing a hat like a fox's head. There was something about her feet that was odd — they looked no bigger than the palm of a human hand. Rachel thought, "She's walking on her toes." The woman looked over towards the taxi and Rachel saw that it wasn't a hat, that the woman had marvelous golden fox eyes and that the tip of her tongue just protruded from her muzzle, doglike. The light changed and the taxi accelerated up a hill, pushing Rachel back into her seat, queasy.

Narrow streets strung overhead with banners. The smells — dried fish and worse — made Rachel feel more and more sick. Nausea brought with it visceral memories of three years of illness before she died, of confusion and fear and pee in the bed. She had not forgotten before, but she hadn't felt it. Now she felt the memories.

The streets were so narrow that the driver's mirror clipped the shoulder of a pedestrian as they passed. The mirror folded in a bit and then snapped out and the angry startled cry dopplered behind them. Rachel kept expecting the face of the driver to change, maybe into a pig, or worse, the demon from the plane.

The taxi lurched to a stop. "Okay," the driver said and grinned into the mirror. His face was the same human face as when they had started. The red letters on the meter said $72.40. And then they blinked three times and said $00.00. When Rachel hadn't moved, the driver said, "Okay," again and said something in Chinese.

She didn't know how to open the car door.

He got out and came around and opened the door. She got out.

"Okay!" he said cheerfully and jumped back in and took off, leaving the smell of exhaust.

She was standing in an alley barely wider than the taxi. Both sides of the alley were long red walls, punctuated by wide doors, all closed. A man jogged past her with a long stick over his shoulders with baskets on both ends. The stick was bowed with the weight and flexed with each step. Directly in front of her was a red door set with studs. If she tilted her head back, above the wall she could see a building with curved eaves, rising tier upon tier like some exotic wedding cake.

The door opened easily when she pushed on it.

Inside was the temple, and in front of it, a slate-stone paved courtyard. A huge bronze cauldron filled with sand had incense sticks smoking in it, and she smelled sandalwood. After the relative quiet of the alley, the temple was loud with people. A Chinese band was playing a cacophony of drums and gongs, *chong, chong, chang-chong,* while a woman stood nodding and smiling. The band was clearly playing for her. Rachel didn't think the music sounded very musical.

There were red pillars holding up the eaves of the temple, and the whole front of the building was open, so that the courtyard simply became the temple. Inside was dim and smelled even more strongly of sandalwood. A huge curl of the incense hung down in a cone from the ceiling. The inside of the temple was full of birds; not the pleasant, comforting and domestic animals her geese were. They had long sweeping tails and sharply pointed wings and they flickered from ground to eaves and watched with bright, black, reptilian eyes. People ignored them.

A man in a narrow white suit came up to her, talking to the air in Chinese. He was wearing sunglasses. It took her a moment to realize that he was not talking to some unseen spirit, but was wearing a headset for a cell phone, most of which was invisible in his jet-black hair. He pushed the mic down away from his face a little and addressed her in Chinese.

"Do you speak English?" she asked. She had not gotten accustomed to this hammering heart of hers.

"No English," he said and said some more in Chinese.

The envelope and letter had Chinese letters on it. She handed it to him. After she had handed it to him, it occurred to her that she didn't know if he had anything to do with the temple or if he was, perhaps, some sort of confidence man.

He pulled the sunglasses down his nose and looked over them to read the letter. His lips moved slightly as he read. He pulled the mic back up and said something into it, then pulled a thin cell phone no bigger than a business card and tapped some numbers out with his thumb.

"Wei!" he shouted into the phone.

He handed her back the letter and beckoned for her to follow, then crossed the temple, walking fast and weaving between people without seeming to have had to adjust. Rachel had to trot to keep up with him, nearly stepping out of her foolish flip-flops.

In an alcove off to one side, the wall was painted with a mural of a Hong Kong street with cars and buses and red-and-white taxis, traffic lights and crosswalks. But no Jade Girls or fox-headed women, no palanquins or tractors. Everything in it looked very contemporary; the light reflecting off the plate-glass windows, the briefcases and fur coats. As contemporary as the white-suited man. The man held up his hand that she was to wait here. He disappeared back into the crowd.

She thought about going back out and getting in a taxi and going back to the airport. Would she need money? She hadn't needed money to get here, although they had told her that the amount of the taxi had been subtracted from her money. Did she have enough to get back? What if she had to stay here? What would she do?

An old woman in a gray tunic and black pants said, "Rachel Ball?"

"Yes?"

"I am Miss Lily. I speak English. I can help you," the woman said. "May I see your notification?"

Rachel did not know what a "notification" was. "All I have is this letter," she said. The letter had marks from handling, as if her hands had been moist. What place was this where the dead perspired?

"Ah," said Miss Lily. "That is it. Very good. Would you like your money in bills or in a debit card?"

"Is it enough to get me home?" Rachel asked.

"Oh, yes," Miss Lily said. "Much more than that."

"Bills," Rachel said. She did not care about debit cards.

"Very good," said Miss Lily. "And would you like to make arrangements to sell your goods, or will you be shipping them?"

"What do people do with money?" Rachel asked.

"They use it to buy things, to buy food and goods, just as they do in life. You are a Christian, aren't you?"

"Baptist," Rachel said. "But is this all there is for Chinese people after they die? The same as being alive? What happens to people who have no money?"

"People who have no money have nothing," said Miss Lily. "So they have to work. But this is the first of the seven heavens. People who are good here progress up through the heavens. And if they continue, they will eventually reach a state of what you would call transcendence, what we call the three realms, when they are beyond this illusion of matter."

"Can they die here?"

Miss Lily inclined her head. "Not die, but if they do not progress, they can go into the seven hells."

"But I have enough money to get back home," Rachel said. "And if I left you the rest of it, the money and the goods, could you give it to someone here who needs it?

"At home you will not progress," Miss Lily said gently.

That stopped Rachel. She would go back to her little clapboard cabin and her geese and everything would become as timeless as it had been before. Here she would progress.

Progress for what? She was dead. Death is eternity.

She had been dead for over seventy years, and she would be dead forever and forever. Dead longer than those buried in the tombs of Egypt, where the dead had been prepared for an afterlife as elaborate as this one. In her mind, forever spread back and forward through the epochs of dinosaurs, her time of seventy years getting smaller and smaller in proportion. Through the four billion years of the earth.

And still farther back and forward, through the time it took the pinwheel galaxy to turn, the huge span of a galactic day, and a galactic year, in which everything recognizable grew dwarfed.

And she would be dead.

Progress meant nothing.

It made no difference what she chose.

And she was back at her gate in Swan Pond standing in the talcum dust and it was no difference if this was 1927 or 2003 or 10,358. Hong Kong left behind in the blink of an eye. She wasn't surprised. In front of her was the empty clapboard cabin, no longer white-painted and tidy but satiny gray with age. The windows were empty of glass and curtains and under a lowering evening sky, a wind rhythmically slapped a shutter against the abandoned house. The tomatoes were gone to weeds, and there were no geese to greet her.

And it did not matter.

A great calm settled over her and her unruly heart quieted in her chest.

Everything was still.

SCARECROW

GREGORY MAGUIRE

WHAT'S THE FIRST thing you know in life? Even before you know words? Sun in the sky. Heart of gold in a field of blue, and the world cracks open. You are knowing something. There you are.

As with all of us, the Scarecrow awoke knowing he had *been* for some time already, though unwoken. There was a sense of vanishing splendor in the world about him, an echo of a lost sound even before he knew what *sound* or *echo* meant. The backward crush of time and, also, time's forward rush. The knife of light between his eyes. The wound of hollowness behind his forehead. There was motion, sound, color; there was scent, depth, hope. There was already, in the first fifteen seconds, *then* and *now*.

Before him were two fields. One was filled with ripening corn. The other was shorn clean, and grew only a gallows tree in the dead center.

Beyond the fields huddled a low farmhouse, painted blue. And beyond the farmhouse rose a hill, also painted blue, or was that just the color of shadow when the cloud passed over?

A tribe of Crows sank from a point too high above for the Scarecrow to see or imagine. Their voices brayed insult at him as they fell to the field, ears of green-husked sweetcorn breaking beneath their attack. "Hey, there," cried the Scarecrow, "well then!" More instinct than anything else, and not to frighten them away, necessarily. More to announce his notice of them. But they were startled, and wheeled around, and disappeared.

Who am I? he said to himself, and then he said it aloud. The sky refused to answer, as did the corn, the wind, the light — or if they were answering, he couldn't understand the language.

The Crows returned to blot the field before him. With weapons of beak and claw and mighty wing, they beat at the corn, feasting.

"Welcome!" called the Scarecrow.

They laughed at him.

One Crow flew nearer. She seemed less interested in the corn than the others. She wore a rhinestone necklace. Her wings were infested with fleas and her eyes, he noticed, rheumy. She was an old Crow and not in the best of health.

"What's wrong with you? You're supposed to scare us," she said.

"Oh, I didn't realize."

She waggled her head. "Brainless fool."

"Brainless? What do you mean?" he said.

"Think about it. Brainless. No brain."

"How can I think about it if I haven't got a brain?" he murmured.

"You haven't got a brain, haven't got a clue, so you haven't got a chance to keep us from the corn. You're supposed to be *protecting the corn*."

Was she being kind, in telling him his life's work, or was she taunting him for being so stupid? She flew nearer, though her cousins were ambushing the ranks of corn with fiercer strength than ever. The Scarecrow wondered if she was too old to attack the corn as fiercely as her kin. Or was she too old to be that hungry? Maybe she just preferred gossip to gluttony.

"Most creatures who can talk can figure out a little," she said. "What's your problem, brother, that you're so dim-witted?"

"My arms hurt. Maybe if they didn't hurt I would be able to think. I need to be able to think. How did I get here?" he said. "At least tell me that."

The Crow hopped onto a fence rail nearby and settled her head at an angle. She looked at him with one black eye, bright as the back of a beetle. "This is my field, I live here," she said, "I notice what goes on. But where to start?"

"The beginning," begged the Scarecrow.

"A farmer sowed a field not far away, some time ago, and from the seeds he scattered there grew a great lot of hay. Every day he watched the rain water it, and the sun nourish it, and he kept the Cows from tramping it down. It grew up bright as a field of bronzy-green swords. He was proud of that field of hay! And just before the rains at the end of summer, his heart bursting with pride, the farmer swept along the field with a huge scythe, and cut the hay to the ground."

The Scarecrow gasped. "He killed it!"

"We call it harvest," said the Crow, "but it looks mighty like killing, I agree. Anyway, the hay lay in fine thick patterns across the field. The farmer picked it up with a fork and loaded it onto a wagon. Later he bound it with twine, and stored the bales in a barn. Most of it he fed to his Cows."

"Cannibals!" snorted the Scarecrow. "He sacrificed his field for the Cows!"

"We call it farming," said the Crow. "And hay cannot talk or think like you and me. But will you pay attention? Sometimes farmers stuff some of their hay into a pair of trousers and a bright red shirt. Then a farmer might put some more into an old farm sack, and paint a face upon it. A farmer could set the sack upon the neck of the shirt, and tie it together with a moldy bit of rope good for little else."

"And then what?" said the Scarecrow.

"Well, that's you," said the Crow.

"Hay and straw and some moldy rope and some secondhand clothes? That's all I am?" said the Scarecrow. "The farmer made me? Did he teach me to talk, did he sing me to sleep, did he bless my forehead? But where did the clothes come from?"

"I don't know if the farmer made you," said the Crow, cagily, hiding something. "But he intended to, as he had set aside enough hay for your limbs, and he had chosen the sack and painted your face upon it. And those are his clothes, anyway, so in a sense he is your father."

"Didn't he need them?" asked the Scarecrow.

"No," said the Crow. "Not after a while. Before he could finish you, he fell sick. I suppose he must have died. No man needs his clothes after he's died."

"What does *after* mean?" said the Scarecrow, who was too new to understand befores and afters.

"It means the *next* that follows the *now*, or the *now* that follows the *once*."

"I wish I had a brain," said the Scarecrow. "I understand a man falling sick and dying, but I do not understand befores and afters."

"The last time I laid eyes on him, I was perched on his windowsill, being nosy. I saw him tossing and turning with a fever. It seemed bad. I know he must have died, for if he had not, he would be running to berate you for letting us Crows eat all the corn. But he is dead, and you are all alone. That's too bad, but it can't be helped. I suppose his farmer neighbors took the clothes off his dead body and finished dressing you, and set you on your stake to do the job you were made to do. Too bad you can't do it very well. And now I will stop chatting and go eat some corn myself." Off she flew, in a fluttery, palsied manner, her jewelry flashing in the sun like splashes of fountain. The Scarecrow could see that she had been waiting to peck at ears of corn already cut open by the stronger crows.

"Stop," called the Scarecrow, "stop!" He did not mean for her to stop eating the corn, for he did not care. He meant to stop her from leaving. But she didn't listen.

The Crows made a mess of the cornfield. The Scarecrow knew that the old Crow must have been telling the truth, for no farmer came running from the nearby house to scold him for the damage. But even more damage lay in store. The next day the sky turned hugely purple. Mountainous clouds swept over, dragging along the ground a smoky funnel of wind. The remaining stalks were flattened. When the Crows returned, they had to settle their spiky pronged feet in the complicated floor of leaves and stalks, and hunt with lowered heads for what corn could still be found.

"Stop," cried the Scarecrow, "look out! Beware!" But he was not trying to protect the corn. He had seen a different danger approaching his friend the Crow. Her hearing was not what it once must have been so she wasn't aware. Her head was down, hunched in her collar of fine glints, digging for an especially rich ear of corn. From a hump of green rubble

　　　　THE SECRET HISTORY OF FANTASY

launched a missile of red fur and black leather boots, and teeth as sharp as the points of rhinestones. Sharper even. The other Crows escaped in an explosion of noisy wings and terrified cries, but the old Crow was too slow. She fell beneath clever paws and hungry jaws, and the jewelry made a bright exclamation mark in the air before it dropped to the ground.

"Yum," said the Fox, after he had finished his meal. "Yes, she was good. But I feel like a little something more." He tried his teeth on the necklace, but it did not appeal to his taste. So the Fox stood up in his black leather boots, and though he could see farther than he would have had the corn not fallen in the wind, he still could not find a suitable sweet morsel to finish his meal. "Straw-head," said the Fox, "you are higher than I. Can you see anything sweet for me to go after?" He licked his chops.

"What do you mean, *after?*" said the Scarecrow, a bit wary, but still curious.

"After?" said the Fox. *"After?* After means *toward.* I go after the Crow, and I get her. I go after my Vixen, and I get her. I go after what I want. What do you want?"

"To understand," said the Scarecrow, sighing.

"Ah, knowledge is sweet, too," said the Fox. He resigned himself to conversation rather than dessert, and he circled himself into a coil of Fox, where he could see how his hind legs ended so magnificently in black leather boots. He settled his bush over himself like a blanket. Then he put his chin upon his front paws and looked up at the Scarecrow. His eyes began to close.

"It seems a brutal world," said the Scarecrow.

"Doesn't it though," said the Fox appreciatively.

"You speak as if you know me," said the Scarecrow.

"I believe I know your clothes," said the Fox. "I recognize them. Your clothes make you seem quite familiar. I am happy not to be running from the farmer who used to wear them. When he would see me in his henhouse he would run for a weapon. But now the clothes have survived the man, for he must be dead. Otherwise he would be out here harvesting what is left of his flattened crop of corn. I notice that his clothes are capable of nothing more than housing straw — rather chatty straw, to my surprise, but straw nonetheless."

"He died of a terrible illness, I hear," said the Scarecrow.

"Is that so? Not what I heard." The Fox purred softly at the thought of treachery. "In all likelihood he died over there on the gallows tree. He was to be hung by the neck until he was dead," said the Fox. "The farmer's friendly neighbors intended to break his neck just as I broke the neck of Madame Crow a few minutes ago."

"But why?" said the Scarecrow, alarmed.

"Before you were born, the farmer had gone off to another village to buy some seedcorn," said the Fox. "When he came back he fell deeply ill. Folks round here are afraid of the plague, and none of them would tend him. He tossed and turned in a raging fever. But somehow he survived, and believed himself to be recovered. He went to the well in the center of the village and greeted all his neighbors — though somewhat coldly, I'll wager, since they had not come to his help. Then a terrible misfortune occurred. Within days the villagers he met succumbed to fevers and fits, and some of them died. The ones who survived blamed him for the outbreak of sickness. They went after him."

"After him," said the Scarecrow, trying hard to understand.

"They said he had caused the death of their loved ones," said the Fox. "They said he had infected them on purpose, so that other families would not have the help to bring in their corn, and he alone would prosper with a good crop. They came after him with pitchforks and accusations. The farmer was not yet well enough to run away with any speed. They caught him in the middle of the corn. I saw them trap him; I was hiding in the weevily shadows, watching. They went to hang him, much as you are hung there on your stake. I would have stayed to watch the execution, but a sudden summer storm came up, and I fled to my hole. But I suppose they did their job and gave him his death."

"Did he not ask for their charity?" said the Scarecrow.

"Oh, anyone can ask," said the Fox. "No doubt the Crow would have asked for my charity if she'd been able to squeeze breath through her gullet. But charity doesn't satisfy the stomach, does it?"

The Scarecrow didn't know. He tried to close his eyes to squeeze out the sight of the gallows tree in the next field over, but his eyes were painted open. He tried not to listen to the Fox, but his ears were painted open. He tried to still the beating in his chest, but he couldn't; this was because a family of Mice had discovered the Scarecrow and were exploring him as a possible home. It was both uncomfortable and slightly embarrassing to have Mice capering about inside his clothes.

"I suggest you should look for lodging elsewhere," said the Scarecrow in as low a voice as he could manage, "for there is a Fox nearby who likes to go after small creatures."

The Mice took heed and removed themselves to a safer neighborhood. The Fox, nearly asleep, began to laugh softly. "Charity is so appealing in the young," he said. Soon thereafter he began to snore.

The Scarecrow had no choice but to look at the farmhouse, the fields, the gallows tree, the hill beyond them all. The world seemed a bitter place, arranged just so: fields, gallows, house, and hill.

Then around the edge of the hill came a girl and a dog. They were both walking briskly, with a little skip in their step, and from time to time the dog would run ahead and sniff at the seams of the world here and there. The Fox was deep in his dream and the dog would soon be upon him. "Stop!" cried the Scarecrow.

The Fox bolted upright from his sleep and his neck twisted around so his ruff stood out like a brush. He saw the child and the dog. Instinctively ready to flee, the Fox took just enough time to glance up at the Scarecrow as if to say: *Why? Why do you save me, when you disapprove of how I am, when you disapprove of how the world is? Why do you bother?*

But he could not take the time to voice the questions, for the dog was almost upon him, and the Fox disappeared in a streak of smoke-red against the green-and-gold wreckage of the cornfield. He vanished so quickly that he left behind his pair of handsome black leather boots.

The dog barked. It seemed unable to make a sensible remark, and the Scarecrow by now was not inclined to question it anyway. The Scarecrow did not know why he had alerted the Fox to danger. Were the clothes that the Scarecrow was born into the clothes of a kindly man or a terrible one? Did it matter who the farmer had been, did that shape who the Scarecrow might be? What manner of creature, what quality of spirit, what variety of soul?

It was very troubling. The Scarecrow merely watched as the girl approached. By now he was not sure that he cared to know any more about the world.

The girl wore her hair in pigtails. She was clothed in a sensible dress with an apron tied neatly behind in a bow. She wore neither rhinestone necklace nor black leather boots, but her shoes were glittering in the afternoon sun. "What's that, then?" she said to the dog in a fond voice. "Did you smell something of interest?"

The dog circled about beneath the Scarecrow's pillar, and looked up and barked.

"Why, a Scarecrow," said the girl. "What do you know?"

Since the Scarecrow knew very little indeed, he did not answer.

"I should like to know which is the best way to proceed," said the girl, almost to herself. "The road divides here, and we could go this way, or that way."

The Scarecrow knew only the house, the fields, the gallows tree, the hill.

"Perhaps it doesn't matter, though," continued the girl, musing. "We didn't choose to come here, after all, so perhaps any choice we make from here has the chance of being the right one."

"What does that mean?" said the Scarecrow.

The girl gave a little start and the dog went and cowered behind the basket she had set down. "I'm a foreigner," she said, "an accidental visitor, and I do not know my way."

"I mean, *after all*," said the Scarecrow. "I do not understand befores and afters. What does *after all* mean? It sounds important."

"After all?" said the girl. She put her head to one side. "It means, when everything is thought about, what you can then conclude."

"If you can't think," said the Scarecrow, "can you have an after all?"

"Of course," said the girl, "but thinking helps."

"I should like to learn to think," said the Scarecrow. "I should like to know about this more, before the world seems too dark to bear."

"Would you like to get down?" said the girl.

This had never occurred to the Scarecrow yet. "May I?" he said.

"I will loosen you off your hook if I can reach," said the girl, but she couldn't. Still, she didn't give up. She wandered across the field to the farmhouse. The Scarecrow watched her knock on the door, and when there was no answer, he saw her enter. Before long she returned with a little chair. She stood on it and worked at the nail on which the Scarecrow hung. She managed to bend it down, and off he slid, into a heap on the ground.

It felt good to move!

"Whyever did you help me?" he asked.

"Whyever not?" she said, and he didn't know the answer since he didn't know much. But he grinned, for it was fun to be asked, and maybe if she asked him again someday, he would have an answer ready.

"How do you come to be a talking Scarecrow?" she said.

"I don't know," he said. "How do you come to be a talking girl?"

"I'm sure I have no idea," said the girl. "I was born this way."

"So was I," said the Scarecrow. "But my clothes were given me by a dead man, I hear."

He told the girl the story of the farmer who had been treacherously ill, and then had shared his disease with his neighbors, though by chance or intention it could not be said for sure. The Scarecrow told how the neighbors had fallen upon the farmer and killed him for the crime.

The girl looked doubtful. "Who tells you such a grim tale?" she said.

"A Crow, rest her soul, and a Fox, luck preserve him," said the Scarecrow.

The girl looked sadly at the Scarecrow. "You believe everything you're told?" she said.

"I haven't been told a whole lot yet," the Scarecrow admitted. "I'm only two days old, I think."

The girl said, "Wait here while I return the chair to where I found it." And off she went with a thoughtful expression on her face. Her dog followed her with a cheery wag of his tail.

The Scarecrow trusted that she would return. And return she did. She had a calmer look on her face. "The Crow did not know and the Fox did not know," she said warmly. "But I can read, and I do know. I saw a letter on the table in the farmhouse. It was a letter written by the farmer."

"Yes?" said the Scarecrow.

"The letter said, 'To my neighbors: You will think that I have died. But I have not. This spring when I went over the hill to buy my seedcorn, I fell in love with a woman there. On my return, I had hoped to sow my fields quickly and then go back to marry her, and bring her here to live, but my sickness prevented my traveling. When you caught me and brought me so close to death on the gallows tree, I thought that was the end. But fate would have it otherwise. The storm came up and you all ran for safety. Then appeared my beloved, who had worried because I hadn't returned to her. She had come to find out why, and she had seen you gather, and hid herself in the corn. Seizing her chance, she leapt up and cut me down. So today I am going to marry her. I will not come back to this farm, for I need to make myself a happily ever after somewhere far from here. I have dressed myself in brand-new clothes to make her pleased with her choice. Here are my old clothes. Please use them for the public good and make a Scarecrow to protect the corn from the Crows. It is your corn now, as it always would have been whenever you needed it. Good-bye.'"

The Scarecrow felt his spirits lift up. "So the owner of these clothes was a man who cared for the well-being of his neighbors, even those who had tried to kill him?"

"I do believe," said the girl, "an unusual man with a good heart."

"We should go tear down the gallows tree in the middle of the next field," said the Scarecrow, "so the neighbors may not try such a scheme again."

The girl peered at it with her hand over her eye. "That is not usually a gallows tree," she decided. "It is really just a pole for you to rest upon when that field is ready to be planted with another crop of corn."

The Scarecrow said, "So the stories of the Crow and the Fox were wrong."

"The Crow and Fox were not wrong," said the girl, "they just did not know what came after." She smiled at the Scarecrow and began to play with bits of corn husk. She made a dolly from an ear of corn, and twisted the leaves of cornstalks to make arms and legs. She dressed it in a rhinestone necklace and a pair of black leather boots.

The Scarecrow waited for the dolly to speak. It was no less than he was, some dead agricultural matter dressed up in human clothes. But it did not speak or move as he did.

"Why does it not tell us something?" he asked the girl. "Why am I alive and it is not?"

"I do not know," said the girl. "I am young too. I do not know why I have arrived here in this strange land, where Scarecrows can talk. There is a lot I don't know. It was all winds and noises when I came —"

This reminded the Scarecrow of the day of his awakening — the day before yesterday. He nodded, for the first time knowing something to be true because of his own experience of it. "And lights," he said.

"Yes, and lights," said the girl. "Lights and darks. And suddenly I was here, where everything seems strange. And I don't know why. Like the Fox and the Crow, I don't know the whole story yet. But that's a good reason to go on, don't you think?"

"Go where?" said the Scarecrow.

"Go forward," said the girl. "See something. Learn something. Figure it out. We won't ever get the whole thing, I bet, but we'll get something. And then we'll have something to tell when we're old about what happened to us when we were young."

"Now?" said the Scarecrow. "Can you tell it now?"

"After," said the girl. "We have to have the *before* first, and that's life."

"And what's life?" said the Scarecrow.

"Moving," said the girl. "Moving on. Shall we move on? Will you come with me?"

"Yes," said the Scarecrow. "For the sake of knowing some more about this, of developing my brains so I can bear this mystery better." Straw limbs and human clothes, perhaps, but still hungry for a life to live before so that there could be a story to tell after.

"Which way shall we go?" said the girl.

"Not toward the fields, the house, the hill, the gallows tree," said the Scarecrow. "Let's go in the direction we have not yet gone."

"Good enough for me," said the girl. She left the corn dolly for some other child to find. Then she picked up her basket and the dog came running to her heels. Now that the Scarecrow was down on the ground, he could see that the two fields that made up his world so far were divided by a road paved with yellow brick.

"This way," said the girl. And she and the Scarecrow turned their heads toward the west.

LADY OF THE SKULLS

PATRICIA A. McKILLIP

THE LADY SAW them ride across the plain: a company of six. Putting down her watering can, which was the bronze helm of some unfortunate knight, she leaned over the parapet, chin on her hand. They were all armed, their war-horses caparisoned; they glittered under the noon sun with silver-edged shields, jeweled bridles, and sword hilts. What, she wondered as always in simple astonishment, did they imagine they had come to fight? She picked up the helm, poured water into a skull containing a miniature rose bush. The water came from within the tower, the only source on the entire barren, sun-cracked plain. The knights would ride around the tower under the hot sun for hours, looking for entry. At sunset, she would greet them, carrying water.

She sighed noiselessly, troweling around the little rose bush with a dragon's claw. If they were too blind to find the tower door, why did they think they could see clearly within it? They, she thought in sudden impatience. They, they, they…they fed the plain with their bleached bones; they never learned….

A carrion-bird circled above her, counting heads. She scowled at it; it cried back at her, mocking. *You,* its black eye said, *never die. But you bring the dead to me.*

"They never listen to me," she said, looking over the plain again, her eyes prickling dryly. In the distance, lightning cracked apart the sky; purple clouds rumbled. But there was no rain in them, never any rain; the sky was as tearless as she. She moved from skull to skull along the parapet wall, watering things she had grown stubbornly from seeds that blew from distant, placid gardens in peaceful kingdoms. Some were grasses, weeds, or wildflowers. She did not care; she watered anything that grew.

The men below began their circling. Their mounts kicked up dust, snorting; she heard cursing, bewildered questions, then silence as they paused to rest. Sometimes they called her, pleading. But she could do nothing for them. They churned around the tower, bright, powerful, richly armed. She read the devices on their shields: three of Grenelief, one of Stoney Head, one of Dulcis Isle, one of Carnelaine. After a time, one man dropped out of the circle, stood back. His shield was simple: a red rose on white. Carnelaine, she thought, looking down at him, and then realized he was looking up at her.

He would see a puff of airy sleeve, a red geranium in an upside-down skull. Lady of the Skulls, they called her, clamoring to enter. Sometimes they were more courteous, sometimes less. She watered, waiting for this one to call her. He did not; he guided his horse into the tower's shadow and dismounted. He took his helm off, sat down to wait, burrowing idly in the ground and flicking stones as he watched her sleeve sometimes, and sometimes the distant storm.

Drawn to his calm, the others joined him finally, flinging off pieces of armor. They cursed the hard ground and sat, their voices drifting up to her in the windless air as she continued her watering.

Like others before them, they spoke of what the most precious thing of the legendary treasure might be, besides elusive. They had made a pact, she gathered: If one obtained the treasure, he would divide it among those left living. She raised a brow. The one of Dulcis Isle, a dark-haired man wearing red jewels in his ears, said:

"Anything of the dragon for me. They say it was a dragon's hoard, once. They say that dragon bones are worm-holed with magic, and if you move one bone the rest will follow. The bones will bring the treasure with them."

"I heard," said the man from Stoney Head, "there is a well and a fountain rising from it, and when the drops of the fountain touch ground they turn to diamonds."

"Don't talk of water," one of the three thick-necked, nut-haired men of Grenelief pleaded. "I drank all mine."

"All we must do is find the door. There's water within."

"What are you going to do?" the man of Carnelaine asked. "Hoist the water on your shoulder and carry it out?"

The straw-haired man from Stoney Head tugged at his long moustaches. He had a plain, blunt, energetic voice devoid of any humor. "I'll carry it out in my mouth. When I come back alive for the rest of it, there'll be plenty to carry in. Skulls, if nothing else. I heard there's a sorceress' cauldron, looks like a rusty old pot —"

"May be that," another of Grenelief said.

"May be, but I'm going for the water. What else could be most precious in this heat-blasted place?"

"That's a point," the man of Dulcis Isle said. Then: "But no, it's dragon-bone for me."

"More to the point," the third of Grenelief said, aggrieved, "how do we get in the cursed place?"

"There's a lady up there watering plants," the man of Carnelaine said, and there were all their faces staring upward; she could have tossed jewels into their open mouths. "She knows we're here."

"It's the Lady," they murmured, hushed.

"Lady of the Skulls."

"Does she have hair, I wonder."

"She's old as the tower. She must be a skull."

"She's beautiful," the man of Stoney Head said shortly. "They always are, the ones who lure, the ones who guard, the ones who give death."

"Is it her tower?" the one of Carnelaine asked. "Or is she trapped?"

"What's the difference? When the spell is gone, so will she be. She's nothing real, just a piece of the tower's magic."

They shifted themselves as the tower shadow shifted. The Lady took a sip of water out of the helm, then dipped her hand in it and ran it over her face. She wanted to lean over the edge and shout at them all: Go home, you silly, brainless fools. If you know so much, what are you doing here sitting on bare ground in front of a tower without a door waiting for a woman to kill you? They moved to one side of the tower, she to the other, as the sun climbed down the sky. She watched the sun set. Still the men refused to leave, though they had not a stick of wood to burn against the dark. She sighed her noiseless sigh and went down to greet them.

The fountain sparkled in the midst of a treasure she had long ceased to notice. She stepped around gold armor, black, gold-rimed dragon bones, the white bones of princes. She took the plain silver goblet beside the rim of the well, and dipped it into the water, feeling the cooling mist from the little fountain. The man of Dulcis Isle was right about the dragon bones. The doorway was the dragon's open yawning maw, and it was invisible by day.

The last ray of sunlight touched the bone, limned a black, toothed opening that welcomed the men. Mute, they entered, and she spoke.

"You may drink the water, you may wander throughout the tower. If you make no choice, you may leave freely. Having left, you may never return. If you choose, you must make your choice by sunset tomorrow. If you choose the most precious thing in the tower, you may keep all that you see. If you choose wrongly, you will die before you leave the plain."

Their mouths were open again, their eyes stunned at what hung like vines from the old dragon's bones, what lay heaped upon the floor. Flicking, flicking, their eyes came across her finally, as she stood patiently holding the cup. Their eyes stopped at her: a tall, broad-shouldered, barefoot woman in a coarse white linen smock, her red hair bundled untidily on top of her head, her long skirt still splashed with the wine she had spilled in the tavern so long ago. In the torchlight it looked like blood.

They chose to sleep, as they always did, tired by the long journey, dazed by too much rich, vague color in the shadows. She sat on the steps and watched them for a little. One cried in his sleep. She went to the top of the tower after a while, where she could watch the stars. Under the moon, the flowers turned odd, secret colors, as if their true colors blossomed in another land's daylight, and they had left their pale shadows behind by night. She fell asleep naming the moon's colors.

In the morning, she went down to see who had had sense enough to leave.

They were all still there, searching, picking, discarding among the treasures on the floor, scattered along the spiraling stairs. Shafts of light from the narrow windows sparked fiery colors that constantly caught their eyes, made them drop what they had, reach out again. Seeing her, the one from Dulcis Isle said, trembling, his eyes stuffed with riches, "May we ask questions? What is this?"

"Don't ask her, Marlebane," the one from Stoney Head said brusquely. "She'll lie. They all do."

She stared at him. "I will only lie to you," she promised. She took the small treasure from the hand of the man from Dulcis Isle. "This is an acorn made of gold. If you swallow it, you will speak all the languages of humans and animals."

"And this?" one of Grenelief said eagerly, pushing next to her, holding something of silver and smoke.

"That is a bracelet made of a dragon's nostril bone. The jewel in it is its petrified eye. It watches for danger when you wear it."

The man of Carnelaine was playing a flute made from a wizard's thigh bone. His eyes, the odd gray-green of the dragon's eye, looked dream-drugged with the music. The man of Stoney Head shook him roughly.

"Is that your choice, Ran?"

"No." He lowered the flute, smiling. "No, Corbeil."

"Then drop it before it seizes hold of you and you choose it. Have you seen yet what you might take?"

"No. Have you changed your mind?"

"No." He looked at the fountain, but, prudent, did not speak.

"Bram, look at this," said one brother of Grenelief to another. "Look!"

"I am looking, Yew."

"Look at it! Look at it, Ustor! Have you ever seen such a thing? Feel it! And watch: It vanishes, in light."

He held a sword; its hilt was solid emerald, its blade like water falling in clear light over stone. The Lady left them, went back up the stairs, her bare feet sending gold coins and jewels spinning down through the cross-hatched shafts of light. She stared at the place on the horizon where the flat dusty gold of the plain met the parched dusty sky. Go, she thought dully. Leave all this and go back to the places where things grow. Go, she willed them, go, go, go, with the beat of her heart's blood. But no one came out the door beneath her. Someone, instead, came up the stairs.

"I have a question," said Ran of Carnelaine.

"Ask."

"What is your name?"

She had all but forgotten; it came to her again, after a beat of surprise. "Amaranth." He was holding a black rose in one hand, a silver lily in the other. If he chose one, the thorns would kill him; the other, flashing its pure light, would sear through his eyes into his brain.

"Amaranth. Another flower."

"So it is," she said indifferently. He laid the magic flowers on the parapet, picked a dying geranium leaf, smelled the miniature rose. "It has no smell," she said. He picked another dead leaf. He seemed always on the verge of smiling; it made him look sometimes wise and sometimes foolish. He drank out of the bronze watering helm; it was the color of his hair.

"This water is too cool and sweet to come out of such a barren plain," he commented. He seated himself on the wall, watching her. "Corbeil says you are not real. You look real enough to me." She was silent, picking dead clover out of the clover pot. "Tell me where you came from."

She shrugged. "A tavern."

"And how did you come here?"

She gazed at him. "How did you come here, Ran of Carnelaine?"

He did smile then, wryly. "Carnelaine is poor; I came to replenish its coffers."

"There must be less chancy ways."

"Maybe I wanted to see the most precious thing there is to be found. Will the plain bloom again, if it is found? Will you have a garden instead of skull-pots?"

"Maybe," she said levelly. "Or maybe I will disappear. Die when the magic dies. If you choose wisely, you'll have answers to your questions."

He shrugged. "Maybe I will not choose. There are too many precious things."

She glanced at him. He was trifling, wanting hints from her, answers couched in riddles. Shall I take rose or lily? Or wizard's thigh bone? Tell me. Sword or water or dragon's eye? Some had questioned her so before.

She said simply, "I cannot tell you what to take. I do not know myself. As far as I have seen, everything kills." It was as close as she could come, as plain as she could make it: Leave. But he said only, his smile gone, "Is that why you never left?" She stared at him again. "Walked out the door, crossed the plain on some dead king's horse and left?"

She said, "I cannot." She moved away from him, tending some wild-flower she called wind-bells, for she imagined their music as the night air tumbled down from the mountains to race across the plain. After a while, she heard his steps again, going down.

A voice summoned her: "Lady of the Skulls!" It was the man of Stoney Head. She went down, blinking in the thick, dusty light. He stood stiffly, his face hard. They all stood still, watching.

"I will leave now," he said. "I may take anything?"

"Anything," she said, making her heart stone against him, a ghost's heart, so that she would not pity him. He went to the fountain, took a mouthful of water. He looked at her, and she moved to show him the hidden lines of the dragon's mouth. He vanished through the stones.

They heard him scream a moment later. The three of Grenelief stared toward the sound. They each wore pieces of a suit of armor that made the wearer invisible: one lacked an arm, another a thigh, the other his hands. Subtly their expressions changed, from shock and terror into something more complex. Five, she saw them thinking. Only five ways to divide it now.

"Anyone else?" she asked coldly. The man of Dulcis Isle slumped down onto the stairs, swallowing. He stared at her, his face gold-green in the light. He swallowed again. Then he shouted at her.

She had heard every name they could think of to shout before she had ever come to the tower. She walked up the stairs past him; he did not have the courage to touch her. She went to stand among her plants. Corbeil of Stoney Head lay where he had fallen, a little brown patch of wet earth beside his open mouth. As she looked, the sun dried it, and the first of the carrion-birds landed.

She threw bones at the bird, cursing, though it looked unlikely that anyone would be left to take his body back. She hit the bird a couple of times, then another came. Then someone took the bone out of her hand, drew her back from the wall.

"He's dead," Ran said simply. "It doesn't matter to him whether you throw bones at the birds or at him."

"I have to watch," she said shortly. She added, her eyes on the jagged line the parapet made against the sky, like blunt worn dragon's teeth, "You keep coming, and dying. Why do you all keep coming? Is treasure worth being breakfast for the carrion crows?"

"It's worth many different things. To the brothers of Grenelief it means adventure, challenge, adulation if they succeed. To Corbeil it was something to be won, something he would have that no one else could get. He would have sat on top of the pile, and let men look up to him, hating and envying."

"He was a cold man. Cold men feed on a cold fire. Still," she added, sighing, "I would have preferred to see him leave on his feet. What does the treasure mean to you?"

"Money." He smiled his vague smile. "It's not in me to lose my life over money. I'd sooner walk empty-handed out the door. But there's something else."

"What?"

"The riddle itself. That draws us all, at heart. What is the most precious thing? To see it, to hold it, above all to recognize it and choose it — that's what keeps us coming and traps you here." She stared at him, saw, in his eyes, the wonder that he felt might be worth his life.

She turned away; her back to him, she watered bleeding heart and columbine, stonily ignoring what the crows were doing below. "If you find the thing itself," she asked dryly, "what will you have left to wonder about?"

"There's always life."

"Not if you are killed by wonder."

He laughed softly, an unexpected sound, she thought, in that place. "Wouldn't you ride across the plain, if you heard tales of this tower, to try to find the most precious thing in it?"

"Nothing's precious to me," she said, heaving a cauldron of dandelions into shadow. "Not down there, anyway. If I took one thing away with me, it would not be sword or gold or dragon bone. It would be whatever is alive."

He touched the tiny rose. "You mean, like this? Corbeil would never have died for this."

"He died for a mouthful of water."

"He thought it was a mouthful of jewels." He sat beside the rose, his back to the air, watching her pull pots into shade against the noon light. "What makes him twice a fool, I suppose. Three times a fool: for being wrong, for being deluded, and for dying. What a terrible place this is. It strips you of all delusions and then it strips your bones."

"It is terrible," she said somberly. "Yet those who leave without choosing never seem to get the story straight. They must always talk of the treasure they didn't take, not of the bones they didn't leave."

"It's true. Always, they take wonder with them out of this tower and they pass it on to every passing fool." He was silent a little, still watching her. "Amaranth," he said slowly. "That's the flower in poetry that never dies. It's apt."

"Yes."

"And there is another kind of Amaranth, that's fiery and beautiful and it dies...." Her hands stilled, her eyes widened, but she did not speak. He leaned against the hot, crumbling stones, his dragon's eyes following her like a sunflower following the sun. "What were you," he asked, "when you were the Amaranth that could die?"

"I was one of those faceless women who brought you wine in a tavern. Those you shout at, and jest about, and maybe give a coin to and maybe not, depending how we smile."

He was silent, so silent she thought he had gone, but when she turned, he was still there; only his smile had gone. "Then I've seen you," he said softly, "many times, in many places. But never in a place like this."

"The man from Stoney Head expected someone else, too."

"He expected a dream."

"He saw what he expected: Lady of the Skulls." She pulled wild mint into a shady spot under some worn tapestry. "And so he found her. That's all I am now. You were better off when all I served was wine."

"You didn't build this tower."

"How do you know? Maybe I got tired of the laughter and the coins and I made a place for myself where I could offer coins and give nothing."

"Who built this tower?"

She was silent, crumbling a mint leaf between her fingers. "I did," she said at last. "The Amaranth who never dies."

"Did you?" He was oddly pale; his eyes glittered in the light as if at the shadow of danger. "You grow roses out of thin air in this blistered plain; you try to beat back death for us with our own bones. You curse our stupidity and our fate, not us. Who built this tower for you?" She turned her face away, mute. He said softly, "The other Amaranth, the one that dies, is also called Love-lies-bleeding."

"It was the last man," she said abruptly, her voice husky, shaken with sudden pain, "who offered me a coin for love. I was so tired of being touched and then forgotten, of hearing my name spoken and then not, as if I were only real when I was looked at, and just something to forget after that, like you never remember the flowers you toss away. So I said to him: no, and no, and no. And then I saw his eyes. They were like amber with thorns of dark in them: sorcerer's eyes. He said, 'Tell me your name.' And I said, 'Amaranth,' and he laughed and laughed and I could only stand there, with the wine I had brought him overturned on my tray, spilling down my skirt. He said, 'Then you shall make a tower of your name, for the tower is already built in your heart.'"

"Love-lies-bleeding," he whispered.

"He recognized that Amaranth."

"Of course he did. It was what died in his own heart."

She turned then, wordless, to look at him. He was smiling again, though his face was still blanched under the hard, pounding light, and the sweat shone in his hair. She said, "How do you know him?"

"Because I have seen this tower before and I have seen in it the woman we all expected, the only woman some men ever know... And every time we come expecting her, the woman who lures us with what's most precious to us and kills us with it, we build the tower around her again and again and again...."

She gazed at him. A tear slid down her cheek, and then another. "I thought it was my tower," she whispered. "The Amaranth that never dies but only lives forever to watch men die."

"It's all of us," he sighed. In the distance, thunder rumbled.

"We all build towers, then dare each other to enter...." He picked up the little rose in its skull pot and stood abruptly; she followed him to the stairs.

"Where are you going with my rose?"

"Out."

She followed him down, protesting. "But it's mine!"

"You said we could choose anything."

"It's just a worthless thing I grew, it's nothing of the tower's treasure. If you must take after all, choose something worth your life!"

He glanced back at her, as they rounded the tower stairs to the bottom. His face was bone-white, but he could still smile. "I will give you back your rose," he said, "if you will let me take the Amaranth."

"But I am the only Amaranth."

He strode past his startled companions, whose hands were heaped with *this, no this,* and *maybe this*. As if the dragon's magical eye had opened in his own eye, he led her himself into the dragon's mouth.

We Are Norsemen

T. C. Boyle

WE ARE NORSEMEN, hardy and bold. We mount the black waves in our doughty sleek ships and go a-raiding. We are Norsemen, tough as stone. At least some of us are. Myself, I'm a skald — a poet, that is. I go along with Thorkell Son of Thorkell the Misaligned and Kolbein Snub when they sack the Irish coast and violate the Irish children, women, dogs and cattle and burn the Irish houses and pitch the ancient priceless Irish manuscripts into the sea. Then I sing about it. Doggerel like this:

> Fell I not nor failed at
> Fierce words, but my piercing
> Blade mouth gave forth bloody
> Bane speech, its harsh teaching.

Catch the kennings? That's the secret of this skaldic verse — make it esoteric and shoot it full of kennings. Anyway, it's a living.

But I'm not here to carp about a skald's life, I'm here to make art. Spin a tale for posterity. Weave a web of mystery.

That year the winter ran at us like a sword, October to May. You know the sort of thing: permafrosting winds, record cold. The hot springs crusted over, birds stiffened on the wing and dropped to the earth like stones, Thorkell the Old froze to the crossbar in the privy. Even worse: thin-ribbed wolves yabbered on our doorstep, chewed up our coats and boots, and then — one snowy night — made off with Thorkell the Young. It was impossible. We crouched round the fire, thatch leaking, and froze our norns off. The days were short, the mead barrel deep. We drank, shivered, roasted a joint, told tales. The fire played off our faces, red-gold and amber, and we fastened on the narrator's voice like a log on a dark sea, entranced, falling in on ourselves, the soft cadences pulling us through the waves, illuminating shorelines, battlefields, mountains of plunder. Unfortunately, the voice was most often mine. Believe me, a winter like that a skald really earns his keep — six months, seven days a week, and an audience of hard-bitten critics with frost in their beards. The nights dragged on.

One bleak morning we saw that yellow shoots had begun to stab through the cattle droppings in the yard — we stretched, yawned, and began to fill our boats with harrying matériel. We took our battle axes, our throwing axes, our hewing axes, our massive stroke-dealing swords, our disemboweling spears, a couple of strips of jerky and a jug of water. As I said, we were tough. Some of us wore our twin-horned battle helmets, the sight of which interrupts the vital functions of our victims and enemies and inspires high-keyed vibrato. Others of us, in view of fifteen-degree temperatures and a stiff breeze whitening the peaks of the waves, felt that the virtue of toughness had its limits. I decided on a lynx hat that gave elaborate consideration to the ears.

We fought over the gravel brake to launch our terrible swift ship. The wind shrieked of graves robbed, the sky was a hearth gone cold. An icy froth soaked us to the waist. Then we were off, manning the oars in smooth Nordic sync, the ship lurching through rocky breakers, heaving up, slapping down. The spray shot needles in our eyes, the oars lifted and dipped. An hour later the mainland winked into oblivion behind the dark lids of sea and sky.

There were thirteen of us: Thorkell Son of Thorkell the Misaligned, Thorkell the Short, Thorkell Thorkellsson, Thorkell Cat, Thorkell Flat-Nose, Thorkell-neb, Thorkell Ale-Lover, Thorkell the Old, Thorkell the Deep-minded, Ofeig, Skeggi, Grim and me. We were tough. We were hardy. We were bold.

Nonetheless the voyage was a disaster. A northeaster roared down on us like a herd of drunken whales and swept us far off course. We missed our landfall — Ireland — by at least two hundred miles and carried past into the open Atlantic. Eight weeks we sailed, looking for land. Thorkell the Old was bailing one gray afternoon and found three menhaden in his bucket. We ate them raw. I speared an albatross and hung it round my neck. It was no picnic.

Then one night we heard the cries of gulls like souls stricken in the dark. Thorkell Ale-Lover, keen of smell, snuffed the breeze. "Landfall near," he said. In the morning the sun threw our shadows on a new land — buff and green, slabs of gray, it swallowed the horizon.

"Balder be praised!" said Thorkell the Old.

"Thank Frigg," I said.

We skirted the coast, looking for habitations to sack. There were none. We'd discovered a wasteland. The Thorkells were for putting ashore to replenish our provisions and make sacrifice to the gods (in those days we hadn't yet learned to swallow unleavened bread and dab our foreheads with ashes. We were real primitives.) We ran our doughty sleek warship up a sandy spit and leaped ashore, fierce as flayed demons. It was an unnecessary show of force, as the countryside was desolate, but it did our hearts good.

The instant my feet touched earth the poetic fit came on me and I composed this verse:

> New land, new-found beyond
> The mickle waves by fell
> Men-fish, their stark battle
> Valor failèd them not.

No *Edda*, I grant you — but what can you expect after six weeks of bailing? I turned to Thorkell Son of Thorkell the Misaligned, my brain charged with creative fever. "Hey!" I shouted, "let's name this new-found land!" The others crowded round. Thorkell Son of Thorkell the Misaligned looked down at me (he was six four, his red beard hung to his waist). "We'll call it — Newfoundland!" I roared. There was silence. The twin horns of Thorkell's helmet pierced the sky, his eyes were like stones. "Thorkell-land," he said.

We voted. The Thorkells had it, 9 to 4.

For two and a half weeks we plumbed the coast, catching conies, shooting deer, pitching camp on islands or guarded promontories. I'd like to tell you it was glorious — golden sunsets, virgin forests, the thrill of discovery and all that — but when your business is sacking and looting, a virgin forest is the last thing you want to see. We grumbled bitterly. But Thorkell Son of Thorkell the Misaligned was loath to admit that the land to which he'd given his name was uninhabited — and consequently of no use whatever. We forged on. Then one morning he called out from his place at the tiller: "Hah!" he said, and pointed toward a rocky abutment a hundred yards ahead. The mist lay on the water like flocks of sheep. I craned my neck, squinted, saw nothing. And then suddenly, like a revelation, I saw them: three tall posts set into the earth and carved with the figures of men and beasts. The sight brought water to my eyes and verse to my lips (but no sense in troubling you with any dilatory stanzas now — this is a climactic moment).

We landed. Crept up on the carvings, sly and wary, silent as stones. As it turned out, our caution was superfluous: the place was deserted. Besides the carvings (fanged monsters, stags, serpents, the grinning faces of a new race) there was no evidence of human presence whatever. Not even a footprint. We hung our heads: another bootyless day. Ofeig — the berserker — was seized with his berserker's rage and wound up hacking the three columns to splinters with his massive stroke-dealing sword.

The Thorkells were of the opinion that we should foray inland in search of a village to pillage. Who was I to argue? Inland we went, ever hardy and bold, up hill and down dale, through brakes and brambles and bogs and clouds of insects that rushed up our nostrils and down our throats. We found nothing. On the way back to the ship we were luckier. Thorkell-neb stumbled over a shadow in the path, and when the shadow leaped up and shot through the trees, we gave chase. After a good rib-heaving run we caught what proved to be a boy, eleven or twelve, his skin the color of copper, the feathers of birds in his hair. Like the Irish, he spoke gibberish.

Thorkell Son of Thorkell the Misaligned drew pictures in the sand and punched the boy in the chest until the boy agreed to lead us to his people, the carvers of wood. We were Norsemen, and we always got our way. All of us warmed to the prospect of spoils, and off we went on another trek. We brought along our short-swords and disemboweling spears — just in case — though judging from the boy's condition (he was bony and naked, his eyes deep and black as the spaces between the stars) we had nothing to fear from his kindred.

We were right. After tramping through the under- and overgrowth for half an hour we came to a village: smoking cook pots, skinny dogs, short and ugly savages, their hair the color of excrement. I counted six huts of branches and mud, the sort of thing that might excite a beaver. When we stepped into the clearing — tall, hardy and bold — the savages set up a fiendish caterwauling and rushed for their weapons. But what a joke their weapons were! Ofeig caught an arrow in the air, looked at the head on it, and collapsed laughing: it was made of flint. Flint. Can you believe it? Here we'd come Frigg knows how many miles for plunder and the best we could do was a bunch of Stone Age aborigines who thought that a necklace of dogs' teeth was the height of fashion. Oh how we longed for those clever Irish and their gold brooches and silver-inlaid bowls. Anyway, we subdued these screechers as we called them, sacrificed the whole lot of them to the gods (the way I saw it we were doing them a favor), and headed back to our terrible swift ship, heavy of heart. There was no longer any room for debate: Ireland, look out!

As we pointed the prow east the westering sun threw the shadow of the new land over us. Thorkell the Old looked back over his shoulder and shook his head in disgust. "That place'll never amount to a hill of beans," he said.

And then it was gone.

Days rose up out of the water and sank behind us. Intrepid Norsemen, we rode the currents, the salt breeze tickling our nostrils and bellying the sail. Thorkell Flat-Nose was our navigator. He kept two ravens on a cord. After five and a half weeks at sea he released one of them and it shot off into the sky and vanished — but in less than an hour the bird was spotted off starboard, winging toward us, growing larger by turns until finally it flapped down on the prow and allowed its leg to be looped to the cord. Three days later Flat-Nose released the second raven. The bird mounted high, winging to the southeast until it became a black rune carved into the horizon. We followed it into a night of full moon, the stars like milk splattered in the cauldron of the sky. The sea whispered at the prow, the tiller hissed behind us. Suddenly Thorkell Ale-Lover cried, "Land-ho!" We were fell and grim and ravenous. We looked up at the black ribbon of the Irish coast and grinned like wolves. Our shoulders dug at the oars, the sea sliced by. An hour later we landed.

Ofeig was for sniffing out habitations, free-booting and laying waste. But dawn crept on apace, and Thorkell Son of Thorkell the Misaligned reminded him that we Norsemen attack only under cover of darkness, swift and silent as a nightmare. Ofeig did not take it well: the berserker's rage came on him and he began to froth and chew at his tongue and howl like a skinned beast. It was a tense moment. We backed off as he grabbed for his battle ax and whirred it about his head. Fortunately he stumbled over a root and began to attack the earth, gibbering and slavering, sparks slashing out from buried stones as if the ground had suddenly caught fire. (Admittedly, berserkers can be tough to live with — but you can't beat them when it comes to seizing hearts with terror or battling trolls, demons or demiurges.)

Our reaction to all this was swift and uncomplicated: we moved up the beach about two hundred yards and settled down to get some rest. I stretched out in a patch of wildflowers and watched the sky, Ofeig's howls riding the breeze like a celestial aria, waves washing the shore. The Thorkells slept on their feet. It was nearly light when we finally dozed off, visions of plunder dancing in our heads.

I woke to the sound of whetstone on ax: we were polishing the blade edges of our fearsome battle weapons. It was late afternoon. We hadn't eaten in days. Thorkell-neb and Skeggi stood naked on the beach, basting one another with black mud scooped from a nearby marsh. I joined them. We darkened our flaxen hair, drew grim black lines under our eyes, chanted fight songs. The sun hit the water like a halved fruit, then vanished. A horned owl shot out across the dunes. Crickets kreeked in the bushes. The time had come. We drummed one another about the neck and shoulders for a while ("Yeah!" We yelled, "yeah!"), fastened our helmets, and then raced our serpent-headed ship into the waves.

A few miles up the coast we came on a light flickering out over the dark corrugations of the sea. As we drew closer it became apparent that the source of light was detached from the coast itself — could it be an island? Our blood quickened, our lips drew back in anticipation. Ravin and rapine at last! And an island no less — what could be more ideal? There would be no escape from our pure silent fury, no chance of secreting treasures, no hope of reinforcements hastily roused from bumpkin beds in the surrounding countryside. Ha!

An island it was — a tiny point of land, slick with ghostly cliffs and crowned with the walls of a monastery. We circled it, shadows on the dark swell. The light seemed to emanate from a stone structure atop the highest crag — some bookish monk with his nose to the paper no doubt, copying by the last of the firelight. He was in for a surprise. We rode the bosom of the sea and waited for the light to fail. Suddenly Thorkell the Old began to cackle. "That'll be Inishmurray," he wheezed. "Fattest monastery on the west coast." Our eyes glowed. He spat into the spume. "Thought it looked familiar," he said. "I helped Thorir Paunch sack it back in '75." Then the light died and the world became night.

We watched the bookish monk in our minds' eyes: kissing the text and laying it on a shelf, scattering the fire, plodding wearily to his cell and the cold gray pallet. I recited an incendiary verse while we waited for the old ecclesiast to tumble into sleep:

> Eye-bleed monk,
> Night his bane.
> Darkness masks
> The sea-wound,
> Mickle fell,
> Mickle stark.

I finished the recitation with a flourish, rolling the mickles like thunder. Then we struck.

It was child's play. The slick ghostly cliffs were like rolling meadows, the outer wall a branch in our path. There was no sentry, no watchdog, no alarm. We dropped down into the courtyard, naked, our bodies basted black, our doughty death-dealing weapons in hand. We were shadows, fears, fragments of a bad dream.

Thorkell Son of Thorkell the Misaligned stole into one of the little stone churches and emerged with a glowing brand. Then he set fire to two or three of the wickerwork cells and a pile of driftwood. From that point on it was pandemonium — Ofeig tumbling stone crosses, the Thorkells murdering monks in their beds, Skeggi and Thorkell the Old chasing women, Thorkell Ale-Lover waving joints of mutton and horns of beer. The Irish defended themselves as best they could, two or three monks coming at us with barbed spears and pilgrim's staffs, but we made short work of them. We were Norsemen, after all.

For my own part, I darted here and there through the smoke and rubble, seized with a destructive frenzy, frightening women and sheep with my hideous blackened features, cursing like a jay. I even cut down a doddering crone for the sake of a gold brooch, my sweetheart Thorkella in mind. Still, despite the lust and chaos and the sweet smell of anarchy, I kept my head and my poet's eye. I observed each of the principal Thorkells with a reporter's acuity, noting each valorous swipe and thrust, the hot skaldic verses already forming on my lips. But then suddenly I was distracted: the light had reappeared in the little chapel atop the crag. I counted Thorkells (no mean feat when you consider the congeries of legs and arms, sounds and odors, the panicked flocks of sheep, pigs and chickens, the jagged flames, the furious womanizing, gormandizing and sodomizing of the crew). As I say, I counted Thorkells. We were all in sight. Up above, the light grew in intensity, flaming like a planet against the night sky. I thought of the bookish monk and started up the hill.

The night susurrated around me: crickets, katydids, cicadas, and far below the rush of waves on the rocks. The glare from the fires behind

THE SECRET HISTORY OF FANTASY

me gave way to blackness, rich and star-filled. I hurried up to the chapel, lashed by malice aforethought and evil intent — bookish monk, bookish monk — and burst through the door. I was black and terrible, right down to the tip of my foreskin. "Arrrrr!" I growled. The monk sat at a table, his hands clenched, head bent over a massive tome. He was just as I'd pictured him: pale as milk, a fringe of dark pubic hair around his tonsure, puny and frail. He did not look up. I growled again, and when I got no response I began to slash at candles and pitchers and icons and all the other superstitious trappings of the place. Pottery splashed to the floor, shelves tumbled. Still he bent over the book.

The book. What in Frigg's name was a book anyway? Scratchings on a sheet of cowhide. Could you fasten a cloak with it, carry mead in it, impress women with it, wear it in your hair? There was gold and silver scattered round the room, and yet he sat over the book as if it could glow or talk or something. The idiot. The pale, puny, unhardy, unbold idiot. A rage came over me at the thought of it — I shoved him aside and snatched up the book, thick pages, dark characters, the mystery and magic. Snatched it up, me, a poet, a Norseman, an annihilator, an illiterate. Snatched it up and watched the old monk's suffering features as I fed it, page by filthy page, into the fire. Ha!

We are Norsemen, hardy and bold. We mount the black waves in our doughty sleek ships and we go a-raiding. We are Norsemen, tough as stone. We are Norsemen.

The Barnum Museum

Steven Millhauser

1

The Barnum Museum is located in the heart of our city, two blocks north of the financial district. The Romanesque and Gothic entranceways, the paired sphinxes and griffins, the gilded onion domes, the corbeled turrets and mansarded towers, the octagonal cupolas, the crestings and crenellations, all these compose an elusive design that seems calculated to lead the eye restlessly from point to point without permitting it to take in the whole. In fact the structure is so difficult to grasp that we cannot tell whether the Barnum Museum is a single complex building with numerous wings, annexes, additions, and extensions, or whether it is many buildings artfully connected by roofed walkways, stone bridges, flowering arbors, booth-lined arcades, colonnaded passageways.

2

The Barnum Museum contains a bewildering and incalculable number of rooms, each with at least two and often twelve or even fourteen doorways. Through every doorway can be seen further rooms and doorways. The rooms are of all sizes, from the small chambers housing single exhibits to the immense halls rising to the height of five floors. The rooms are never simple, but contain alcoves, niches, roped-off divisions, and screened corners; many of the larger halls hold colorful tents and pavilions. Even if, theoretically, we could walk through all the rooms of the Barnum Museum in a single day, from the pyramidal roof of the highest tower to the darkest cave of the third subterranean level, in practice it is impossible, for we inevitably come to a closed door, or a blue velvet rope stretching across a stairway, or a sawhorse in an open doorway before which sits a guard in a dark green uniform. This repeated experience of refused admittance, within the generally open expanses of the museum, only increases our sense of unexplored regions. Can it be a deliberately calculated effect on the part of the museum directors? It remains true that new rooms are continually being added, old ones relentlessly eliminated or rebuilt. Sometimes the walls between old rooms are knocked down, sometimes large halls are divided into smaller chambers, sometimes a new extension is built into one of the gardens or courtyards; and so constant is the work of renovation and rearrangement that we perpetually hear, beneath the hum of voices, the shouts of children, the shuffle of footsteps, and the cries of the peanut vendors, the faint undersound of hammers, pickaxes, and crumbling plaster. It is said that if you enter the Barnum Museum by a particular doorway at noon and manage to find your way back by three, the doorway through which you entered will no longer lead to the street, but to a new room, whose doors give glimpses of further rooms and doorways.

3

The Hall of Mermaids is nearly dark, lit only by lanterns at the tops of posts. Most of the hall is taken up by an irregular black lake or pool, which measures some hundred yards across at its widest point and is entirely surrounded by boulders that rise from the water. In the center of the pool stands a shadowy rock-island with many peaks and hollows. The water and its surrounding boulders are themselves surrounded by a low wooden platform to which we ascend by three steps. Along the inner rim of the platform stand many iron posts about six feet apart, joined by velvet ropes; at the top of every third post glows a red or yellow lantern. Standing on the platform, we can see over the lower boulders into the black water with its red and yellow reflections. From time to time we hear a light splash and, if we are lucky, catch a sudden glimpse of glimmering dark fishscales or yellow hair. Between the velvet ropes and the boulders lies a narrow strip of platform where two guards ceaselessly patrol; despite their vigilance, now and then a hand, glowing red in the lantern-light, extends across the ropes and throws into the water a peanut, a piece of popcorn, a dime. There are said to be three mermaids in the pool. In the dark hall, in the uncertain light, you can see the faces at the ropes, peering down intently.

4

The enemies of the Barnum Museum say that its exhibits are fraudulent; that its deceptions harm our children, who are turned away from the realm of the natural to a false realm of the monstrous and fantastic; that certain displays are provocative, erotic, and immoral; that this temple of so-called wonders draws us out of the sun, tempts us away from healthy pursuits, and renders us dissatisfied with our daily lives; that the presence of the museum in our city encourages those elements which, like confidence men, sharpers, palmists, and astrologers, prey on the gullible; that the very existence of this grotesque eyesore and its repellent collection of monstrosities disturbs our tranquility, undermines our strength, and reveals our secret weakness and confusion. Some say that these arguments are supported and indeed invented by the directors of the museum, who understand that controversy increases attendance.

5

In one hall there is a marble platform surrounded by red velvet ropes. In the center of the platform a brown man sits cross-legged. He has glossy black eyebrows and wears a brilliant white turban. Before him lies a rolled-up carpet. Bending forward from the waist, he unrolls the carpet with delicate long fingers. It is about four feet by six feet, dark blue, with an intricate design of arabesques in crimson and green. Each of the two ends bears a short white fringe. The turbaned man stands up, steps to the center of the carpet, turns to face one of the fringed ends, and sits down with his legs crossed. His long brown hands rest on his lap. He utters two syllables, which sound like "ah-lek" or "ahg-leh," and as we watch, the carpet rises and begins to fly slowly about the upper reaches of the hall. Unlike the Hall of Mermaids, this hall is brightly lit, as if to encourage our detailed observation. He flies back and forth some thirty feet above our heads, moving in and out among the great chandeliers, sometimes swooping down to skim the crowd, sometimes rising to the wide ledge of a high window, where he lands for a moment before continuing his flight. The carpet does not lie stiffly beneath him, but appears to have a slight undulation; the weight of his seated body shows as a faint depression in the carpet's underside. Sometimes he remains aloft for an entire afternoon, pausing only on the shadowy ledges of the upper windows, and because it is difficult to strain the neck in a continual act of attention, it is easy to lose sight of him there, high up in the great spaces of the hall.

6

In the rooms and halls of the Barnum Museum there is often an atmosphere of carnival, of adventure. Wandering jugglers toss their brightly colored balls in the air, clowns jump and tumble, the peanut vendors in their red-white-and-blue caps shout for attention; here and there, in roped-off corners, an artist standing at an easel paints a picture of a bird that suddenly flies from the painting and perches on a window ledge, a magician shakes from his long black hat a plot of grass, an oak tree hung with colored lanterns, and white chairs and tables disposed beneath the branches. In such a hall it is difficult to know where to turn our eyes, and it is entirely possible that we will give only a casual glance to the blue-and-yellow circus cage in the corner where, tired of trailing his great wings in the straw, the griffin bows his weary head.

7

One school of thought maintains that the wonders of the Barnum Museum deliberately invite mechanical explanations that appear satisfactory without quite satisfying, thereby increasing our curiosity and wonder. Thus some claim that the flying carpet is guided by invisible wires, others argue that it must conceal a small motor, still others insist that it is controlled electronically from within the marble platform. One branch of this school asserts that if in fact the explanation is mechanical, then the mechanism is more marvelous than magic itself. The mermaids are readily explained as real women with false fishtails covering their bottom halves, but it must be reported that no one has ever been able to expose the imposture, even though photographs are permitted on Sundays from three o'clock to five. The lower halves, which all of us have seen, give every appearance of thickness and substance, and behave in every way like fish bodies; no trace of concealed legs is visible; the photographs reveal a flawless jointure of flesh and scale. Many of us who visit the Hall of Mermaids with a desire to glimpse naked breasts soon find our attention straying to the lower halves, gleaming mysteriously for a moment before vanishing into the black pool.

8

There are three subterranean levels of the Barnum Museum. The first resembles any of the upper levels, with the exception that there are no windows and that no sunlight dilutes the glow of the fluorescent ceiling lights. The second level is darker and rougher; old-fashioned gas lamps hiss in the air, and winding corridors lead in and out of a maze of chambers. Crumbling stone stairways lead down to the third level. Here the earthen paths are littered with stones, torches crackle on the damp stone walls, bands of swarthy dwarfs appear suddenly and scamper into the dark. Moldering signs, of which only a few letters are legible, stand before the dark caves. Few venture more than a step or two into the black openings, which are said to contain disturbing creatures dangerous to behold. Some believe that the passageways of the third level extend beyond the bounds of the upper museum, burrowing their way to the very edges of the city. Now and then along the dark paths an opening appears, with black stairs going down. Some say the stairways of the third level lead to a fourth level, which is pitch black and perilous; to descend is to go mad. Others say that the stairways lead nowhere, continuing down and dizzyingly down, beyond the endurance of the boldest venturer, beyond the bounds of imagination itself.

9

It may be thought that the Barnum Museum is a children's museum, and it is certainly true that our children enjoy the flying carpet, the griffin in his cage, the winged horse, the homunculus in his jar, the grelling, the lorax, the giant in his tower, the leprechauns, the Invisibles, the great birds with the faces and breasts of women, the transparent man, the city in the lake, the woman of brass. But quite apart from the fact that adults also enjoy these exhibits, I would argue that the Barnum Museum is not intended solely or even primarily for children. For although there are always children in the halls, there are also elderly couples, teenagers, men in business suits, slim women in blue jeans and sandals, lovers holding hands; in short, adults of all kinds, who return again and again. Even if one argues that certain exhibits appeal most directly to children, it may be argued that other exhibits puzzle or bewilder them; and children are expressly forbidden to descend to the third subterranean level and to enter certain tents and pavilions. But the real flaw in the suggestion that the Barnum Museum is a children's museum lies in the assumption that children are an utterly identical tribe consisting of simple creatures composed of two or three abstract traits, such as innocence and wonder. In fact our children are for the most part shrewd and skeptical, astonished in spite of themselves, suspicious, easily bored, impatient for mechanical explanations. It is not always pleasing to take a child to the Barnum Museum, and many parents prefer to wander the seductive halls alone, in the full freedom of adult yearning, monotony, and bliss.

10

Passing through a doorway, we step into a thick forest and make our way along dark winding paths bordered by velvet ropes. Owls hoot in the nearby branches. The ceiling is painted to resemble a night sky and the forest is illuminated by the light of an artificial moon. We come out onto a moonlit grassy glade. The surrounding wood is encircled by posts joined by velvet ropes; here and there an opening between posts indicates a dark path winding into the trees. It is in the glade that the Invisibles make themselves known. They brush lightly against our arms, bend down the grass blades as they pass, breathe against our cheeks and eyelids, step lightly on our feet. The children shriek in joyful fear, wives cling to their husbands' arms, fathers look about with uncertain smiles. Now and then it happens that a visitor bursts into sobs and is led quickly away by a museum guard. Sometimes the Invisibles do not manifest themselves, and it is only when the visitor, glancing irritably at his watch, begins to make his way toward one of the roped paths, that he may feel, suddenly against his hair, a touch like a caress.

II

It is probable that at some moment between birth and death, every inhabitant of our city will enter the Barnum Museum. It is less probable, but not impossible, that at some moment in the history of the museum our entire citizenry, by a series of overlapping impulses, will find themselves within these halls: mothers pushing their baby carriages, old men bent over canes, *au pair* girls, policemen, fast-food cooks, Little League captains. For a moment the city will be deserted. Our collective attention, directed at the displays of the Barnum Museum, will cause the halls to swell with increased detail. Outside, the streets and buildings will grow vague; street corners will begin to dissolve; unobserved, a garbage-can cover, blown by the wind, will roll silently toward the edge of the world.

12

The Chamber of False Things contains museum guards made of wax, *trompe l'oeil* doorways, displays of false mustaches and false beards, false-bottomed trunks, artificial roses, forged paintings, spurious texts, quack medicines, faked fossils, cinema snow, joke-shop ink spills, spirit messages, Martian super-bees, ectoplasmic projections, the footprints of extraterrestrials, Professor Ricardo and Bobo the Talking Horse, false noses, glass eyes, wax grapes, pubic wigs, hollow novels containing flasks of whiskey, and, in one corner, objects from false places: porphyry figurines from Atlantis, golden cups from El Dorado, a crystalline vial of water from the Fountain of Youth. The meaning of the exhibit is obscure. Is it possible that the directors of the museum wish to enhance the reality of the other displays by distinguishing them from this one? Or is it rather that the directors here wittily or brazenly allude to the nature of the entire museum? Another interpretation presents itself: that the directors intend no meaning, but merely wish to pique our interest, to stimulate our curiosity, to lure us by whatever means deeper and deeper into the museum.

13

As we wander the halls of the Barnum Museum, our attention is struck by all those who cannot, as we can, leave the museum whenever they like. These are the museum workers, of whom the most striking are the guards in their dark green uniforms and polished black shoes. The museum is known to be strict in its hiring practices and to demand of all workers long hours, exemplary performance, and unremitting devotion. Thus the guards are expected to be attentive to the questions of visitors, as well as unfailingly courteous, alert, and cheerful. The guards are offered inexpensive lodgings for themselves and their families on the top floor of one wing; few are wealthy enough to resist such enticements, and so it comes about that the guards spend their lives within the walls of the museum. In addition to the guards, whom we see in every room, there are the janitors in their loose gray uniforms, the peanut vendors, the gift-shop salesgirls, the ticket sellers, the coat-check women, the guides in their maroon uniforms, the keepers of the caged griffin, of the unicorn in the wooded hill, of the grelling in his lair, the wandering clowns and jugglers, the balloon men, the lamplighters and torchlighters of the second and third subterranean levels, as well as the carpenters, plasterers, and electricians, who appear to work throughout the museum's long day, from nine to nine. These are the workers we see, but there are others we have heard about: the administrators in small rooms in remote corridors on the upper floors, the researchers and historians, the archivists, the typists, the messengers, the accountants and legal advisers. What is striking is not that there are so many workers, but that they spend so much of their lives inside the museum — as if, absorbed by this realm of enchantments, they are gradually becoming a different race, who enter our world uneasily, in the manner of revenants or elves.

14

Hannah Goodwin was in her junior year of high school. She was a plain, quiet girl with lank pale-brown hair parted in the middle and a pale complexion marred by always erupting whiteheads that she covered with a flesh-colored ointment. She wore plain, neat shirts and drab corduroys.

She walked the halls alone, with lowered eyes; she never initiated a conversation, and if asked a question would raise her startled eyes and answer quickly, shifting her gaze to one side. She worked hard, never went out with boys, and had one girlfriend, who moved away in the middle of the year. Hannah seemed somewhat depressed at the loss of her friend, and for several weeks was more reserved than usual. It was about this time that she began to visit the Barnum Museum every day after school. Her visits grew longer, and she soon began returning at night. And a change came over her: although she continued to walk the halls alone, and to say nothing in class, there was about her an inner animation, an intensity, that expressed itself in her gray eyes, in her partly open lips, in the very fall of her hair on her shoulders. Even her walk was subtly altered, as if some stiffness or constraint had left her. One afternoon at the lockers a boy asked her to go to the movies; she refused with a look of surprised irritation, as if he were interrupting a conversation. Although her schoolwork did not suffer, for discipline was an old habit, she was visibly impatient with the dull routines of the day; and as her step grew firmer and her gaze surer, and her bright gray eyes, burning with anticipation, swept up to the big round clock above the green blackboard, it was clear that she had been released from some inner impediment, and like a woman in love had abandoned herself utterly to the beckoning halls, the high towers and winding tunnels, the always alluring doorways of the Barnum Museum.

15

The bridges of the Barnum Museum are external and internal. The external bridges span the courtyards, the statued gardens, the outdoor cafès with their striped umbrellas, so that visitors on the upper floors of one wing can pass directly across the sky to a nearby wing simply by stepping through a window; while down below, the balloon man walks with his red and green balloons shaped like griffins and unicorns, the hurdy-gurdy man turns his crank, a boy in brown shorts looks up from his lemon ice and shades his eyes, a young woman with long yellow hair sits down in the grass in a laughing statue's shade. The internal bridges span the upper reaches of the larger halls. At any moment, on an upper floor, we may step through an arched doorway and find ourselves not on the floor of an adjacent room, but on a bridge high above a hall that plunges down through five stories. Some of these bridges are plain wooden arches with sturdy rails, permitting us to see not only the floor below but pieces of rooms through open doorways with ironwork balconies. Other bridges are broad stone spans lined on both sides with toss-penny booths, puppet theaters, and shops selling jack-in-the-boxes, chocolate circus animals, and transparent glass marbles containing miniature mermaids, winged horses, and moonlit forests; between the low roofs, between the narrow alleys separating the shops, we catch glimpses of the tops of juggled balls, the pointed top of a tent, the arched doorway of a distant room.

16

There are times when we do not enjoy the Barnum Museum. The exhibits cease to enchant us; the many doorways, leading to further halls, fill us with a sense of boredom and nausea; beneath the griffin's delicate eyelids we see the dreary, stupefied eyes. In hatred we rage through the gaudy halls, longing for the entire museum to burst into flame. It is best, at such moments, not to turn away, but to abandon oneself to desolation. Gaze in despair at the dubious halls, the shabby illusions, the fatuous faces; drink down disillusion; for the museum, in its patience, will survive our heresies, which only bind us to it in yet another way.

17

Among the festive rooms and halls of the Barnum Museum, with their flying carpets, their magic lamps, their mermaids and grellings, we come now and then to a different kind of room. In it we may find old paint cans and oilcans, a green-stained gardening glove in a battered pail, a rusty bicycle against one wall; or perhaps old games of Monopoly, Sorry, and Risk, stacks of dusty 78 records with a dog and Victrola pictured on the center labels, a thick oak table-base dividing into four claw feet. These rooms appear to be errors or oversights, perhaps proper rooms awaiting renovation and slowly filling with the discarded possessions of

THE SECRET HISTORY OF FANTASY

museum personnel, but in time we come to see in them a deeper mean-ing. The Barnum Museum is a realm of wonders, but do we not need a rest from wonder? The plain rooms scattered through the museum release us from the oppression of astonishment. Such is the common explanation of these rooms, but it is possible to find in them a deeper meaning still. These everyday images, when we come upon them suddenly among the marvels of the Barnum Museum, startle us with their strangeness before settling to rest. In this sense the plain rooms do not interrupt the halls of wonder; they themselves are those halls.

18

It must be admitted that among the many qualities of the Barnum Museum there is a certain coarseness, which expresses itself in the stridency of its architecture, the sensual appeal of certain displays, and the brash abundance of its halls, as well as in smaller matters that attract attention from time to time. Among the latter are the numerous air ducts concealed in the floors of many halls and passageways. Erratically throughout the day, jets of air are released upward, lifting occasional skirts and dresses. This crude echo of the fun house has been criticized sharply by enemies of the museum, and it is certainly no defense to point out that the ducts were installed in an earlier era, when women of all ages wore elaborate dresses to the Barnum Museum — a fact advertised by framed photographs that show well-dressed women in broad-brimmed hats attempting to hold down their skirts and petticoats, which blow up above the knees as gallants in straw hats look on in amusement. For despite the apparent absurdity of air ducts in a world of pants, it remains true that we continue to see a fair number of checked gingham dresses, pleated white skirts, trim charcoal suits, belted poplin shirtwaists, jungle-print shifts, flowery wraparounds, polka-dot dirndls, ruffled jumpers, all of which are continually blowing up in the air to reveal sudden glimpses of green or pink panty hose, lace-trimmed white slips, gartered nylon stockings, and striped bikini underpants amidst laughter and shrill whistles. Our women can of course defeat the ducts by refusing to wear anything but pants to the Barnum Museum, but in fact the ducts appear to have encouraged certain

women, in a spirit either of rebellion or capitulation, to dress up in long skirts and decorative underwear, a fad especially popular among girls in junior high school. These girls of twelve and thirteen, who often visit the museum in small bands, make themselves up in bright red or bright green lipstick and false eyelashes, carry shiny leather pocketbooks, and wear flowing ankle-length skirts over glossy plastic boots. The skirts rise easily in the jets of air and reveal a rich array of gaudy underwear: preposterous bloomers with pink bows, candy-colored underpants with rosettes and streamers, black net stockings attached to black lacy garter belts over red lace underwear, old-fashioned white girdles with grotesque pictures of winking eyes and stuck-out tongues printed on the back. Whatever we may think of such displays, the presence of fun-house air ducts in the Barnum Museum is impossible to ignore. To defend them is not to assert their irrelevance; rather, it is to insist that they lend to the museum an air of the frivolous, the childish, the provocative, the irresponsible. For is it not this irresponsibility, this freedom from solemnity, that permits the museum to elude the mundane, and to achieve the beauty and exaltation of its most daring displays?

19

The museum researchers work behind closed doors in small rooms in remote sections of the uppermost floors. The general public is not admitted to the rooms, but some visitors, wandering among the upper exhibits, have claimed to catch glimpses of narrow corridors and perhaps a suddenly opened door. The rooms are said to be filled with piles of dusty books, reaching from floor to ceiling. Although the existence of the researchers is uncertain, we do not doubt its likelihood; although the nature of their task is unknown, we do not doubt its necessity. It is in these remote rooms that the museum becomes conscious of itself, reflects upon itself, and speaks about itself in words that no one reads. The results of research are said to be published rarely, in heavy volumes that are part of immense multivolume collections stored in upper rooms of the museum and consulted only by other researchers. Sometimes, in a narrow corridor on an upper floor, a door opens and a chalk-pale man appears. The figure

vanishes so swiftly behind the door that we can never be certain whether we have actually seen one of the legendary researchers, elusive as elves, or whether, unable to endure the stillness, the empty corridors, and the closed doors, we have summoned him into existence through minuscule tremors of our eye muscles, photochemical reactions in our rods and cones, the firing of cells in the visual cortex.

20

In the gift shops of the Barnum Museum we may buy old sepia postcards of mermaids and sea dragons, little flip-books that show flying carpets rising into the air, peep-show pens with miniature colored scenes from the halls of the Barnum Museum, mysterious rubber balls from Arabia that bounce once and remain suspended in the air, jars of dark blue liquid from which you can blow bubbles shaped like tigers, elephants, lions, polar bears, and giraffes, Chinese kaleidoscopes showing ceaselessly changing forms of dragons, enchanting pleniscopes and phantatropes, boxes of animate paint for drawing pictures that move, lacquered wooden balls from the Black Forest that, once set rolling, never come to a stop, bottles of colorless jellylike stuff that will assume the shape and color of any object it is set before, shiny red boxes that vanish in direct sunlight, Japanese paper airplanes that glide through houses and over gardens and rooftops, storybooks from Finland with tissue-paper-covered illustrations that change each time the paper is lifted, tin sets of specially treated watercolors for painting pictures on air. The toys and trinkets of the Barnum Museum amuse us and delight our children, but in our apartments and hallways, in air thick with the smells of boiling potatoes and furniture polish, the gifts quickly lose their charm, and soon lie neglected in dark corners of closets beside the eyeless Raggedy Ann doll and the dusty Cherokee headdress. Those who disapprove of the Barnum Museum do not spare the gift shops, which they say are dangerous. For they say it is here that the museum, which by its nature is contemptuous of our world, connects to that world by the act of buying and selling, and indeed insinuates itself into our lives by means of apparently innocent knickknacks carried off in the pockets of children.

21

The museum eremites must be carefully distinguished from the drifters and beggars who occasionally attempt to take up residence in the museum, lurking in dark alcoves, disturbing visitors, and sleeping in the lower passageways. The guards are continually on the lookout for such intruders, whom they usher out firmly but discreetly. The eremites, in contrast, are a small and rigorously disciplined sect who are permitted to dwell permanently in the museum. Their hair is short, their dark robes simple and neat, their vows of silence inviolable. They drink water, eat leftover rolls from the outdoor cafés, and sleep on bare floors in roped-off corners of certain halls. They are said to believe that the world outside the museum is a delusion and that only within its walls is a true life possible. These beliefs are attributed to them without their assent or dissent; they themselves remain silent. The eremites tend to be young men and women in their twenties or early thirties; they are not a foreign sect, but were born in our city and its suburbs; they are our children. They sit cross-legged with their backs straight against the wall and their hands resting lightly on their knees; they stare before them without appearing to take notice of anything. We are of two minds about the eremites. Although on the one hand we admire their dedication to the museum, and acknowledge that there is something praiseworthy in their extreme way of life, on the other hand we reproach them for abandoning the world outside the museum, and feel a certain contempt for the exaggeration and distortion we sense in their lives. In general they make us uneasy, perhaps because they seem to call into question our relation to the museum, and to demand of us an explanation that we are unprepared to make. For the most part we pass them with tense lips and averted eyes.

22

Among the myriad halls and chambers of the Barnum Museum we come to a crowded room that looks much like the others, but when we place a hand on the blue velvet rope our palm falls through empty air. In this room we pass with ease through the painted screens, the glass display cases, the stands and pedestals, the dark oak chairs and benches against the walls, and as we do so we stare intently, moving our hands about and wriggling our fingers. The images remain undisturbed by our penetration. Sometimes, passing a man or woman in the crowd, we see our arms move through the edges of arms. Here and there we notice people who rest their hands on the ropes or the glass cases; a handsome young woman, smiling and fanning herself with a glossy postcard, sits down gratefully on a chair; and it is only because they behave in this manner that we are able to tell they are not of our kind.

23

It has been said, by those who do not understand us well, that our museum is a form of escape. In a superficial sense, this is certainly true. When we enter the Barnum Museum we are physically free of all that binds us to the outer world, to the realm of sunlight and death; and sometimes we seek relief from suffering and sorrow in the halls of the Barnum Museum. But it is a mistake to imagine that we flee into our museum in order to forget the hardships of life outside. After all, we are not children, we carry our burdens with us wherever we go. But quite apart from the impossibility of such forgetfulness, we do not enter the museum only when we are unhappy or discontent, but far more often in a spirit of peacefulness or inner exuberance. In the branching halls of the Barnum Museum we are never forgetful of the ordinary world, for it is precisely our awareness of that world which permits us to enjoy the wonders of the halls. Indeed I would argue that we are most sharply aware of our town when we leave it to enter the Barnum Museum; without our museum, we would pass through life as in a daze or dream.

24

For some, the moment of highest pleasure is the entrance into the museum: the sudden plunge into a world of delights, the call of the far doorways. For others, it is the gradual losing of the way: the sense, as we wander from hall to hall, that we can no longer find our way back. This, to be sure, is a carefully contrived pleasure, for although the museum is constructed so as to help us lose our way, we know perfectly well that at any moment we may ask a guard to lead us to an exit. For still others, what pierces the heart is the stepping forth: the sudden opening of the door, the brilliant sunlight, the dazzling shop windows, the momentary confusion on the upper stair.

25

We who are not eremites, we who are not enemies, return and return again to the Barnum Museum. We know nothing except that we must. We walk the familiar and always changing halls now in amusement, now in skepticism, now seeing little but cleverness in the whole questionable enterprise, now struck with enchantment. If the Barnum Museum were to disappear, we would continue to live our lives much as before, but we know we would experience a terrible sense of diminishment. We cannot explain it. Is it that the endless halls and doorways of our museum seem to tease us with a mystery, to promise perpetually a revelation that never comes? If so, then it is a revelation we are pleased to be spared. For in that moment the museum would no longer be necessary, it would become transparent and invisible. No, far better to enter those dubious and enchanting halls whenever we like. If the Barnum Museum is a little suspect, if something of the sly and gimcrack clings to it always, that is simply part of its nature, a fact among other facts. We may doubt the museum, but we do not doubt our need to return. For we are restless, already we are impatient to move through the beckoning doorways, which lead to rooms with other doorways that give dark glimpses of distant rooms, distant doorways, unimaginable discoveries. And is it possible that the secret of the museum lies precisely here, in its knowledge that we can never be satisfied? And still the hurdy-gurdy plays, the jugglers' bright balls turn in the air, somewhere the griffin stirs in his sleep. Welcome to the Barnum Museum! For us it's enough, for us it is almost enough.

THE SECRET HISTORY OF FANTASY

Mrs. Todd's Shortcut

Stephen King

"There goes the Todd woman," I said.

Homer Buckland watched the little Jaguar go by and nodded. The woman raised her hand to Homer. Homer nodded his big, shaggy head to her but didn't raise his own hand in return. The Todd family had a big summer home on Castle Lake, and Homer had been their caretaker since time out of mind. I had an idea that he disliked Worth Todd's second wife every bit as much as he'd liked 'Phelia Todd, the first one.

This was just about two years ago and we were sitting on a bench in front of Bell's Market, me with an orange soda-pop, Homer with a glass of mineral water. It was October, which is a peaceful time in Castle Rock. Lots of the lake places still get used on the weekends, but the aggressive, boozy summer socializing is over by then and the hunters with their big guns and their expensive nonresident permits pinned to their orange caps haven't started to come into town yet. Crops have been mostly laid by. Nights are cool, good for sleeping, and old joints like mine haven't yet started to complain. In October the sky over the lake is passing fair, with those big white clouds that move so slow; I like how they seem so flat on the bottoms, and how they are a little gray there, like with a shadow of sundown foretold, and I can watch the sun sparkle on the water and not be bored for some space of minutes. It's in October, sitting on the bench in front of Bell's and watching the lake from afar off, that I still wish I was a smoking man.

"She don't drive as fast as 'Phelia," Homer said. "I swan I used to think what an old-fashion name she had for a woman that could put a car through its paces like she could."

Summer people like the Todds are nowhere near as interesting to the year-round residents of small Maine towns as they themselves believe. Year-round folk prefer their own love stories and hate stories and scandals and rumors of scandal. When that textile fellow from Amesbury shot himself, Estonia Corbridge found that after a week or so she couldn't even get invited to lunch on her story of how she found him with the pistol still in one stiffening hand. But folks are still not done talking about Joe Camber, who got killed by his own dog.

Well, it don't matter. It's just that they are different racecourses we run on. Summer people are trotters; us others that don't put on ties to do our week's work are just pacers. Even so there was quite a lot of local interest when Ophelia Todd disappeared back in 1973. Ophelia was a genuinely nice woman, and she had done a lot of things in town. She worked to raise money for the Sloan Library, helped to refurbish the war memorial, and that sort of thing. But *all* the summer people like the idea of raising money. You mention raising money and their eyes light up and commence to gleam. You mention raising money and they can get a committee together and appoint a secretary and keep an agenda. They like that. But you mention *time* (beyond, that is, one big long walloper of a combined cocktail party and committee meeting) and you're out of luck. Time seems to be what summer people mostly set a store by. They lay it by, and if they could put it up in Ball jars like preserves, why, they would. But 'Phelia Todd seemed willing to *spend* time — to do desk duty in the library as well as to raise money for it. When it got down to using scouring pads and elbow grease on the war memorial, 'Phelia was right out there with town women who had lost sons in three different wars, wearing an overall with her hair done up in a kerchief. And when kids needed ferrying to a summer swim program, you'd be as apt to see her as anyone headed down Landing Road with the back of Worth Todd's big shiny pickup full of kids. A good woman. Not a town woman, but a good woman. And when she disappeared, there was concern. Not grieving, exactly, because a disappearance is not exactly like a death. It's not like chopping something off with a cleaver; more like something running down the sink so slow you don't know it's all gone until long after it is.

THE SECRET HISTORY OF FANTASY

"'Twas a Mercedes she drove," Homer said, answering the question I hadn't asked. "Two-seater sportster. Todd got it for her in sixty-four or sixty-five, I guess. You remember her taking the kids to the lake all those years they had Frogs and Tadpoles?"

"Ayuh."

"She'd drive 'em no more than forty, mindful they was in the back. But it chafed her. That woman had lead in her foot and a ball bearing sommers in the back of her ankle."

It used to be that Homer never talked about his summer people. But then his wife died. Five years ago it was. She was plowing a grade and the tractor tipped over on her and Homer was taken bad off about it. He grieved for two years or so and then seemed to feel better. But he was not the same. He seemed waiting for something to happen, waiting for the next thing. You'd pass his neat little house sometimes at dusk and he would be on the porch smoking a pipe with a glass of mineral water on the porch rail and the sunset would be in his eyes and pipe smoke around his head and you'd think — I did, anyway — *Homer is waiting for the next thing*. This bothered me over a wider range of my mind than I liked to admit, and at last I decided it was because if it had been me, I wouldn't have been waiting for the next thing, like a groom who has put on his morning coat and finally has his tie right and is only sitting there on a bed in the upstairs of his house and looking first at himself in the mirror and then at the clock on the mantel and waiting for it to be eleven o'clock so he can get married. If it had been me, I would not have been waiting for the next thing; I would have been waiting for the last thing.

But in that waiting period — which ended when Homer went to Vermont a year later — he sometimes talked about those people. To me, to a few others.

"She never even drove fast with her husband, s'far as I know. But when I drove with her, she made that Mercedes strut."

A fellow pulled in at the pumps and began to fill up his car. The car had a Massachusetts plate.

"It wasn't one of these new sports cars that run on unleaded gasoline and hitch every time you step on it; it was one of the old ones, and the speedometer was calibrated all the way up to a hundred and sixty. It was a funny color of brown and I ast her one time what you called that color and she said it was Champagne. Ain't that *good*, I says, and she laughs fit to split. I like a woman who will laugh when you don't have to point her right at the joke, you know."

The man at the pumps had finished getting his gas.

"Afternoon, gentlemen," he says as he comes up the steps.

"A good day to you," I says, and he went inside.

"'Phelia was always lookin for a shortcut," Homer went on as if we had never been interrupted. "That woman was mad for a shortcut. I never saw the beat of it. She said if you can save enough distance, you'll save time as well. She said her father swore by that scripture. He was a salesman, always on the road, and she went with him when she could, and he was always lookin for the shortest way. So she got in the habit.

"I ast her one time if it wasn't kinda funny — here she was on the one hand, spendin her time rubbin up that old statue in the Square and takin the little ones to their swimmin lessons instead of playing tennis and swimming and getting boozed up like normal summer people, and on the other hand bein so damn set on savin fifteen minutes between here and Fryeburg that thinkin about it probably kep her up nights. It just seemed to me the two things went against each other's grain, if you see what I mean. She just looks at me and says, 'I like being helpful, Homer. I like driving, too — at least sometimes, when it's a challenge — but I don't like the *time* it takes. It's like mending clothes — sometimes you take tucks and sometimes you let things out. Do you see what I mean?'

"'I guess so, missus,' I says, kinda dubious.

"'If sitting behind the wheel of a car was my idea of a really good time *all* the time, I would look for long-cuts,' she says, and that tickled me s'much I had to laugh."

The Massachusetts fellow came out of the store with a six-pack in one hand and some lottery tickets in the other.

"You enjoy your weekend," Homer says.

"I always do," the Massachusetts fellow says. "I only wish I could afford to live here all year round."

"Well, we'll keep it all in good order for when you *can* come," Homer says, and the fellow laughs.

We watched him drive off toward someplace, that Massachusetts plate showing. It was a green one. My Marcy says those are the ones the Massachusetts Motor Registry gives to drivers who ain't had a accident in that strange, angry, fuming state for two years. If you have, she says, you got to have a red one so people know to watch out for you when they see you on the roll.

"They was in-state people, you know, the both of them," Homer said, as if the Massachusetts fellow had reminded him of the fact.

"I guess I did know that," I said.

"The Todds are just about the only birds we got that fly north in the winter. The new one, I don't think she likes flying north too much."

He sipped his mineral water and fell silent a moment, thinking.

"*She* didn't mind it, though," Homer said. "At least, I *judge* she didn't although she used to complain about it something fierce. The complaining was just a way to explain why she was always lookin for a shortcut."

"And you mean her husband didn't mind her traipsing down every wood-road in tarnation between here and Bangor just so she could see if it was nine-tenths of a mile shorter?"

"He didn't care piss-all," Homer said shortly, and got up, and went in the store. There now, Owens, I told myself, you know it ain't safe to ast him questions when he's yarning, and you went right ahead and ast one, and you have buggered a story that was starting to shape up promising.

I sat there and turned my face up into the sun and after about ten minutes he come out with a boiled egg and sat down. He ate her and I took care not to say nothing and the water on Castle Lake sparkled as blue as something as might be told of in a story about treasure. When Homer had finished his egg and had a sip of mineral water, he went on. I was surprised, but still said nothing. It wouldn't have been wise.

"They had two or three different chunks of rolling iron," he said. "There was the Cadillac, and his truck, and her little Mercedes go-devil. A couple of winters he left the truck, 'case they wanted to come down and do some skiin. Mostly when the summer was over he'd drive the Caddy back up and she'd take her go-devil."

I nodded but didn't speak. In truth, I was afraid to risk another comment. Later I thought it would have taken a lot of comments to shut Homer Buckland up that day. He had been wanting to tell the story of Mrs. Todd's shortcut for a long time.

"Her little go-devil had a special odometer in it that told you how many miles was in a trip, and every time she set off from Castle Lake to Bangor she'd set it to ooo-point-o and let her clock up to whatever. She had made a game of it, and she used to chafe me with it."

He paused, thinking that back over.

"No, that ain't right."

He paused more and faint lines showed up on his forehead like steps on a library ladder.

"She *made* like she made a game of it, but it was a serious business to her. Serious as anything else, anyway." He flapped a hand and I think he meant the husband. "The glovebox of the little go-devil was filled with maps, and there was a few more in the back where there would be a seat in a regular car. Some was gas station maps, and some was pages that had been pulled from the Rand-McNally Road Atlas; she had some maps from Appalachian Trail guidebooks and a whole mess of topographical survey-squares, too. It wasn't her having those maps that made me think it wa'n't a game; it was how she'd drawed lines on all of them, showing routes she'd taken or at least tried to take.

"She'd been stuck a few times, too, and had to get a pull from some farmer with a tractor and chain.

"I was there one day laying tile in the bathroom, sitting there with grout squittering out of every damn crack you could see — I dreamed of nothing but squares and cracks that was bleeding grout that night — and she come stood in the doorway and talked to me about it for quite a while. I used to chafe her about it, but I was also sort of interested, and not just because my brother Franklin used to live down-Bangor and I'd traveled most of the roads she was telling me of. I was interested just because a man like me is always uncommon interested in knowing the shortest way, even if he don't always want to take it. You that way too?"

"Ayuh," I said. There's something powerful about knowing the shortest way, even if you take the longer way because you know your mother-in-law is sitting home. Getting there quick is often for the birds, although no one holding a Massachusetts driver's license seems to know it. But *knowing* how to get there quick — or even knowing how to get there a way that the person sitting beside you don't know...that has power.

"Well, she had them roads like a Boy Scout has his knots," Homer said, and smiled his large, sunny grin. "She says, 'Wait a minute, wait a minute,' like a little girl, and I hear her through the wall rummaging through her desk, and then she comes back with a little notebook that looked like she'd had it a good long time. Cover was all rumpled, don't you know, and some of the pages had pulled loose from those little wire rings on one side.

"'The way Worth goes — the way *most* people go — is Route 97 to Mechanic Falls, then Route 11 to Lewiston, and then the Interstate to Bangor. 156.4 miles.'

I nodded.

"'If you want to skip the turnpike — and save some distance — you'd go to Mechanic Falls, Route 11 to Lewiston, Route 202 to Augusta, then up Route 9 through China Lake and Unity and Haven to Bangor. That's 144.9 miles.'

"'You won't save no time that way, missus,' I says, 'not going through Lewiston *and* Augusta. Although I will admit that drive up the Old Derry Road to Bangor is real pretty.'

"'Save enough miles and soon enough you'll save time,' she says. 'And I didn't say that's the way I'd go, although I have a good many times; I'm just running down the routes most people use. Do you want me to go on?'

"'No,' I says, 'just leave me in this cussed bathroom all by myself starin at all these cussed cracks until I start to rave.'

"'There are four major routes in all,' she says. 'The one by Route 2 is 163.4 miles. I only tried it once. Too long.'

"'That's the one I'd hosey if my wife called and told me it was left-overs,' I says, kinda low.

"'What was that?' she says.

"'Nothin,' I says. 'Talkin to the grout.'

"'Oh. Well, the fourth — and there aren't too many who know about it, although they are all good roads — paved, anyway — is across Speckled Bird Mountain on 219 to 202 *beyond* Lewiston. Then, if you take Route 19, you can get around Augusta. Then you take the Old Derry Road. That way is just 129.2.'

"I didn't say nothing for a little while and p'raps she thought I was doubting her because she says, a little pert, 'I know it's hard to believe, but it's so.'

"I said I guessed that was about right, and I thought — looking back — it probably was. Because that's the way I'd usually go when I went down to Bangor to see Franklin when he was still alive. I hadn't been that way in years, though. Do you think a man could just — well — forget a road, Dave?"

I allowed it was. The turnpike is easy to think of. After a while it almost fills a man's mind, and you think not how could I get from here to there but how can I get from here to the turnpike ramp that's *closest* to there. And that made me think that maybe there are lots of roads all over that are just going begging; roads with rock walls beside them, real roads with blackberry bushes growing alongside them but nobody to eat the berries but the birds and gravel pits with old rusted chains hanging down in low curves in front of their entryways, the pits themselves as forgotten as a child's old toys with scrumgrass growing up their deserted unremembered sides. Roads that have just been forgot except by the people who live on them and think of the quickest way to get off them and onto the turnpike where you can pass on a hill and not fret over it. We like to joke in Maine that you can't get there from here, but maybe the joke is on us. The truth is there's about a damn thousand ways to do it and man doesn't bother.

Homer continued: "I grouted tile all afternoon in that hot little bathroom and she stood there in the doorway all that time, one foot crossed behind the other, bare-legged, wearin loafers and a khaki-colored skirt and a sweater that was some darker. Hair was drawed back in a hosstail.

She must have been thirty-four or -five then, but her face was lit up with what she was tellin me and I swan she looked like a sorority girl home from school on vacation.

"After a while she musta got an idea of how long she'd been there cuttin the air around her mouth because she says, 'I must be boring the hell out of you, Homer.'

"'Yes'm,' I says, 'you are. I druther you went away and left me to talk to this damn grout.'

"'Don't be sma'at, Homer,' she says.

"'No, missus, you ain't borin me,' I says.

"So she smiles and then goes back to it, pagin through her little notebook like a salesman checkin his orders. She had those four main ways — well, really three because she gave up on Route 2 right away — but she must have had forty different other ways that were play-offs on those. Roads with state numbers, roads without, roads with names, roads without. My head fair spun with 'em. And finally she says to me, 'You ready for the blue-ribbon winner, Homer?'

"'I guess so,' I says.

"'At least it's the blue-ribbon winner *so far,*' she says. 'Do you know, Homer, that a man wrote an article in *Science Today* in 1923 proving that no man could run a mile in under four minutes? He *proved* it, with all sorts of calculations based on the maximum length of the male thigh-muscles, maximum length of stride, maximum lung capacity, maximum heart-rate, and a whole lot more. I was *taken* with that article! I was so taken that I gave it to Worth and asked him to give it to Professor Murray in the math department at the University of Maine. I wanted those figures checked because I was sure they must have been based on the wrong postulates, or something. Worth probably thought I was being silly — "Ophelia's got a bee in her bonnet" is what he says — but he took them. Well, Professor Murray checked through the man's figures quite carefully…and do you know *what,* Homer?'

"'No, missus.'

"'Those figures were *right.* The man's criteria were *solid.* He proved, back in 1923, that a man couldn't run a mile in under four minutes. He *proved* that. But people do it all the time, and do you know what that means?'

"'No, missus,' I said, although I had a glimmer.

"'It means that no blue ribbon is forever,' she says. 'Someday — if the world doesn't explode itself in the meantime — someone will run a two-minute mile in the Olympics. It may take a hundred years or a thousand, but it will happen. Because there is no ultimate blue ribbon. There is zero, and there is eternity, and there is mortality, but there is no *ultimate*.'

"And there she stood, her face clean and scrubbed and shinin, that darkish hair of hers pulled back from her brow, as if to say 'Just you go ahead and disagree if you can.' But I couldn't. Because I believe something like that. It is much like what the minister means, I think, when he talks about grace.

"'You ready for the blue-ribbon winner *for now?'* she says.

"'Ayuh,' I says, and I even stopped groutin for the time bein. I'd reached the tub anyway and there wasn't nothing left but a lot of those frikkin squirrelly little corners. She drawed a deep breath and then spieled it out at me as fast as that auctioneer goes over in Gates Falls when he has been putting the whiskey to himself, and I can't remember it all, but it went something like this."

Homer Buckland shut his eyes for a moment, his big hands lying perfectly still on his long thighs, his face turned up toward the sun. Then he opened his eyes again and for a moment I swan he *looked* like her, yes he did, a seventy-year-old man looking like a woman of thirty-four who was at that moment in her time looking like a college girl of twenty, and I can't remember exactly what *he* said any more than *he* could remember exactly what *she* said, not just because it was complex but because I was so fetched by how he looked sayin it, but it went close enough like this:

"'You set out Route 97 and then cut up Denton Street to the Old Townhouse Road and that way you get around Castle Rock downtown but back to 97. Nine miles up you can go an old logger's road a mile and a half to Town Road #6, which takes you to Big Anderson Road by Sites' Cider Mill. There's a cut-road the old-timers call Bear Road, and that gets you to 219. Once you're on the far side of Speckled Bird Mountain you grab the Stanhouse Road, turn left onto the Bull Pine Road — there's a swampy patch there but you can spang right through it if you get up enough speed on the gravel — and so you come out on Route 106. 106 cuts through Alton's Plantation to the Old Derry Road — and there's two or three woods roads there that you follow and so come out on Route 3 just beyond Derry Hospital. From there it's only four miles to Route 2 in Etna, and so into Bangor.'

"She paused to get her breath back, then looked at me. 'Do you know how long that is, all told?'

"'No'm,' I says, thinking it sounds like about a hundred and ninety miles and four bust springs.

"'It's 116.4 miles,' she says."

I laughed. The laugh was out of me before I thought I wasn't doing myself any favor if I wanted to hear this story to the end. But Homer grinned himself and nodded.

"I know. And *you* know I don't like to argue with anyone, Dave. But there's a difference between having your leg pulled and getting it shook like a damn apple tree.

"'You don't believe me,' she says.

"'Well, it's *hard* to believe, missus,' I said.

"'Leave that grout to dry and I'll show you,' she says. 'You can finish behind the tub tomorrow. Come on, Homer. I'll leave a note for Worth — he may not be back tonight anyway — and you can call your wife! We'll be sitting down to dinner in the Pilot's Grille in' — she looks at her watch — 'two hours and forty-five minutes from right now. And if it's a minute longer, I'll buy you a bottle of Irish Mist to take home with you. You see, my dad was right. Save enough miles and you'll save time, even if you have to go through every damn bog and sump in Kennebec County to do it. Now what do you say?'

"She was lookin at me with her brown eyes just like lamps, there was a devilish look in them that said turn your cap around back'rds, Homer, and climb aboard this hoss, I be first and you be second and let the devil take the hindmost, and there was a grin on her face that said the exact same thing, and I tell you, Dave, I wanted to *go*. I didn't even want to top that damn can of grout. And I *certain* sure didn't want to drive that go-devil of hers. I wanted just to sit in it on the shotgun side and watch her get in, see her skirt come up a little, see her pull it down over her knees or not, watch her hair shine."

He trailed off and suddenly let off a sarcastic, choked laugh. That laugh of his sounded like a shotgun loaded with rock salt.

"Just call up Megan and say, 'You know 'Phelia Todd, that woman you're halfway to being so jealous of now you can't see straight and can't ever find a good word to say about her? Well, her and me is going to make this speed-run down to Bangor in that little champagne-colored go-devil Mercedes of hers, so don't wait dinner.'

"Just call her up and say that. Oh *yes*. Oh *ayuh*."

And he laughed again with his hands lying there on his legs just as natural as ever was and I seen something in his face that was almost hateful and after a minute he took his glass of mineral water from the railing there and got outside some of it.

"You didn't go," I said.

"Not *then*."

He laughed, and this laugh was gentler.

"She must have seen something in my face, because it was like she found herself again. She stopped looking like a sorority girl and just looked like 'Phelia Todd again. She looked down at the notebook like she didn't know what it was she had been holding and put it down by her side, almost behind her skirt.

"I says, 'I'd like to do just that thing, missus, but I got to finish up here, and my wife has got a roast on for dinner.'

"She says, 'I understand, Homer — I just got a little carried away. I do that a lot. All the time, Worth says.' Then she kinda straightened up and says, 'But the offer holds, any time you want to go. You can even throw your shoulder to the back end if we get stuck somewhere. Might save me five dollars.' And she laughed.

"'I'll take you up on it, missus,' I says, and she seen that I meant what I said and wasn't just being polite.

"And before you just go believing that a hundred and sixteen miles to

Bangor is out of the question, get out your own map and see how many miles it would be as the crow flies.'

"I finished the tiles and went home and ate leftovers — there wa'n't no roast, and I think 'Phelia Todd knew it — and after Megan was in bed, I got out my yardstick and a pen and my Mobil map of the state, and I did what she had told me…because it had laid hold of my mind a bit, you see. I drew a straight line and did out the calculations accordin to the scale of miles. I was some surprised. Because if you went from Castle Rock up there to Bangor like one of those little Piper Cubs could fly on a clear day — if you didn't have to mind lakes, or stretches of lumber company woods that was chained off, or bogs, or crossing rivers where there wasn't no bridges, why, it would just be seventy-nine miles, give or take."

I jumped a little.

"Measure it yourself, if you don't believe me," Homer said. "I never knew Maine was so small until I seen that."

He had himself a drink and then looked around at me.

"There come a time the next spring when Megan was away in New Hampshire visiting with her brother. I had to go down to the Todds' house to take off the storm doors and put on the screens, and her little Mercedes go-devil was there. She was down by herself.

"She come to the door and says: 'Homer! Have you come to put on the screen doors?'

"And right off I says: 'No, missus, I come to see if you want to give me a ride down to Bangor the short way.'

"Well, she looked at me with no expression on her face at all, and I thought she had forgotten all about it. I felt my face gettin red, the way it will when you feel you just pulled one hell of a boner. Then, just when I was getting ready to 'pologize, her face busts into that grin again and she says, 'You just stand right there while I get my keys. And don't change your mind, Homer!'

"She come back a minute later with 'em in her hand. 'If we get stuck, you'll see mosquitoes just about the size of dragonflies.'

"'I've seen 'em as big as English sparrows up in Rangely, missus,' I said, 'and I guess we're both a spot too heavy to be carried off.'

"She laughs. 'Well, I warned you, anyway. Come on, Homer.'

"'And if we ain't there in two hours and forty-five minutes,' I says, kinda sly, 'you was gonna buy me a bottle of Irish Mist.'

"She looks at me kinda surprised, the driver's door of the go-devil open and one foot inside. 'Hell, Homer,' she says, 'I told you that was the Blue Ribbon for *then*. I've found a way up there that's *shorter*. We'll be there in two and a half hours. Get in here, Homer. We are going to roll.'"

He paused again, hands lying calm on his thighs, his eyes dulling, perhaps seeing that champagne-colored two-seater heading up the Todds' steep driveway.

"She stood the car still at the end of it and says, 'You sure?'

"'Let her rip,' I says. The ball bearing in her ankle rolled and that heavy foot come down. I can't tell you nothing much about whatall happened after that. Except after a while I couldn't hardly take my eyes off her. There was somethin wild that crep into her face, Dave — something *wild* and something *free,* and it frightened my heart. She was beautiful, and I was took with love *for* her, anyone would have been, any man, anyway, and maybe any woman too, but I was scairt *of* her too, because she looked like she could kill you if her eye left the road and fell on you and she decided to love you back. She was wearin blue jeans and a old white shirt with the sleeves rolled up — I had a idea she was maybe fixin to paint somethin on the back deck when I came by — but after we had been goin for a while seemed like she was dressed in nothin but all this white billowy stuff like a pitcher in one of those old gods-and-goddesses books."

He thought, looking out across the lake, his face very somber.

"Like the huntress that was supposed to drive the moon across the sky."

"Diana?"

"Ayuh. Moon was her go-devil. 'Phelia looked like that to me and I just tell you fair out that I was stricken in love for her and never would have made a move, even though I was some younger then than I am now. I would not have made a move even had I been twenty, although I suppose I might of at sixteen, and been killed for it — killed if she looked at me was the way it felt.

"She was like that woman drivin the moon across the sky, halfway up over the splashboard with her gossamer stoles all flyin out behind her in silver cobwebs and her hair streamin back to show the dark little hollows of her temples, lashin those horses and tellin me to get along faster and never mind how they blowed, just faster, faster, *faster.*

"We went down a lot of woods roads — the first two or three I knew, and after that I didn't know none of them. We must have been a sight to those trees that had never seen nothing with a motor in it before but big old pulp-trucks and snowmobiles; that little go-devil that would most likely have looked more at home on the Sunset Boulevard than shooting through those woods, spitting and bulling its way up one hill and then slamming down the next through those dusty green bars of afternoon sunlight — she had the top down and I could smell everything in those woods, and you know what an old fine smell that is, like something which has been mostly left alone and is not much troubled. We went on across corduroy which had been laid over some of the boggiest parts, and black mud squelched up between some of those cut logs and she laughed like a kid. Some of the logs was old and rotted, because there hadn't been nobody down a couple of those roads — except for her, that is — in I'm going to say five or ten years. We was *alone,* except for the birds and whatever animals seen us. The sound of that go-devil's engine, first buzzin along and then windin up high and fierce when she punched in the clutch and shifted down... that was the only motor-sound I could hear. And although I knew we had to be close to *someplace* all the time — I mean, these days you always are — I started to feel like we had gone back in time, and there wasn't *nothing.* That if we stopped and I climbed a high tree, I wouldn't see nothing in any direction but woods and woods and more woods. And all the time she's just *hammering* that thing along, her hair all out behind her, smilin, her eyes flashin. So we come out on the Speckled Bird Mountain Road and for a while I known where we were again, and then she turned off and for just a little bit I *thought* I knew, and then I didn't even bother to kid myself no more. We went cut-slam down another woods road, and then we come out — I swear it — on a nice paved road with a sign that said MOTORWAY B. You ever heard of a road in the state of Maine that was called Motorway B?"

"No," I says. "Sounds English."

"Ayuh. *Looked* English. These trees like willows overhung the road. 'Now watch out here, Homer,' she says, 'one of those nearly grabbed me a month ago and gave me an Indian burn.'

"I didn't know what she was talkin about and started to say so, and then I seen that even though there was no wind, the branches of those trees was dippin down — they was *waverin* down. They looked black and wet inside the fuzz of green on them. I couldn't believe what I was seein. Then one of 'em snatched off my cap and I knew I wasn't asleep. 'Hi!' I shouts. 'Give that back!'

"'Too late now, Homer,' she says, and laughs. 'There's daylight, just up ahead...we're okay.'

"Then another one of 'em comes down, on her side this time, and snatches at her — I swear it did. She ducked, and it caught in her hair and pulled a lock of it out. 'Ouch, dammit that *hurts!*' she yells, but she was laughin, too. The car swerved a little when she ducked and I got a look into the woods and holy God, Dave! *Everythin* in there was movin. There was grasses wavin and plants that was all knotted together so it seemed like they made faces, and I seen somethin sittin in a squat on top of a stump, and it looked like a tree-toad, only it was as big as a full-growed cat.

"Then we come out of the shade to the top of a hill and she says, 'There! That was exciting, wasn't it?' as if she was talkin about no more than a walk through the Haunted House at the Fryeburg Fair.

"About five minutes later we swung onto another of her woods roads. I didn't want no more woods right then — I can tell you that for sure — but these were just plain old woods. Half an hour after that, we was pulling into the parking lot of the Pilot's Grille in Bangor. She points to that little odometer for trips and says, 'Take a gander, Homer.' I did, and it said 111.6. 'What do you think now? Do you believe in my shortcut?'

"That wild look had mostly faded out of her, and she was just 'Phelia Todd again. But that other look wasn't entirely gone. It was like she was two women, 'Phelia and Diana, and the part of her that was Diana was so much in control when she was driving the back roads that the part that was 'Phelia didn't have no idea that her shortcut was taking her through places...places that ain't on any map of Maine, not even on those survey-squares.

"She says again, 'What do you think of my shortcut, Homer?'

"And I says the first thing to come into my mind, which ain't something you'd usually say to a lady like 'Phelia Todd. 'It's a real piss-cutter, missus,' I says.

"She laughs, just as pleased as punch, and I seen it then, just as clear as glass: She didn't remember none of the funny stuff. Not the willow-branches — except they weren't willows, not at all, not really anything like 'em, or anything else — that grabbed off m'hat, not that MOTORWAY B sign, or that awful-lookin toad-thing. *She didn't remember none of that funny stuff!* Either I had dreamed it was there or she had dreamed it wasn't. All I knew for sure, Dave, was that we had rolled only a hundred and eleven miles and gotten to Bangor, and that wasn't no daydream; it was right there on the little go-devil's odometer, in black and white.

"'Well, it is,' she says. 'It *is* a piss-cutter. I only wish I could get Worth to give it a go sometime...but he'll never get out of his rut unless someone blasts him out of it, and it would probably take a Titan II missile to do that, because I believe he has built himself a fallout shelter at the bottom of that rut. Come on in, Homer, and let's dump some dinner into you.'

"And she bought me one hell of a dinner, Dave, but I couldn't eat very much of it. I kep thinkin about what the ride back might be like, now that it was drawing down dark. Then, about halfway through the meal, she excused herself and made a telephone call. When she came back she ast me if I would mind drivin the go-devil back to Castle Rock for her. She said she had talked to some woman who was on the same school committee as her, and the woman said they had some kind of problem about somethin or other. She said she'd grab herself a Hertz car if Worth couldn't see her back down. 'Do you mind awfully driving back in the dark?' she ast me.

"She looked at me, kinda smilin, and I knew she remembered *some* of it all right — Christ knows how much, but she remembered enough to know I wouldn't want to try her way after dark, if ever at all...although I seen by the light in her eyes that it wouldn't have bothered her a bit.

"So I said it wouldn't bother me, and I finished my meal better than when I started it. It was drawin down dark by the time we was done, and she run us over to the house of the woman she'd called. And when she gets out she looks at me with that same light in her eyes and says, 'Now, you're *sure* you don't want to wait, Homer? I saw a couple of side roads just today, and although I can't find them on my maps, I think they might chop a few miles.'

"I says, 'Well, missus, I would, but at my age the best bed to sleep in is my own, I've found. I'll take your car back and never put a ding in her... although I guess I'll probably put on some more miles than you did.'

"Then she laughed, kind of soft, and she give me a kiss. That was the best kiss I ever had in my whole life, Dave. It was just on the cheek, and it was the chaste kiss of a married woman, but it was as ripe as a peach, or like those flowers that open in the dark, and when her lips touched my skin I felt like...I don't know exactly what I felt like, because a man can't easily hold on to those things that happened to him with a girl who was ripe when the world was young or how those things felt — I'm talking around what I mean, but I think you understand. Those things all get a red cast to them in your memory and you cannot see through it at all.

"'You're a sweet man, Homer, and I love you for listening to me and riding with me,' she says. 'Drive safe.'

"Then in she went, to that woman's house. Me, I drove home."

"How did you go?" I asked.

He laughed softly. "By the turnpike, you damned fool," he said, and I never seen so many wrinkles in his face before as I did then.

He sat there, looking into the sky.

"Came the summer she disappeared. I didn't see much of her...that was the summer we had the fire, you'll remember, and then the big storm that knocked down all the trees. A busy time for caretakers. Oh, I *thought* about her from time to time, and about that day, and about that kiss, and it started to seem like a dream to me. Like one time, when I was about sixteen and couldn't think about nothing but girls. I was out plowing George Bascomb's west field, the one that looks acrost the lake at the mountains, dreamin about what teenage boys dream of. And I pulled up this rock with the harrow blades, and it split open, and it *bled*. At least, it looked to me like it bled. Red stuff come runnin out of the cleft in the rock and soaked into the soil. And I never told no one but my mother, and I never told her what it meant to me, or what happened to me, although she washed my drawers and maybe she knew. Anyway, she suggested I ought to pray on it. Which I did, but I never got no enlightenment, and after a while something started to suggest to my mind that it had been a dream. It's that way, sometimes. There is holes in the *middle*, Dave. Do you know that?"

"Yes," I says, thinking of one night when I'd seen something. That was in '59, a bad year for us, but my kids didn't know it was a bad year; all they knew was that they wanted to eat just like always. I'd seen a bunch of whitetail in Henry Brugger's back field, and I was out there after dark with a jacklight in August. You can shoot two when they're summer-fat; the second'll come back and sniff at the first as if to say *What the hell? Is it fall already?* and you can pop him like a bowlin pin. You can hack off enough meat to feed yowwens for six weeks and bury what's left. Those are two whitetails the hunters who come in November don't get a shot at, but kids have to eat. Like the man from Massachusetts said, *he'd* like to be able to afford to live here the year around, and all I can say is sometimes you pay for the privilege after dark. So there I was, and I seen this big orange light in the sky; it come down and down, and I stood and watched it with my mouth hung on down to my breastbone and when it hit the lake the whole of it was lit up for a minute a purple-orange that seemed to go right up to the sky in rays. Wasn't nobody ever said nothing to me about that light, and I never said nothing to nobody myself, partly because I was afraid they'd laugh, but also because they'd wonder what the hell I'd been doing out there after dark to start with. And after a while it was like Homer said — it seemed like a dream I had once had, and it didn't signify to me because I couldn't make nothing of it which would turn under my hand. It was like a moonbeam. It didn't have no handle and it didn't have no blade. I couldn't make it work so I left it alone, like a man does when he knows the day is going to come up nevertheless.

"There are *holes* in the middle of things," Homer said, and he sat up straighter, like he was mad. "Right in the damn *middle* of things, not even to the left or right where your p'riph'ral vision is and you could say 'Well, but hell —' They are there and you go around them like you'd go around a pothole in the road that would break an axle. You know? And you forget it. Or like if you are plowin, you can plow a dip. But if there's somethin like a *break* in the earth, where you see darkness, like a cave might be there, you say 'Go around, old hoss. Leave that alone! I got a good shot over here to the left'ards.' Because it wasn't a cave you was lookin for, or some kind of college excitement, but good plowin.

"*Holes* in the *middle* of things."

He fell still a long time then and I let him be still. Didn't have no urge to move him. And at last he says:

"She disappeared in August. I seen her for the first time in early July, and she looked…" Homer turned to me and spoke each word with careful, spaced emphasis. "Dave Owens, she looked *gorgeous!* Gorgeous and wild and almost untamed. The little wrinkles I'd started to notice around her eyes all seemed to be gone. Worth Todd, he was at some conference or something in Boston. And she stands there at the edge of the deck — I was out in the middle with my shirt off — and she says, 'Homer, you'll never believe it.'

"'No, missus, but I'll try,' I says.

"'I found two new roads,' she says, 'and I got up to Bangor this last time in just sixty-seven miles.'

"I remembered what she said before and I says, 'That's not possible, missus. Beggin your pardon, but I did the mileage on the map myself, and seventy-nine is tops…as the crow flies.'

"She laughed, and she looked prettier than ever. Like a goddess in the sun, on one of those hills in a story where there's nothing but green grass and fountains and no puckies to tear at a man's forearms at all. 'That's right,' she says, 'and you can't run a mile in under four minutes. It's been mathematically *proved*.'

"'It ain't the same,' I says.

"'It's the same,' she says. 'Fold the map and see how many miles it is then, Homer. It can be a little less than a straight line if you fold it a little, or it can be a lot less if you fold it a lot.'

"I remembered our ride then, the way you remember a dream, and I says, 'Missus, you can fold a map on paper but you can't fold *land*. Or at least you shouldn't ought to try. You want to leave it alone.'

"'No sir,' she says. 'It's the one thing right now in my life that I won't leave alone, because it's *there*, and it's *mine*.'

"Three weeks later — this would be about two weeks before she disappeared — she give me a call from Bangor. She says, 'Worth has gone to New York, and I am coming down. I've misplaced my damn key, Homer. I'd like you to open the house so I can get in.'

"Well, that call come at eight o'clock, just when it was starting to come down dark. I had a sanwidge and a beer before leaving — about twenty minutes. Then I took a ride down there. All in all, I'd say I was forty-five minutes. When I got down there to the Todds', I seen there was a light on in the pantry I didn't leave on while I was comin down the driveway. I was lookin at that, and I almost run right into her little go-devil. It was parked kind of on a slant, the way a drunk would park it, and it was splashed with muck all the way up to the windows, and there was this stuff stuck in that mud along the body that looked like seaweed...only when my lights hit it, it seemed to be *movin*. I parked behind it and got out of my truck. That stuff wasn't seaweed, but it *was* weeds, and it *was* movin...kinda slow and sluggish, like it was dyin. I touched a piece of it, and it tried to wrap itself around my hand. It felt nasty and awful. I drug my hand away and wiped it on my pants. I went around to the front of the car. It looked like it had come through about ninety miles of splash and low country. Looked *tired*, it did. Bugs was splashed all over the windshield — only they didn't look like no kind of bugs *I* ever seen before. There was a moth that was about the size of a sparrow, its wings still flappin a little, feeble and dyin. There was things like mosquitoes, only they had real eyes that you could see — and they seemed to be seein *me*. I could hear those weeds scrapin against the body of the go-devil, dyin, tryin to get a hold on somethin. And all I could think was Where in the hell has she been? And how did she get here in only three-quarters of an hour? Then I seen somethin else. There was some kind of a animal half-smashed onto the radiator grille, just under where that Mercedes ornament is — the one that looks kinda like a star looped up into a circle? Now most small animals you kill on the road is bore right under the car, because they are crouching when it hits them, hoping it'll just go over and leave them with their hide still attached to their meat. But every now and then one will Jump, not away, but right at the damn car, as if to get in one good bite of whatever the buggardly thing is that's going to kill it — I have known that to happen. This thing had maybe done that. And it looked mean enough to jump a Sherman tank. It looked like something which come of a mating between a wood-chuck and a weasel, but there was other stuff thrown in that a body didn't even want to look at. It hurt your eyes, Dave; worse'n that, it hurt your *mind*. Its pelt was matted with blood, and there was claws sprung out of the pads on its feet like a cat's claws, only longer. It had big yellowy eyes, only they was glazed. When I was a kid I had a porcelain marble — a croaker — that looked like that. And teeth. Long thin needle teeth that looked almost like darning needles, stickin out of its mouth. Some of them was sunk right into that steel grillwork. That's why it was still hanging on; it had hung its *own* self on by the teeth. I looked at it and knowed it had a headful of poison just like a rattlesnake, and it jumped at that go-devil when it saw it was about to be run down, tryin to bite it to death. And I wouldn't be the one to try and yonk it offa there because I had cuts on my hands—hay-cuts — and I thought it would kill me as dead as a stone parker if some of that poison seeped into the cuts.

"I went around to the driver's door and opened it. The inside light come on, and I looked at that special odometer that she set for trips... and what I seen there was 31.6.

"I looked at that for a bit, and then I went to the back door. She'd forced the screen and broke the glass by the lock so she could get her hand through and let herself in. There was a note that said: 'Dear Homer — got here a little sooner than I thought I would. Found a shortcut, and it is a dilly! You hadn't come yet so I let myself in like a burglar. Worth is coming day after tomorrow. Can you get the screen fixed and the door

THE SECRET HISTORY OF FANTASY

reglazed by then? Hope so. Things like that always bother him. If I don't come out to say hello, you'll know I'm asleep. The drive was very tiring, but I was here in no time! Ophelia.'

"*Tirin!* I took another look at that bogey-thing hangin offa the grille of her car, and I thought Yessir, it *must* have been tiring. By God, *yes.*"

He paused again, and cracked a restless knuckle.

"I seen her only once more. About a week later. Worth was there, but he was swimmin out in the lake, back and forth, back and forth, like he was sawin wood or signin papers. More like he was signin papers, I guess.

"'Missus,' I says, 'this ain't my business, but you ought to leave well enough alone. That night you come back and broke the glass of the door to come in, I seen somethin hangin off the front of your car —'

"'Oh, the chuck! I took care of that,' she says.

"'Christ!' I says. 'I hope you took some care!'

"'I wore Worth's gardening gloves,' she said. 'It wasn't anything anyway, Homer, but a jumped-up woodchuck with a little poison in it.'

"'But missus,' I says, 'where there's woodchucks there's bears. And if that's what the woodchucks look like along your shortcut, what's going to happen to you if a bear shows up?'

"She looked at me, and I seen that other woman in her — that Diana-woman. She says, 'If things are different along those roads, Homer, maybe I am different, too. Look at this.'

"Her hair was done up in a clip at the back, looked sort of like a butterfly and had a stick through it. She let it down. It was the kind of hair that would make a man wonder what it would look like spread out over a pillow. She says, 'It was coming in gray, Homer. Do you see any gray?' And she spread it with her fingers so the sun could shine on it.

"'No'm,' I says.

"She looks at me, her eyes all a-sparkle, and she says, 'Your wife is a good woman, Homer Buckland, but she has seen me in the store and in the post office, and we've passed the odd word or two, and I have seen her looking at my hair in a kind of satisfied way that only women know. I know what she says, and what she tells her friends...that Ophelia Todd has started dyeing her hair. But I have not. I have lost my way looking for a shortcut more than once…lost my way…and lost my gray.' And she laughed, not like a college girl but like a girl in high school. I admired her and longed for her beauty, but I seen that other beauty in her face as well just then…and I felt afraid again. Afraid *for* her, and afraid *of* her.

"'Missus,' I says, 'you stand to lose more than a little sta'ch in your hair.'

"'No,' she says. 'I tell you I am different over there…I am *all myself* over there. When I am going along that road in my little car I am not Ophelia Todd, Worth Todd's wife who could never carry a child to term, or that woman who tried to write poetry and failed at it, or the woman who sits and takes notes in committee meetings, or anything or anyone else. When I am on that road I am in the heart of myself, and I feel like —'

"'*Diana,*' I said.

"She looked at me kind of funny and kind of surprised, and then she laughed. 'O like some goddess, I suppose,' she said. 'She will do better than most because I am a night person — I love to stay up until my book is done or until the National Anthem comes on the TV, and because I am very pale, like the moon — Worth is always saying I need a tonic, or blood tests or some sort of similar bosh. But in her heart what every woman wants to be is some kind of goddess, I think — men pick up a ruined echo of that thought and try to put them on pedestals (a woman, who will pee down her own leg if she does not squat! it's funny when you stop to think of it) — but what a man senses is not what a woman wants. A woman wants to be in the clear, is all. To stand if she will, or walk…' Her eyes turned toward that little go-devil in the driveway, and narrowed. Then she smiled. 'Or to *drive,* Homer. A man will not see that. He thinks a goddess wants to loll on a slope somewhere on the foothills of Olympus and eat fruit, but there is no god or goddess in that. All a woman wants is what a man wants — a woman wants to *drive.*'

"'Be careful where you drive, missus, is all,' I says, and she laughs and give me a kiss spang in the middle of the forehead.

"She says, 'I will, Homer,' but it didn't mean nothing, and I known it, because she said it like a man who says he'll be careful to his wife or his girl when he knows he won't…can't.

THE SECRET HISTORY OF FANTASY

"I went back to my truck and waved to her once, and it was a week later that Worth reported her missing. Her and that go-devil both. Todd waited seven years and had her declared legally dead, and then he waited another year for good measure — I'll give the sucker that much — and then he married the second Missus Todd, the one that just went by. And I don't expect you'll believe a single damn word of the whole yarn."

In the sky one of those big flat-bottomed clouds moved enough to disclose the ghost of the moon — half-full and pale as milk. And something in my heart leaped up at the sight, half in fright, half in love.

"I do though," I said. "Every frigging damned word. And even if it ain't true, Homer, it ought to be."

He give me a hug around the neck with his forearm, which is all men can do since the world don't let them kiss but only women, and laughed, and got up.

"Even if it *shouldn't* ought to be, it is," he said. He got his watch out of his pants and looked at it. "I got to go down the road and check on the Scott place. You want to come?"

"I believe I'll sit here for a while," I said, "and think."

He went to the steps, then turned back and looked at me, half-smiling. "I believe she was right," he said. "She *was* different along those roads she found...wasn't nothing that would dare touch her. You or me, maybe, but not her.

"And I believe she's young."

Then he got in his truck and set off to check the Scott place.

That was two years ago, and Homer has since gone to Vermont, as I think I told you. One night he come over to see me. His hair was combed, he had a shave, and he smelled of some nice lotion. His face was clear and his eyes were alive. That night he looked sixty instead of seventy, and I was glad for him and I envied him and I hated him a little, too. Arthritis is one buggardly great old fisherman, and that night Homer didn't look like arthritis had any fishhooks sunk into his hands the way they were sunk into mine.

"I'm going," he said.

"Ayuh?"

"Ayuh."

"All right; did you see to forwarding your mail?"

"Don't want none forwarded," he said. "My bills are paid. I am going to make a clean break."

"Well, give me your address. I'll drop you a line from one time to the another, old hoss." Already I could feel loneliness settling over me like a cloak...and looking at him, I knew that things were not quite what they seemed.

"Don't have none yet," he said.

"All right," I said. "*Is* it Vermont, Homer?"

"Well," he said, "it'll do for people who want to know."

I almost didn't say it and then I did. "What does she look like now?"

"Like Diana," he said. "But she is kinder."

"I envy you, Homer," I said, and I did.

I stood at the door. It was twilight in that deep part of summer when the fields fill with perfume and Queen Anne's Lace. A full moon was beating a silver track across the lake. He went across my porch and down the steps. A car was standing on the soft shoulder of the road, its engine idling heavy, the way the old ones do that still run full bore straight ahead and damn the torpedoes. Now that I think of it, that car *looked* like a torpedo. It looked beat up some, but as if it could go the ton without breathin hard. He stopped at the foot of my steps and picked something up — it was his gas can, the big one that holds ten gallons. He went down my walk to the passenger side of the car. She leaned over and opened the door. The inside light came on and just for a moment I saw her, long red hair around her face, her forehead shining like a lamp. Shining like the *moon*. He got in and she drove away. I stood out on my porch and watched the taillights of her little go-devil twinkling red in the dark...getting smaller and smaller. They were like embers, then they were like flickerflies, and then they were gone.

Vermont, I tell the folks from town, and Vermont they believe, because it's as far as most of them can see inside their heads. Sometimes I almost believe it myself, mostly when I'm tired and done up. Other times I think

THE SECRET HISTORY OF FANTASY

about them, though — all this October I have done so, it seems, because October is the time when men think mostly about far places and the roads which might get them there. I sit on the bench in front of Bell's Market and think about Homer Buckland and about the beautiful girl who leaned over to open his door when he come down that path with the full red gasoline can in his right hand — she looked like a girl of no more than sixteen, a girl on her learner's permit, and her beauty *was* terrible, but I believe it would no longer kill the man it turned itself on; for a moment her eyes lit on me, I was not killed, although part of me died at her feet.

Olympus must be a glory to the eyes and the heart, and there are those who crave it and those who find a clear way to it, mayhap, but I know Castle Rock like the back of my hand and I could never leave it for no shortcuts where the roads may go; in October the sky over the lake is no glory but it is passing fair, with those big white clouds that move so slow; I sit here on the bench, and think about 'Phelia Todd and Homer Buckland, and I don't necessarily wish I was where they are...but I still wish I was a smoking man.

BEARS DISCOVER FIRE

TERRY BISSON

I WAS DRIVING with my brother, the preacher, and my nephew, the preacher's son, on I-65 just north of Bowling Green when we got a flat. It was Sunday night and we had been to visit Mother at the Home. We were in my car. The flat caused what you might call knowing groans since, as the old-fashioned one in my family (so they tell me), I fix my own tires, and my brother is always telling me to get radials and quit buying old tires.

But if you know how to mount and fix tires yourself, you can pick them up for almost nothing.

Since it was a left rear tire, I pulled over to the left, onto the median grass. The way my Caddy stumbled to a stop, I figured the tire was ruined. "I guess there's no need asking if you have any of that FlatFix in the trunk," said Wallace.

"Here, son, hold the light," I said to Wallace Jr. He's old enough to want to help and not old enough (yet) to think he knows it all. If I'd married and had kids, he's the kind I'd have wanted.

An old Caddy has a big trunk that tends to fill up like a shed. Mine's a '56. Wallace was wearing his Sunday shirt, so he didn't offer to help while I pulled magazines, fishing tackle, a wooden tool box, some old clothes, a comealong wrapped in a grass sack, and a tobacco sprayer out of the way, looking for my jack. The spare looked a little soft.

The light went out. "Shake it, son," I said.

It went back on. The bumper jack was long gone, but I carry a little quarter-ton hydraulic. I found it under Mother's old *Southern Living*s, 1978–1986. I had been meaning to drop them at the dump. If Wallace hadn't been along, I'd have let Wallace Jr. position the jack under the axle, but I got on my knees and did it myself. There's nothing wrong with a boy learning to change a tire. Even if you're not going to fix and mount them, you're still going to have to change a few in this life. The light went off again before I had the wheel off the ground. I was surprised at how dark the night was already. It was late October and beginning to get cool. "Shake it again, son," I said.

It went back on but it was weak. Flickery.

"With radials you just don't *have* flats," Wallace explained in that voice he uses when he's talking to a number of people at once; in this case, Wallace Jr. and myself. "And even when you *do*, you just squirt them with this stuff called FlatFix and you just drive on. Three ninety-five the can."

"Uncle Bobby can fix a tire hisself," said Wallace Jr., out of loyalty I presume.

"*Him*self," I said from halfway under the car. If it was up to Wallace, the boy would talk like what Mother used to call "a helot from the gorges of the mountains." But drive on radials.

"Shake that light again," I said. It was about gone. I spun the lugs off into the hubcap and pulled the wheel. The tire had blown out along the sidewall. "Won't be fixing this one," I said. Not that I cared. I have a pile as tall as a man out by the barn.

The light went out again, then came back better than ever as I was fitting the spare over the lugs. "Much better," I said. There was a flood of dim orange flickery light. But when I turned to find the lug nuts, I was surprised to see that the flashlight the boy was holding was dead. The light was coming from two bears at the edge of the trees, holding torches. They were big, three-hundred-pounders, standing about five feet tall. Wallace Jr. and his father had seen them and were standing perfectly still. It's best not to alarm bears.

I fished the lug nuts out of the hubcap and spun them on. I usually like to put a little oil on them, but this time I let it go. I reached under the car and let the jack down and pulled it out. I was relieved to see that the spare was high enough to drive on. I put the jack and the lug wrench and the flat into the trunk. Instead of replacing the hubcap, I put it in there too. All this time, the bears never made a move. They just held the torches, whether out of curiosity or helpfulness, there was no way of knowing. It

THE SECRET HISTORY OF FANTASY

looked like there may have been more bears behind them, in the trees.

Opening three doors at once, we got into the car and drove off. Wallace was the first to speak. "Looks like bears have discovered fire," he said.

When we first took Mother to the Home almost four years (forty-seven months) ago, she told Wallace and me she was ready to die. "Don't worry about me, boys," she whispered, pulling us both down so the nurse wouldn't hear. "I've drove a million miles and I'm ready to pass over to the other shore. I won't have long to linger here." She drove a consolidated school bus for thirty-nine years. Later, after Wallace left, she told me about her dream. A bunch of doctors were sitting around in a circle discussing her case. One said, "We've done all we can for her, boys, let's let her go." They all turned their hands up and smiled. When she didn't die that fall she seemed disappointed, though as spring came she forgot about it, as old people will.

In addition to taking Wallace and Wallace Jr. to see Mother on Sunday nights, I go myself on Tuesdays and Thursdays. I usually find her sitting in front of the TV, even though she doesn't watch it. The nurses keep it on all the time. They say the old folks like the flickering. It soothes them down.

"What's this I hear about bears discovering fire?" she said on Tuesday. "It's true," I told her as I combed her long white hair with the shell comb Wallace had brought her from Florida. Monday there had been a story in the Louisville *Courier-Journal*, and Tuesday one on NBC or CBS nightly news. People were seeing bears all over the state, and in Virginia as well. They had quit hibernating, and were apparently planning to spend the winter in the medians of the interstates. There have always been bears in the mountains of Virginia, but not here in western Kentucky, not for almost a hundred years. The last one was killed when Mother was a girl. The theory in the *Courier-Journal* was that they were following I-65 down from the forests of Michigan and Canada, but one old man from Allen County (interviewed on nationwide TV) said that there had always been a few bears left back in the hills, and they had come out to join the others now that they had discovered fire.

"They don't hibernate anymore," I said. "They make a fire and keep it going all winter."

"I declare," Mother said. "What'll they think of next!"

The nurse came to take her tobacco away, which is the signal for bed-time.

Every October, Wallace Jr. stays with me while his parents go to camp. I realize how backward that sounds, but there it is. My brother is a Minister (House of the Righteous Way, Reformed) but he makes two-thirds of his living in real estate. He and Elizabeth go to a Christian Success Retreat in South Carolina, where people from all over the country practice selling things to one another. I know what it's like not because they've ever bothered to tell me, but because I've seen the Revolving Equity Success Plan ads late at night on TV.

The school bus let Wallace Jr. off at my house on Wednesday, the day they left. The boy doesn't have to pack much of a bag when he stays with me. He has his own room here. As the eldest of our family, I hung onto the old home place near Smiths Grove. It's getting run down, but Wallace Jr. and I don't mind. He has his own room in Bowling Green, too, but since Wallace and Elizabeth move to a different house every three months (part of the Plan), he keeps his .22 and his comics, the stuff that's important to a boy his age, in his room here at the home place. It's the room his dad and I used to share.

Wallace Jr. is twelve. I found him sitting on the back porch that over-looks the interstate when I got home from work. I sell crop insurance.

After I changed clothes I showed him how to break the bead on a tire two ways, with a hammer, and by backing a car over it. Like making sorghum, fixing tires by hand is a dying art. The boy caught on fast, though. "Tomorrow I'll show you how to mount your tire with the hammer and a tire iron," I said.

"What I wish is I could see the bears," he said. He was looking across the field to I-65, where the northbound lanes cut off the corner of our field. From the house at night, sometimes the traffic sounds like a waterfall.

"Can't see their fire in the daytime," I said. "But wait till tonight." That night CBS or NBC (I forget which is which) did a special on the bears, which were becoming a story of nationwide interest. They were seen in

Kentucky, West Virginia, Missouri, Illinois (southern), and, of course, Virginia. There have always been bears in Virginia. Some characters there were even talking about hunting them. A scientist said they were heading into the states where there is some snow but not too much, and where there is enough timber in the medians for firewood. He had gone in with a video camera, but his shots were just blurry figures sitting around a fire. Another scientist said the bears were attracted by the berries on a new bush that grew only in the medians of the interstates. He claimed this berry was the first new species in recent history, brought about by the mixing of seeds along the highway. He ate one on TV, making a face, and called it a "newberry." A climatic ecologist said that the warm winters (there was no snow last winter in Nashville, and only one flurry in Louisville) had changed the bears' hibernation cycle, and now they were able to remember things from year to year. "Bears may have discovered fire centuries ago," he said, "but forgot it." Another theory was that they had discovered (or remembered) fire when Yellowstone burned, several years ago.

The TV showed more guys talking about bears than it showed bears, and Wallace Jr. and I lost interest. After the supper dishes were done I took the boy out behind the house and down to our fence. Across the interstate and through the trees, we could see the light of the bears' fire. Wallace Jr. wanted to go back to the house and get his .22 and go shoot one, and I explained why that would be wrong. "Besides," I said, "a twenty-two wouldn't do much more to a bear than make it mad.

"Besides," I added, "it's illegal to hunt in the medians."

The only trick to mounting a tire by hand, once you have beaten or pried it onto the rim, is setting the bead. You do this by setting the tire upright, sitting on it, and bouncing it up and down between your legs while the air goes in. When the bead sets on the rim, it makes a satisfying "pop." On Thursday, I kept Wallace Jr. home from school and showed him how to do this until he got it right. Then we climbed our fence and crossed the field to get a look at the bears.

In northern Virginia, according to *Good Morning America*, the bears were keeping their fires going all day long. Here in western Kentucky, though, it was still warm for late October and they only stayed around the fires at night. Where they went and what they did in the daytime, I don't know. Maybe they were watching from the newberry bushes as Wallace Jr. and I climbed the government fence and crossed the northbound lanes. I carried an axe and Wallace Jr. brought his .22, not because he wanted to kill a bear but because a boy likes to carry some kind of a gun. The median was all tangled with brush and vines under the maples, oaks, and sycamores. Even though we were only a hundred yards from the house, I had never been there, and neither had anyone else that I knew of. It was like a created country. We found a path in the center and followed it down across a slow, short stream that flowed out of one grate and into another. The tracks in the gray mud were the first bear signs we saw. There was a musty, but not really unpleasant smell. In a clearing under a big hollow beech, where the fire had been, we found nothing but ashes. Logs were drawn up in a rough circle and the smell was stronger. I stirred the ashes and found enough coals to start a new flame, so I banked them back the way they had been left.

I cut a little firewood and stacked it to one side, just to be neighborly.

Maybe the bears were watching us from the bushes even then. There's no way to know. I tasted one of the newberries and spit it out. It was so sweet it was sour, just the sort of thing you would imagine a bear would like.

That evening after supper I asked Wallace Jr. if he might want to go with me to visit Mother. I wasn't surprised when he said yes. Kids have more consideration than folks give them credit for. We found her sitting on the concrete front porch of the Home, watching the cars go by on I-65. The nurse said she had been agitated all day. I wasn't surprised by that, either. Every fall as the leaves change, she gets restless, maybe the word is "hopeful," again. I brought her into the dayroom and combed her long white hair. "Nothing but bears on TV anymore," the nurse complained, flipping the channels. Wallace Jr. picked up the remote after the nurse left, and we watched a CBS or NBC Special Report about some hunters in Virginia who had gotten their houses torched. The TV interviewed a hunter and his wife whose $117,500 Shenandoah Valley home had burned. She blamed the

THE SECRET HISTORY OF FANTASY

bears. He didn't blame the bears, but he was suing for compensation from the state since he had a valid hunting license. The state hunting commissioner came on and said that possession of a hunting license didn't prohibit ("enjoin," I think, was the word he used) *the hunted* from striking back. I thought that was a pretty liberal view for a state commissioner. Of course, he had a vested interest in not paying off. I'm not a hunter myself.

"Don't bother coming on Sunday," Mother told Wallace Jr. with a wink. "I've drove a million miles and I've got one hand on the gate." I'm used to her saying stuff like that, especially in the fall, but I was afraid it would upset the boy. In fact, he looked worried after we left and I asked him what was wrong.

"How could she have drove a million miles?" he asked. She had told him forty-eight miles a day for thirty-nine years, and he had worked it out on his calculator to be 336,960 miles.

"Have *driven*," I said. "And it's forty-eight in the morning and forty-eight in the afternoon. Plus there were the football trips. Plus, old folks exaggerate a little." Mother was the first woman school-bus driver in the state. She did it every day and raised a family, too. Dad just farmed.

I usually get off the interstate at Smiths Grove, but that night I drove north all the way to Horse Cave and doubled back so Wallace Jr. and I could see the bears' fires. There were not as many as you would think from the TV — one every six or seven miles, hidden back in a clump of trees or under a rocky ledge. Probably they look for water as well as wood. Wallace Jr. wanted to stop, but it's against the law to stop on the interstate and I was afraid the state police would run us off.

There was a card from Wallace in the mailbox. He and Elizabeth were doing fine and having a wonderful time. Not a word about Wallace Jr., but the boy didn't seem to mind. Like most kids his age, he doesn't really enjoy going places with his parents.

On Saturday afternoon the Home called my office (Burley Belt Drought & Hail) and left word that Mother was gone. I was on the road. I work Saturdays. It's the only day a lot of part-time farmers are home. My heart literally missed a beat when I called in and got the message, but only a beat. I had long been prepared. "It's a blessing," I said when I got the nurse on the phone.

"You don't understand," the nurse said. "Not *passed* away, gone. *Ran* away, gone. Your mother has escaped." Mother had gone through the door at the end of the corridor when no one was looking, wedging the door with her comb and taking a bedspread which belonged to the Home. What about her tobacco? I asked. It was gone. That was a sure sign she was planning to stay away. I was in Franklin, and it took me less than an hour to get to the Home on I-65. The nurse told me that Mother had been acting more and more confused lately. Of course they are going to say that. We looked around the grounds, which is only a half acre with no trees between the interstate and a soybean field. Then they had me leave a message at the sheriff's office. I would have to keep paying for her care until she was officially listed as Missing, which would be Monday.

It was dark by the time I got back to the house, and Wallace Jr. was fixing supper. This just involves opening a few cans, already selected and grouped together with a rubber band. I told him his grandmother had gone, and he nodded, saying, "She told us she would be." I called South Carolina and left a message. There was nothing more to be done. I sat down and tried to watch TV, but there was nothing on. Then, I looked out the back door, and saw the firelight twinkling through the trees across the northbound lane of I-65, and realized I just might know where to find her.

It was definitely getting colder, so I got my jacket. I told the boy to wait by the phone in case the sheriff called, but when I looked back, halfway across the field, there he was behind me. He didn't have a jacket. I let him catch up. He was carrying his .22 and I made him leave it leaning against our fence. It was harder climbing the government fence in the dark, at my age, than it had been in the daylight. I am sixty-one. The highway was busy with cars heading south and trucks heading north.

Crossing the shoulder, I got my pants cuffs wet on the long grass, already wet with dew. It is actually bluegrass.

The first few feet into the trees it was pitch-black and the boy grabbed my hand. Then it got lighter. At first I thought it was the moon, but it was the high beams shining like moonlight into the treetops, allowing Wallace Jr. and me to pick our way through the brush. We soon found the path and its familiar bear smell.

I was wary of approaching the bears at night. If we stayed on the path we might run into one in the dark, but if we went through the bushes we might be seen as intruders. I wondered if maybe we shouldn't have brought the gun.

We stayed on the path. The light seemed to drip down from the canopy of the woods like rain. The going was easy, especially if we didn't try to look at the path but let our feet find their own way.

Then through the trees I saw their fire.

The fire was mostly of sycamore and beech branches, the kind that puts out very little heat or light and lots of smoke. The bears hadn't learned the ins and outs of wood yet. They did okay at tending it, though. A large cin-namon-brown northern-looking bear was poking the fire with a stick, add-ing a branch now and then from a pile at his side. The others sat around in a loose circle on the logs. Most were smaller black or honey bears, one was a mother with cubs. Some were eating berries from a hubcap. Not eating, but just watching the fire, my mother sat among them with the bedspread from the Home around her shoulders.

If the bears noticed us, they didn't let on. Mother patted a spot right next to her on the log and I sat down. A bear moved over to let Wallace Jr. sit on her other side.

The bear smell is rank but not unpleasant, once you get used to it. It's not like a barn smell, but wilder. I leaned over to whisper something to Mother and she shook her head. *It would be rude to whisper around these creatures that don't possess the power of speech*, she let me know without speaking. Wallace Jr. was silent too. Mother shared the bedspread with us and we sat for what seemed hours, looking into the fire.

The big bear tended the fire, breaking up the dry branches by holding one end and stepping on them, like people do. He was good at keeping it going at the same level. Another bear poked the fire from time to time but the others left it alone. It looked like only a few of the bears knew how to use fire, and were carrying the others along. But isn't that how it is with everything? Every once in a while, a smaller bear walked into the circle of firelight with an armload of wood and dropped it onto the pile. Median wood has a silvery cast, like driftwood.

Wallace Jr. isn't fidgety like a lot of kids. I found it pleasant to sit and stare into the fire. I took a little piece of Mother's *Red Man*, though I don't generally chew. It was no different from visiting her at the Home, only more interesting, because of the bears. There were about eight or ten of them. Inside the fire itself, things weren't so dull, either: little dramas were being played out as fiery chambers were created and then destroyed in a crashing of sparks. My imagination ran wild. I looked around the circle at the bears and wondered what *they* saw. Some had their eyes closed. Though they were gathered together, their spirits still seemed solitary, as if each bear was sitting alone in front of its own fire.

The hubcap came around and we all took some newberries. I don't know about Mother, but I just pretended to eat mine. Wallace Jr. made a face and spit his out. When he went to sleep, I wrapped the bedspread around all three of us. It was getting colder and we were not provided, like the bears, with fur. I was ready to go home, but not Mother. She pointed up toward the canopy of trees, where a light was spreading, and then pointed to herself. Did she think it was angels approaching from on high? It was only the high beams of some southbound truck, but she seemed mighty pleased. Holding her hand, I felt it grow colder and colder in mine.

Wallace Jr. woke me up by tapping on my knee. It was past dawn, and his grandmother had died sitting on the log between us. The fire was banked up and the bears were gone and someone was crashing straight through the woods, ignoring the path. It was Wallace. Two state troopers were right behind him. He was wearing a white shirt, and I realized it was Sunday morning. Underneath his sadness on learning of Mother's death, he looked peeved.

The troopers were sniffing the air and nodding. The bear smell was still strong. Wallace and I wrapped Mother in the bedspread and started with

THE SECRET HISTORY OF FANTASY

her body back out to the highway. The troopers stayed behind and scattered the bears' fire ashes and flung their firewood away into the bushes. It seemed a petty thing to do. They were like bears themselves, each one solitary in his own uniform.

There was Wallace's Olds 98 on the median, with its radial tires looking squashed on the grass. In front of it there was a police car with a trooper standing beside it, and behind it a funeral home hearse, also an Olds 98.

"First report we've had of them bothering old folks," the trooper said to Wallace. "That's not hardly what happened at all," I said, but nobody asked me to explain. They have their own procedures. Two men in suits got out of the hearse and opened the rear door. That to me was the point at which Mother departed this life. After we put her in, I put my arms around the boy. He was shivering even though it wasn't that cold. Sometimes death will do that, especially at dawn, with the police around and the grass wet, even when it comes as a friend.

We stood for a minute watching the cars and trucks pass. "It's a blessing," Wallace said. It's surprising how much traffic there is at 6:22 A.M.

That afternoon, I went back to the median and cut a little firewood to replace what the troopers had flung away. I could see the fire through the trees that night.

I went back two nights later, after the funeral. The fire was going and it was the same bunch of bears, as far as I could tell. I sat around with them a while but it seemed to make them nervous, so I went home. I had taken a handful of newberries from the hubcap, and on Sunday I went with the boy and arranged them on Mother's grave. I tried again, but it's no use, you can't eat them.

Unless you're a bear.

BONES

FRANCESCA LIA BLOCK

I DREAMED OF being a part of the stories — even terrifying ones, even horror stories — because at least the girls in stories were alive before they died.

My ears were always ringing from the music cranked to pain-pitch in the clubs. Cigarette smoke perfumed my hair, wove into my clothes. I took the occasional drug when it came my way. The more mind-altering the better. I had safe sex with boys I didn't know — usually pretty safe. I felt immortal, which is how you are supposed to feel when you are young, I guess, no matter what anybody older tells you. But I'm not sure I wanted immortality that much then.

I met him at a party that a girl from my work told me about. It was at this house in the hills, a small castle that some movie star had built in the fifties with turrets and balconies and balustrades. People were bringing offerings — bottles of booze and drugs and guitars and drums and paints and canvases. It was the real bohemian scene. I thought that in it I could become something else, that I could become an artist, alive. And everyone else wanted that, too; they were coming there for him.

Once he'd come into the restaurant late at night and I took his order but he didn't seem to notice me at all. I noticed him because of the color of his hair and goatee. I heard that he was this big promoter guy, managed bands, owned some clubs and galleries. A real patron of the arts, Renaissance man. Derrick Blue they called him, or just Blue. It was his house, his party, they were all making the pilgrimage for him.

It was summer and hot. I was sweating, worried my makeup would drip off. Raccoon pools of mascara and shadow around my eyes. The air had that grilled smell, meat and gasoline, that it gets in Los Angeles when the temperature soars. It was a little cooler in the house so I went in and sat on this overstuffed antique couch under some giant crimson painting of a girl's face with electric lights for her pupils, and drank my beer and watched everybody. There was a lot of posing going on, a kind of auditioning or something. More and more scantily clad girls kept coming, boys were playing music or drawing the girls or just lying back, smoking.

Derrick Blue came out after a while and he made the rounds — everybody upped the posing a little for him. I just watched. Then he came over and smiled and took my hand and looked into my eyes and how hungry I was, in every way. I was always hungry for food — blueberry pancakes and root beer floats and pizza gluey with cheese — I thought about it all the time. And other things. I'd sit around dreaming that the boys I saw at shows or at work — the boys with silver earrings and big boots — would tell me I was beautiful, take me home and feed me Thai food or omelets and undress me and make love to me all night with the palm trees whispering windsongs about a tortured, gleaming city and the moonlight like flame melting our candle bodies. And then I was hungry for him, this man who seemed to have everything, and to actually be looking at me. I didn't realize why he was looking.

He found out pretty fast that I wasn't from around there, didn't know too many people well, lived alone in a crummy hotel apartment in Koreatown, ate what I could take home from work. He knew how hungry I was. He asked everything as if he really cared and I just stared back at him and answered. He had blue eyes, so blue that they didn't dim next to his blue-dyed hair. Cold beveled eyes. They made the sweat on my temples evaporate and I felt like I was high on coke coke coke when he looked at me.

The crimson girl on the wall behind me, the girl with the open mouth and the bared teeth and the electric eyes, looked like she was smiling — until you looked closely.

Derrick Blue caught my arm as I was leaving — I was pretty drunk by then, the hillside was sliding and the flowers were blurry and glowy like in those 3-D postcards — and it was pretty late, and he said, stay.

He said he wanted to talk to me, we could stay up all night talking and then have some breakfast. It was maybe two or three in the morning but the air was still hot like burning flowers. I felt sweat trickle down my ribs under my T-shirt.

We were all over his house. On the floor and the couches and tables and beds. He had music blasting from speakers everywhere and I let it take me like when I was at shows, thrashing around, losing the weight of who I was, the self-consciousness and anxiety, to the sound. He said, You're so tiny, like a doll, you look like you might break. I wanted him to break me. Part of me did. He said, I can make you whatever you want to be. I wanted him to. But what did I want to be? Maybe that was the danger.

The night was blue, like drowning in a cocktail. I tasted it bittersweet and felt the burning of ice on my skin. I reeled through the rooms of antiques and statues and huge-screen TVs and monster stereo systems and icy lights in frosted glass. If you asked me then if I would have died at that moment I might have said yes. What else was there? This was the closest thing to a story I'd ever known. Inside me it felt like nothing.

That night he told all the tales. You know, I am still grateful to him for that. I hadn't heard them since I was little. They made me feel safe. Enchanted. Alive. Charmed. He said he had named himself for Bluebeard, if I hadn't guessed. He said it had become a metaphor for his whole life. He took a key from his pocket. I wasn't afraid. I couldn't quite remember the story. I felt the enchantment around us like stepping into a big blue glitter storybook with a little mirror on the cover and princesses dancing inside, dwarves and bears and talking birds. And dying girls. He said, the key, it had blood on it, remember? It was a fairy, and she couldn't get the blood off, no matter what she did. It gave her away. I knew that Bluebeard had done something terrible. I was starting to remember. When I first heard that story I couldn't understand it — why is this a fairy tale? Dead girls in a chamber, a psychotic killer with blue hair. I tried to speak but the enchantment had seeped into my mouth like choking electric blue frosting from a cake. I looked up at him. I wondered how he managed it. If anyone came looking for the women. Not if they were a bunch of lost girls without voices or love. No one would have come then.

Part of me wanted to swoon into nothing, but the other women's bones were talking. I didn't see the bones but I knew they were there, under the house. The little runaway bones of skinny, hungry girls who didn't think they were worth much — anything — so they stayed after the party was over and let Derrick Blue tell them his stories. He probably didn't even have to use much force on most of them.

I will rewrite the story of Bluebeard. The girl's brothers don't come to save her on horses, baring swords, full of power and at exactly the right moment. There are no brothers. There is no sister to call out a warning. There is only a slightly feral one-hundred-pound girl with choppy black hair, kohl-smeared eyes, torn jeans, and a pair of boots with steel toes. This girl has a little knife to slash with, a little pocket knife, and she can run. That is one thing about her — she has always been able to run. Fast. Not because she is strong or is running toward something but because she has learned to run away.

I pounded through the house, staggering down the hallways, falling down the steps. It was a hot streaky dawn full of insecticides, exhaust, flowers that could make you sick or fall in love. My battered Impala was still parked there on the side of the road and I opened it and collapsed inside. I wanted to lie down on the shredded seats and sleep and sleep.

But I thought of the bones; I could hear them singing. They needed me to write their song.

SNOW, GLASS, APPLES

NEIL GAIMAN

I DO NOT know what manner of thing she is. None of us do. She killed her mother in the birthing, but that's never enough to account for it.

They call me wise, but I am far from wise, for all that I foresaw fragments of it, frozen moments caught in pools of water or in the cold glass of my mirror. If I were wise I would not have tried to change what I saw. If I were wise I would have killed myself before ever I encountered her, before ever I caught him.

Wise, and a witch, or so they said, and I'd seen his face in my dreams and in reflections for all my life: sixteen years of dreaming of him before he reined his horse by the bridge that morning, and asked my name. He helped me onto his high horse and we rode together to my little cottage, my face buried in the gold of his hair. He asked for the best of what I had; a king's right, it was.

His beard was red-bronze in the morning light, and I knew him, not as a king, for I knew nothing of kings then, but as my love. He took all he wanted from me, the right of kings, but he returned to me on the following day, and on the night after that: his beard so red, his hair so gold, his eyes the blue of a summer sky, his skin tanned the gentle brown of ripe wheat.

His daughter was only a child: no more than five years of age when I came to the palace. A portrait of her dead mother hung in the princess's tower room; a tall woman, hair the colour of dark wood, eyes nut-brown. She was of a different blood to her pale daughter.

The girl would not eat with us.

I do not know where in the palace she ate.

I had my own chambers. My husband the king, he had his own rooms also. When he wanted me he would send for me, and I would go to him, and pleasure him, and take my pleasure with him.

One night, several months after I was brought to the palace, she came to my rooms. She was six. I was embroidering by lamplight, squinting my eyes against the lamp's smoke and fitful illumination. When I looked up, she was there.

"Princess?"

She said nothing. Her eyes were black as coal, black as her hair; her lips were redder than blood. She looked up at me and smiled. Her teeth seemed sharp, even then, in the lamplight.

"What are you doing away from your room?"

"I'm hungry," she said, like any child.

It was winter, when fresh food is a dream of warmth and sunlight; but I had strings of whole apples, cored and dried, hanging from the beams of my chamber, and I pulled an apple down for her.

"Here."

Autumn is the time of drying, of preserving, a time of picking apples, of rendering the goose fat. Winter is the time of hunger, of snow, and of death; and it is the time of the midwinter feast, when we rub the goose-fat into the skin of a whole pig, stuffed with that autumn's apples, then we roast it or spit it, and we prepare to feast upon the crackling.

She took the dried apple from me and began to chew it with her sharp yellow teeth.

"Is it good?"

She nodded. I had always been scared of the little princess, but at that moment I warmed to her and, with my fingers, gently, I stroked her cheek. She looked at me and smiled — she smiled but rarely — then she sank her teeth into the base of my thumb, the Mound of Venus, and she drew blood.

I began to shriek, from pain and from surprise; but she looked at me and I fell silent.

The little princess fastened her mouth to my hand and licked and sucked and drank. When she was finished, she left my chamber. Beneath my gaze the cut that she had made began to close, to scab, and to heal.

THE SECRET HISTORY OF FANTASY

The next day it was an old scar: I might have cut my hand with a pocket-knife in my childhood.

I had been frozen by her, owned and dominated. That scared me, more than the blood she had fed on. After that night I locked my chamber door at dusk, barring it with an oaken pole, and I had the smith forge iron bars, which he placed across my windows.

My husband, my love, my king, sent for me less and less, and when I came to him he was dizzy, listless, confused. He could no longer make love as a man makes love; and he would not permit me to pleasure him with my mouth: the one time I tried, he started, violently, and began to weep. I pulled my mouth away and held him tightly, until the sobbing had stopped, and he slept, like a child.

I ran my fingers across his skin as he slept. It was covered in a multitude of ancient scars. But I could recall no scars from the days of our courtship, save one, on his side, where a boar had gored him when he was a youth.

Soon he was a shadow of the man I had met and loved by the bridge. His bones showed, blue and white, beneath his skin. I was with him at the last: his hands were cold as stone, his eyes milky-blue, his hair and beard faded and lustreless and limp. He died unshriven, his skin nipped and pocked from head to toe with tiny, old scars.

He weighed near to nothing. The ground was frozen hard, and we could dig no grave for him, so we made a cairn of rocks and stones above his body, as a memorial only, for there was little enough of him left to protect from the hunger of the beasts and the birds.

So I was queen.

And I was foolish, and young — eighteen summers had come and gone since first I saw daylight — and I did not do what I would do, now.

If it were today, I would have her heart cut out, true. But then I would have her head and arms and legs cut off. I would have them disembowel her. And then I would watch, in the town square, as the hangman heated the fire to white-heat with bellows, watch unblinking as he consigned each part of her to the fire. I would have archers around the square, who would shoot any bird or animal who came close to the flames, any raven or dog or hawk or rat. And I would not close my eyes until the princess was ash, and a gentle wind could scatter her like snow.

I did not do this thing, and we pay for our mistakes.

They say I was fooled; that it was not her heart. That it was the heart of an animal — a stag, perhaps, or a boar. They say that, and they are wrong.

And some say (but it is *her* lie, not mine) that I was given the heart, and that I ate it. Lies and half-truths fall like snow, covering the things that I remember, the things I saw. A landscape, unrecognisable after a snowfall; that is what she has made of my life.

There were scars on my love, her father's thighs, and on his ballock-pouch, and on his male member, when he died.

I did not go with them. They took her in the day, while she slept, and was at her weakest. They took her to the heart of the forest, and there they opened her blouse, and they cut out her heart, and they left her dead, in a gully, for the forest to swallow.

The forest is a dark place, the border to many kingdoms; no one would be foolish enough to claim jurisdiction over it. Outlaws live in the forest. Robbers live in the forest, and so do wolves. You can ride through the forest for a dozen days and never see a soul; but there are eyes upon you the entire time.

They brought me her heart. I know it was hers — no sow's heart or doe's would have continued to beat and pulse after it had been cut out, as that one did.

I took it to my chamber.

I did *not* eat it: I hung it from the beams above my bed, placed it on a length of twine that I strung with rowan-berries, orange-red as a robin's breast; and with bulbs of garlic.

Outside, the snow fell, covering the footprints of my huntsmen, covering her tiny body in the forest where it lay.

I had the smith remove the iron bars from my windows, and I would spend some time in my room each afternoon through the short winter days, gazing out over the forest, until darkness fell.

There were, as I have already stated, people in the forest. They would come out, some of them, for the Spring Fair: a greedy, feral, dangerous people; some were stunted — dwarfs and midgets and hunchbacks; others had the huge teeth and vacant gazes of idiots; some had fingers like flippers or crab-claws. They would creep out of the forest each year for the Spring Fair, held when the snows had melted.

As a young lass I had worked at the fair, and they had scared me then, the forest folk. I told fortunes for the fairgoers, scrying in a pool of still water; and, later, when I was older, in a disc of polished glass, its back all silvered — a gift from a merchant whose straying horse I had seen in a pool of ink.

The stallholders at the fair were afraid of the forest folk; they would nail their wares to the bare boards of their stalls — slabs of gingerbread or leather belts were nailed with great iron nails to the wood. If their wares were not nailed, they said, the forest folk would take them, and run away, chewing on the stolen gingerbread, flailing about them with the belts.

The forest folk had money, though: a coin here, another there, sometimes stained green by time or the earth, the face on the coin unknown to even the oldest of us. Also they had things to trade, and thus the fair continued, serving the outcasts and the dwarfs, serving the robbers (if they were circumspect) who preyed on the rare travellers from lands beyond the forest, or on gypsies, or on the deer. (This was robbery in the eyes of the law. The deer were the queen's.)

The years passed by slowly, and my people claimed that I ruled them with wisdom. The heart still hung above my bed, pulsing gently in the night. If there were any who mourned the child, I saw no evidence: she was a thing of terror, back then, and they believed themselves well rid of her.

Spring Fair followed Spring Fair: five of them, each sadder, poorer, shoddier than the one before. Fewer of the forest folk came out of the forest to buy. Those who did seemed subdued and listless. The stallholders stopped nailing their wares to the boards of their stalls. And by the fifth year but a handful of folk came from the forest — a fearful huddle of little hairy men, and no one else.

The Lord of the Fair, and his page, came to me when the fair was done. I had known him slightly, before I was queen.

"I do not come to you as my queen," he said.

I said nothing. I listened.

"I come to you because you are wise," he continued. "When you were a child you found a strayed foal by staring into a pool of ink; when you were a maiden you found a lost infant who had wandered far from her mother, by staring into that mirror of yours. You know secrets and you can seek out things hidden. My queen," he asked, "what is taking the forest folk? Next year there will be no Spring Fair. The travellers from other kingdoms have grown scarce and few, the folk of the forest are almost gone. Another year like the last, and we shall all starve."

I commanded my maidservant to bring me my looking-glass. It was a simple thing, a silver-backed glass disc, which I kept wrapped in a doe-skin, in a chest, in my chamber.

They brought it to me, then, and I gazed into it:

She was twelve and she was no longer a little child. Her skin was still pale, her eyes and hair coal-black, her lips as red as blood. She wore the clothes she had worn when she left the castle for the last time — the blouse, the skirt — although they were much let-out, much mended. Over them she wore a leather cloak, and instead of boots she had leather bags, tied with thongs, over her tiny feet.

She was standing in the forest, beside a tree.

As I watched, in the eye of my mind, I saw her edge and step and flitter and pad from tree to tree, like an animal: a bat or a wolf. She was following someone.

He was a monk. He wore sackcloth, and his feet were bare, and scabbed and hard. His beard and tonsure were of a length, overgrown, unshaven.

She watched him from behind the trees. Eventually he paused for the night, and began to make a fire, laying twigs down, breaking up a robin's nest as kindling. He had a tinder-box in his robe, and he knocked the flint against the steel until the sparks caught the tinder and the fire flamed. There had been two eggs in the nest he had found, and these he ate, raw. They cannot have been much of a meal for so big a man.

He sat there in the firelight, and she came out from her hiding place. She crouched down on the other side of the fire, and stared at him. He

THE SECRET HISTORY OF FANTASY

grinned, as if it were a long time since he had seen another human, and beckoned her over to him.

She stood up and walked around the fire, and waited, an arm's-length away. He pulled in his robe until he found a coin — a tiny, copper penny — and tossed it to her. She caught it, and nodded, and went to him. He pulled at the rope around his waist, and his robe swung open. His body was as hairy as a bear's. She pushed him back onto the moss. One hand crept, spider-like, through the tangle of hair, until it closed on his manhood; the other hand traced a circle on his left nipple. He closed his eyes, and fumbled one huge hand under her skirt. She lowered her mouth to the nipple she had been teasing, her smooth skin white on the furry brown body of him.

She sank her teeth deep into his breast. His eyes opened, then they closed again, and she drank.

She straddled him, and she fed. As she did so a thin blackish liquid began to dribble from between her legs...

"Do you know what is keeping the travellers from our town? What is happening to the forest people?" asked the Head of the Fair.

I covered the mirror in doe-skin, and told him that I would personally take it upon myself to make the forest safe once more.

I had to, although she terrified me. I was the queen.

A foolish woman would have gone then into the forest and tried to capture the creature; but I had been foolish once and had no wish to be so a second time.

I spent time with old books, for I could read a little. I spent time with the gypsy women (who passed through our country across the mountains to the south, rather than cross the forest to the north and the west).

I prepared myself, and obtained those things I would need, and when the first snows began to fall, then I was ready.

Naked, I was, and alone in the highest tower of the palace, a place open to the sky. The winds chilled my body; goose-pimples crept across my arms and thighs and breasts. I carried a silver basin, and a basket in which I had placed a silver knife, a silver pin, some tongs, a grey robe and three green apples.

I put them down and stood there, unclothed, on the tower, humble before the night sky and the wind. Had any man seen me standing there, I would have had his eyes; but there was no one to spy. Clouds scudded across the sky, hiding and uncovering the waning moon.

I took the silver knife, and slashed my left arm — once, twice, three times. The blood dripped into the basin, scarlet seeming black in the moonlight.

I added the powder from the vial that hung around my neck. It was a brown dust, made of dried herbs and the skin of a particular toad, and from certain other things. It thickened the blood, while preventing it from clotting.

I took the three apples, one by one, and pricked their skins gently with my silver pin. Then I placed the apples in the silver bowl, and let them sit there while the first tiny flakes of snow of the year fell slowly onto my skin, and onto the apples, and onto the blood.

When dawn began to brighten the sky I covered myself with the grey cloak, and took the red apples from the silver bowl, one by one, lifting each into my basket with silver tongs, taking care not to touch it. There was nothing left of my blood or of the brown powder in the silver bowl, save nothing save a black residue, like a verdigris, on the inside.

I buried the bowl in the earth. Then I cast a glamour on the apples (as once, years before, by a bridge, I had cast a glamour on myself), that they were, beyond any doubt, the most wonderful apples in the world; and the crimson blush of their skins was the warm colour of fresh blood.

I pulled the hood of my cloak low over my face, and I took ribbons and pretty hair ornaments with me, placed them above the apples in the reed basket, and I walked alone into the forest, until I came to her dwelling: a high, sandstone cliff, laced with deep caves going back a way into the rock wall.

There were trees and boulders around the cliff-face, and I walked quietly and gently from tree to tree, without disturbing a twig or a fallen leaf. Eventually I found my place to hide, and I waited, and I watched.

After some hours a clutch of dwarfs crawled out of the cave-front — ugly, misshapen, hairy little men, the old inhabitants of this country. You saw them seldom now.

They vanished into the wood, and none of them spied me, though one of them stopped to piss against the rock I hid behind.

I waited. No more came out.

I went to the cave entrance and hallooed into it, in a cracked old voice.

The scar on my Mound of Venus throbbed and pulsed as she came towards me, out of the darkness, naked and alone.

She was thirteen years of age, my stepdaughter, and nothing marred the perfect whiteness of her skin save for the livid scar on her left breast, where her heart had been cut from her long since.

The insides of her thighs were stained with wet black filth.

She peered at me, hidden, as I was, in my cloak. She looked at me hungrily. "Ribbons, goodwife," I croaked. "Pretty ribbons for your hair..."

She smiled and beckoned to me. A tug; the scar on my hand was pulling me towards her. I did what I had planned to do, but I did it more readily than I had planned: I dropped my basket, and screeched like the bloodless old pedlar woman I was pretending to be, and I ran.

My grey cloak was the colour of the forest, and I was fast; she did not catch me.

I made my way back to the palace.

I did not see it. Let us imagine though, the girl returning, frustrated and hungry, to her cave, and finding my fallen basket on the ground.

What did she do?

I like to think she played first with the ribbons, twined them into her raven hair, looped them around her pale neck or her tiny waist.

And then, curious, she moved the cloth to see what else was in the basket; and she saw the red, red apples.

They smelled like fresh apples, of course; and they also smelled of blood. And she was hungry. I imagine her picking up an apple, pressing it against her cheek, feeling the cold smoothness of it against her skin.

And she opened her mouth and bit deep into it...

By the time I reached my chambers, the heart that hung from the roof-beam, with the apples and hams and the dried sausages, had ceased to beat. It hung there, quietly, without motion or life, and I felt safe once more.

That winter the snows were high and deep, and were late melting. We were all hungry come the spring.

The Spring Fair was slightly improved that year. The forest folk were few, but they were there, and there were travellers from the lands beyond the forest.

I saw the little hairy men of the forest-cave buying and bargaining for pieces of glass, and lumps of crystal and of quartz-rock. They paid for the glass with silver coins — the spoils of my stepdaughter's depredations, I had no doubt. When it got about what they were buying, townsfolk rushed back to their homes, came back with their lucky crystals, and, in a few cases, with whole sheets of glass.

I thought, briefly, about having them killed, but I did not. As long as the heart hung, silent and immobile and cold, from the beam of my chamber, I was safe, and so were the folk of the forest, and, thus, eventually, the folk of the town.

My twenty-fifth year came, and my stepdaughter had eaten the poisoned fruit two winters' back, when the prince came to my palace. He was tall, very tall, with cold green eyes and the swarthy skin of those from beyond the mountains.

He rode with a small retinue: large enough to defend him, small enough that another monarch — myself, for instance — would not view him as a potential threat.

I was practical: I thought of the alliance of our lands, thought of the Kingdom running from the forests all the way south to the sea; I thought of my golden-haired bearded love, dead these eight years; and, in the night, I went to the prince's room.

I am no innocent, although my late husband, who was once my king, was truly my first lover, no matter what they say.

At first the prince seemed excited. He bade me remove my shift, and made me stand in front of the opened window, far from the fire, until my skin was chilled stone-cold. Then he asked me to lie upon my back, with my hands folded across my breasts, my eyes wide open — but staring only at the beams above. He told me not to move, and to breathe as little as possible. He implored me to say nothing. He spread my legs apart.

It was then that he entered me.

As he began to thrust inside me, I felt my hips raise, felt myself begin to match him, grind for grind, push for push. I moaned. I could not help myself.

His manhood slid out of me. I reached out and touched it, a tiny, slippery thing.

"Please," he said, softly. "You must neither move, nor speak. Just lie there on the stones, so cold and so fair."

I tried, but he had lost whatever force it was that had made him virile; and, some short while later, I left the Prince's room, his curses and tears still resounding in my ears.

He left early the next morning, with all his men, and they rode off into the forest.

I imagine his loins, now, as he rode, a knot of frustration at the base of his manhood. I imagine his pale lips pressed so tightly together. Then I imagine his little troupe riding through the forest, finally coming upon the glass-and-crystal cairn of my stepdaughter. So pale. So cold. Naked, beneath the glass, and little more than a girl, and dead.

In my fancy, I can almost feel the sudden hardness of his manhood inside his britches, envision the lust that took him then, the prayers he muttered beneath his breath in thanks for his good fortune. I imagine him negotiating with the little hairy men — offering them gold and spices for the lovely corpse under the crystal mound.

Did they take his gold willingly? Or did they look up to see his men on their horses, with their sharp swords and their spears, and realize they had no alternative?

I do not know. I was not there; I was not scrying. I can only imagine...

Hands, pulling off the lumps of glass and quartz from her cold body. Hands, gently caressing her cold cheek, moving her cold arm, rejoicing to find the corpse still fresh and pliable.

Did he take her there, in front of them all? Or did he have her carried to a secluded nook before he mounted her?

I cannot say.

Did he shake the apple from her throat? Or did her eyes slowly open as he pounded into her cold body; did her mouth open, those red lips part, those sharp yellow teeth close on his swarthy neck, as the blood, which is the life, trickled down her throat, washing down and away the lump of apple, my own, my poison?

I imagine; I do not know.

This I do know: I was woken in the night by her heart pulsing and beating once more. Salt blood dripped onto my face from above. I sat up. My hand burned and pounded as if I had hit the base of my thumb with a rock.

There was a hammering on the door. I felt afraid, but I am a queen, and I would not show fear. I opened the door.

First his men walked in to my chamber, and stood around me, with their sharp swords, and their long spears.

Then he came in; and he spat in my face.

Finally, she walked into my chamber, as she had when I was first a queen, and she was a child of six. She had not changed. Not really.

She pulled down the twine on which her heart was hanging. She pulled off the dried rowan-berries, one by one; pulled off the garlic bulb — now a dried thing, after all these years; then she took up her own, her pumping heart — a small thing, no larger than that of a nanny-goat or a she-bear — as it brimmed and pumped its blood into her hand.

Her fingernails must have been as sharp as glass: she opened her breast with them, running them over the purple scar. Her chest gaped, suddenly, open and bloodless. She licked her heart, once, as the blood ran over her hands, and she pushed the heart deep into her breast.

I saw her do it. I saw her close the flesh of her breast once more. I saw the purple scar begin to fade.

Her prince looked briefly concerned, but he put his arm around her nonetheless, and they stood, side by side, and they waited.

And she stayed cold, and the bloom of death remained on her lips, and his lust was not diminished in any way.

They told me they would marry, and the kingdoms would indeed be joined. They told me that I would be with them on their wedding day.

It is starting to get hot in here.

They have told the people bad things about me; a little truth to add savour to the dish, but mixed with many lies.

I was bound and kept in a tiny stone cell beneath the palace, and I remained there through the autumn. Today they fetched me out of the cell; they stripped the rags from me, and washed the filth from me, and then they shaved my head and my loins, and they rubbed my skin with goose grease.

The snow was falling as they carried me — two men at each hand, two men at each leg— utterly exposed, and spread-eagled and cold, through the midwinter crowds; and brought me to this kiln.

My stepdaughter stood there with her prince. She watched me, in my indignity, but she said nothing.

As they thrust me inside, jeering and chaffing as they did so, I saw one snowflake land upon her white cheek, and remain there without melting.

They closed the kiln-door behind me. It is getting hotter in here, and outside they are singing and cheering and banging on the sides of the kiln.

She was not laughing, or jeering, or talking. She did not sneer at me or turn away. She looked at me, though; and for a moment I saw myself reflected in her eyes.

I will not scream. I will not give them that satisfaction. They will have my body, but my soul and my story are my own, and will die with me.

The goose-grease begins to melt and glisten upon my skin. I shall make no sound at all. I shall think no more on this.

I shall think instead of the snowflake on her cheek.

I think of her hair as black as coal, her lips as red as blood, her skin, snow-white.

Fruit and Words

Aimee Bender

So THERE WE were, Steve and I, smack in the middle of the same fight we'd had a million times before, a fight I knew so well I could graph it. We were halfway down the second slope of resignation, the place where we usually went to different rooms and despaired quietly on our own, and right at the moment that I thought, for the first time in seven years, that maybe things were just not going to work out after all, that was the moment he suggested we drive to Vegas right then and tie the knot. "Now?" I said and he nodded, with gravity. "Now." We packed as fast as we could, hoping we could pack faster than those winged feet of doubt, driving 100 miles per hour in silence, from sand to trees to mountains to dry plains to that tall, electric glitter. Parked. Checked in. Changed clothes. Held hands. Together we walked up to the casino chapel but as soon as Steve put his nose in the room, well, that's when those winged feet fluttered to rest on his shoulder. Reeling, he said he had a migraine and needed to lie down. An hour later he told me, washcloth on forehead, that he had to fly home that instant and could I drive back by myself? I stood at the doorway and watched him pack his nicest suit, folding it into corners and angles, his chest and legs and back and butt in squares and triangles, shut and carried.

"Goodbye," we said to each other, and the kiss was an old dead sock.

I spent the day there floating in the glowing blue swimming pool in my brand-new black swimming suit, cocooning myself in a huge white towel that smelled of sunshine, walking past tigers and dolphins. I slept diagonal on the king bed. After checking out, I went to the car, which was boiling hot, and put my bag in the trunk and geared up the engine and turned on the air conditioner and pulled out of the parking structure. The road extended through the desert, a long dry tongue. I didn't feel like listening to music and was speeding along, wondering if to all people the idea of marrying felt so much like being buried alive, as in particular the idea of marrying this man did. Anticipating the talks we were going to have, to get to the point where we both admitted we were only in it out of loyalty and fear, my mouth dried up and I had a sudden and very intense craving for a mango.

I'd never eaten a mango in my life. But the craving was vast, sweeping, feverish.

Great, I thought. It is not mango season and it is not mango country. And I knew those bright flavored gums would not cut it.

After half an hour, the craving was so bad I stopped at a gas station and tried anyway, bought a pack of orange-pink candy — Mango Tango! — but the taste of each flat circle, so sugary and similar to all other sugar flavors, made me long for the real one even more. I stopped at every market I saw but the fruit they had was pathetic: soft mealy apples, gray bananas, the occasional hard green plum.

The road was quiet and empty of cars. I sped past gas stations and fast food.

I was thinking, seriously, of driving straight to the airport and emptying my savings to fly myself to Africa so I could find one there, easy off the tree, the gentle give at the touch of my thumb, when far ahead, several miles up the road, I caught a glimpse of what appeared to be a shack. It was part of a tiny commercial strip facing a doughnut store and an oil lube filter station. From a distance it looked colorful and lively and as I got closer and closer, I thought I might be hallucinating from the heat because as far as I could tell, the front of the shack was full of trays and tables and shelves and piles of ripe beautiful fruit. My mouth started to water and I pulled over and parked my car on the shoulder of the road.

The highway was still empty of cars and the fast food doughnut chain was empty of cars and the oil lube filter was closed, so crossing the street was a breeze. The awning of the store was a sweet blue-and-white gingham and sure enough, there were huge tables burgeoning with fruit: vivid clementines, golden apples, dark plums, swollen peaches, three patterns of yellow and brown pears.

THE SECRET HISTORY OF FANTASY

The awning said FRUIT AND WORDS.

I went inside. I found a tan woman behind the counter perched on a stool, dusting a deep red apple with her sleeve.

"Hello," I said. "Wow, you have such beautiful fruit here!"

She had a flat face, so flat I was scared to see her in profile.

"Hello," she said mildly.

My hopes were swelling as I walked by a luscious stack of papayas, surging as I passed a group of star fruit and then, indeed, next to a humble pile of four, I found the small sign that said what I wanted to hear. And there they were, gentle and orange, the smell emanating from their skin, so rich I could pick up a whiff from a distance.

She nodded at me. "They're very good," she said. "Those mangoes are excellent quality."

She placed the polished apple in front of herself like she was teacher and student all at once. I scooped up all four and took them to the counter. I felt a wave of utter unearned competence. Ha ha to everyone else. Finding fresh mangoes fifty miles out of Las Vegas seemed to me, in no uncertain terms, like some kind of miracle.

"You have no idea how wonderful this is," I told her, beaming. "I have been having the most powerful mango craving. And here we are, in the desert of all places!"

She shrugged, agreeable. She'd heard this before.

"Where do you get them?" I asked.

She picked at the point of her eye.

"I get the fruit as a trade," she said. "There's a buyer who likes the salt here so he brings me fruit as payment."

"What a deal for you," I said, "getting all this gorgeous fruit for just a little salt."

I brought a mango up to my nose and smelled the sweetness inside its skin.

The woman sniffed. "It's not regular salt," she said. She indicated behind me with her chin.

"Ah," I said. "What's all that?"

"Those are the words," she said.

I kept my arms full of mangoes and took a step nearer. As far as I could tell, the entire back wall of the shop was covered, floor to ceiling, with cutout letters. They were piled high on shelves, making big words and small words, crammed close together, letters overlapping.

"Go closer," she said. "You can't see as well from here." She gave me a shove on my shoulder blade.

As I approached, I could see that the words weren't just cut from cardboard. Each word was different. I first saw the word NUT; it was a large capitalized word NUT and it was made out of something beige. I couldn't really tell what it was but then I saw the word GRASS, which was woven from tall blades, green and thready, and LEMON, cleverly twisted into cursive with peels and pulp, letting off a wonderful smell, so I went right up to NUT and discovered that it was in fact crumbled pieces of nuts all mixed together into a tan gluey paste.

"Isn't this interesting," I said to the woman.

I found PAPER, cut clean with an X-Acto knife, and a calligraphied ORGANDY, fluffing out so frothy I could hardly read it, and HAIR which was strawberry blond and curled up at the edge of the H and the leg of the R. The man who'd left Las Vegas had strawberry blond hair so I ignored that one and picked up PEARL instead.

"This is pricey, I bet," I said, and she gave me an anxious look, like I was going to drop it. It was stunning, not made of tiny pearls, but somehow of one solid piece of pearl, rippling out rainbow colors across its capitals. I put it back carefully on the shelf next to BARNACLE, prickly and dry looking.

"Why do you make these?" I said. "They're so beautiful!"

And they were. They were beautiful on their own and they were beautiful all together. I thought of her in her desert studio, hands dusty, apron splattered, sweat pouring, hammering down the final O in RADIO. She was making the world simple. She made the world steady somehow.

"People like the words," she told me, picking up her apple to shine some more. "I made them for fun and then I got rich."

"Well, I'd definitely like to buy these four mangoes," I said.

She pressed the register. "Ten dollars."

"And just curiously, how much are the words?" I kept my eyes on that wall, wanting to lean my head on PILLOW.

"Depends," she said. "They vary. Plus, you see, those are just the solids."

"What?" I stroked the petals that made up ROSE.

"I mean those are just the solids. I put the solids on display first because they're easiest to understand."

"Solid colors?" I said, staring at PLAID.

"Solid solids," she said. "Liquids are in the back. Gases are in the back of the back. Both are very pricey," she said, "but I'll charge you just three dollars to look. Three dollars for the tour."

"Liquid words?" I said, and I brought out my wallet. She rang up my mangoes and the tour. I moved closer to the register. "I think I'd like to buy a solid too," I said.

I was feeling, suddenly, more liberated than I had in seven years. I wanted to take over the store. I wanted to bathe in plum juice, rediscover my body and adorn it in kiwi circles. I bit into a mango. The skin broke quick, and the flesh, meaty and wet, slid inside my mouth, the nearly embarrassing free-for-all lusciousness of ripe fruit.

"Oh!" I said. "Incredible!"

She gave me two dollars in change. I licked mango juice off my wrist and turned back to the words.

"Can I buy a solid?" I asked.

She shrugged. "Of course," she said. "Which one?"

I wanted them all so I just pointed to the first I'd seen. "How much for NUT?"

"Interesting choice," she said, walking over and pulling it off the shelf. "NUT. There are seven different kinds of nuts in here. Macadamia, peanut, walnut, pecan, cashew, garbanzo, and almond."

I raised my eyebrows, impressed.

"Wow," I said.

She just stood there.

"Isn't garbanzo a bean?" I asked.

She held it out to me. "I'll give it to you for fourteen," she said. "Two dollars a nut."

There was a ten in my wallet between four ones and I lifted them all out. I had another drippy bite of mango.

"I won't eat it," I told her, indicating NUT.

She gave me a lip smile and took my money. "You can eat it," she said. "I don't care."

Scooping all my purchases into a brown bag, she lifted a simple silver key off the wall behind her and beckoned for me to follow. We stopped at a gray door. Before she inserted the key, the woman put a hand on my sleeve.

"Be careful," she said. "These are very delicate words. Don't drip mango on anything."

I had almost finished that first mango by now, the most incredible piece of food I had ever eaten in my life, and I held the remains of the pit away from me. My lips were sticky with juice. I felt the horror of Vegas dissipating, clarity descending like a window wrapped around my heart. She turned the knob, and I followed her in.

The back room was a square with a glass door at the far wall. This room was full of shelves too but the words were even harder to read from far away. I walked quietly up to them.

"Don't touch," she hissed.

The liquid words were set up in two ways. Most of them were shooting through glass pipes that shaped the letters. This looked really neat but I felt a little bit like it was cheating. Some of the others were liquids spilled onto a glass board, forming the letters. This was less cheating but looked cheaper. I walked down the row. I was not thrilled by WATER or COKE. I was drawn to RUBBING ALCOHOL, which was done with the piping and took up almost a whole shelf. It was a good one because it looked just like the water but I trusted that it wasn't. There was one called POISON, no specification, and the liquid was dark brown. The letters were fancy on that one, like an old-fashioned theater brochure. I found BLOOD.

"Real blood?" I whispered, and brought the mango back close to me. Licked its pulpy pit.

She nodded. "Of course."

"From what?" I asked, voice a little higher, and she didn't answer. It shot bright through the pipe as if in a huge loose vein.

I didn't like that blood one. I was recording all of this in a monologue in my head and I wondered then who I would tell the story to, and for the moment I couldn't think of anyone. This made me feel bad, so I went over to LAKE and held that and it had little tiny ferns floating in it and I thought it was pretty. It was next to OCEAN, which was looking more or less exactly like LAKE and that's when I wondered if the woman was really truthful and how would anyone know? I wanted to buy OCEAN too, I wanted to have the word OCEAN with me all the time, it was way better than NUT, but I didn't really trust it. It seemed likely that it was, deep down, TAP.

I paused by MILK. The sole white liquid. Soothing, just to look at.

"Gases?" she said.

"Okay," I said. "Sure. I'd like to see the gases, why not."

My hands were now hardening with stickiness, each finger gluing slightly to its neighbor. I wanted to wash them, but instead I dropped the gooey pit into my purse near my wallet. The woman gave me a disapproving look and brought out another silver key, this one from her pocket. She turned and clicked and we went through the glass door in the back of the back room.

The gas room was empty.

"Oh," I said, "hmm." I worried for a second that she'd been robbed and was just now finding out.

"Be very very careful," she whispered then. "This is expensive." She looked tense beneath her tan, each of her features tight in its place.

"More expensive than PEARL?" I said.

"Much more," she said. "This takes very difficult concentration. This is my most challenging work. Look here," she said, "come here and look."

She walked over to one of the shelves on the wall and close up I could see there was more glass tubing — not much, but one word's worth. It spelled SMOKE. Soft granules of ash floated through the M.

"It's a good one," I said. "I like it."

"Most of them," she said, still whispering, "in this room, don't have the tubing."

"Oh." I bobbed my head, not understanding.

"See," she continued, "there are many many gas words in this room but you might not be able to read them."

I looked to the shelves and saw nothing, saw shelves that were empty, saw how my apartment would look in a month when Steve had cleared out his books and his bookends.

"Top shelf: XENON," the woman said. "It's there, it's just very hard to see. I can see it because I have very good eyes for it, because it is my medium."

I looked to the top shelf. "There's no XENON there," I said. "There's nothing."

"Trust me," she said. "There's XENON."

I shook my head. I shifted my feet a few times. There was POISON in the room before, dark and available, and a thin wire of fear started to cut and coil in my stomach.

"ARGON," she said, "is on shelf four, below XENON."

"Noble gas number two," I said.

She nodded. "I prefer the noble gases."

"I bet," I said. "There's no ARGON there," I said.

"It's there," she said. "Be extremely careful."

I spoke slowly, coated now in a very mild shellac of panic. "How," I said, "how can it be there, it would dissipate. I took chemistry. It can't just sit there. Argon," I said, "can't just *sit* there."

"I put guidelines in the air," she said. "I make a formation in the air."

I turned toward the entrance.

"I think it's time for me to go," I said.

"NEON," she said, "is on shelf number three."

But right before I walked to the door, I reached out a hand which was so hard and gluey from the mango juice, reached out just to wipe it slightly on the very tip of the shelf. The coil in my stomach took my fingers there. I barely even noticed what I was doing.

The woman drew in her breath in agony.

"Aaghh!" she choked as I got in my little wipe wipe. "You broke it!"

"I broke what?" I said. "Broke what?"

"You broke AIR," she said. "You need to pay for it, you broke it, you broke AIR."

Then she pointed to a sign I hadn't seen before, tucked half behind a shelf, a half-hidden laminated sign that said: VISITORS MUST PAY FOR BROKEN MERCHANDISE.

"There's air there still," I said, "that's no special air."

"It was air in the shape of AIR," she said. "It took me a while to train that space, it was AIR. That's three hundred dollars."

"What?" I said. "I won't pay that," I said, speaking louder. "I didn't even break it, look, there's tons of air around, there's air everywhere."

I waved my hand in the space, indicating air, and she let out another, louder, shriek.

"That was HOPE," she said, "you just broke HOPE!"

"HOPE?" I said, and now I went straight to the glass door. "Broke hope? Hope is not a gas, you can't form hope!"

The door, thank God, was unlocked, and I swung it open and stalked into the liquid room. The woman was right on my heels.

"I caught hope," she said. "I made it into a gas."

"I want to go now," I said. "There's no possible way to catch hope, please."

My voice was gaining height. I didn't believe her but still. Of all things to wreck.

"Well," she said. "I went to wedding after wedding after wedding in Las Vegas. And I capped the bottle each time right when they said 'I do.'"

This made me laugh for a second but then I had to stop because I thought I might choke. I could just see those couples now, perched at opposite ends of a living-room couch, bookending the air between them, the thickest, most formed air around, that uncrossable, unbreakable, impossible air, finally signing the papers that would send them to different addresses.

I thought of the seven years I'd spent with Steve, and how at first when we'd kissed his lips had been a boat made of roses and how now they were a freight train of lead.

So that I wouldn't cry, I put my hand near my face and made a pushing motion, moved some wind toward her. "I'm Queen of Hope," I said. "Here. Have some of mine."

She grabbed BLOOD from the liquid room shelves.

"Give me my money for AIR!" she said, waving the BLOOD in my face.

I opened the door to the solid room and ran through it. I kept my back arched so she wouldn't touch me. I couldn't pay the money and I wouldn't pay it, it was air, for God's sake, but I didn't want that blood on me, didn't want that blood anywhere close to me.

"I'm sorry," I yelled as I edged out the front, "sorry!"

I looked past the fruit to locate my car and as I did, my eye grazed over the solid words, familiar now, but on the bottom shelf I suddenly saw CAT and DOG in big brown capitals which I hadn't seen before and my stomach balked. The woman kept yelling "You Owe Me Money!" and I hit the dead warmth of the outside air.

Everything was still. My car sat across the street, waiting for me, placid.

The woman was right behind me, yelling, "You owe me three hundred dollars!" and I took NUT out of my bag and threw it behind me where it broke on the street into a million shavings. "Nut!" I yelled. I got into my car, key shaking.

"Vandal!" she yelled back, and she didn't even try to cross the street but just stood at the front of the blue-awninged store with BLOOD in her arms and then she reached back and pelted my car with a tangelo and a pineapple and one huge hard cantaloupe. I locked my doors and right when I put my key into the ignition, she took BLOOD and threw that too; it hit the car square on the passenger-side window, cracking on the top and opening up like an egg, dripping red down the window until the letters ran clear. Maybe it was just juice, but that one I trusted, that one seemed real to me.

Hands trembling, I put my foot on the accelerator and the car started quickly, warmed from the sunlight, the desert spreading out hot and fruitless. The window to my right was streaking with red now. I kept a hand on the car lock, making sure it was down. Across the street, the woman pulled back her arm, which was an awfully good arm, by the way, she was some kind of baseball superstar, and she let fly a few guavas, which splatted blue against my rear window.

I drove away fast as I could. The shack and the woman, still throwing, grew small in my rearview mirror. I drove and drove for eighty miles without pausing, just getting away, just speeding away as the blood dried on the window, away from the piles of tangerines, from the star fruit clumped in stolen constellations, from the seven different mutations of apple.

In an hour I desperately needed to go to the bathroom, so I pulled into a gas station. I still had the brown bag of mangoes with me. When I opened it up, they were all black and rotten, with flies crawling over them. I dumped the whole bag. The one I'd eaten was just a pit, which I removed from my purse and kept on the passenger seat, but by the time I got home and pulled into the empty driveway, it too had rotted away into a soft, weak ball.

THE EMPIRE OF ICE CREAM

JEFFREY FORD

ARE YOU FAMILIAR with the scent of extinguished birthday candles? For me, their aroma is superseded by a sound like the drawing of a bow across the bass string of a violin. This note carries all of the melancholic joy I have been told the scent engenders — the loss of another year, the promise of accrued wisdom. Likewise, the notes of an acoustic guitar appear before my eyes as a golden rain, falling from a height just above my head only to vanish at the level of my solar plexus. There is a certain imported Swiss cheese I am fond of that is all triangles, whereas the feel of silk against my fingers rests on my tongue with the flavor and consistency of lemon meringue. These perceptions are not merely thoughts, but concrete physical experiences. Depending upon how you see it, I, like approximately nine out of every million individuals, am either cursed or blessed with a condition known as *synesthesia*.

It has only recently come to light that the process of synesthesia takes place in the hippocampus, part of the ancient limbic system, where remembered perceptions triggered in diverse geographical regions of the brain as the result of an external stimulus come together. It is believed that everyone, at a point somewhere below consciousness, experiences this coinciding of sensory association, yet in most it is filtered out and only a single sense is given predominance in one's waking world. For we lucky few, the filter is broken or perfected, and what is usually subconscious becomes conscious. Perhaps, at some distant point in history, our early ancestors were completely synesthetic and touched, heard, smelled, tasted, and saw, at once, each specific incident, the mixing of sensoric memory along with the perceived sense, without affording precedence to the findings of one of the five portals through which "reality" invades us. The scientific explanations, as far as I can follow them, seem to make sense now, but when I was young and told my parents about the whisper of vinyl, the stench of purple, the spinning blue gyres of the church bell, they feared I was defective and that my mind was brimming with hallucinations like an abandoned house choked with ghosts.

As an only child, I wasn't afforded the luxury of being anomalous. My parents were well on in years — my mother nearly forty, my father already forty-five — when I arrived after a long parade of failed pregnancies. The fact that, at age five, I heard what I described as an angel crying whenever I touched velvet would never be allowed to stand, but was seen as an illness to be cured by whatever methods were available. Money was no object in the pursuit of perfect normalcy. And so my younger years were a torment of hours spent in the waiting rooms of psychologists, psychiatrists, and therapists. I can't find words to describe the depths of medical quackery I was subjected to by a veritable army of so-called professionals who diagnosed me with everything from schizophrenia to bipolar depression to low IQ caused by muddled potty training. Being a child, I was completely honest with them about what I experienced, and this, my first mistake, resulted in blood tests, brain scans, special diets, and the forced consumption of a demon's pharmacopeia of mind-deadening drugs that diminished my will but not the vanilla scent of slanting golden sunlight on late autumn afternoons.

My only-child status along with the added complication of my "condition," as they called it, led my parents to perceive me as fragile. For this reason I was kept fairly isolated from other children. Part of it, I'm sure, had to do with the way my abnormal perceptions and utterances would reflect upon my mother and father, for they were the type of people who could not bear to be thought of as having been responsible for the production of defective goods. I was tutored at home by my mother instead of being allowed to attend school. She was actually a fine teacher, having a PhD in history and a firm grasp of classical literature. My father, an actuary, taught me math, and in this subject I proved to be an unquestionable failure until I reached college age. Although x=y might have been a suitable metaphor for the phenomenon of synesthesia, it made no sense on paper. The number 8, by the way, reeks of withered flowers.

What I *was* good at was music. Every Thursday at 3:00 in the afternoon, Mrs. Brithnic would arrive at the house to give me a piano lesson. She was a kind old lady with thinning white hair and the most beautiful fingers — long and smooth, as if they belonged to a graceful young giantess. Although something less than a virtuoso at the keys, she was a veritable genius at teaching me to allow myself to enjoy the sounds I produced. Enjoy them I did, and when I wasn't being dragged hither and yon in the pursuit of losing my affliction, home base for me was the piano bench. In my imposed isolation from the world, music became a window of escape I would crawl through as often as possible.

When I would play, I could see the notes before me like a fireworks display of colors and shapes. By my twelfth year I was writing my own compositions, and my notations on the pages accompanying the notes referred to the visual displays that coincided with them. In actuality, when I played, I was really painting — in midair before my eyes — great abstract works in the tradition of Kandinsky. Many times, I planned a composition on a blank piece of paper using the crayon set of sixty-four colors I'd had since early childhood. The only difficulty in this was with colors like magenta and cobalt blue, which I perceive primarily as tastes, so I would have to write them down in pencil as licorice and tapioca on my colorfully scribbled drawing where they would appear in the music.

My punishment for having excelled at the piano was to lose my only real friend, Mrs. Brithnic. I remember distinctly the day my mother let her go. She calmly nodded, smiling, understanding that I had already surpassed her abilities. Still, though I knew this was the case, I cried when she hugged me goodbye. When her face was next to mine, she whispered into my ear, "Seeing is believing," and in that moment I knew she had completely understood my plight. Her lilac perfume, the sound of one nearly inaudible B-flat played by an oboe, still hung about me as I watched her walk down the path and out of my life for good.

I believe it was the loss of Mrs. Brithnic that made me rebel. I became desultory and despondent. Then one day, soon after my thirteenth birthday, instead of obeying my mother, who had just told me to finish reading a textbook chapter while she showered, I went to her pocketbook, took five dollars, and left the house. As I walked along beneath the sunlight and blue sky, the world around me seemed brimming with life. What I wanted more than anything else was to meet other young people my own age. I remembered an ice-cream shop in town where, when passing by in the car returning from whatever doctor's office we had been to, there always seemed to be kids hanging around. I headed directly for that spot while wondering if my mother would catch up to me before I made it. When I pictured her drying her hair, I broke into a run.

Upon reaching the row of stores that contained The Empire of Ice Cream, I was out of breath as much from the sheer exhilaration of freedom as from the half-mile sprint. Peering through the glass of the front door was like looking through a portal into an exotic other world. Here were young people, my age, gathered in groups at tables, talking, laughing, eating ice cream — not by night, after dinner, but in the middle of broad daylight. I opened the door and plunged in. The magic of the place seemed to brush by me on its way out as I entered, for the conversation instantly died away. I stood in the momentary silence as all heads turned to stare at me.

"Hello," I said, smiling, and raised my hand in greeting, but I was too late. They had already turned away, the conversation resumed, as if they had merely afforded a grudging glimpse to see the door open and close at the behest of the wind. I was paralyzed by my inability to make an impression, the realization that finding friends was going to take some real work.

"What'll it be?" said a large man behind the counter.

I broke from my trance and stepped up to order. Before me, beneath a bubble dome of glass, lay the Empire of Ice Cream. I'd never seen so much of the stuff in so many colors and incarnations — with nuts and fruit, cookie and candy bits, mystical swirls the sight of which sounded to me like a distant siren. There were deep vats of it set in neat rows totaling thirty flavors. My diet had never allowed for the consumption of confections or desserts of any type, and rare were the times I had so much as a thimbleful of vanilla ice cream after dinner. Certain doctors had told my parents that my eating these treats might seriously exacerbate my condition. With this in mind, I ordered a large bowl of coffee ice cream. My choice of coffee stemmed from the fact that that beverage was another item on the list of things I should never taste.

After paying, I took my bowl and spoon and found a seat in the corner of the place from which I could survey all the other tables. I admit that I had some trepidations about digging right in, since I'd been warned against it for so long by so many adults. Instead, I scanned the shop, watching the other kids talking, trying to overhear snatches of conversation. I made eye contact with a boy my own age two tables away. I smiled and waved to him. He saw me and then leaned over and whispered something to the other fellows he was with. All four of them turned, looked at me, and then broke into laughter. It was a certainty they were making fun of me, but I basked in the victory of merely being noticed. With this, I took a large spoonful of ice cream and put it in my mouth.

There is an attendant phenomenon of the synesthetic experience I have yet to mention. Of course I had no term for it at this point in my life, but when one is in the throes of the remarkable transference of senses, it is accompanied by a feeling of "epiphany," a "eureka" of contentment that researchers of the anomalous condition would later term *noetic*, borrowing from William James. That first taste of coffee ice cream elicited a deeper noetic response than I'd ever before felt, and along with it came the appearance of a girl. She coalesced out of thin air and stood before me, obscuring my sight of the group that was still laughing. Never before had I seen through tasting, hearing, touching, smelling, something other than simple abstract shapes and colors.

She was turned somewhat to the side and hunched over, wearing a plaid skirt and a white blouse. Her hair was the same dark brown as my own, but long and gathered in the back with a green rubber band. There was a sudden shaking of her hand, and it became clear to me that she was putting out a match. Smoke swirled away from her. I could see now that she had been lighting a cigarette. I got the impression that she was wary of being caught in the act of smoking. When she turned her head sharply to look back over her shoulder, I dropped the spoon on the table. Her look instantly enchanted me.

As the ice cream melted away down my throat, she began to vanish, and I quickly lifted the spoon to restoke my vision, but it never reached my lips. She suddenly went out like a light when I felt something land softly upon my left shoulder. I heard the incomprehensible murmur of recrimination, and knew it as my mother's touch. She had found me. A great wave of laughter accompanied my removal from The Empire of Ice Cream. Later I would remember the incident with embarrassment, but for the moment, even as I spoke words of apology to my mother, I could think only of what I'd seen.

The ice-cream incident — followed hard by the discovery of the cigar box of pills I hid in my closet, all of the medication that I'd supposedly swallowed for the past six months — led my parents to believe that heaped upon my condition was now a tendency toward delinquency that would grow, if unchecked, in geometrical proportion with the passing of years. It was decided that I should see yet another specialist to deal with my behavior, a therapist my father had read about who would prompt me to talk my willfulness into submission. I was informed of this in a solemn meeting with my parents. What else was there to do but acquiesce? I knew that my mother and father wanted, in their pedestrian way, what they believed was best for me. Whenever the situation would infuriate me, I would go to the piano and play, sometimes for three or four hours at a time.

Dr. Stullin's office was in a ramshackle Victorian house on the other side of town. My father accompanied me on the first visit, and, when he pulled up in front of the sorry old structure, he checked the address at least twice to make sure we'd come to the right place. The doctor, a round little man with a white beard and glasses with small circular lenses, met us at the front door. Why he laughed when we shook hands at the introductions, I hadn't a clue, but he was altogether jolly, like a pint-sized Santa Claus dressed in a wrinkled brown suit one size too small. He swept out his arm to usher me into his house, but when my father tried to enter, the doctor held up his hand and said, "You will return in one hour and five minutes."

My father gave some weak protest and said that he thought he might be needed to help discuss my history to this point. Here the doctor's demeanor instantly changed. He became serious, official, almost commanding.

"I'm being paid to treat the boy. You will have to find your own therapist."

My father was obviously at a loss. He looked as if he was about to object, but the doctor said, "One hour and five minutes." Following me inside, he quickly shut the door behind him.

As he led me through a series of unkempt rooms lined with crammed bookshelves, and one in which piles of paper covered the tops of tables and desks, he said, laughing, "Parents — so essential, yet sometimes like something you have stepped in and cannot get off your shoe. What else is there but to love them?"

We wound up in a room at the back of the house made from a skeleton of thin steel girders and paneled with glass panes. The sunlight poured in, and surrounding us, at the edges of the place, and also hanging from some of the girders, were green plants. There was a small table on which sat a teapot and two cups and saucers. As I took the seat he motioned for me to sit in, I looked out through the glass and saw that the backyard was one large, magnificent garden, blooming with all manner of colorful flowers.

After he poured me a cup of tea, the questioning began. I'd had it in my mind to be as recalcitrant as possible, but there was something in the manner in which he had put my father off that I admired about him. Also, he was unlike other therapists I had been to, who would listen to my answers with complete reservation of emotion or response. When he asked why I was here and I told him it was because I had escaped in order to go to the ice-cream shop, he scowled and said, "Patently ridiculous." I was unsure if he meant me or my mother's response to what I'd done. I told him about playing the piano, and he smiled warmly and nodded. "That is a good thing," he said.

After he asked me about my daily routine and my home life, he sat back and said, "So, what's the problem? Your father has told me that you hallucinate. Can you explain?"

No matter how ingratiating he had been, I'd already decided that I would no longer divulge any of my perceptions to anyone. Then he did something unexpected.

"Do you mind?" he asked as he took out a pack of cigarettes.

Before I could shake my head no, he had one out of the pack and lit. Something about this, perhaps because I'd never seen a doctor smoke in front of a patient before, perhaps because it reminded me of the girl who had appeared before me in the ice-cream shop, weakened my resolve to say nothing. When he flicked his ashes into his half-empty teacup, I started talking. I told him about the taste of silk, the various corresponding colors for the notes of the piano, the nauseating stench of purple.

I laid the whole thing out for him and then sat back in my chair, now somewhat regretting my weakness, for he was smiling and the smoke was leaking out of the corners of his mouth. He exhaled, and in that cloud came the word that would validate me, define me, and haunt me for the rest of my life — *synesthesia*.

By the time I left Stullin's office that day, I was a new person. The doctor spoke to my father and explained the phenomenon to him. He cited historical cases and gave him the same general overview of the neurological workings of the condition. He also added that most synesthetes don't experience the condition in such a variety of senses as I did, although it was not unheard of. My father nodded every now and then but was obviously perplexed at the fact that my long-suffered *condition* had, in an instant, vanished.

"There's nothing wrong with the boy," said Stullin, "except for the fact that he is, in a way, exceptional. Think of it as a gift, an original way of sensing the world. These perceptions are as real for him as are your own to you."

Stullin's term for my condition was like a magic incantation from a fairy tale, for through its power I was released from the spell of my parents' control. In fact, their reaction to it was to almost completely relinquish interest in me, as if after all of their intensive care I'd been found out to be an imposter now unworthy of their attention. When it became clear that I would have the ability to go about my life as any normal child might, I relished the concept of freedom. The sad fact was, though, that I didn't know how to. I lacked all experience at being part of society. My uncertainty made me shy, and my first year in public school was a disaster. What I wanted was a friend my own age, and this goal continued to elude me until I was well out of high school and in college. My desperation to connect made me ultimately nervous, causing me to act and speak without reserve. This was the early 1960s, and if anything was important in high school social circles at the time, it was remaining *cool*. I was the furthest thing from cool you might imagine.

For protection, I retreated into my music and spent hours working out compositions with my crayons and pens, trying to corral the sounds and resultant visual pyrotechnics, odors, and tastes into cohesive scores. All along, I continued practicing and improving my abilities at the keyboard, but I had no desire to become a performer. Quite a few of my teachers through the years had it in their minds that they could shape me into a brilliant concert pianist. I would not allow it, and when they insisted, I'd drop them and move on. Nothing frightened me more than the thought of sitting in front of a crowd of onlookers. The weight of judgment lurking behind even one set of those imagined eyes was too much for me to bear. I'd stayed on with Stullin, visiting once a month, and no matter his persistent proclamations as to my relative normalcy, it was impossible for me, after years of my parents' insisting otherwise, to erase the fact that I was, in my own mind, a freak.

My greatest pleasure away from the piano at this time was to take the train into the nearby city and attend concerts given by the local orchestra or small chamber groups that would perform in more intimate venues. Rock and roll was all the rage, but my training at the piano and the fact that calm solitude, as opposed to raucous socializing, was the expected milieu of the symphony drew me in the direction of classical music. It was a relief that most of those who attended the concerts were adults who paid no attention to my presence. From the performances I witnessed, from the stereo I goaded my parents into buying for me, and my own reading, I, with few of the normal distractions of the typical teenager, gathered an immense knowledge of my field.

My hero was J. S. Bach. It was from his works that I came to understand mathematics and, through a greater understanding of math, came to a greater understanding of Bach — the golden ratio, the rise of complexity through the reiteration of simple elements, the presence of the cosmic in the common.

Whereas others simply heard his work, I could also feel it, taste it, smell it, visualize it, and in doing so was certain I was witnessing the process by which all of Nature had moved from a single cell to a virulent, diverse forest. Perhaps part of my admiration for the good cantor of Leipzig was his genius with counterpoint, a practice where two or more distinct melodic lines delicately join at certain points to form a singularly cohesive listening experience. I saw in this technique an analogy to my desire that some day my own unique personality might join with that of another's and form a friendship. Soon after hearing the fugue pieces that are part of *The Well-Tempered Clavier,* I decided I wanted to become a composer.

Of course, during these years, both dreadful for my being a laughingstock in school and delightful for their musical revelations, I couldn't forget the image of the girl who momentarily appeared before me during my escape to The Empire of Ice Cream. The minute that Dr. Stullin pronounced me sane, I made plans to return and attempt to conjure her again. The irony of the situation was that just that single first taste of coffee ice cream had ended up making me ill, either because I'd been sheltered from rich desserts my whole life or because my system actually was inherently delicate. Once my freedom came, I found I didn't have the stomach for all of those gastronomic luxuries I had at one time so desired. Still, I was willing to chance the stomachache in order to rediscover her.

On my second trip to The Empire, after taking a heaping spoonful of coffee ice cream and experiencing again that deep noetic response, she appeared as before, her image forming in the empty space between me and the front window of the shop. This time she seemed to be sitting at the end of a couch situated in a living room or parlor, reading a book. Only her immediate surroundings within a foot or two of her body were clear to me. As my eyes moved away from her central figure, the rest of the couch and the table beside her, holding a lamp, became increasingly ghostlike; images from the parking lot outside the shop window showed through. At the edges of the phenomenon there was nothing but the merest wrinkling of the atmosphere. She turned the page, and I

THE SECRET HISTORY OF FANTASY

was drawn back to her. I quickly fed myself another bit of ice cream and marveled at her beauty. Her hair was down, and I could see that it came well past her shoulders. Bright green eyes, a small, perfect nose, smooth skin, and full lips that silently moved with each word of the text she was scanning. She was wearing some kind of very sheer, powder-blue pajama top, and I could see the presence of her breasts beneath it.

I took two spoonfuls of ice cream in a row, and, because my desire had tightened my throat and I couldn't swallow, their cold burned my tongue. In the time it took for the mouthful of ice cream to melt and trickle down my throat, I simply watched her chest subtly heave with each breath, her lips move, and I was enchanted. The last thing I noticed before she disappeared was the odd title of the book she was reading: *The Centrifugal Rickshaw Dancer.* I'd have taken another spoonful, but a massive headache had blossomed behind my eyes, and I could feel my stomach beginning to revolt against the ice cream. I got up and quickly left the shop. Out in the open air I walked for over an hour, trying to clear my head of the pain while at the same time trying to retain her image in my memory. I stopped three times along my meandering course, positive I was going to vomit, but never did.

My resistance to the physical side effects of the ice cream never improved, but I returned to the shop again and again, like a binge drinker to the bottle, hangover be damned, whenever I was feeling most alone. Granted, there was something of a voyeuristic thrill underlying the whole thing, especially when the ice cream would bring her to me in various states of undress — in the shower, in her bedroom. But you must believe me when I say that there was much more to it than that. I wanted to know everything about her. I studied her as assiduously as I did *The Goldberg Variations* or Schoenberg's serialism. She was, in many ways, an even more intriguing mystery, and the process of investigation was like constructing a jigsaw puzzle, reconfiguring a blasted mosaic.

I learned that her name was Anna. I saw it written on one of her sketchpads. Yes, she was an artist, and I believe she had great aspirations in this direction as I did in music. I spent so many spoonfuls of coffee ice cream, initiated so many headaches, just watching her draw. She never lifted a paintbrush or pastel, but was tied to the simple tools of pencil and paper. I never witnessed her using a model or photograph as a guide. Instead she would place the sketchpad flat on a table and hunker over it. The tip of her tongue would show itself from the right corner of her lips when she was in deepest concentration. Every so often she would take a drag on a cigarette that burned in an ashtray to her left. The results of her work, the few times I was lucky enough to catch a glimpse, were astonishing. Sometimes she was obviously drawing from life, the portraits of people whom she must have known. At other times she would conjure strange creatures or mandala-like designs of exotic blossoms. The shading was incredible, giving weight and depth to her creations. All of this from the tip of a graphite pencil one might use to work a calculation or jot a memo. If I did not adore her, I might've envied her innate talent.

To an ancillary degree, I was able to catch brief glimpses of her surroundings, and this was fascinating for she seemed to move through a complete, separate world of her own, some kind of *other* reality that was very much like ours. I'd garnered enough to know that she lived in a large old house with many rooms, the windows covered with long drapes to block out the light. Her work area was chaotic, stacks of her drawings covering the tops of tables and pushed to the sides of her desk. A black-and-white cat was always prowling in and out of the tableau. She was very fond of flowers and often worked in some sun-drenched park or garden, creating painstaking portraits of amaryllis or pansies, and although the rain would be falling outside my own window, there the skies were bottomless blue.

Although over the course of years I'd told Stullin much about myself, revealed my ambitions and most secret desires, I had never mentioned Anna. It was only after I graduated high school and was set to go off to study at Gelsbeth Conservatory in the nearby city that I decided to reveal her existence to him. The doctor had been a good friend to me, albeit a remunerated one, and was always most congenial and understanding when I'd give vent to my frustrations. He persistently argued the optimistic viewpoint for me when all was as inky black as the aroma of my father's aftershave. My time with him never resulted in a palpable difference in my ability to attract friends or feel more comfortable in public, but I enjoyed his company. At the same time, I was somewhat relieved to be severing all ties to my troubled past and escaping my childhood once and for all. I was willing to jettison Stullin's partial good to be rid of the rest.

We sat in the small sunroom at the back of his house, and he was questioning me about what interests I would pursue in my forthcoming classes. He had a good working knowledge of classical music and had told me at one of our earliest meetings that he had studied the piano when he was younger. He had a weakness for the Romantics, but I didn't hold it against him. Somewhere in the midst of our discussion I simply blurted out the details of my experiences with coffee ice cream and the resultant appearances of Anna. He was obviously taken aback. He leaned forward in his chair and slowly went through the procedure of lighting a cigarette.

"You know," he said, releasing a cascade of smoke, the aroma of which always manifested itself for me in the faint sound of a mosquito, "that is quite unusual. I don't believe there has ever been a case of a synesthetic vision achieving a figurative resemblance. They are always abstract. Shapes, colors, yes, but never an image of an object, not to mention a person."

"I know it's the synesthesia," I said. "I can feel it. The exact same experience as when I summon colors from my keyboard."

"And you say she always appears in relation to your eating ice cream?" he asked, squinting.

"Coffee ice cream," I said.

This made him laugh briefly, but his smile soon diminished, and he brought his free hand up to stroke his beard. I knew this action to be a sign of his concern. "What you are describing to me would be, considering the current medical literature, a hallucination."

I shrugged.

"Still," he went on, "the fact that it is always related to your tasting the ice cream, and that you can identify an associated noetic feeling, I would have to agree with you that it seems related to your condition."

"I knew it was unusual," I said. "I was afraid to mention it."

"No, no, it's good that you did. The only thing troubling me about it is that I am too aware of your desire to connect with another person your age. To be honest, it has all the earmarks of wish fulfillment that points back to a kind of hallucination. Look, you don't need this distraction now. You are beginning your life, you are moving on, and there is every indication that you will be successful in your art. When the other students at the conservatory understand your abilities, you will make friends, believe me. It will not be like high school. Chasing this insubstantial image could impede your progress. Let it go."

And so, not without a large measure of regret, I did. To an extent, Stullin was right about Gelsbeth. It wasn't like high school, and I did make the acquaintance of quite a few like-minded people with whom I could at least connect on the subject of music. I wasn't the only odd fish in that pond, believe me. To be a young person with an overriding interest in Bach or Mozart or Scriabin was its own eccentricity for those times. The place was extremely competitive, and I took the challenge. My fledgling musical compositions were greeted with great interest by the faculty, and I garnered a degree of notoriety when one day a fellow student discovered me composing a chamber piece for violins and cello using my set of crayons. I would always work in my corresponding synesthetic colors and then transpose the work, scoring it in normal musical notation.

The years flew by, and I believe they were the most rewarding of my entire life. I rarely went home to visit, save on holidays when the school was closed, even though it was only a brief train ride from the city. The professors were excellent but unforgiving of laziness and error. It wasn't a labor for me to meet their expectations. For the first time in my life, I felt what it meant to play, an activity I'd never experienced in childhood. The immersion in great music, the intricate analysis of its soul, kept me constantly engaged, filled with a sense of wonder.

Then, in my last year, I became eligible to participate in a competition for composers. There was a large cash prize, and the winner's work would be performed by a well-known musician at a concert in the city's symphony hall. The difficulty of being a composer was always the near-impossibility of getting one's work performed by competent musicians in a public venue. The opportunity presented by the competition was one I couldn't let slip away. More important than the money or the accolades would be a kind of recognition that would bring me to the attention of potential patrons who might commission a work. I knew that it was time to finally compose the fugue I'd had in mind for so many years. The utter complexity of the form, I believed, would be the best way to showcase all of my talents.

When it came time to begin the composition of the fugue, I took the money I'd made tutoring young musicians on the weekends and put it toward renting a beach house out on Varion Island for two weeks. In the summer the place was a bustling tourist spot for the wealthy, with a small central town that could be termed quaint. In those months, I wouldn't have been able to touch the price of the lowliest dwelling for a single day's rent. It was the heart of winter, though, when I took a leave from the school, along with crayons, books, a small tape player, and fled by way of bus and cab to my secret getaway.

The house I came to wasn't one of the grand wooden mansions on stilts that lined the road along the causeway, but instead a small bungalow, much like a concrete bunker. It was painted an off-putting yellow that tasted to me for all the world like cauliflower. It sat atop a small rise, and its front window faced the ocean, giving me a sublime view of the dunes and beach. What's more, it was within walking distance of the tiny village. There was sufficient heat, a telephone, a television, a kitchen with all the appliances, and I instantly felt as at home there as I had anywhere in my life. The island itself was deserted. On my first day I walked down to the ocean, along the shore the mile and a half to the eastern point, and then back by way of the main road, passing empty houses, and I saw no one. I'd been told over the phone by the realtor that the diner in town and a small shop that sold cigarettes and newspapers stayed open through the winter. Thankfully, she was right, for without the diner, I would have starved.

The setting of the little bungalow was deliciously melancholic, and for my sensibilities that meant conducive to work. I could hear the distant breaking of waves and, above that, the winter wind blowing sand against the window glass, but these were not distractions. Instead, they were the components of a silence that invited one to dream wide awake, to let the imagination open, and so I dove into the work straightaway. On the first afternoon, I began recording in my notebook my overall plan for the fugue. I'd decided that it would have only two voices. Of course, some had been composed with as many as eight, but I didn't want to be ostentatious. Showing reserve is as important a trait of technical mastery as is that of complexity.

I already had the melodic line of the subject, which had been a castoff from another project I'd worked on earlier in the year. Even though I decided it wasn't right for the earlier piece, I couldn't forget it and kept revising it here and there, playing it over and over. In the structure of a fugue, one posits the melodic line or subject, and then there is an answer (counterpoint), a reiteration of that line with differing degrees of variation, so that what the listener hears is like a dialogue (or a voice and its echo) of increasing complexity. After each of the voices has entered the piece, there is an episode that leads to the reentry of the voices and given answers, now in different keys. I had planned to use a technique called *stretto,* in which the answers, as they are introduced, overlap somewhat the original subject lines. This allows for a weaving of the voices so as to create an intricate tapestry of sound.

All this would be difficult to compose but nothing outlandishly original. It was my design, though, to impress the judges by trying something new. Once the fugue had reached its greatest state of complication, I wanted the piece to slowly, almost logically at first, but then without rhyme or meter, crumble into chaos. At the very end, from that chaotic cacophony, there would emerge one note, drawn out to great length, which would eventually diminish into nothing.

For the first week, the work went well. I took a little time off every morning and evening for a walk on the beach. At night I would go to the diner and then return to the bungalow to listen to Bach's *Art of the Fugue* or *Toccata and Fugue in D Minor,* some Brahms, Haydn, Mozart, and then pieces from the inception of the form by composers like Sweelinck and Froberger. I employed the crayons on a large piece of good drawing paper, and although to anyone else it wouldn't look like musical notation, I knew exactly how it would sound when I viewed it. Somewhere after the first week, though, I started to slow down, and by Saturday night my work came to a grinding halt. What I'd begun with such a clear sense of direction had me trapped. I was lost in my own complexity. The truth was, I was exhausted and could no longer pick apart the threads of the piece — the subject, the answer, the counter-subject snarled like a ball of yarn.

I was thoroughly weary and knew I needed rest, but even though I went to bed and closed my eyes, I couldn't sleep. All day Sunday I sat in a chair and surveyed the beach through the front window. I was too tired to work but too frustrated about not working to sleep. That evening, after having done nothing all day, I stumbled down to the diner and took my usual seat. The place was empty, save for one old man sitting in the far corner reading a book while eating his dinner. This solitary character looked somewhat like Stullin for his white beard, and at first glance, had I not known better, I could've sworn the book he was reading was *The Centrifugal Rickshaw Dancer*. I didn't want to get close enough to find out for fear he might strike up a conversation.

The waitress came and took my order. When she was finished writing on her pad, she said, "You look exhausted tonight."

I nodded.

"You need to sleep," she said.

"I have work to do," I told her.

"Well, then, let me bring you some coffee."

I laughed. "You know, I've never had a cup of coffee in my life," I said.

"Impossible," she said. "It looks to me like tonight might be a good time to start."

"I'll give it a try," I told her, and this seemed to make her happy.

While I ate, I glanced through my notebook and tried to reestablish the architecture of the fugue. As always, when I looked at my notes, everything was crystal clear, but when it came time to continue on the score, every potential further step seemed the wrong way to go. Somewhere in the midst of my musing, I pushed my plate away and drew toward me the cup and saucer. My usual drink was tea, and I'd forgotten I had changed my order. I took a sip, and the dark, bitter taste of black coffee startled me. I looked up, and there was Anna, staring at me, having just lowered a cup away from her lips. In her eyes I saw a glint of recognition, as if she were actually seeing me, and I'm sure she saw the same in mine.

I whispered, "I see you."

She smiled. "I see you too," she said.

I would have been less surprised if a dog had spoken to me. Sitting dumbfounded, I reached slowly out toward where she seemed to sit across from me in the booth. As my hand approached, she leaned back away from it.

"I've been watching you for years," she said.

"The coffee?" I said.

She nodded. "You are a synesthete, am I right?"

"Yes," I said. "But you're a figment of my imagination, a product of a neurological anomaly."

Here she laughed out loud. "No," she said, "you are."

After our initial exchange, neither of us spoke. I was in a mild state of shock, I believe. *This can't be,* I kept repeating in my mind, but there she was, and I could hear her breathing. Her image appeared even sharper than it had previously under the influence of the coffee ice cream. And now, with the taste that elicited her presence uncompromised by cream and sugar and the cold, she remained without dissipating for a good few minutes before beginning to mist at the edges and I had to take another sip to sharpen the focus. When I brought my cup up to drink, she also did at the same exact time, as if she were a reflection, as if I were her reflection, and we both smiled.

"I can't speak to you where I am. They'll think I've lost my mind," I whispered.

"I'm in the same situation," she said.

"Give me a half-hour and then have another cup of coffee, and I'll be able to speak to you in private."

She nodded in agreement and watched as I called for the check.

By the time the waitress arrived at my booth, Anna had dissolved into a vague cloud, like the exhalation of a smoker. It didn't matter, as I knew she couldn't be seen by anyone else. As my bill was being tallied, I ordered three cups of coffee to go.

"That coffee is something, isn't it?" said the waitress. "I swear by it. Amazing you've never had any up to this point. My blood is three-quarters coffee, I drink so much of it," she said.

"Wonderful stuff," I agreed.

Wonderful it was, for it had awakened my senses, and I walked through the freezing, windy night, carrying in a box my containers of elixir, with all the joy of a child leaving school on Friday afternoon. The absurdity of the whole affair didn't escape me, and I laughed out loud remembering my whispered plan to wait a half-hour and then drink another cup. The conspiratorial nature of it excited me, and I realized for the first time since seeing her that Anna had matured and grown more beautiful in the years I had forsaken her.

Back at the bungalow, I put the first of the large Styrofoam containers into the microwave in the kitchen and heated it for no more than thirty seconds. I began to worry that perhaps in Anna's existence time was altogether different and a half-hour for me might be two or three or a day for her. The instant the bell sounded on the appliance, I took the cup out, seated myself at the small kitchen table, and drank a long draught of the dark potion. Before I set the cup down, she was there, sitting in the seat opposite me.

"I know your name is Anna," I said to her. "I saw it on one of your drawing pads."

She flipped her hair behind her ear on the left side and asked, "What's yours?"

"William," I said. Then I told her about the coffee ice cream and first time I encountered her image.

"I remember," she said, "when I was a child of nine, I snuck a sip of my father's coffee he had left in the living room, and I saw you sitting at a piano. I thought you were a ghost. I ran to get my mother to show her, but when I returned you had vanished. She thought little of it since the synesthesia was always prompting me to describe things that made no sense to her."

"When did you realize it was the coffee?" I asked.

"Oh, some time later. I again was given a taste of it at breakfast one morning, and there you were, sitting at our dining room table, looking rather forlorn. It took every ounce of restraint not to blurt out that you were there. Then it started to make sense to me. After that, I would try to see you as much as possible. You were often very sad when you were younger. I know that."

The look on her face, one of true concern for me, almost brought tears to my eyes. She was a witness to my life. I hadn't been as alone as I'd always thought.

"You're a terrific artist," I said.

She smiled. "I'm great with a pencil, but my professors are demanding a piece in color. That's what I'm working on now."

Intermittently in the conversation we'd stop and take sips of coffee to keep the connection vital. As it turned out, she too had escaped her normal routine and taken a place in order to work on a project for her final portfolio review. We discovered all manner of synchronicities between our lives. She admitted to me that she had also been a loner as a child and that her parents had a hard time dealing with her synesthetic condition. As she put it, "Until we discovered the reality of it, I think they thought I was crazy." She laughed, but I could tell by the look in her eyes how deeply it had affected her.

"Have you ever told anyone about me?" I asked.

"Only my therapist," she said. "I was relieved when he told me he had heard of rare cases like mine."

This revelation brought me up short, for Stullin had told me he had never encountered anything of the sort in the literature. The implications of this inconsistency momentarily reminded me that she was not real, but I quickly shoved the notion from my thoughts and continued the conversation.

That night, by parsing out the coffee I had, and she doing the same, we stayed together until two in the morning, telling each other about our lives, our creative ideas, our dreams for the future. We found that our synesthetic experiences were similar and that our sense impressions were often transposed with the same results. For instance, for both of us, the aroma of new-mown grass was circular and the sound of a car horn tasted of citrus. She told me that her father was an amateur musician who loved the piano and classical music. In the middle of my recounting for her the intricacies of the fugue I was planning, she suddenly looked up from her cup and said, "Oh no, I'm out of coffee." I looked down at my own cup and realized I'd just taken the last sip.

"Tomorrow at noon," she said as her image weakened.

"Yes!" I yelled, afraid she would not hear me.

Then she became a phantom, a miasma, a notion, and I was left staring at the wall of the kitchen. With her gone, I could not sit still for long. All the coffee I'd drunk was coursing through me, and because my frail system had never before known the stimulant, my hands literally shook from it. I knew sleep was out of the question, so after walking around the small rooms of the bungalow for an hour, I sat down to my fugue to see what I could do.

Immediately, I picked up the trail of where I had been headed before Saturday's mental block had set in. Everything was piercingly clear to me, and I could hear the music I was noting in various colors as if there were a tape of the piece playing as I created it. I worked like a demon, quickly, unerringly, and the ease with which the answers to the musical problems presented themselves gave me great confidence and made my decisions ingenious. Finally, around eight in the morning (I hadn't noticed the sunrise), the coffee took its toll on me, and I became violently ill. The stomach pains, the headache, were excruciating. At ten, I vomited, and that relieved the symptoms somewhat. But by eleven A.M. I was at the diner buying another four cups of coffee.

The waitress tried to interest me in breakfast, but I said I wasn't hungry. She told me I didn't look well, and I tried to laugh off her concern. When she pressed the matter, I made some surly comment to her that I can't now remember, and she understood I was interested in nothing but the coffee. I took my hoard and went directly to the beach. The temperature was milder that day and the fresh air cleared my head. I sat in the shelter of a deep hollow amidst the dunes to block the wind, drank, and watched Anna at work, wherever she was, on her project — a large, color-ful abstract drawing. After spying on her for a few minutes, I realized that the composition of the piece, its arrangement of color, presented itself to me as the melodic line of Symphony no. 8 in B Minor by Franz Schubert. This amused me at first, to think that my own musical knowledge was inherent in the existence of her world, that my imagination was its es-sence. What was also interesting was that such a minor interest of mine, Schubert, should manifest itself. I supposed that any aspect of my life, no matter how minor, was fodder for this imaginative process. It struck me just as quickly, though, that I didn't want this to be so. I wanted her to be apart from me, her own separate entity, for without that, what would her friendship mean? I physically shook my head to rid myself of the idea. When at noon she appeared next to me in my nest among the dunes, I'd already managed to forget this worm in the apple.

We spent the morning together talking and laughing, strolling along the edge of the ocean, climbing on the rocks at the point. When the cof-fee ran low around three, we returned to the diner for me to get more. I asked them to make me two whole pots and just pour them into large, plastic takeout containers. The waitress said nothing but shook her head. In the time I was on my errand, Anna, in her own world, brewed another vat of it.

We met up back at my bungalow, and as evening came on, we took out our respective projects and worked together, across from each other at the kitchen table. In her presence my musical imagination was on fire, and she admitted to me that she saw for the first time the overarching structure of her drawing and where she was headed with it. At one point I became so immersed in the work, I reached out and picked up what I thought would be one of my crayons but instead it turned out to be a violet pastel. I didn't own pastels, Anna did.

"Look," I said to her, and at that moment felt a wave of dizziness pass over me. A headache was beginning behind my eyes.

She lifted her gaze from her work and saw me holding the violet stick. We both sat quietly, in awe of its implications. Slowly, she put her hand out across the table toward me. I dropped the pastel and reached toward her. Our hands met, and I swear I could feel her fingers entangled with mine.

"What does this mean, William?" she said with a note of fear in her voice and let go of me.

As I stood up, I lost my balance and needed to support myself by clutching the back of the chair. She also stood, and as I approached her, she backed away. "No, this isn't right," she said.

"Don't worry," I whispered. "It's me." I took two wobbly steps and drew so close to her I could smell her perfume. She cringed but did not try to get away. I put my arms around her and attempted to kiss her.

"No," she cried. Then I felt the force of both her hands against my chest, and I stumbled backward onto the floor. "I don't want this. It's not real," she said, and began to hurriedly gather her things.

"Wait, I'm sorry," I said. I tried to scrabble to my feet, and that's when the sum total of my lack of sleep, the gallons of caffeine, the fraying of my nerves came together like the twining voices in a fugue and struck me in the head as if I'd been kicked by a horse. My body was shaking, my vision grew hazy, and I could feel myself phasing in and out of consciousness. I managed to watch Anna turn and walk away as if passing through the living room. Somehow I got to my feet and followed her, using the furniture as support. The last thing I remember was flinging open the front door of the small house and screaming her name.

I was found the next morning lying on the beach, unconscious. It was the old man with the white beard from the diner, who, on his daily early-morning beachcombing expedition, came across me. The police were summoned. An ambulance was called. I came to in a hospital bed the next day, the warm sun, smelling of antique rose, streaming through a window onto me.

They kept me at the small shore hospital two days for psychological observation. A psychiatrist visited me, and I managed to convince him that I'd been working too hard on a project for school. Apparently the waitress at the diner had told the police that I'd been consuming ridiculous amounts of coffee and going without sleep. Word of this had gotten back to the doctor who attended to me. When I told him it was the first time I had tried coffee and that I'd gotten carried away, he warned me to stay off it, telling me they found me in a puddle of my own vomit. "It obviously disagrees with your system. You could have choked to death when you passed out." I thanked him for his advice and promised him I'd stay well away from it in the future.

In the days I was at the hospital, I tried to process what had happened with Anna. Obviously, my bold advance had frightened her. It crossed my mind that it might be better to leave her alone in the future. The very fact that I was sure I'd made physical contact with her was, in retrospect, unsettling. I wondered if perhaps Stullin was right, and what I perceived to be a result of synesthesia was actually a psychotic hallucination. I left it an open issue in my mind as to whether I would seek her out again. One more meeting might be called for, I thought, at least to simply apologize for my mawkish behavior.

I asked the nurse if my things from the beach house had been brought to the hospital, and she told me they had. I spent the entirety of my last day there dressed and waiting to get the okay for my release. That afternoon, they brought me my belongings. I went carefully through everything, but it became obvious to me that my crayon score for the fugue was missing. Everything else was accounted for, but there was no large sheet of drawing paper. I asked the nurse, who was very kind, and actually reminded me somewhat of Mrs. Brithnic, to double-check and see if everything had been brought to me. She did and told me there was nothing else. I called the Varion Island police on the pretense of thanking them and asked if they had seen the drawing. My fugue had vanished. I knew a grave depression would descend upon me soon due to its disappearance, but for the moment I was numb and slightly pleased to merely be alive.

I decided to return to my parents' house for a few days and rest up before returning to the conservatory in order to continue my studies. In the bus station near the hospital, while I was waiting, I went to the small newspaper stand in order to buy a pack of gum and a paper with which to pass the time. As I perused the candy rack, my sight lighted upon something that made me feel the way Eve must have when she first saw the apple, for there was a bag of Thompson's Coffee-Flavored Hard Candy.

The moment I read the words on the bag, I reached for them. There was a spark in my solar plexus, and my palms grew damp. *No Caffeine* the package read, and I was hard-pressed to believe my good fortune. I looked nervously over my shoulder while purchasing three bags of them, and when, on the bus, I tore a bag open, I did so with such violence, a handful of them scattered across the seat and into the aisle.

I arrived by cab at my parents' house and had to let myself in. Their car was gone, and I supposed they were out for the day. I hadn't seen them in some months and almost missed their presence. When night descended and they didn't return, I thought it odd but surmised they were on one of the short vacations they often took. It didn't matter. I sat at my old home base on the piano bench and sucked on coffee-flavored hard candies until I grew too weary to sit up. Then I got into my childhood bed, turned to face the wall as I always had when I was little, and fell asleep.

The next day, after breakfast, I resumed my vigil that had begun on the long bus trip home. By that afternoon my suspicions as to what had become of my fugue were confirmed. The candy didn't bring as clear a view of Anna as did the ice cream, let alone the black coffee, but it was focused enough for me to follow her through her day. I was there when she submitted my crayon score as her art project for the end-of-the-semester review. How she was able to appropriate it, I have no idea. It defied logic. In the fleeting glimpses I got of the work, I tried to piece together how I had gone about weaving the subjects and their answers. The second I would see it, the music would begin to sound for me, but I never got a good-enough look at it to sort out the complex structure of the piece. The two things I was certain of were that the fugue had been completed right up to the point where it was supposed to fall into chaos, and that Anna did quite well with her review because of it.

By late afternoon, I'd come to the end of my Thompson's candies and had but one left. Holding it in my hand, I decided it would be the last time I would conjure a vision of Anna. I came to the conclusion that her theft of my work had canceled out my untoward advance and we were now even, so to speak. I would leave her behind as I had before, but this time for good. With my decision made, I opened the last of the hard confections and placed it on my tongue. That dark, amber taste slowly spread through my mouth and, as it did, a cloudy image formed and crystallized into focus. She had the cup to her mouth, and her eyes widened as she saw me seeing her.

"William," she said. "I was hoping to see you one more time."

"I'm sure," I said, trying to seem diffident, but just hearing her voice made me weak.

"Are you feeling better?" she asked. "I saw what happened to you. I was with you on the beach all that long night, but couldn't reach you."

"My fugue," I said. "You took it."

She smiled. "It's not yours. Let's not kid ourselves, you know you are merely a projection of my synesthetic process."

"Who is a projection of whose?" I asked.

"You're nothing more than my muse," she said.

I wanted to contradict her, but I didn't have the meanness to subvert her belief in her own reality. Of course, I could have brought up the fact that she was told that figurative synesthesia was a known version of the disease. This was obviously not true. Also, there was the fact that her failed drawing, the one she had abandoned for mine, was based on Schubert's Eighth, a product of my own knowledge working through her. How could I convince her she wasn't real? She must've seen the doubt in my eyes because she became defensive in her attitude. "I'll not see you again," she said. "My therapist has given me a pill he says will eradicate my synesthesia. We have that here, in the true reality. It's already begun to work. I no longer hear my cigarette smoke as the sound of a faucet dripping. Green no longer tastes of lemon. The ring of the telephone doesn't feel like burlap."

This pill was the final piece of evidence. A pill to cure synesthesia? "You may be harming yourself," I said, "by taking that drug. If you cut yourself off from me, you may cease to exist. Perhaps we are meant to be together." I felt a certain panic at the idea that she would lose her special perception and I would lose the only friend I'd ever had who understood my true nature.

THE SECRET HISTORY OF FANTASY

"Dr. Stullin says it will not harm me, and I will be like everyone else. Goodbye, William," she said, and pushed the coffee cup away from her.

"Stullin," I said. "What do you mean, Stullin?"

"My therapist," she said, and although I could still see her before me, I could tell I had vanished from her view. As I continued to watch, she lowered her face into her hands and appeared to be crying. Then my candy turned from the thinnest sliver into nothing but saliva, and I swallowed. A few seconds more, and she was completely gone.

It was three in the afternoon when I put my coat on and started across town to Stullin's place. I had a million questions, and foremost was whether or not he treated a young woman named Anna. My thoughts were so taken by my last conversation with her that when I arrived in front of the doctor's walkway, I realized I hadn't noticed the sun go down. It was as if I had walked in my sleep and awakened at his address. The street was completely empty of people or cars, reminding me of Varion Island. I took the steps up to his front door and knocked. It was dark inside except for a light on the second floor, but the door was slightly ajar, which I thought odd given it was the middle of the winter. Normally, I would have turned around and gone home after my third attempt to get his attention, but there was too much I needed to discuss.

I stepped inside, closing the door behind me. "Dr. Stullin?" I called. There was no answer. "Doctor?" I tried again and then made my way through the foyer to the room where the tables were stacked with paper. In the meager light coming in through the window, I found a lamp and turned it on. I continued to call out as I went from room to room, turning on lights, heading for the sunroom at the back of the place where we always had our meetings. When I reached that room, I stepped inside, and my foot came down on something alive. There was a sudden screech that nearly made my heart stop, and then I saw the black-and-white cat whose tail I had trod upon, race off into another room.

It was something of a comfort to be again in that plant-filled room. The sight of it brought back memories of it as the single safe place in the world when I was younger. Oddly enough, there was a lit cigarette in the ashtray on the table between the two chairs that faced each other. Lying next to it, opened to the middle and turned down on its pages, was a copy of *The Centrifugal Rickshaw Dancer*. I'd have preferred to see a ghost to that book. The sight of it chilled me. I sat down in my old seat and watched the smoke from the cigarette twirl up toward the glass panes. Almost instantly a great weariness seized me, and I closed my eyes.

That was days ago. When I discovered the next morning that I could not open the doors to leave, that I could not even break the glass in order to crawl out, it became clear to me what was happening. At first I was frantic, but then a certain calm descended upon me, and I learned to accept my fate. Those stacks of paper in that room on the way to the sunroom — each sheet held a beautiful pencil drawing. I explored the upstairs, and there, on the second floor, found a piano and the sheet music for Bach's *Grosse Fugue*. There was a black-and-white photograph of Mrs. Brithnic in the upstairs hallway and one of my parents standing with Anna as a child.

That hallway, those rooms, are gone, vanished. Another room has disappeared each day I have been trapped here. I sit in Stullin's chair now, in the only room still remaining (this one will be gone before tonight), and compose this tale — in a way, my fugue. The black-and-white cat sits across from me, having fled from the dissipation of the house as it closes in around us. Outside, the garden, the trees, the sky have all lost their color and now appear as if rendered in graphite — wonderfully shaded to give them an appearance of weight and depth. So too with the room around us: the floor, the glass panels, the chairs, the plants, even the cat's tail and my shoes and legs have lost their life and become the shaded gray of a sketch. I imagine Anna will soon be free of her condition. As for me, who always believed himself to be unwanted, unloved, misunderstood, I will surpass being a mere artist and become instead a work of art that will endure. The cat meows loudly, and I feel the sound as a hand upon my shoulder.

The Edge of the World

Michael Swanwick

The day that Donna and Piggy and Russ went to see the Edge of the World was a hot one. They were sitting on the curb by the gas station that noontime, sharing a Coke and watching the big Starlifters lumber up into the air, one by one, out of Toldenarba AFB. The sky rumbled with their passing. There'd been an incident in the Persian Gulf, and half the American forces in the Twilight Emirates were on alert.

"My old man says when the Big One goes up, the base will be the first to go," Piggy said speculatively. "Treaties won't allow us to defend it. One bomber comes in high and whaboom —" he made soft nuclear explosion noises —"it's all gone." He was wearing camouflage pants and a khaki teeshirt with an iron-on reading KILL 'EM ALL AND LET GOD SORT 'EM OUT. Donna watched as he took off his glasses to polish them on his shirt. His face went slack and vacant, then livened as he put them back on again, as if he were playing with a mask.

"You should be so lucky," Donna said. "Mrs. Khashoggi is still going to want that paper done on Monday morning, Armageddon or not."

"Yeah, can you believe her?" Piggy said. "That weird accent! And all that memorization! Cut me some slack. I mean, who cares whether Ackronnion was part of the Mezentian Dynasty?"

"You ought to care, dipshit," Russ said. "Local history's the only decent class the school's got." Russ was the smartest boy Donna had ever met, never mind the fact that he was flunking out. He had soulful eyes and a radical haircut, short on the sides with a dyed-blond punklock down the back of his neck. "Man, I opened the *Excerpts from Epics* text that first night, thinking it was going to be the same old bullshit, and I stayed up 'til dawn. Got to school without a wink of sleep, but I'd managed to read every last word. This is one weird part of the world; its history is full of dragons and magic and all kinds of weird monsters. Do you realize that in the eighteenth century three members of the British legation were eaten by demons? That's in the historical record!"

Russ was an enigma to Donna. The first time they'd met, hanging with the misfits at an American School dance, he'd tried to put a hand down her pants, and she'd slugged him good, almost breaking his nose. She could still hear his surprised laughter as blood ran down his chin. They'd been friends ever since. Only there were limits to friendship, and now she was waiting for him to make his move and hoping he'd get down to it before her father was rotated out.

In Japan she'd known a girl who had taken a razor blade and carved her boyfriend's name in the palm of her hand. How could she do that? Donna had wanted to know. Her friend had shrugged, said, "As long as it gets me noticed." It wasn't until Russ that Donna understood.

"Strange country," Russ said dreamily. "The sky beyond the Edge is supposed to be full of demons and serpents and shit. They say that if you stare into it long enough, you'll go mad."

They all three looked at one another.

"Well, hell," Piggy said. "What are we waiting for?"

The Edge of the World lay beyond the railroad tracks. They bicycled through the American enclave into the old native quarter. The streets were narrow here, the sideyards crammed with broken trucks, rusted-out buses, even yachts up in cradles with stoven-in sides. Garage doors were black mouths hissing and spitting welding sparks, throbbing to the hammered sound of worked metal. They hid their bikes in a patch of scrub apricot trees where the railroad crossed the industrial canal and hiked across.

Time had altered the character of the city where it bordered the Edge. Gone were the archers in their towers, vigilant against a threat that never came. Gone were the rose quartz palaces with their thousand windows, not a one of which overlooked the Edge. The battlements where blind musicians once piped up the dawn now survived only in Mrs. Khashoggi's texts. Where they had been was now a drear line of weary factory buildings, their lower windows cinderblocked or bricked up and those beyond reach of vandals' stones painted over in patchwork squares of grey and faded blue.

A steam whistle sounded and lines of factory workers shambled back inside, brown men in chinos and white shirts, Syrian and Lebanese laborers imported to do work no native Toldenarban would touch. A shredded net waved forlornly from a basketball hoop set up by the loading dock.

There was a section of hurricane fence down. They scrambled through.

As they cut across the grounds, a loud whine arose from within the factory building. Down the way another plant lifted its voice in a solid wham-wham-wham as rhythmic and unrelenting as a headache. One by one the factories shook themselves from their midday drowse and went back to work. "Why do they locate these things along the Edge?" Donna asked.

"It's so they can dump their chemical waste over the Edge," Russ explained. "These were all erected before the Emir nationalized the culverts that the Russian Protectorate built."

Behind the factory was a chest-high concrete wall, rough-edged and pebbly with the slow erosion of cement. Weeds grew in clumps at its foot. Beyond was nothing but sky.

Piggy ran ahead and spat over the Edge. "Hey, remember what Nixon said when he came here? *It is indeed a long way down.* What a guy!"

Donna leaned against the wall. A film of haze tinted the sky grey, intensifying at the focal point to dirty brown, as if a dead spot were burned into the center of her vision. When she looked down, her eyes kept grabbing for ground and finding more sky. There were a few wispy clouds in the distance and nothing more. No serpents coiled in the air. She should have felt disappointed but, really, she hadn't expected better. This was of a piece with all the natural wonders she had ever seen, the waterfalls, geysers and scenic vistas that inevitably included power lines, railings and parking lots absent from the postcards. Russ was staring intently ahead, hawklike, frowning. His jaw worked slightly, and she wondered what he saw.

"Hey, look what I found!" Piggy whooped. "It's a stairway!"

They joined him at the top of an institutional-looking concrete-and-iron stairway. It zigzagged down the cliff toward an infinitely distant and nonexistent Below, dwindling into hazy blue. Quietly, as if he'd impressed himself, Piggy said, "What do you suppose is down there?"

"Only one way to find out, isn't there?" Russ said.

Russ went first, then Piggy, then Donna, the steps ringing dully under their feet. Graffiti covered the rocks, worn spraypaint letters in yellow and black and red scrawled one over the other and faded by time and weather into mutual unreadability, and on the iron railings, words and arrows and triangles had been markered onto or dug into the paint with knife or nail: JURGEN BIN SCHEISSKOPF. MOTLEY CRUE. DEATH TO SATAN AMERICA IMPERIALIST. Seventeen steps down, the first landing was filthy with broken brown glass, bits of crumbled concrete, cigarette butts, soggy, half-melted cardboard. The stairway folded back on itself and they followed it down.

"You ever had *fugu?*" Piggy asked. Without waiting for an answer, he said, "It's Japanese poisonous blowfish. It has to be prepared very carefully — they license the chefs — and even so, several people die every year. It's considered a great delicacy."

"Nothing tastes that good," Russ said.

"It's not the flavor," Piggy said enthusiastically. "It's the poison. Properly prepared, see, there's a very small amount left in the sashimi and you get a threshold dose. Your lips and the tips of your fingers turn cold. Numb. That's how you know you're having the real thing. That's how you know you're living right on the edge."

"I'm already living on the edge," Russ said. He looked startled when Piggy laughed.

A fat moon floated in the sky, pale as a disk of ice melting in blue water. It bounced after them as they descended, kicking aside loose soda bottles in Styrofoam sleeves, crushed Marlboro boxes, a scattering of carbonized sparkplugs. On one landing they found a crumpled shopping cart, and Piggy had to muscle it over the railing and watch it fall. "Sure is

THE SECRET HISTORY OF FANTASY

a lot of crap here," he observed. The landing smelled faintly of urine.

"It'll get better farther down," Russ said. "We're still near the top, where people can come to get drunk after work." He pushed on down. Far to one side they could see the brown flow from the industrial canal where it spilled into space, widening and then slowly dispersing into rainbowed mist, distance glamoring it beauty.

"How far are we planning to go?" Donna asked apprehensively.

"Don't be a weak sister," Piggy sneered. Russ said nothing.

The deeper they went, the shabbier the stairway grew, and the spottier its maintenance. Pipes were missing from the railing. Where patches of paint had fallen away the bolts anchoring the stair to the rock were walnut-sized lumps of rust.

Needle-clawed marsupials chittered warningly from niches in the rock as they passed. Tufts of grass and moth-white gentians grew in the loess-filled cracks.

Hours passed. Donna's feet and calves and the small of her back grew increasingly sore, but she refused to be the one to complain. By degrees she stopped looking over the side and out into the sky, and stared instead at her feet flashing in and out of sight while one hand went slap grab tug on the rail. She felt sweaty and miserable.

Back home she had a half-finished paper on the Three Days Incident of March, 1810, when the French Occupation, by order of Napoleon himself, had fired cannonade after cannonade over the Edge into nothingness. They had hoped to make rainstorms of devastating force that would lash and destroy their enemies, and created instead only a gunpowder haze, history's first great failure in weather control. This descent was equally futile, Donna thought, an endless and wearying exercise in nothing. Just the same as the rest of her life. Every time her father was reposted, she had resolved to change, to be somebody different this time around, whatever the price, even if — no, especially if — it meant playacting something she was not. Last year in Germany when she'd gone out with that local boy with the Alfa Romeo and instead of jerking him off had used her mouth, she had thought: Everything's going to be different now. But no.

Nothing ever changed.

"Heads up!" Russ said. "There's some steps missing here!" He leaped, and the landing gonged hollowly under his sneakers. Then again as Piggy jumped after.

Donna hesitated. There were five steps gone and a drop of twenty feet before the stairway cut back beneath itself. The cliff bulged outward here, and if she slipped she'd probably miss the stairs altogether.

She felt the rock draw away from her to either side, and was suddenly aware that she was connected to the world by the merest speck of matter, barely enough to anchor her feet. The sky wrapped itself about her, extending to infinity, depthless and absolute. She could extend her arms and fall into it forever. What would happen to her then? she wondered. Would she die of thirst and starvation, or would the speed of her fall grow so great that the oxygen would be sucked from her lungs, leaving her to strangle in a sea of air? "Come on, Donna!" Piggy shouted up at her. "Don't be a pussy!"

"Russ —" she said quaveringly.

But Russ wasn't looking her way. He was frowning downward, anxious to be going. "Don't push the lady," he said. "We can go on by ourselves."

Donna choked with anger and hurt and desperation all at once. She took a deep breath and, heart scudding, leaped. Sky and rock wheeled over her head. For an instant she was floating, falling, totally lost and filled with a panicky awareness that she was about to die. Then she crashed onto the landing. It hurt like hell, and at first she feared she'd pulled an ankle. Piggy grabbed her shoulders and rubbed the side of her head with his knuckles. "I knew you could do it, you wimp."

Donna knocked away his arm. "Okay, wiseass. How are you expecting to get us back up?"

The smile disappeared from Piggy's face. His mouth opened, closed. His head jerked fearfully upward. An acrobat could leap across, grab the step and flip up without any trouble at all. "I — I mean, I —"

"Don't worry about it," Russ said impatiently. "We'll think of something." He started down again.

It wasn't natural, Donna realized, his attitude. There was something obsessive about his desire to descend the stairway. It was like the time he'd brought his father's revolver to school along with a story about playing Russian roulette that morning before breakfast. "Three times!" he'd said proudly.

He'd had that same crazy look on him, and she hadn't the slightest notion then or now how she could help him.

Russ walked like an automaton, wordlessly, tirelessly, never hurrying up or slowing down. Donna followed in concerned silence, while Piggy scurried between them, chattering like somebody's pet Pekinese. This struck Donna as so apt as to be almost allegorical: the two of them together yet alone, the distance between filled with noise. She thought of this distance, this silence, as the sun passed behind the cliff and the afternoon heat lost its edge.

The stairs changed to cement-jacketed brick with small buttresses cut into the rock. There was a pile of stems and cherry pits on one landing, and the railing above them was white with bird droppings. Piggy leaned over the rail and said, "Hey, I can see seagulls down there. Flying around."

"Where?" Russ leaned over the railing, then said scornfully, "Those are pigeons. The Ghazoddis used to release them for rifle practice."

As Piggy turned to follow Russ down again, Donna caught a glimpse into his eyes, liquid and trembling with helplessness and despair. She'd seen that fear in him only once before, months ago when she'd stopped by his house on the way to school, just after the Emir's assassination.

The living room windows were draped and the room seemed unnaturally gloomy after being out in the morning sun. Blue television light flickered over shelves of shadowy ceramic figurines: Dresden milkmaids, Chantilly Chinamen, Meissen pug-dogs connected by a gold chain held in their champed jaws, naked Delft nymphs dancing.

Piggy's mother sat in a limp dressing gown, hair unbrushed, watching the funeral. She held a cup of oily looking coffee in one hand. Donna was surprised to see her up so early. Everyone said that she had a bad problem with alcohol, that even by service wife standards she was out of control.

"Look at them," Piggy's mother said. On the screen were solemn processions of camels and Cadillacs, sheikhs in jellaba, keffigeh and mirrorshades, European dignitaries with wives in tasteful grey Parisian fashions. "They've got their nerve."

"Where did you put my lunch?" Piggy said loudly from the kitchen.

"Making fun of the Kennedys, like that!" The Emir's youngest son, no more than four years old, salaamed his father's casket as it passed before him. "That kid's bad enough, but you should see the mother, crying as if her heart were broken. It's enough to turn your stomach. If I were Jackie, I'd —"

Donna and Piggy and Russ had gone bowling the night the Emir was shot. This was out in the ruck of cheap joints that surrounded the base, catering almost exclusively to servicemen. When the Muzak piped through overhead speakers was interrupted for the news bulletin, everyone had stood up and cheered. *Up we go* someone had begun singing, and the rest had joined in, *into the wild blue yonder...* Donna had felt so sick with fear and disgust she had thrown up in the parking lot. "I don't think they're making fun of anyone," Donna said. "They're just —"

"Don't talk to her!" The refrigerator door slammed shut. A cupboard door slammed open.

Piggy's mother smiled bitterly. "This is exactly what you'd expect from these ragheads. Pretending they're white people, deliberately mocking their betters. Filthy brown animals."

"Mother! Where is my fucking lunch?"

She looked at him then, jaw tightening. "Don't you use that kind of language on me, young man."

"All right!" Piggy shouted. "All right, I'm going to school without lunch! Shows how much you care!"

He turned to Donna and in the instant before he grabbed her wrist and dragged her out of the house, Donna could no longer hear the words, could only see that universe of baffled futility haunting Piggy's eyes. That same look she glimpsed today.

The railings were wooden now, half the posts rotting at their bases, with an occasional plank missing, wrenched off and thrown over the side by previous visitors. Donna's knees buckled and she stumbled, almost lurching into the rock. "I have to stop," she said, hating herself for it. "I cannot go one more step."

Piggy immediately collapsed on the landing. Russ hesitated, then climbed up to join them. The three sat staring out into nothing, legs over the Edge, arms clutching the rail.

Piggy found a Pepsi can, logo in flowing Arabic, among the rubble. He held it in his left hand and began sticking holes in it with his butterfly knife, again and again, cackling like a demented sex criminal. "Exterminate the brutes!" he said happily. Then, with absolutely no transition he asked, "How are we ever going to get back up?" so dolorously Donna had to bite back her laughter.

"Look, I just want to go on down a little bit more," Russ said.

"Why?" Piggy sounded petulant.

"So I can get down enough to get away from this garbage." He gestured at the cigarette butts, the broken brown glass, sparser than above but still there. "Just a little farther, okay guys?" There was an edge to his voice, and under that the faintest hint of a plea. Donna felt helpless before those eyes. She wished they were alone, so she could ask him what was wrong.

Donna doubted that Russ himself knew what he expected to find down below. Did he think that if he went down far enough, he'd never have to climb back? She remembered the time in Mr. Herriman's algebra class when a sudden tension in the air had made her glance across the room at Russ, and he was, with great concentration, tearing the pages out of his math text and dropping them one by one on the floor. He'd taken a five-day suspension for that, and Donna had never found out what it was all about. But there was a kind of glorious arrogance to the act; Russ had been born out of time. He really should have been a medieval prince, a Medici or one of the Sabakan pretenders.

"Okay," Donna said, and Piggy of course had to go along.

Seven flights farther down the modern stairs came to an end. The wooden railing of the last short, septambic flight had been torn off entirely, and laid across the steps. They had to step carefully between the uprights and the rails. But when they stood at the absolute bottom, they saw that there were stairs beyond the final landing, steps that had been cut into the stone itself. They were curving swaybacked things that millennia of rain and foot traffic had worn so uneven they were almost impassable.

Piggy groaned. "Man, you can't expect us to go down that thing."

"Nobody's asking you," Russ said.

They descended the old stairway backwards and on all fours. The wind breezed up, hitting them with the force of an unexpected shove first to one side and then the other. There were times when Donna was so frightened she thought she was going to freeze up and never move again. But at last the stone broadened and became a wide, even ledge, with caves leading back into the rock.

The cliff face here was greenwhite with lichen, and had in ancient times been laboriously smoothed and carved. Between each cave (their mouths alone left in a natural state, unaltered) were heavy-thighed women — goddesses, perhaps, or demons or sacred dancers — their breasts and faces chipped away by the image-hating followers of the Prophet at a time when Mohammed yet lived. Their hands held loops of vines in which were entangled moons, cycling from new through waxing quarter and gibbous to full and then back through gibbous and waning quarter to dark. Piggy was gasping, his face bright with sweat, but he kept up his blustery front. "What the fuck is all this shit, man?"

"It was a monastery," Russ said. He walked along the ledge dazedly, a wondering half- smile on his lips. "I read about this." He stopped at a turquoise automobile door someone had flung over the Edge to be caught and tossed by fluke winds, the only piece of trash that had made it down this far. "Give me a hand."

He and Piggy lifted the door, swung it back and forth three times to build up momentum, then lofted it over the lip of the rock. They all three lay down on their stomachs to watch it fall away, turning end over end and seeming finally to flicker as it dwindled smaller and smaller, still falling. At last it shrank below the threshold of visibility and became one of a number of shifting motes in the downbelow, part of the slow, mazy movement of dead blood cells in the eyes' vitreous humors.

Donna turned over on her back, drew her head back from the rim, stared upward. The cliff seemed to be slowly tumbling forward, all the world inexorably, dizzyingly leaning down to crush her.

"Let's go explore the caves," Piggy suggested.

They were empty. The interiors of the caves extended no more than thirty feet into the rock, but they had all been elaborately worked, arched ceilings carved with thousands of faux tesserae, walls adorned with bas-relief pillars. Between the pillars the walls were taken up with long shelves carved into the stone. No artifacts remained, not so much as a potsherd or a splinter of bone. Piggy shone his pocket flash into every shadowy niche. "Somebody's been here before us and taken everything," he said.

"The Historic Registry people, probably." Russ ran a hand over one shelf. It was the perfect depth and height for a line of three-pound coffee cans. "This is where they stowed the skulls. When a monk grew so spiritually developed he no longer needed the crutch of physical existence, his fellows would render the flesh from his bones and enshrine his skull. They poured wax in the sockets, then pushed in opals while it was still warm. They slept beneath the faintly gleaming eyes of their superiors."

When they emerged it was twilight, the first stars appearing from behind a sky fading from blue to purple. Donna looked down on the moon. It was as big as a plate, full and bright. The rilles, dry seas and mountain chains were preternaturally distinct. Somewhere in the middle was Tranquility Base, where Neil Armstrong had planted the American flag.

"Jeez, it's late," Donna said. "If we don't start home soon, my mom is going to have a cow."

"We still haven't figured a way to get back up," Piggy reminded her. Then: "We'll probably have to stay here. Learn to eat owls and grow crops sideways on the cliff face. Start our own civilization. Our only serious problem is the imbalance of sexes, but even that's not insurmountable." He put an arm around Donna's shoulders, grabbed at her breast. "You'd pull the train for us, wouldn't you, Donna?"

Angrily she pushed him away and said, "You keep a clean mouth! I'm so tired of your juvenile talk and behavior."

"Hey, calm down, it's cool." That panicky look was back in his eyes, the forced knowledge that he was not in control, could never be in control, that there was no such thing as control. He smiled weakly, placatingly.

"No, it is not. It is most emphatically not 'cool.'" Suddenly she was white and shaking with fury. Piggy was a spoiler. His simple presence ruined any chance she might have had to talk with Russ, find out just what was bugging him, get him to finally, really notice her. "I am sick of having to deal with your immaturity, your filthy language and your crude behavior."

Piggy turned pink and began stuttering.

Russ reached a hand into his pocket, pulled out a chunk of foil-wrapped hash, and a native tin pipe with a carved coral bowl. The kind of thing the local beggar kids sold for twenty-nine cents. "Anybody want to get stoned?" he asked suavely.

"You bastard!" Piggy laughed. "You told me you were out!"

Russ shrugged. "I lied." He lit the pipe carefully, drew in, passed it to Donna. She took it from his fingers, felt how cold they were to her touch, looked up over the pipe and saw his face, thin and ascetic, eyelids closed, pale and Christlike through the blue smoke. She loved him intensely in that instant and wished she could sacrifice herself for his happiness. The pipe's stem was overwarm, almost hot, between her lips. She drew in deep.

The smoke was raspy in her throat, then tight and swirling in her lungs. It shot up into her head, filled it with buzzing harmonics: the air, the sky, the rock behind her back all buzzing, ballooning her skull outward in a visionary rush that forced wide open first her eyes and then her mouth. She choked and spasmodically coughed. More smoke than she could imagine possibly holding in her lungs gushed out into the universe.

"Hey, watch that pipe!" Piggy snatched it from her distant fingers. They tingled with pinpricks of pain like tiny stars in the darkness of her flesh. "You were spilling the hash!" The evening light was abuzz with energy, the sky swarming up into her eyes. Staring out into the darkening air, the moon rising below her and the stars as close and friendly as those in a children's book illustration, she felt at peace, detached from worldly cares. "Tell us about the monastery, Russ," she said, in the same voice she might have used a decade before to ask her father for a story.

THE SECRET HISTORY OF FANTASY

"Yeah, tell us about the monastery, Unca Russ," Piggy said, but with jeering undertones. Piggy was always sucking up to Russ, but there was tension there too, and his sarcastic little challenges were far from rare. It was classic beta male jealousy, straight out of Primate Psychology 101.

"It's very old," Russ said. "Before the Sufis, before Mohammed, even before the Zoroastrians crossed the gulf, the native mystics would renounce the world and go to live in cliffs on the Edge of the World. They cut the steps down, and once down, they never went back up again."

"How did they eat then?" Piggy asked skeptically.

"They wished their food into existence. No, really! It was all in their creation myth: In the beginning all was Chaos and Desire. The world was brought out of Chaos — by which they meant unformed matter — by Desire, or Will. It gets a little inconsistent after that, because it wasn't really a religion, but more like a system of magic. They believed that the world wasn't complete yet, that for some complicated reason it could never be complete. So there's still traces of the old Chaos lingering just beyond the Edge, and it can be tapped by those who desire it strongly enough, if they have distanced themselves from the things of the world. These mystics used to come down here to meditate against the moon and work miracles.

"This wasn't sophisticated stuff like the Tantric monks in Tibet or anything, remember. It was like a primitive form of animism, a way to force the universe to give you what you wanted. So the holy men would come down here and they'd wish for...like riches, you know? Filigreed silver goblets with rubies, mounds of moonstones, elfinbone daggers sharper than Damascene steel. Only once they got them they weren't supposed to want them. They'd just throw them over the Edge. There were these monasteries all along the cliffs. The farther from the world they were, the more spiritually advanced."

"So what happened to the monks?"

"There was a king — Althazar? I forget his name. He was this real greedhead, started sending his tax collectors down to gather up everything the monks brought into existence. Must've figured, hey, the monks weren't using them. Which as it turned out was like a real major blasphemy, and the monks got pissed. The boss mystics, all the real spiritual heavies, got together for this big confab. Nobody knows how. There's one of the classics claims they could run sideways on the cliff just like it was the ground, but I don't know. Doesn't matter. So one night they all of them, every monk in the world, meditated at the same time. They chanted together, they said, It is not enough that Althazar should die, for he has blasphemed. He must suffer a doom such as has been visited on no man before. He must be un-made, uncreated, reduced to less than has ever been. And they prayed that there be no such king as Althazar, that his life and history be unmade, so that there never had been such a king as Althazar.

"And he was no more.

"But so great was their yearning for oblivion that when Althazar ceased to be, his history and family as well, they were left feeling embittered and did not know why. And not knowing why, their hatred turned upon themselves, and their wish for destruction, and they too all of a single night, ceased to be." He fell silent.

At last Piggy said, "You believe that crap?" Then, when there was no answer: "It's none of it true, man! Got that? There's no magic, and there never was." Donna could see that he was really angry, threatened on some primal level by the possibility that someone he respected could even begin to believe in magic. His face got pink, the way it always did when he lost control.

"No, it's all bullshit," Russ said bitterly. "Like everything else."

They passed the pipe around again. Then Donna leaned back, stared straight out, and said, "If I could wish for anything, you know what I'd wish for?"

"Bigger tits?"

She was so weary now, so pleasantly washed out, that it was easy to ignore Piggy. "I'd wish I knew what the situation was."

"What situation?" Piggy asked. Donna was feeling languorous, not at all eager to explain herself, and she waved away the question. But he persisted. "What situation?"

"Any situation. I mean, all the time, I find myself talking with people and I don't know what's really going on. What games they're playing.

Why they're acting the way they are. I wish I knew what the situation was."

The moon floated before her, big and fat and round as a griffin's egg, shining with power. She could feel that power washing through her, the background radiation of decayed chaos spread across the sky at a uniform three degrees Kelvin. Even now, spent and respent, a coin fingered and thinned to the worn edge of nonexistence, there was power out there, enough to flatten planets.

Staring out at that great fat boojum snark of a moon, she felt the flow of potential worlds, and within the cold silver disk of that jester's skull, rank with magic, sensed the invisible presence of Russ's primitive monks, men whose minds were nowhere near comprehensible to her, yet vibrated with power, existing as matrices of patterned stress, no more actual than Donald Duck, but no less powerful either. She was caught in a waking fantasy, in which the sky was full of power and all of it accessible to her. Monks sat empty handed over their wishing bowls, separated from her by the least fictions of time and reality. For an eternal instant all possibilities fanned out to either side, equally valid, no one more real than any other. Then the world turned under her, and her brain shifted back to realtime.

"Me," Piggy said, "I just wish I knew how to get back up the stairs."

They were silent for a moment. Then it occurred to Donna that here was the perfect opportunity to find out what was bugging Russ. If she asked cautiously enough, if the question hit him just right, if she were just plain lucky, he might tell her everything. She cleared her throat. "Russ? What do you wish?"

In the bleakest voice imaginable, Russ said, "I wish I'd never been born."

She turned to ask him why, and he wasn't there.

"Hey," Donna said. "Where'd Russ go?"

Piggy looked at her oddly. "Who's Russ?"

It was a long trip back up. They carried the length of wooden railing between them, and every now and then Piggy said, "Hey, wasn't this a great idea of mine? This'll make a swell ladder."

"Yeah, great," Donna would say, because he got mad when she didn't respond. He got mad too, whenever she started to cry, but there wasn't anything she could do about that. She couldn't even explain why she was crying, because in all the world — of all his friends, acquaintances, teachers, even his parents — she was the only one who remembered that Russ had ever existed.

The horrible thing was that she had no specific memories of him, only a vague feeling of what his presence had been like, and a lingering sense of longing and frustration.

She no longer even remembered his face.

"Do you want to go first or last?" Piggy had asked her.

When she'd replied, "Last. If I go first, you'll stare at my ass all the way up," he'd actually blushed. Without Russ to show off in front of, Piggy was a completely different person, quiet and not at all abusive. He even kept his language clean.

But that didn't help, for just being in his presence was enough to force understanding on her: That his bravado was fueled by his insecurities and aspirations, that he masturbated nightly and with self-loathing, that he despised his parents and longed in vain for the least sign of love from them. That the way he treated her was the sum and total of all of this and more.

She knew exactly what the situation was.

Dear God, she prayed, let it be that I won't have this kind of understanding when I reach the top. Or else make it so that situations won't be so painful up there, that knowledge won't hurt like this, that horrible secrets won't lie under the most innocent word.

They carried their wooden burden upward, back toward the world.

Super Goat Man

Jonathan Lethem

When Super Goat Man moved into the commune on our street I was ten years old. Though I liked superheroes, I wasn't familiar with Super Goat Man. His presence didn't mean anything, particularly, to myself or to the other kids in the neighborhood. For us, as we ran and screamed and played secret games on the sidewalk, Super Goat Man was only another of the men who sat on stoops in sleeveless undershirts on hot summer days, watching the slow progress of life on the block. The two little fleshy horns on his forehead didn't make him especially interesting. We weren't struck by his fall from grace, out of the world of comic-book heroes, among which he had been at best a minor star, to land here in Cobble Hill, Brooklyn, in a single room in what was basically a dorm for college dropouts, a hippie group shelter, any more than we were by the tufts of extra hair at his throat and behind his ears. We had eyes only for Spider-Man or Batman in those days, superheroes in two dimensions, with lunch boxes and television shows and theme songs. Super Goat Man had none of those.

It was our dads who cared. They were unmistakably drawn to the strange figure who'd moved to the block, as though for them he represented some lost possibility in their own lives. My father in particular seemed fascinated with Super Goat Man, though he covered this interest by acting as though it were on my behalf. One day toward the end of that summer he and I walked to Montague Street, to visit the comics shop there. This was a tiny storefront filled with long white boxes, crates full of carefully archived comics, protected by plastic bags and cardboard backing. The boxes contained ancient runs of back issues of titles I'd heard of, as well as thousands of other comics featuring characters I'd never encountered. The shop was presided over by a nervous young pedant with long hair and a beard, a collector-type himself, an old man in spirit who distrusted children in his store, as he ought to have. He assisted my father in finding what he sought, deep in the alphabetical archive — a five-issue run of *The Remarkable Super Goat Man,* from Electric Comics. These were the only comics in which Super Goat Man had appeared. There were just five issues because after five the title had been forever canceled. My father seemed satisfied with what he'd found. We paid for the five issues and left.

I didn't know how to explain to my father that Electric wasn't one of the major comics publishers. The stories the comics contained, when we inspected them together, were both ludicrous and boring. Super Goat Man's five issues showed him rescuing old ladies from swerving trucks and kittens from lightning-struck trees, and battling dull villains like Vest Man and False Dave. The drawings were amateurish, cut-rate, antiquated. I couldn't have articulated these judgments then, of course. I only knew I disliked the comics, found them embarrassing, for myself, for Super Goat Man, and for my dad. They languished in my room, unread, and were eventually cleaned up — I mean, thrown out — by my mom.

For the next few years Super Goat Man was less than a minor curiosity to me. I didn't waste thought on him. The younger men and women who lived in the commune took him for granted, as anyone should, so far as I knew. We kids would see him in their company, moving furniture up the stoop and into the house, discarded dressers and couches and lamps they'd found on the street, or taping posters on lampposts announcing demonstrations against nuclear power or in favor of day-care centers, or weeding in the commune's pathetic front yard, which was intended as a vegetable garden but was choked not only with uninvited growth but with discarded ice-cream wrappers and soda bottles — we kids used the commune's yard as a dumping ground. It didn't occur to me that Super Goat Man was much older, really, than the commune's other occupants, that in fact they might be closer to my age than to his. However childish their behavior, the hippies all seemed as dull and remote as grown-ups to me.

THE SECRET HISTORY OF FANTASY

It was the summer when I was thirteen that my parents allowed me to accompany them to one of the commune's potluck dinners. The noise and vibrancy of that house's sporadic celebrations were impossible to ignore on our street, and I knew my parents had attended a few earlier parties — warily, I imagined. The inhabitants of the commune were always trying to sweep their neighbors into dubious causes, and it might be a mistake to be seduced by frivolity into some sticky association. But my parents liked fun too. And had too little of it. Their best running jokes concerned the dullness of their friends' dinner parties. This midsummer evening they brought me along to see inside the life of the scandalous, anomalous house.

The house was already full, many bearded and jeweled and scruffy, reeking of patchouli and musk, others, like my parents, dressed in their hippest collarless shirts and paisley blouses, wearing their fattest beads and bracelets. The offerings, nearly all casseroles brimming with exotic gray proteins, beans and tofu and eggplant and more I couldn't name, were lined on a long side table, mostly ignored. This was a version of cocktail hour, with beer drunk from the bottle and well-rolled marijuana cigarettes. I didn't see whether my parents indulged in the latter. My mother accepted a glass of orange juice, surely spiked. I meant not to pay them any attention, so I moved for the stairs. There were partiers leaning on the banister at the first landing, and evidence of music playing in upstairs rooms, so I didn't doubt the whole house was open to wandering.

There was no music coming from the garden-facing room on the second floor, but the door was open and three figures were visible inside, seated on cushions on a mattress on the floor. A young couple, and Super Goat Man. From his bare hairy feet on the mattress, I guessed it was his room I'd entered. The walls were sparse apart from a low bookcase, on which I spotted, laid crosswise in the row of upright spines, Norman Mailer's *Armies of the Night*, Sergei Eisenstein's *Film Form / The Film Sense*, and Thomas Pynchon's *V.* The three titles stuck in my head; I would later attempt to read each of the three at college, succeeding only with the Mailer. Beside the bookcase was a desk heaped with papers, and behind it a few black-and-white postcards had been thumbtacked to the wall. These looked less like a considered decoration than as if they'd been pinned up impulsively by a sitter at the desk. One of the postcard images I recognized as Charlie Parker, clutching a saxophone with his meaty hands. The jazzman was an idol of my father's, perhaps a symbol of his vanished youth.

The young man on the mattress was holding a book: *Memories, Dreams, Reflections,* by Carl Jung. Super Goat Man had evidently just pressed it on him, and had likely been extolling its virtues when I walked into the room.

"Hello," said the young woman, her voice warm. I must have been staring, from my place in the middle of the room.

"You're Everett, aren't you?" said Super Goat Man, before I could speak.

"How'd you know my name?"

"You live on the block," said Super Goat Man. "I've seen you running around."

"I think we'll head down, Super Goat Man," said the young man abruptly, tucking the book under his arm as he got up from the mattress. "Get something to eat before it's too late."

"I want to hit the dance floor," said the young woman.

"See you down there," said Super Goat Man. With that the young couple were gone.

"You checking out the house?" said Super Goat Man to me once we were alone. "Casing the joint?"

"I'm looking for my friend," I lied.

"I think some kids are hanging out in the backyard."

"No, she went upstairs." I wanted him to think I had a girlfriend.

"Okay, cool," said Super Goat Man. He smiled. I suppose he was waiting for me to leave, but he didn't give any sign that I was bothering him by staying.

"Why do you live here?" I asked.

"These are my friends," he said. "They helped me out when I lost my job."

"You're not a superhero anymore, are you?"

Super Goat Man shrugged. "Some people felt I was being too outspoken about the war. Anyway, I wanted to accomplish things on a more local level."

"Why don't you have a secret identity?"

"I wasn't that kind of superhero."

"But what was your name, before?"

"Ralph Gersten."

"What did Ralph Gersten do?"

"He was a college teacher, for a couple of years."

"So why aren't you Ralph Gersten now?"

"Sometime around when they shot Kennedy I just realized Ralph Gersten wasn't who I was. He was a part of an old life I was holding on to. So I became Super Goat Man. I've come to understand that this is who I am, for better or worse."

This was a bit much for me to assimilate, so I changed the subject. "Do you smoke pot?"

"Sometimes."

"Were Mr. and Mrs. Gersten sad when you gave up your secret identity?"

"Who?"

"Your parents."

Super Goat Man smiled. "They weren't my real parents. I was adopted."

Suddenly I was done. "I'm going downstairs, Super Goat Man."

"Okay, Everett," he said. "See you down there, probably."

I made my way downstairs, and lurked in the commune's muddy and ill-lit backyard, milling with the other teenagers and children stranded there by the throngs of frolickers — for the party was now overflowing its bounds, and we were free to steal beers from the counter and carry on our own tentative party, our own fumbling flirtations. I had no girlfriend, but I did play spin the bottle that night, crouched on the ground beneath a fig tree.

Then, near midnight, I went back inside. The living room was jammed with bodies — dancers on a parquet floor that had been revealed when the vast braided rug had been curled up against the base of the mantel. Colored Christmas lights were bunched in the corner, and some of them blinked to create a gently eerie strobe. I smelled sweat and smoke. Feeling perverse and thrilled by the kisses I'd exchanged in the mud beneath the tree, I meandered into the web of celebrants.

Super Goat Man was there. He was dancing with my mother. She was as I'd never seen her, braceleted wrists crossed above her head, swaying to the reggae — I think it was the sound track to *The Harder They Come.* Super Goat Man was more dressed-up than he'd been in his room upstairs. He wore a felt brocade vest and striped pants. He danced in tiny little steps, almost as though losing and regaining his balance, his arms loose at his sides, fingers snapping. Mostly he moved his head to the beat, shaking it back and forth as if saying *no-no-no, no-no-no.* He shook his head at my mother's dancing, as if he couldn't approve of the way she was moving, but couldn't quit paying attention either.

My father? He was seated on the rolled-up rug, his back against the mantel, elbows on his knees, dangling with forefinger and thumb a nearly empty paper cup of red wine. Like me, he was watching my mom and Super Goat Man. It didn't look as if it bothered him at all.

My junior year at Corcoran College, in Corcoran, New Hampshire, Super Goat Man was brought in to fill the Walt Whitman Chair in the Humanities. This was 1981, the dawn of Reagan. The chair was required to offer one course; Super Goat Man's was listed in the catalogue as Dissidence and Desire: Marginal Heroics in American Life 1955–1975. The reading included Frantz Fanon, Roland Barthes, and Timothy Leary. It was typical of Corcoran that it would choose that particular moment to recuperate a figure associated with sixties protest, to enshrine what had once been at the vigorous center of the culture in the harmless pantheon of academia. It was Super Goat Man's first teaching job since the fifties. The commune on our street had shut down at some point in my high-school years, and I don't know where Super Goat Man had been in the intervening time. I certainly hadn't thought about him since departing for college.

He'd gained a little weight, but was otherwise unchanged. I first spotted him moving across the Commons lawn on a September afternoon, one with the scent of fallen and fermenting crab apples on the breeze. It was one of those rare, sweet days on either side of the long New Hampshire winter, when a school year was either falsely fresh before its plunge into bleak December, or exhausted and ready to give way to summer. Super Goat Man wore a forest green corduroy suit and a wide salmon tie, but his feet were still bare. A couple of Corcoran girls trailed alongside him. He had a book open as he walked — perhaps he was reading them a poem.

The college had assigned Super Goat Man one of the dormitory apartments — a suite of rooms built into Sweeney House, one of the student residences. That is to say, he lived on the edge of the vast commons lawn, and we students felt his watchful presence much as I had in Cobble Hill, on our street. I didn't take Super Goat Man's class, which was mostly full of freshmen, and of those renegade history and rhetoric majors who'd been seduced by French strains of philosophy and literary theory. I fancied myself a classics scholar then — though I'd soon divert into a major in history — and wasn't curious about contemporary political theory, even if I'd believed Super Goat Man to be a superior teacher, which I didn't. I wasn't certain he had nothing to offer the Corcoran students, but whatever it might be it wasn't summed up by the title of his class.

I did, however, participate in one of the late-night salons in the living room of Sweeney House. Super Goat Man had begun appearing there casually, showing up after a few students had occupied the couches, and had lit a fire or opened a bottle of red wine. Increasingly his presence was relied upon; soon it was a given that he was the center of an unnamed tradition. Though Corcoran College was then in the throes of a wave of glamorous eighties-style binge parties, and cocaine had begun to infiltrate our sanctum in the New Hampshire woods as if we were all denizens of Andy Warhol's Factory, the Sweeney House salons were a throwback to another, earlier temperature of college socializing. Bearded art students who disdained dancing in favor of bull sessions, Woolfian-Plathian girls in long antique dresses, and lonely gay virgins of both genders — these were the types who found their way to Sweeney to sit at

Super Goat Man's feet. There were also, from what I observed, a handful of quiet superhero comic-book fans who revered Super Goat Man in that capacity and were covertly basking in his aura, ashamed to ask the sorts of questions I'd peppered him with in his room in the communal house, so long ago.

The evening I sat in, Super Goat Man had dragged his phonograph out from his apartment and set it up in the living room so that he could play Lenny Bruce records for his acolytes. Super Goat Man had five or six of the records. He spoke intermittently, his voice unhurried and reflective, explaining the context of the famous comedian's arrests and court-room battles before dropping the needle on a given track. After a while conversation drifted to other subjects. Cross talk arose, though whenever Super Goat Man began to speak in his undemonstrative way all chatter fell deferentially silent. Then Super Goat Man went into his apartment and brought out an Ornette Coleman LP.

"You know a bit about jazz, don't you, Everett?" It was the first time he'd addressed me directly. I hadn't known he'd recognized me.

"A thing or two, I guess."

"Everett's father was the one who turned me on to Rahsaan Roland Kirk," Super Goat Man told a teenager I recognized, a bespectacled sophomore who'd impressively talked his way into a classics seminar that was meant for upperclassmen. "I always thought that stuff was too gim-micky, but I'd never really listened."

I tried to imagine when Super Goat Man and my dad had spent so much time together. It was almost impossible to picture, but Super Goat Man didn't have any reason to be lying about it. It was one of the first times I was forced to consider the possibility that my parents had social lives — that they had lives.

"Does your father write about jazz?" the sophomore asked me, wide-eyed. I suppose he'd misunderstood Super Goat Man's remark. There were plenty of famous — or at least interesting — fathers at Corcoran College, but mine wasn't one of them.

"My father works for New York State," I said. "Department of Housing and Urban Development. Well, he just lost his job, in fact."

"He's a good five-card-stud player too," said Super Goat Man. "Cleaned me out a few times, I don't mind saying."

"Oh yeah, my dad's a real supervillain," I said with the heaviest sarcasm I could muster. I was embarrassed to think of my father sucking up to Super Goat Man, as he surely had during their long evenings together, whoever had taken the bulk of the chips.

Then the squeaky jazz began playing, and Super Goat Man, though seated in one of the dormitory's ratty armchairs, closed his eyes and began shaking his head as if transported back to the commune's dance floor, or perhaps to some even earlier time. I studied his face. The tufts around his ears and throat were graying. I puzzled over his actual age. Had Super Goat Man once spent decades frozen in a block of ice, like Captain America? If Ralph Gersten had been a college teacher in the fifties, he was probably older than my dad.

Eight months later the campus was green again. The term was almost finished, all of us nearly freed to summer, when it happened: the incident at the Campanile. A Saturday, late in a balmy night of revels, the Commons lawn full of small groups crossing from dorm to dorm, cruising at the parties which still flared like bonfires in the landscape of the campus. Many of us yet owed papers, others would have to sit in a final class the following Monday, but the mood was one of expulsive release from our labors. It was nearly three in the morning when Rudy Krugerrand and Seth Brummell, two of the wealthiest and most widely reviled frat boys at Corcoran, scaled the Campanile tower and began bellowing.

I was among those awake and near enough to be drawn by the commotion, into the small crowd at the dark base of the Campanile tower. When I first gazed up at Rudy and Seth I was confused by what I saw: Were there four figures spotlit against the clock beneath the bells? And where were the campus authorities? It was as though this night had been officially ceded to some bacchanalian imperative.

That spring a sculpture student had, as his thesis project, decorated the Commons with oversize office supplies — a stapler in the dimensions of a limousine, a log painted as a number two pencil, and a pile of facsimile paper clips each the height of a human being, fashioned out of plastic piping and silver paint. I suppose the work was derivative of Claes Oldenburg, but the result made an impressive spectacle. It was two of the paper-clip sculptures that Rudy Krugerrand and Seth Brummell had managed to attach to their belts like mannequin dance partners and drag with them out onto the ledge of the Campanile clock, where they stood now, six stories from the ground. On the precipice at the clockface, their faces uplit in the floodlights, Rudy and Seth were almost like players in the climax of some Gothic silent-film drama, but they didn't have the poise or imagination to know it. They were only college pranksters, reelingly drunk, Seth with a three-quarters empty bottle of Jack Daniel's still in his hand, and at first it was hard to make out what they were shouting. We on the ground predictably shouted *"Jump!"* back at them, knowing they loved themselves too dearly ever to consider it.

Then Rudy Krugerrand's slurred voice rose out above the din — or perhaps it was only that I picked it out of the din for the first time. "Calling Super Goat Man! Calling Super Goat Man!" He shouted this until his voice broke hoarse. "This looks like a job for Super Goat Man! Come out, come out, wherever you are!"

"What's going on?" I asked a student beside me.

He shrugged. "I guess they're calling out Super Goat Man. They want to see if he can get them down from the ledge."

"What do you mean?"

"They want to see him use his powers."

From the clock tower Seth Brummell screamed now, in a girlish falsetto: "Oh, Super Goat Man, where are you?"

A stirring had begun in the crowd, which had grown by now to a hundred or more. A murmuring. Super Goat Man's name was planted like a seed. Under the guise of concern for Rudy and Seth, but certainly with a shiver of voyeuristic anticipation, some had begun to speak of going to the Sweeney House apartment, to see if Super Goat Man could be located. There was a hint of outrage: Why wasn't he here already? What kind of Super Goat Man was he, anyway?

Now a group of fifteen or twenty broke out and streamed down the hill, toward Sweeney House. Others trailed after them, myself included.

I hid in this crowd, feeling like an observer, though I suppose I was as complicit as anyone. Were we only curious, or a part of a mob? It seemed, anyway, that we were under the direction of Rudy and Seth.

"That's right," mocked Rudy. "Only Super Goat Man can save us now!"

Those who'd led the charge hammered on Super Goat Man's apartment door for a good few minutes before getting a result. Bold enough to have woken him, they inched backward at the sight of him on his threshold, dressed only in a flowery silk kimono, blinking groggily at the faces arrayed on the hill. Then someone stepped forward and took his arm, pointed him toward the Campanile. Any conversation was drowned in murmurs, and by the sound of sirens, now belatedly pulling up at the base of the tower. Super Goat Man shook his head sorrowfully, but he began to trek up the hill to the Commons, toward the Campanile. We all fell in around and behind him, emboldened at marching to the beat of a super-hero's step, feeling the pulse of the script it now appeared would be played out, ignoring the fact that it had been written by Rudy and Seth and Jack Daniel's. Super Goat Man's kimono fluttered slightly, not quite a cape. He tightened the sash, and strode, rubbing at his eyes with balled fists.

This success only seemed to enrage Rudy and Seth, who writhed and scorned from atop their perch. "Baaahh, baaahh, Super Goat Man!" they roared. "What's the matter with your goaty senses? Smoke too much dope tonight? *Fuck* you, Super Goat Man!" Seth lifted his giant paper clip above his head, to shake it like a fake strongman's prop dumbbell.

The campus police began to herd the students from the base of the tower, but our arriving throng pushed the opposite way. In the confusion, the young policemen seemed utterly helpless, and fell back. Straining on tiptoe to see over the heads of the crowd, I followed the progress of the lime green kimono as Super Goat Man was thrust to the fore, not necessarily by his own efforts. Above, Seth was strumming air-guitar chords on his paper clip, then waggling it over our heads like an enormous phallus.

"Bite my crank, Super Goat Man!"

The crowd gasped as Super Goat Man shed his garb — for mobility I suppose — and started shimmying, almost scampering, up the face of the tower. His pelt was glossy in the moonlight, but nobody could have mistaken the wide swath of white above his dusky buttocks for sheen. Super Goat Man was aging. He scurried through the leaf-blobby shade a tree branch cast against the side of the tower, then back into the light. Whether it was the pressure of expectation on a still-sleepy mind, or possibly a genuine calling to heroics, a hope he could do some good here, Super Goat Man had taken the bait. His limbs worked miraculously in ascending the tower, yet one could only dread what would come if he reached the idiot boys at the top, who grew more agitated and furious at every inch he achieved. Rudy had lifted his own paper clip, to match Seth, and now he swung it out over us.

The plummet silenced us. It was over before we could swallow our words and form a cry to replace them. Six stories is no distance at all, only enough. Rudy's paper clip had overbalanced him. Super Goat Man had braced three limbs, and reached out with a fourth — some number of us saw, others only imagined afterward — but he didn't come away with Rudy. Super Goat Man caught the paper clip in mid-flight with the prehensile toes of his left foot, and the sculpture was jerked free from Rudy as he fell. That's how firm was Super Goat Man's hold on the tower's third story: it was left for later to speculate whether he might have been able to halt a human body's fall. Rudy came to earth, shattering at the feet of the policemen there at the tower's base. Now the nude furry figure could only undertake a sober, methodical descent, paper clip tucked beneath one arm. At the clockface, Seth Brummell was mute, clinging to a post, to wait for the security men who would soon unlock the small door in the tower behind him and angrily yank him to safety.

Rudy Krugerrand survived his fall. His ruined spine cost him the use of his legs, cost him all feeling below some point at his middle. Only a junior, he rather courageously reappeared in a mechanical wheelchair the following September, resumed his studies, resumed drinking too, though his temperament was mellowed, reflective now. He'd be seen at parties dozing in the corner after the dance floor had filled — it took very little beer to knock his dwindled body out. If Rudy had died, or never returned, the incident likely would have been avidly discussed, etched into campus legend. Instead it was covered in a clumsy hush. The coexistence in the same small community of Rudy and Super Goat Man — who'd been offered a seat in the social sciences, and accepted — comprised a kind of odd, insoluble puzzle: Had the hero failed the crisis? Caused it, by some innate provocation? Or was the bogus crisis unworthy, and the outcome its own reward? Who'd shamed whom?

I contemplated this koan, or didn't, for just another year. My graduate studies took me to the University of California at Irvine, three thousand grateful miles from Corcoran, now Super Goat Man's province. I didn't see him, or think of him again, for more than a decade.

The sweetest student I ever had was an Italian girl named Angela Verucci. Tall, bronze-skinned, with a quizzical, slightly humorless cast, dressed no matter the weather in neat pantsuits or skirts with stockings, in heavy tortoise-shell glasses frames and with her blond hair knit in a tight, almost Japanese bun, her aura of seriousness and her Mediterranean luster outshone the blandly corn-fed and T-shirted students in whose midst she had materialized. Angela Verucci was not so much a girl, really: twenty-four years old, she'd already studied at Oxford before taking the Reeves Fellowship that had brought her to America. She spoke immaculate English, and though her accreditation was a mess, truly she was nearly as accomplished a medievalist as I was the day she appeared in my class. This was at Oregon State University, in Corvallis, where I'd been given a two-year postdoc after my six years at Irvine. Oregon State was the third stop in Angela Verucci's American tour — she'd also spent a year at Columbia and, as it happened, a term at Corcoran.

What does a single, thirty-year-old history professor do with the sweetest student he's ever had? He waits until the end of the semester, files a Circular of Intent with the Faculty Appropriateness Committee, and in early spring asks her to hike with him to the highest point in the county, a lookout over three mountain ranges called Sutter's Parlor. Angela Verucci arrived in heels, perhaps not completely grasping the sense of the invitation. We forsook the ascent in favor of a glass of Oregon Pinot Noir on a restaurant patio perched on the Willamette River — near enough, for the Brooklynite and the Sicilian, to an expedition.

We were married two years later, on the Italian island itself. The ceremony was deferentially Catholic; I didn't care. The wider circle of my acquaintances learned the happy details in a mass e-mail. Then Angela and I returned to our quiet rented bungalow in New Brunswick, New Jersey. I was at Rutgers then, on a second postdoc, and hungry for a tenure-track position. My job interviews were hardly unsuccessful: I was never summarily dismissed, instead always called back for second and third visits, always asked to teach a sample class. Afterward, polite notes flew back and forth, candidate and committee reassuring one another of how fine the experience had been, how glad we both were to have met. Only I never got a job.

So by the time I got the invitation to interview for a position at Corcoran, the New England pastures of my alma mater didn't appear such a poor fate. It was the week of Halloween, the weather glorious, so at the very least the day of the interview would be a nice jaunt. We left early, to roam a few New Hampshire back roads, then ate a picnic lunch beside Corcoran Pond before I checked in for an afternoon of meetings.

Corcoran looked implacable, though I knew it was changed. The school had been through financial shake-ups and tenure scandals; those had, in turn, purged most of the administrators and faculty I'd known. But the grounds, the crab apple trees and white clapboard, were eternal as a country-store calendar. While Angela took a memory tour, heading for her old dorm, I turned up for my scheduled tribunal. There, I was debriefed by peers, a couple of them younger than myself. The room was full of the usual tensions: some of these people had an investment in my candidacy, some had bets on other tables. No one was in the least sentimental about my status as alumnus — that was reserved, I supposed, for the dinner tonight, arranged in my honor at the president's house. After a finishing round of polite handclasps I was ferried to the president's office. On top of tonight's dinner, she'd also wanted to meet me alone. I figured it was a good sign.

The president asked how I'd liked the interview; we made this and other small talk. She asked about my years at Corcoran, which I painted in rosy tones. Then she said: "Did you know Super Goat Man when you were a student here?"

THE SECRET HISTORY OF FANTASY

"Sure," I said. "I mean, I never took a class with him."

"He surprised me by asking to join us at the dinner tonight — he usually doesn't bother with faculty socializing anymore."

"He's still here?" I was amazed Super Goat Man, of all people, had threaded his way through so many personnel shake-ups.

"Yes, though he's reduced to a kind of honorary presence. He doesn't actually teach now. I don't know if he'd be capable of it. But he's beloved. The students joke that he can be spotted strolling across Commons lawn twice a semester. And that if you want to get any time with him, you can join him on the stroll."

"He recognized my name?"

"He seemed to, yes. You should prepare yourself. He's quite infirm."

"How — how old is he?"

"Measured in years, I don't know. But there's been an accelerated aging process. You'll see."

Perhaps superheroism was a sort of toxin, like a steroid, one with a punitive cost to the body. I mused on this as I departed the president's office, crossed the Commons, and headed through the parking lot and downhill, to find the bench beside Corcoran Creek, a favorite spot, where Angela had said she'd wait. I saw my wife before she saw me, her feet tucked up on the slats, abandoned shoes beneath, her body curled around a big hardback biography of Rousseau. In the distance, dying October light drew long saddle-shaped curves on the White Mountains of New Hampshire. Suddenly I could picture us here for a long time, and picture it happily.

"How did it go?" she asked when she noticed me.

"Par: two friends, two enemies, one sleeper."

"And the president?"

"Nice, but she wasn't giving anything away." I put my hands on her shoulders. She closed the book.

"You seem distant," Angela said. "Memories?"

"Yes." In fact, I was thinking about Super Goat Man. I'd never before considered the sacrifice he'd made, enunciating his political views so long ago. Fruitlessly, it seemed to me. In exchanging his iconic, trapped-in-amber status, what had he gained? Had Super Goat Man really accomplished much outside the parameters of his comics? However unglamorous the chores, didn't kittens *need* rescuing from trees? Didn't Vest Man require periodic defeating? Why jettison Ralph Gersten if in the end all you attained was life as a campus mascot?

I wanted to convey some of this to Angela, but didn't know where to begin. "When you were here —" I began, then stopped.

"Yes?"

"Did you know Super Goat Man?"

I felt her stiffen. "Of course, everybody knew him," she said.

"He's still here." I watched her as I spoke. Her gaze dipped to the ground.

"You saw him?"

"No, but we will at dinner tonight."

"How...unexpected." Now Angela was the one in fugue.

"Did you study with him?"

"He rarely taught. I attended a few talks."

"I thought you didn't like that stuff."

She shrugged. "I was curious."

I waited to understand. Crickets had begun a chorus in the grass. The sun ebbed. Soon we'd need to visit our bed-and-breakfast outside campus, to change into fresh clothes for the dinner party. Ordinarily such gatherings were clumsy at best, with grudges incompletely smothered under the surface of the talk, among tenured faculty who knew one another far too well. Something in me now curdled at the prospect of this one. In fact, I'd begun to dread it.

"Everett." There was something Angela wanted to tell me.

I made a preemptive guess. "Did you have some sort of something with Super Goat Man?" This was how she and I blundered through one another's past liaisons — we'd never been systematic.

I moved around the bench, to try and look her in the eye.

"Just an — affair. Nothing."

"What's nothing?"

She shrugged, and flipped her fingers as though dispelling a small fog.

"We fooled around a few times. It was stupid."

I felt the poison of bitterness leach into my bloodstream. "I don't know why but I find that totally disgusting."

"Oh, Everett." Angela raised her arms, moved to assuage me, knowing as she did my visceral possessiveness, the bolt of jealousy that shot through me when contemplating her real past, anytime it arose. Of course, she couldn't understand my special history with Super Goat Man. How could she if I didn't? I'd never even mentioned him.

"I was a silly girl." She spoke gently. "And I didn't know you yet."

Unsatisfied, I wished her to declare that the encounter had been abusive, an ethical violation. Not that I had any ground to stand on. Anyway, she was Italian in this, as in all things. It was just an affair.

"Do you want to skip the dinner?"

She scowled. "That's silly. He wouldn't even remember. And I don't care. It's really nothing, my darling. My love."

At the president's house Super Goat Man was the last to arrive, so I was allowed to fantasize briefly that I'd been spared. The sight, when he did come in, was startling. He'd not only aged, but shrunk — I doubted if he was even five feet tall. He was, as ever, barefooted, and wore white muslin pajamas, with purple piping. The knees of the pajama bottoms were smudged with mud. As he entered the room, creeping in among us as we stood with our cocktail glasses, I quickly saw the reason for the smudges: as Super Goat Man's rickety steps faltered he dropped briefly to all fours. There, on the ground, he'd shake himself, almost like a wet dog. Then he'd rise again, on palsied limbs.

No one took notice of this. The guests, the other faculty, were inured, polite. In this halting manner Super Goat Man made his way past us, to the dining room. Apparently he wasn't capable of mingling, or even necessarily of speech. He took a seat at the long table, his bunched face, his squinting eyes and wrinkled horns, nearly at the level of his place setting. So Super Goat Man's arrival curtailed cocktail hour, as we began drifting in behind him, almost guiltily. The president's husband showed us to our places, which had been carefully designated, though an accommodation was evidently being made for Super Goat Man, who'd plopped down where he liked and wasn't to be budged. I was at the right hand of the president, and the left of the chair of the hiring committee. Again, a good sign. Angela sat across from me, Super Goat Man many places away, at the other end of the table.

I actually managed to forget him for the duration of the meal. He was, so far as I could tell, silent at his feed, and the women on either side of him turned to their other partners, or conversed across the width of the table. Toward the end we were served a course of cognac and dessert, and the president's husband passed around cigars, which he bragged were Cuban. Some of the women fled their chairs to avoid the smoke; other guests rose and mingled again in the corners of the room. It was in this interval of disarrangement that Super Goat Man pushed himself off his chair and made his way to the seat at my left, which the president had vacated. He had to collapse to his knees only once on the way, and he offered no evidence of sacrificed dignity as he rose from the floor.

Angela remained in her seat. Unlike any of the American women, she'd accepted a cigar, and now leaned it into the flame of a lighter proffered by an older professor she'd been entertaining throughout the meal. Her eyes found mine as Super Goat Man approached. Her expression was curious, and not unsympathetic.

Super Goat Man prodded my arm with a finger. I turned and considered him. Black pupils gleamed behind a hedge of eyebrows. His resplendent tufts had thinned and spread — the hair of his face had been redistributed, to form a merciful gauze across his withered features.

"I...knew...your...father." His voice was mossy, sepulchral.

"Yes," I said simply, keeping my voice low. No one was paying us any attention, yet. Not apart from Angela.

"You...remember...?"

"Of course."

"We...love...jazz..."

I wondered whether he meant my father or, somehow, me. I had in fact over the years come around to my father's love of jazz, though my preference was not so much Ornette Coleman and Rahsaan Roland Kirk as Duke Ellington and Fletcher Henderson.

"…poker…"

"He cleaned you out," I reminded him.

"Yezz…good times…beautiful women…" He struggled, swallowed hard, blinked. "All this controversy…not worth it…"

"My father was never involved in any controversy," I heard myself say, though I knew Super Goat Man was speaking only of himself, his lost career.

"No…absolutely true…knew how to live…"

Angela had leaned back, pursing her lips to savor the cigar. I might have noticed the room's gabble of conversation had dampened somewhat — might have noticed it sooner, I mean.

"So…many…hangovers…"

"But you and I have something in common besides my father," I told Super Goat Man.

"Yezz…yezz…?"

"Of course we do," I began, and though I now understood we had the attention of the entire room, that the novelty of Super Goat Man's reminiscences had drawn every ear, I found myself unable to quit before I finished the thought. Further, having gained their attention, I allowed my voice to rise to a garrulous, plummy tone, as if I were starring in dinner theater. Before the line was half out of my mouth, I knew that the words, by airing the sort of laundry so desperately repressed in a community as precious as Corcoran, damned my candidacy. But that was a prize I no longer sought. Broader repercussions I could only guess at. My wife's eyes were on me now, her cigar's blunt tip flaring. I'd answer to her, later, if she gave me the chance.

It was the worst thing I could think to say. The impulse had formed in the grip of sexual jealousy, of course. But before it crossed my lips I knew my loathing had its origins in an even deeper place, the mind of a child wondering at his father's own susceptibility to the notion of a hero.

What I said was this: "I once saw you rescue a paper clip."

John Uskglass and the Cumbrian Charcoal Burner

Susanna Clarke

Many summers ago in a clearing in a wood in Cumbria there lived a Charcoal Burner. He was a very poor man. His clothes were ragged and he was generally sooty and dirty. He had no wife or children, and his only companion was a small pig called Blakeman. Most of the time he stayed in the clearing which contained just two things: an earth-covered stack of smoldering charcoal and a hut built of sticks and pieces of turf. But in spite of all this he was a cheerful soul — unless crossed in any way.

One bright summer's morning a stag ran into the clearing. After the stag came a large pack of hunting dogs, and after the dogs came a crowd of horsemen with bows and arrows. For some moments nothing could be seen but a great confusion of baying dogs, sounding horns, and thundering hooves. Then, as quickly as they had come, the huntsmen disappeared among the trees at the far end of the clearing — all but one man.

The Charcoal Burner looked around. His grass was churned to mud; not a stick of his hut remained standing; and his neat stack of charcoal was half-dismantled and fires were bursting forth from it. In a blaze of fury he turned upon the remaining huntsman and began to heap upon the man's head every insult he had ever heard.

But the huntsman had problems of his own. The reason that he had not ridden off with the others was that Blakeman was running, this way and that, beneath his horse's hooves, squealing all the while. Try as he might, the huntsman could not get free of him. The huntsman was very finely dressed in black, with boots of soft black leather and a jeweled harness. He was in fact John Uskglass (otherwise called the Raven King), King of Northern England and parts of Faerie, and the greatest magician that ever lived. But the Charcoal Burner (whose knowledge of events outside the woodland clearing was very imperfect) guessed nothing of this. He only knew that the man would not answer him and this infuriated him more than ever. "Say something!" he cried.

A stream ran through the clearing. John Uskglass glanced at it, then at Blakeman running about beneath his horse's hooves. He flung out a hand and Blakeman was transformed into a salmon. The salmon leapt through the air into the brook and swam away. Then John Uskglass rode off.

The Charcoal Burner stared after him. "Well, now what am I going to do?" he said.

He extinguished the fires in the clearing and he repaired the stack of charcoal as best he could. But a stack of charcoal that has been trampled over by hounds and horses cannot be made to look the same as one that has never received such injuries, and it hurt the Charcoal Burner's eyes to look at such a botched, broken thing.

He went down to Furness Abbey to ask the monks to give him some supper because his own supper had been trodden into the dirt. When he reached the Abbey he inquired for the Almoner whose task it is to give food and clothes to the poor. The Almoner greeted him in a kindly manner and gave him a beautiful round cheese and a warm blanket and asked what had happened to make his face so long and sad.

So the Charcoal Burner told him; but the Charcoal Burner was not much practiced in the art of giving clear accounts of complicated events. For example he spoke at great length about the huntsman who had got left behind, but he made no mention of the man's fine clothes or the jeweled rings on his fingers, so the Almoner had no suspicion that it might be the King. In fact the Charcoal Burner called him "a black man" so that the Almoner imagined he meant a dirty man — just such another one as the Charcoal Burner himself.

The Almoner was all sympathy. "So poor Blakeman is a salmon now, is he?" he said. "If I were you, I would go and have a word with Saint Kentigern. I am sure he will help you. He knows all about salmon."

"Saint Kentigern, you say? And where will I find such a useful person?" asked the Charcoal Burner eagerly.

"He has a church in Grizedale. That is the road over there."

THE SECRET HISTORY OF FANTASY

So the Charcoal Burner walked to Grizedale, and when he came to the church he went inside and banged on the walls and bawled out Saint Kentigern's name, until Saint Kentigern looked out of Heaven and asked what the matter was.

Immediately the Charcoal Burner began a long indignant speech describing the injuries that had been done to him, and in particular the part played by the solitary huntsman.

"Well," said Saint Kentigern, cheerfully. "Let me see what I can do. Saints, such as I, ought always to listen attentively to the prayers of poor, dirty, ragged men, such as you. No matter how offensively those prayers are phrased. You are our special care."

"I am though?" said the Charcoal Burner, who was rather flattered to hear this.

Then Saint Kentigern reached down from Heaven, put his hand into the church font and pulled out a salmon. He shook the salmon a little and the next moment there was Blakeman, as dirty and clever as ever.

The Charcoal Burner laughed and clapped his hands. He tried to embrace Blakeman but Blakeman just ran about, squealing, with his customary energy.

"There," said Saint Kentigern, looking down on this pleasant scene with some delight. "I am glad I was able to answer your prayer."

"Oh, but you have not!" declared the Charcoal Burner. "You must punish my wicked enemy!"

Then Saint Kentigern frowned a little and explained how one ought to forgive one's enemies. But the Charcoal Burner had never practiced Christian forgiveness before and he was not in a mood to begin now. "Let Blencathra fall on his head!" he cried, with his eyes ablaze and his fists held high. (Blencathra is a high hill some miles to the north of Grizedale.)

"Well, no," said Saint Kentigern diplomatically. "I really cannot do that. But I think you said this man was a hunter? Perhaps the loss of a day's sport will teach him to treat his neighbours with more respect."

The moment that Saint Kentigern said these words, John Uskglass (who was still hunting) tumbled down from his horse and into a cleft in some rocks. He tried to climb out but found that he was held there by some mysterious power. He tried to do some magic to counter it, but the magic did not work. The rocks and earth of England loved John Uskglass well. They would always wish to help him if they could, but this power — whatever it was — was something they respected even more.

He remained in the cleft all day and all night, until he was thoroughly cold, wet, and miserable. At dawn the unknown power suddenly released him — why, he could not tell. He climbed out, found his horse, and rode back to his castle at Carlisle.

"Where have you been?" asked William of Lanchester. "We expected you yesterday."

Now John Uskglass did not want any one to know that here might be a magician in England more powerful than himself. So he thought for a moment. "France," he said.

"France!" William of Lanchester looked surprised. "And did you see the King? What did he say? Are they planning new wars?"

John Uskglass gave some vague, mystical, and magician-like reply. Then he went up to his room and sat down upon the floor by his silver dish of water. Then he spoke to Persons of Great Importance (such as the West Wind or the Stars) and asked them to tell him who had caused him to be thrown into the cleft. Into his dish came a vision of the Charcoal Burner.

John Uskglass called for his horse and his dogs, and he rode to the clearing in the wood.

Meanwhile the Charcoal Burner was toasting some of the cheese the Almoner had given him. Then he went to look for Blakeman, because there were few things in the world that Blakeman liked as much as toasted cheese.

While he was gone John Uskglass arrived with his dogs. He looked around at the clearing for some clue as to what had happened. He wondered why a great and dangerous magician would choose to live in a wood and earn his living as a charcoal burner. His eye fell upon the toasted cheese.

Now toasted cheese is a temptation few men can resist, be they charcoal burners or kings. John Uskglass reasoned thus: all of Cumbria belonged to him — therefore this wood belonged to him — therefore this toasted cheese belonged to him. So he sat down and ate it, allowing his dogs to lick his fingers when he was done.

At that moment the Charcoal Burner returned. He stared at John Uskglass and at the empty green leaves where his toasted cheese had been. "You!" he cried. "It is you! You ate my dinner!" He took hold of John Uskglass and shook him hard. "Why? Why do you these things?"

John Uskglass said not a word. (He felt himself to be at something of a disadvantage.) He shook himself free from the Charcoal Burner's grasp, mounted upon his horse and rode out of the clearing.

The Charcoal Burner went down to Furness Abbey again. "That wicked man came back and ate my toasted cheese!" he told the Almoner.

The Almoner shook his head sadly at the sinfulness of the world. "Have some more cheese," he offered. "And perhaps some bread to go with it?"

"Which saint is it that looks after cheeses?" demanded the Charcoal Burner.

The Almoner thought for a moment. "That would be Saint Bridget," he said.

"And where will I find her ladyship?" asked the Charcoal Burner, eagerly.

"She has a church at Beckermet," replied the Almoner, and he pointed the way the Charcoal Burner ought to take.

So the Charcoal Burner walked to Beckermet and when he got to the church he banged the altar plates together and roared and made a great deal of noise until Saint Bridget looked anxiously out of Heaven and asked if there was anything she could do for him.

The Charcoal Burner gave a long description of the injuries his silent enemy had done him.

Saint Bridget said she was sorry to hear it. "But I do not think I am the proper person to help you. I look after milkmaids and dairymen. I encourage the butter to come and the cheeses to ripen. I have nothing to do with cheese that has been eaten by the wrong person. Saint Nicholas looks after thieves and stolen property. Or there is Saint Alexander of Comana who loves Charcoal Burners. Perhaps," she added hopefully, "you would like to pray to one of them?"

The Charcoal Burner declined to take an interest in the persons she mentioned. "Poor, ragged, dirty men like me are your special care!" he insisted. "Do a miracle!"

"But perhaps," said Saint Bridget, "this man does not mean to offend you by his silence. Have you considered that he may be mute?"

"Oh, no! I saw him speak to his dogs. They wagged their tails in delight to hear his voice. Saint, do your work! Let Blencathra fall on his head!"

Saint Bridget sighed. "No, no, we cannot do that; but certainly he is wrong to steal your dinner. Perhaps it might be as well to teach him a lesson. Just a small one."

At that moment John Uskglass and his court were preparing to go hunting. A cow wandered into the stable yard. It ambled up to where John Uskglass stood by his horse and began to preach him a sermon in Latin on the wickedness of stealing. Then his horse turned its head and told him solemnly that it quite agreed with the cow and that he should pay good attention to what the cow said.

All the courtiers and the servants in the stable yard fell silent and stared at the scene. Nothing like this had ever happened before.

"This is magic!" declared William of Lanchester. "But who would dare...?"

"I did it myself," said John Uskglass quickly.

"Really?" said William. "Why?"

There was a pause. "To help me contemplate my sins and errors," said John Uskglass at last, "as a Christian should from time to time."

"But stealing is not a sin of yours! So why...?"

"Good God, William!" cried John Uskglass. "Must you ask so many questions? I shall not hunt today!"

He hurried away to the rose garden to escape the horse and the cow. But the roses turned their red-and-white faces toward him and spoke at length about his duty to the poor; and some of the more ill-natured flowers hissed, "Thief! Thief!" He shut his eyes and put his fingers in his ears, but his dogs came and found him and pushed their noses in his face and told him how very, very disappointed they were in him. So he went and hid in a bare little room at the top of the castle. But all that day the

THE SECRET HISTORY OF FANTASY

stones of the walls loudly debated the various passages in the Bible that condemn stealing.

John Uskglass had no need to inquire who had done this (the cow, horse, dogs, stones and roses had all made particular mention of toasted cheese); and he was determined to discover who this strange magician was and what he wanted. He decided to employ that most magical of all creatures — the raven. An hour later a thousand or so ravens were despatched in a flock so dense that it was as if a black mountain were flying through the summer sky. When they arrived at the Charcoal Burner's clearing, they filled every part of it with a tumult of black wings. The leaves were swept from the trees, and the Charcoal Burner and Blakeman were knocked to the ground and battered about. The ravens searched the Charcoal Burner's memories and dreams for evidence of magic. Just to be on the safe side, they searched Blakeman's memories and dreams too. The ravens looked to see what man and pig had thought when they were still in their mothers' wombs; and they looked to see what both would do when finally they came to Heaven. They found not a scrap of magic anywhere.

When they were gone, John Uskglass walked into the clearing with his arms folded, frowning. He was deeply disappointed at the ravens' failure.

The Charcoal Burner got slowly up from the ground and looked around in amazement. If a fire had ravaged the wood, the destruction could scarcely have been more complete. The branches were torn from the trees and a thick, black layer of raven feathers lay over everything. In a sort of ecstasy of indignation, he cried, "Tell me why you persecute me!"

But John Uskglass said not a word.

"I will make Blencathra fall on your head! I will do it! You know I can!" He jabbed his dirty finger in John Uskglass's face. "You — know — I — can!"

The next day the Charcoal Burner appeared at Furness Abbey before the sun was up. He found the Almoner, who was on his way to Prime. "He came back and shattered my wood," he told him. "He made it black and ugly!"

"What a terrible man!" said the Almoner, sympathetically.

"What saint is in charge of ravens?" demanded the Charcoal Burner.

"Ravens?" said the Almoner. "None that I know of." He thought for a moment. "Saint Oswald had a pet raven of which he was extremely fond."

"And where would I find his saintliness?"

"He has a new church at Grasmere."

So the Charcoal Burner walked to Grasmere and when he got there, he shouted and banged on the walls with a candlestick.

Saint Oswald put his head out of Heaven and cried, "Do you have to shout so loud? I am not deaf! What do you want? And put down that candlestick! It was expensive!" During their holy and blessed lives Saint Kentigern and Saint Bridget had been a monk and a nun respectively; they were full of mild, saintly patience. But Saint Oswald had been a king and a soldier, and he was a very different sort of person.

"The Almoner at Furness Abbey says you like ravens," explained the Charcoal Burner.

"'Like' is putting it a little strong," said Saint Oswald. "There was a bird in the seventh century that used to perch on my shoulder. It pecked my ears and made them bleed."

The Charcoal Burner described how he was persecuted by the silent man.

"Well, perhaps he has reason for behaving as he does?" said Saint Oswald, sarcastically. "Have you, for example, made great big dents in his expensive candlesticks?"

The Charcoal Burner indignantly denied ever having hurt the silent man.

"Hmm," said Saint Oswald, thoughtfully. "Only kings can hunt deer, you know."

The Charcoal Burner looked blank.

"Let us see," said Saint Oswald. "A man in black clothes, with powerful magic and ravens at his command, and the hunting rights of a king. This suggests nothing to you? No, apparently it does not. Well, it so happens that I think I know the person you mean. He is indeed very arrogant and perhaps the time has come to humble him a little. If I understand you aright, you are angry because he does not speak to you?"

"Yes."

"Well then, I believe I shall loosen his tongue a little."

"What sort of punishment is that?" asked the Charcoal Burner. "I want you to make Blencathra fall on his head!"

Saint Oswald made a sound of irritation. "What do you know of it?" he said. "Believe me, I am a far better judge than you of how to hurt this man!"

As Saint Oswald spoke John Uskglass began to talk in a rapid and rather excited manner. This was unusual but did not at first seem sinister. All his courtiers and servants listened politely. But minutes went by — and then hours — and he did not stop talking. He talked through dinner; he talked through mass; he talked through the night. He made prophecies, recited Bible passages, told the histories of various fairy kingdoms, gave recipes for pies. He gave away political secrets, magical secrets, infernal secrets, Divine secrets, and scandalous secrets — as a result of which the Kingdom of Northern England was thrown into various political and theological crises. Thomas of Dundale and William of Lanchester begged and threatened and pleaded, but nothing they said could make the King stop talking. Eventually they were obliged to lock him in the little room at the top of the castle so that no one else could hear him. Then, since it was inconceivable that a king should talk without someone listening, they were obliged to stay with him, day after day. After exactly three days he fell silent.

Two days later he rode into the Charcoal Burner's clearing. He looked so pale and worn that the Charcoal Burner was in high hopes that Saint Oswald might have relented and pushed Blencathra on his head.

"What is it that you want from me?" asked John Uskglass, warily.

"Ha!" said the Charcoal Burner with triumphant looks. "Ask my pardon for turning poor Blakeman into a fish!"

A long silence.

Then with gritted teeth, John Uskglass asked the Charcoal Burner's pardon. "Is there anything else you want?" he asked.

"Repair all the hurts you did me!"

Immediately the Charcoal Burner's stack and hut reappeared just as they had always been; the trees were made whole again; fresh, green leaves covered their branches; and a sweet lawn of soft grass spread over the clearing.

"Anything else?"

The Charcoal Burner closed his eyes and strained to summon up an image of unthinkable wealth. "Another pig!" he declared.

John Uskglass was beginning to suspect that he had made a miscalculation somewhere — though he could not for his life tell where it was. Nevertheless he felt confident enough to say, "I will grant you a pig — if you promise that you will tell no one who gave it to you or why."

"How can I?" said the Charcoal Burner. "I do not know who you are. Why?" he said, narrowing his eyes. "Who are you?"

"No one," said John Uskglass quickly.

Another pig appeared, the very twin of Blakeman, and while the Charcoal Burner was exclaiming over his good fortune, John Uskglass got on his horse and rode away in a condition of the most complete mystification.

Shortly after that he returned to his capital city of Newcastle. In the next fifty or sixty years his lords and servants often reminded him of the excellent hunting to be had in Cumbria, but he was careful never to go there again until he was sure the Charcoal Burner was dead.

The Book of Martha

Octavia E. Butler

"It's DIFFICULT, ISN'T it?" God said with a weary smile. "You're truly free for the first time. What could be more difficult than that?"

Martha Bes looked around at the endless grayness that was, along with God, all that she could see. In fear and confusion, she covered her broad black face with her hands. "If only I could wake up," she whispered.

God kept silent but was so palpably, disturbingly present that even in the silence Martha felt rebuked. "Where is this?" she asked, not really wanting to know, not wanting to be dead when she was only forty-three. "Where am I?"

"Here with me," God said.

"Really here?" she asked. "Not at home in bed dreaming? Not locked up in a mental institution? Not…not lying dead in a morgue?"

"Here," God said softly. "With me."

After a moment, Martha was able to take her hands from her face and look again at the grayness around her and at God. "This can't be heaven," she said. "There's nothing here, no one here but you."

"Is that all you see?" God asked.

This confused her even more. "Don't you know what I see?" she demanded and then quickly softened her voice. "Don't you know everything?"

God smiled. "No, I outgrew that trick long ago. You can't imagine how boring it was."

This struck Martha as such a human thing to say that her fear diminished a little — although she was still impossibly confused. She had, she remembered, been sitting at her computer, wrapping up one more day's work on her fifth novel. The writing had been going well for a change, and she'd been enjoying it. For hours, she'd been spilling her new story onto paper in that sweet frenzy of creation that she lived for. Finally, she had stopped, turned the computer off, and realized that she felt stiff. Her back hurt. She was hungry and thirsty, and it was almost five A.M. She had worked through the night. Amused in spite of her various aches and pains, she got up and went to the kitchen to find something to eat.

And then she was *here,* confused and scared. The comfort of her small, disorderly house was gone, and she was standing before this amazing figure who had convinced her at once that he was God — or someone so powerful that he might as well be God. He had work for her to do, he said — work that would mean a great deal to her and to the rest of humankind.

If she had been a little less frightened, she might have laughed. Beyond comic books and bad movies, who said things like that?

"Why," she dared to ask, "do you look like a twice-life-sized, bearded white man?" In fact, seated as he was on his huge thronelike chair, he looked, she thought, like a living version of Michelangelo's *Moses,* a sculpture that she remembered seeing pictured in her college art-history textbook about twenty years before. Except that God was more fully dressed than Michelangelo's *Moses,* wearing, from neck to ankles, the kind of long, white robe that she had so often seen in paintings of Christ.

"You see what your life has prepared you to see," God said.

"I want to see what's really here!"

"Do you? What you see is up to you, Martha. Everything is up to you."

She sighed. "Do you mind if I sit down?"

And she was sitting. She did not sit down, but simply found herself sitting in a comfortable armchair that had surely not been there a moment before. Another trick, she thought resentfully — like the grayness, like the giant on his throne, like her own sudden appearance here. Everything was just one more effort to amaze and frighten her. And, of course, it was working. She was amazed and badly frightened. Worse, she disliked the giant for manipulating her, and this frightened her even more. Surely he could read her mind. Surely he would punish...

She made herself speak through her fear. "You said you had work for me." She paused, licked her lips, tried to steady her voice. "What do you want me to do?"

He didn't answer at once. He looked at her with what she read as amusement — looked at her long enough to make her even more uncomfortable.

"What do you want me to do?" she repeated, her voice stronger this time.

"I have a great deal of work for you," he said at last. "As I tell you about it, I want you to keep three people in mind: Jonah, Job, and Noah. Remember them. Be guided by their stories."

"All right," she said because he had stopped speaking, and it seemed that she should say something. "All right."

When she was a girl, she had gone to church and to Sunday school, to Bible class and to vacation Bible school. Her mother, only a girl herself, hadn't known much about being a mother, but she had wanted her child to be "good," and to her, "good" meant "religious." As a result, Martha knew very well what the Bible said about Jonah, Job, and Noah. She had come to regard their stories as parables rather than literal truths, but she remembered them. God had ordered Jonah to go to the city of Nineveh and to tell the people there to mend their ways. Frightened, Jonah had tried to run away from the work and from God, but God had caused him to be shipwrecked, swallowed by a great fish, and given to know that he could not escape.

Job had been the tormented pawn who lost his property, his children, and his health in a bet between God and Satan. And when Job proved faithful in spite of all that God had permitted Satan to do to him, God rewarded Job with even greater wealth, new children, and restored health.

As for Noah, of course, God ordered him to build an ark and save his family and a lot of animals because God had decided to flood the world and kill everyone and everything else.

Why was she to remember these three Biblical figures in particular? What had they do with her — especially Job and all his agony?

"This is what you're to do," God said. "You will help humankind to survive its greedy, murderous, wasteful adolescence. Help it to find less destructive, more peaceful, sustainable ways to live."

Martha stared at him. After a while, she said feebly, "...what?"

"If you don't help them, they will be destroyed."

"You're going to destroy them...again?" she whispered.

"Of course not," God said, sounding annoyed. "They're well on the way to destroying billions of themselves by greatly changing the ability of the earth to sustain them. That's why they need help. That's why you will help them."

"How?" she asked. She shook her head. "What can I do?"

"Don't worry," God said. "I won't be sending you back home with another message that people can ignore or twist to suit themselves. It's too late for that kind of thing anyway." God shifted on his throne and looked at her with his head cocked to one side. "You'll borrow some of my power," he said. "You'll arrange it so that people treat one another better and treat their environment more sensibly. You'll give them a better chance to survive than they've given themselves. I'll lend you the power, and you'll do this." He paused, but this time she could think of nothing to say. After a while, he went on.

"When you've finished your work, you'll go back and live among them again as one of their lowliest. You're the one who will decide what that will mean, but whatever you decide is to be the bottom level of society, the lowest class or caste or race, that's what you'll be."

This time when he stopped talking, Martha laughed. She felt overwhelmed with questions, fears, and bitter laughter, but it was the laughter that broke free. She needed to laugh. It gave her strength somehow.

"I was born on the bottom level of society," she said. "You must have known that."

God did not answer.

"Sure you did." Martha stopped laughing and managed, somehow, not to cry. She stood up, stepped toward God. "How could you not know? I was born poor, black, and female to a fourteen-year-old mother who could barely read. We were homeless half the time while I was growing up. Is that bottom-level enough for you? I was born on the bottom, but I didn't stay there. I didn't leave my mother there, either. And I'm not going back there!"

Still God said nothing. He smiled.

Martha sat down again, frightened by the smile, aware that she had been shouting — shouting at God! After a while, she whispered, "Is that why you chose me to do this...this work? Because of where I came from?"

"I chose you for all that you are and all that you are not," God said. "I could have chosen someone much poorer and more downtrodden. I chose you because you were the one I wanted for this."

Martha couldn't decide whether he sounded annoyed. She couldn't decide whether it was an honor to be chosen to do a job so huge, so poorly defined, so *impossible*.

"Please let me go home," she whispered. She was instantly ashamed of herself. She was begging, sounding pitiful, humiliating herself. Yet these were the most honest words she'd spoken so far.

"You're free to ask me questions," God said as though he hadn't heard her plea at all. "You're free to argue and think and investigate all of human history for ideas and warnings. You're free to take all the time you need to do these things. As I said earlier, you're truly free. You're even free to be terrified. But I assure you, you will do this work."

Martha thought of Job, Jonah, and Noah. After a while, she nodded.

"Good," God said. He stood up and stepped toward her. He was at least twelve feet high and inhumanly beautiful. He literally glowed. "Walk with me," he said.

And abruptly, he was not twelve feet high. Martha never saw him change, but now he was her size — just under six feet — and he no longer glowed. Now when he looked at her, they were eye to eye. He did look at her. He saw that something was disturbing her, and he asked, "What is it now? Has your image of me grown feathered wings or a blinding halo?"

"Your halo's gone," she answered. "And you're smaller. More normal."

"Good," he said. "What else do you see?"

"Nothing. Grayness."

"That will change."

It seemed that they walked over a smooth, hard, level surface, although when she looked down, she couldn't see her feet. It was as though she walked through ankle-high, ground-hugging fog.

"What are we walking on?" she asked.

"What would you like?" God asked. "A sidewalk? Beach sand? A dirt road?"

"A healthy, green lawn," she said, and was somehow not surprised to find herself walking on short, green grass. "And there should be trees," she said, getting the idea and discovering she liked it. "There should be sunshine — blue sky with a few clouds. It should be May or early June."

And it was so. It was as though it had always been so. They were walking through what could have been a vast city park.

Martha looked at God, her eyes wide. "Is that it?" she whispered. "I'm supposed to change people by deciding what they'll be like, and then just…just saying it?"

"Yes," God said.

And she went from being elated to — once again — being terrified. "What if I say something wrong, make a mistake?"

"You will."

"But…people could get hurt. People could die."

God went to a huge deep-red Norway maple tree and sat down beneath it on a long wooden bench. Martha realized that he had created both the ancient tree and the comfortable-looking bench only a moment before. She knew this, but again, it had happened so smoothly that she was not jarred by it.

"It's so easy," she said. "Is it always this easy for you?"

God sighed. "Always," he said.

She thought about that — his sigh, the fact that he looked away into the trees instead of at her. Was an eternity of absolute ease just another name for hell? Or was that just the most sacrilegious thought she'd had so far? She said, "I don't want to hurt people. Not even by accident."

THE SECRET HISTORY OF FANTASY

God turned away from the trees, looked at her for several seconds, then said, "It would be better for you if you had raised a child or two."

Then, she thought with irritation, he should have chosen someone who'd raised a child or two. But she didn't have the courage to say that. Instead, she said, "Won't you fix it so I don't hurt or kill anyone? I mean, I'm new at this. I could do something stupid and wipe people out and not even know I'd done it until afterward."

"I won't fix things for you," God said. "You have a free hand."

She sat down next to him because sitting and staring out into the endless park was easier than standing and facing him and asking him questions that she thought might make him angry. She said, "Why should it be my work? Why don't you do it? You know how. You could do it without making mistakes. Why make me do it? I don't know anything."

"Quite right," God said. And he smiled. "That's why."

She thought about this with growing horror. "Is it just a game to you, then?" she asked. "Are you playing with us because you're bored?"

God seemed to consider the question. "I'm not bored," he said. He seemed pleased somehow. "You should be thinking about the changes you'll make. We can talk about them. You don't have to just suddenly proclaim."

She looked at him, then stared down at the grass, trying to get her thoughts in order. "Okay. How do I start?"

"Think about this: What change would you want to make if you could make only one? Think of one important change."

She looked at the grass again and thought about the novels she had written. What if she were going to write a novel in which human beings had to be changed in only one positive way? "Well," she said after a while, "the growing population is making a lot of the other problems worse. What if people could only have two children? I mean, what if people who wanted children could only have two, no matter how many more they wanted or how many medical techniques they used to try to get more?"

"You believe the population problem is the worst one, then?" God asked.

"I think so," she said. "Too many people. If we solve that one, we'll have more time to solve other problems. And we can't solve it on our own. We all know about it, but some of us won't admit it. And nobody wants some big government authority telling them how many kids to have." She glanced at God and saw that he seemed to be listening politely. She wondered how far he would let her go. What might offend him. What might he do to her if he were offended? "So everyone's reproductive system shuts down after two kids," she said. "I mean, they get to live as long as before, and they aren't sick. They just can't have kids any more."

"They'll try," God said. "The effort they put into building pyramids, cathedrals, and moon rockets will be as nothing to the effort they'll put into trying to end what will seem to them a plague of barrenness. What about people whose children die or are seriously disabled? What about a woman whose first child is a result of rape? What about surrogate motherhood? What about men who become fathers without realizing it? What about cloning?"

Martha stared at him, chagrined. "That's why you should do this. It's too complicated."

Silence.

"All right," Martha sighed and gave up. "All right. What if even with accidents and modern medicine, even something like cloning, the two-kid limit holds. I don't know how that could be made to work, but you do."

"It could be made to work," God said, "but keep in mind that you won't be coming here again to repair any changes you make. What you do is what people will live with. Or in this case, die with."

"Oh," Martha said. She thought for a moment, then said, "Oh, no."

"They would last for a good many generations," God said. "But they would be dwindling all the time. In the end, they would be extinguished. With the usual diseases, disabilities, disasters, wars, deliberate childlessness, and murder, they wouldn't be able to replace themselves. Think of the needs of the future, Martha, as well as the needs of the present."

"I thought I was," she said. "What if I made four kids the maximum number instead of two?"

God shook his head. "Free will coupled with morality has been an interesting experiment. Free will is, among other things, the freedom to make mistakes. One group of mistakes will sometimes cancel another. That's saved any number of human groups, although it isn't dependable. Sometimes mistakes cause people to be wiped out, enslaved, or driven from their homes because they've so damaged or altered their land or their water or their climate. Free will isn't a guarantee of anything, but it's a potentially useful tool — too useful to erase casually."

"I thought you wanted me to put a stop to war and slavery and environmental destruction!" Martha snapped, remembering the history of her own people. How could God be so casual about such things?

God laughed. It was a startling sound — deep, full, and, Martha thought, inappropriately happy. Why would this particular subject make him laugh? Was he God? Was he Satan? Martha, in spite of her mother's efforts, had not been able to believe in the literal existence of either. Now, she did not know what to think — or what to do.

God recovered himself, shook his head, and looked at Martha. "Well, there's no hurry," he said. "Do you know what a nova is Martha?"

Martha frowned. "It's...a star that explodes," she said, willing, even eager, to be distracted from her doubts.

"It's a pair of stars," God said. "A large one — a giant — and a small, very dense dwarf. The dwarf pulls material from the giant. After a while, the dwarf has taken more material than it can control, and it explodes. It doesn't necessarily destroy itself, but it does throw off a great deal of excess material. It makes a very bright, violent display. But once the dwarf has quieted down, it begins to siphon material from the giant again. It can do this over and over. That's what a nova is. If you change it — move the two stars farther apart or equalize their density, then it's no longer a nova."

Martha listened, catching his meaning even though she didn't want to. "Are you saying that if...if humanity is changed, it won't be humanity any more?"

"I'm saying more than that," God told her. "I'm saying that even though this is true, I will permit you to do it. What you decide should be done with humankind *will* be done. But whatever you do, your decisions will have consequences. If you limit their fertility, you will probably destroy them. If you limit their competitiveness or their inventiveness, you might destroy their ability to survive the many disasters and challenges that they must face."

Worse and worse, Martha thought, and she actually felt nauseous with fear. She turned away from God, hugging herself, suddenly crying, tears streaming down her face. After a while, she sniffed and wiped her face on her hands, since she had nothing else. "What will you do to me if I refuse?" she asked, thinking of Job and Jonah in particular.

"Nothing." God didn't even sound annoyed. "You won't refuse."

"But what if I do? What if I really can't think of anything worth doing?"

"That won't happen. But if it did somehow, and if you asked, I would send you home. After all, there are millions of human beings who would give anything to do this work."

And, instantly, she thought of some of these — people who would be happy to wipe out whole segments of the population whom they hated and feared, or people who would set up vast tyrannies that forced everyone into a single mold, no matter how much suffering that created. And what about those who would treat the work as fun — as nothing more than a good-guys-versus-bad-guys computer game, and damn the consequences. There were people like that. Martha knew people like that.

But God wouldn't choose that kind of person. If he was God. Why had he chosen her, after all? For all of her adult life, she hadn't even believed in God as a literal being. If this terrifyingly powerful entity, God or not, could choose her, he could make even worse choices.

After a while, she asked, "Was there really a Noah?"

"Not one man dealing with a worldwide flood," God said. "But there have been a number of people who've had to deal with smaller disasters."

"People you ordered to save a few and let the rest die?"

"Yes," God said.

She shuddered and turned to face him again. "And what then? Did they go mad?" Even she could hear the disapproval and disgust in her voice.

God chose to hear the question as only a question. "Some took refuge in madness, some in drunkenness, some in sexual license. Some killed themselves. Some survived and lived long, fruitful lives."

Martha shook her head and managed to keep quiet.

"I don't do that any longer," God said.

No, Martha thought. Now he had found a different amusement. "How big a change do I have to make?" she asked. "What will please you and cause you to let me go and not bring in someone else to replace me?"

"I don't know," God said, and he smiled. He rested his head back against the tree. "Because I don't know what you will do. That's a lovely sensation — anticipating, not knowing."

"Not from my point of view," Martha said bitterly. After a while, she said in a different tone, "Definitely not from my point of view. Because I don't know what to do. I really don't."

"You write stories for a living," God said. "You create characters and situations, problems and solutions. That's less than I've given you to do."

"But you want me to tamper with real people. I don't want to do that. I'm afraid I'll make some horrible mistake."

"I'll answer your questions," God said. "Ask."

She didn't want to ask. After a while, though, she gave in. "What, exactly, do you want? A utopia? Because I don't believe in them. I don't believe it's possible to arrange a society so that everyone is content, every-one has what he or she wants."

"Not for more than a few moments," God said. "That's how long it would take for someone to decide that he wanted what his neighbor had — or that he wanted his neighbor as a slave of one kind or another, or that he wanted his neighbor dead. But never mind. I'm not asking you to create a utopia, Martha, although it would be interesting to see what you could come up with."

"So what are you asking me to do?"

"To help them, of course. Haven't you wanted to do that?"

"Always," she said. "And I never could in any meaningful way. Famines, epidemics, floods, fires, greed, slavery, revenge, stupid, stupid wars..."

"Now you can. Of course, you can't put an end to all of those things without putting an end to humanity, but you can diminish some of the problems. Fewer wars, less covetousness, more forethought and care with the environment… What might cause that?"

She looked at her hands, then at him. Something had occurred to her as he spoke, but it seemed both too simple and too fantastic, and to her personally, perhaps, too painful. Could it be done? Should it be done? Would it really help if it were done? She asked, "Was there really anything like the Tower of Babel? Did you make people suddenly unable to understand each other?"

God nodded. "Again, it happened several times in one way or another."

"So what did you do? Change their thinking somehow, alter their memories?"

"Yes, I've done both. Although before literacy, all I had to do was divide them physically, send one group to a new land or give one group a custom that altered their mouths — knocking out the front teeth during puberty rites, for instance. Or give them a strong aversion to something others of their kind consider precious or sacred or —"

To her amazement, Martha interrupted him. "What about changing people's… I don't know, their brain activity. Can I do that?"

"Interesting," God said. "And probably dangerous. But you can do that if you decide to. What do you have in mind?"

"Dreams," she said. "Powerful, unavoidable, realistic dreams that come every time people sleep."

"Do you mean," God asked, "that they should be taught some lesson through their dreams?"

"Maybe. But I really mean that somehow people should spend a lot of their energy in their dreams. They would have their own personal best of all possible worlds during their dreams. The dreams should be much more realistic and intense than most dreams are now. Whatever people love to do most, they should dream about doing it, and the dreams should change to keep up with their individual interests. Whatever grabs their attention, whatever they desire, they can have it in their sleep. In fact, they can't avoid having it. Nothing should be able to keep the dreams away — not drugs, not surgery, not anything. And the dreams should satisfy much more deeply, more thoroughly, than reality can. I mean, the satisfaction should be in the dreaming, not in trying to make the dream real."

God smiled. "Why?"

"I want them to have the only possible utopia." Martha thought for a moment. "Each person will have a private, perfect utopia every night — or an imperfect one. If they crave conflict and struggle, they get that. If they want peace and love, they get that. Whatever they want or need comes to them. I think if people go to a...well, a private heaven every night, it might take the edge off their willingness to spend their waking hours trying to dominate or destroy one another." She hesitated. "Won't it?"

God was still smiling. "It might. Some people will be taken over by it as though it were an addictive drug. Some will try to fight it in themselves or others. Some will give up on their lives and decide to die because nothing they do matters as much as their dreams. Some will enjoy it and try to go on with their familiar lives, but even they will find that the dreams interfere with their relations with other people. What will humankind in general do? I don't know." He seemed interested, almost excited. "I think it might dull them too much at first — until they're used to it. I wonder whether they can get used to it."

Martha nodded. "I think you're right about it dulling them. I think at first most people will lose interest in a lot of other things — including real, wide-awake sex. Real sex is risky to both the health and the ego. Dream sex will be fantastic and not risky at all. Fewer children will be born for a while."

"And fewer of those will survive," God said.

"What?"

"Some parents will certainly be too involved in dreams to take care of their children. Loving and raising children is risky, too, and it's hard work."

"That shouldn't happen. Taking care of their kids should be the one thing that parents want to do for real in spite of the dreams. I don't want to be responsible for a lot of neglected kids."

"So you want people — adults and children — to have nights filled with vivid, wish-fulfilling dreams, but parents should somehow see child care as more important than the dreams, and the children should not be seduced away from their parents by the dreams, but should want and need a relationship with them as though there were no dreams?"

"As much as possible." Martha frowned, imagining what it might be like to live in such a world. Would people still read books? Perhaps they would to feed their dreams. Would she still be able to write books? Would she want to? What would happen to her if the only work she had ever cared for was lost? "People should still care about their families and their work," she said. "The dreams shouldn't take away their self-respect. They shouldn't be content to dream on a park bench or in an alley. I just want the dreams to slow things down a little. A little less aggression, as you said, less covetousness. Nothing slows people down like satisfaction, and this satisfaction will come every night."

God nodded. "Is that it, then? Do you want this to happen?"

"Yes. I mean, I think so."

"Are you sure?"

She stood up and looked down at him. "Is it what I should do? Will it work? Please tell me."

"I truly don't know. I don't want to know. I want to watch it all un-fold. I've used dreams before, you know, but not like this."

His pleasure was so obvious that she almost took the whole idea back. He seemed able to be amused by terrible things. "Let me think about this," she said. "Can I be by myself for a while?"

God nodded. "Speak aloud to me when you want to talk. I'll come to you."

And she was alone. She was alone inside what looked and felt like her home — her little house in Seattle, Washington. She was in her living room.

Without thinking, she turned on a lamp and stood looking at her books. Three of the walls of the room were covered with bookshelves. Her books were there in their familiar order. She picked up several, one after another — history, medicine, religion, art, crime. She opened them to see that they were, indeed, her books, highlighted and written in by her own hand as she researched this novel or that short story.

She began to believe she really was at home. She had had some sort of strange waking dream about meeting with a God who looked like Michelangelo's *Moses* and who ordered her to come up with a way to make humanity a less self-destructive species. The experience felt completely, unnervingly real, but it couldn't have been. It was too ridiculous.

She went to her front window and opened the drapes. Her house was on a hill and faced east. Its great luxury was that it offered a beautiful view of Lake Washington just a few blocks down the hill.

But now, there was no lake. Outside was the park that she had wished into existence earlier. Perhaps twenty yards from her front window was the big red Norway maple tree and the bench where she had sat and talked with God.

The bench was empty now and in deep shadow. It was getting dark outside.

She closed the drapes and looked at the lamp that lit the room. For a moment, it bothered her that it was on and using electricity in this Twilight Zone of a place. Had her house been transported here, or had it been duplicated? Or was it all a complex hallucination?

She sighed. The lamp worked. Best to just accept it. There was light in the room. There was a room, a house. How it all worked was the least of her problems.

She went to the kitchen and there found all the food she had had at home. Like the lamp, the refrigerator, the electric stovetop, and the ovens worked. She could prepare a meal. It would be at least as real as anything else she'd run across recently. And she was hungry.

She took a small can of solid white albacore tuna and containers of dill weed and curry power from the cupboard and got bread, lettuce, dill pickles, green onions, mayonnaise, and chunky salsa from the refrigerator. She would have a tuna-salad sandwich or two. Thinking about it made her even hungrier.

Then she had another thought, and she said aloud, "May I ask you a question?"

And they were walking together on a broad, level dirt pathway bordered by dark, ghostly silhouettes of trees. Night had fallen, and the darkness beneath the trees was impenetrable. Only the pathway was a ribbon of pale light — starlight and moonlight. There was a full moon, brilliant, yellow-white, and huge. And there was a vast canopy of stars. She had seen the night sky this way only a few times in her life. She had always lived in cities where the lights and the smog obscured all but the brightest few stars.

She looked upward for several seconds, then looked at God and saw, somehow, without surprise, that he was black now, and clean-shaven. He was a tall, stocky black man wearing ordinary, modern clothing — a dark sweater over a white shirt and dark pants. He didn't tower over her, but he was taller than the human-sized version of the white God had been. He didn't look anything like the white Moses-God, and yet he was the same person. She never doubted that.

"You're seeing something different," God said. "What is it?" Even his voice was changed, deepened.

She told him what she was seeing, and he nodded. "At some point, you'll probably decide to see me as a woman," he said.

"I didn't decide to do this," she said. "None of it is real, anyway."

"I've told you," he said. "Everything is real. It's just not as you see it."

She shrugged. It didn't matter — not compared to what she wanted to ask. "I had a thought," she said, "and it scared me. That's why I called you. I sort of asked about it before, but you didn't give me a direct answer, and I guess I need one."

He waited.

"Am I dead?"

"Of course not," he said, smiling. "You're here."

"With you," she said bitterly.

Silence.

"Does it matter how long I take to decide what to do?"

"I've told you, no. Take as long as you like."

That was odd, Martha thought. Well, everything was odd. On impulse, she said, "Would you like a tuna-salad sandwich?"

"Yes," God said. "Thank you."

They walked back to the house together instead of simply appearing there. Martha was grateful for that. Once inside, she left him sitting in her living room, paging through a fantasy novel and smiling. She went through the motions of making the best tuna-salad sandwiches she could. Maybe effort counted. She didn't believe for a moment that she was preparing real food or that she and God were going to eat it.

And yet, the sandwiches were delicious. As they ate, Martha remembered the sparkling apple cider that she kept in the refrigerator for company. She went to get it, and when she got back to the living room, she saw that God had, in fact, become a woman.

Martha stopped, startled, then sighed. "I see you as female now," she said. "Actually, I think you look a little like me. We look like sisters." She smiled wearily and handed over a glass of cider.

God said, "You really are doing this yourself, you know. But as long as it isn't upsetting you, I suppose it doesn't matter."

"It does bother me. If I'm doing it, why did it take so long for me to see you as a black woman — since that's no more true than seeing you as a white or a black man?"

"As I've told you, you see what your life has prepared you to see." God looked at her, and for a moment, Martha felt that she was looking into a mirror.

Martha looked away. "I believe you. I just thought I had already broken out of the mental cage I was born and raised in — a human God, a white God, a male God…"

"If it were truly a cage," God said, "you would still be in it, and I would still look the way I did when you first saw me."

"There is that," Martha said. "What would you call it then?"

"An old habit," God said. "That's the trouble with habits. They tend to outlive their usefulness."

Martha was quiet for a while. Finally she said, "What do you think about my dream idea? I'm not asking you to foresee the future. Just find fault. Punch holes. Warn me."

God rested her head against the back of the chair. "Well, the evolving environmental problems will be less likely to cause wars, so there will probably be less starvation, less disease. Real power will be less satisfying than the vast, absolute power they can possess in their dreams, so fewer people will be driven to try to conquer their neighbors or exterminate their minorities. All in all, the dreams will probably give humanity more time than it would have without them."

Martha was alarmed in spite of herself. "Time to do what?"

"Time to grow up a little. Or at least, time to find some way of surviving what remains of its adolescence." God smiled. "How many times have you wondered how some especially self-destructive individual managed to survive adolescence? It's a valid concern for humanity as well as for individual human beings."

"Why can't the dreams do more than that?" she asked. "Why can't the dreams be used not just to give them their heart's desire when they sleep, but to push them toward some kind of waking maturity. Although I'm not sure what species maturity might be like."

"Exhaust them with pleasure," God mused, "while teaching them that pleasure isn't everything."

"They already know that."

"Individuals usually know that by the time they reach adulthood. But all too often, they don't care. It's too easy to follow bad but attractive leaders, embrace pleasurable but destructive habits, ignore looming disaster because maybe it won't happen after all — or maybe it will only happen to other people. That kind of thinking is part of what it means to be adolescent."

"Can the dreams teach — or at least promote — more thoughtfulness when people are awake, promote more concern for real consequences?"

"It can be that way if you like."

"I do. I want them to enjoy themselves as much as they can while they're asleep, but to be a lot more awake and aware when they are awake, a lot less susceptible to lies, peer pressure, and self-delusion."

"None of this will make them perfect, Martha."

Martha stood looking down at God, fearing that she had missed something important, and that God knew it and was amused. "But this will help?" she said. "It will help more than it will hurt."

"Yes, it will probably do that. And it will no doubt do other things. I don't know what they are, but they are inevitable. Nothing ever works smoothly with humankind."

"You like that, don't you?"

"I didn't at first. They were mine, and I didn't know them. You cannot begin to understand how strange that was." God shook her head. "They were as familiar as my own substance, and yet they weren't."

"Make the dreams happen." Martha said.

"Are you sure?"

"Make them happen."

"You're ready to go home, then."

"Yes."

God stood and faced her. "You want to go. Why?"

"Because I don't find them interesting in the same way you do. Because your ways scare me."

God laughed — a less disturbing laugh now. "No, they don't," she said. "You're beginning to like my ways."

After a time, Martha nodded. "You're right. It did scare me at first, and now it doesn't. I've gotten used to it. In just the short time that I've been here, I've gotten used to it, and I'm starting to like it. That's what scares me."

In mirror image, God nodded, too. "You really could have stayed here, you know. No time would pass for you. No time has passed."

"I wondered why you didn't care about time."

"You'll go back to the life you remember, at first. But soon, I think you'll have to find another way of earning a living. Beginning again at your age won't be easy."

Martha stared at the neat shelves of books on her walls. "Reading will suffer, won't it — pleasure reading, anyway?"

"It will — for a while, anyway. People will read for information and for ideas, but they'll create their own fantasies. Did you think of that before you made your decision?"

Martha sighed. "Yes," she said. "I did." Sometime later, she added, "I want to go home."

"Do you want to remember being here?" God asked.

"No." On impulse, she stepped to God and hugged her — hugged her hard, feeling the familiar woman's body beneath the blue jeans and black T-shirt that looked as though it had come from Martha's own closet. Martha realized that somehow, in spite of everything, she had come to like this seductive, childlike, very dangerous being. "No," she repeated. "I'm afraid of the unintended damage that the dreams might do."

"Even though in the long run they'll almost certainly do more good than harm?" God asked.

"Even so," Martha said. "I'm afraid the time might come when I won't be able to stand knowing that I'm the one who caused not only the harm, but the end of the only career I've ever cared about. I'm afraid knowing all that might drive me out of my mind someday." She stepped away from God, and already God seemed to be fading, becoming translucent, transparent, gone.

"I want to forget," Martha said, and she stood alone in her living room, looking blankly past the open drapes of her front window at the surface of Lake Washington and the mist that hung above it. She wondered at the words she had just spoken, wondered what it was she wanted so badly to forget.

THE VITA ÆTERNA MIRROR COMPANY
MIRRORS TO LAST TILL KINGDOM COME

YANN MARTEL

I remember how I met
my husband. My dear,
sweet husband. It was
the summer of 1928.
I was sixteen and I was
dressed in white. I was also
wearing a straw hat, only
it was too small and
I was always losing it
in the wind. This was
in Grande-Rivière.
I was staying with
Father Bouillon for a
few weeks during the
summer. I was
standing on the veranda,
considering whether
I should go for a walk
with this too-small hat
and always have to keep
my hand on my head to
hold it down, or fetch
another hat that fit me
perfectly but didn't go
as well with my dress.
I was standing on the

veranda, thinking about
it, when a car with two
men stalled just in front
of the house, maybe fifty
feet away. The driver,
a doctor, got out.
I knew he was a doctor
because his car had the
special licence plate that
doctors had in those days.
He opened the hood, leaned
in and did I don't know
what. He seemed in a
hurry. The other man
didn't help; he just sat
in the car, listless.
I found out later that my
future husband was
driving him to the
hospital. He fiddled
about with the engine
for a minute or two and
then fetched the crank.
He turned the crank
and the engine started
up. He hurried back into
the car. I watched this
scene without moving or
saying a word. He didn't
see me, the doctor. The
other man did. The car
disappeared down the
road and then the wind
blew my hat away. I

THE SECRET HISTORY OF FANTASY

blah-blah-blah-blah-
blah-blah-blah-blah-
blah-blah-blah-blah-
blah-blah-blah-blah-
blah-blah-blah-blah-
blah-blah-blah-blah-
blah-blah-blah-blah-
blah-blah-blah-blah-
blah-blah-blah-blah-
blah-blah-blah-blah-
blah-blah-blah-blah-
blah-blah-blah-blah-
blah-blah-blah-blah-
blah-blah-blah-blah-

Man, she can go on.

And always the same
stories.

My head will explode
soon.

blah-blah-blah-blah-
blah-blah-blah-blah-
blah-blah-blah-blah-
blah-blah-blah-blah-
blah-blah-blah-blah-
blah-blah-blah-blah-
blah-blah-blah-blah-
blah-blah-blah-blah-
blah-blah-blah-blah-
blah-blah-blah-blah-

(Meanwhile, the machine was chugging away industriously. I put my hand on it. I could feel vibrations.)

blah-blah-blah-blah-
next day, a bright sunny
day, I was walking back
home from the post office
when I saw the very
same car coming towards

me. The sun was behind
me, in the doctor's eyes.
His car didn't have
visors, so he was wearing
a long cap. As the car
came closer, I could see
something written on
it. SEARCHING FOR
A BRIDE, it said in
bright red letters. He
was a bachelor, of course.
He told me later that the
cap was a gift from a
friend. And so, squinting
at the road ahead, as if
actually searching for a
bride at that very
moment, he drove by.
Without seeing me, once
again. He was so
charmingly distracted
sometimes. Once he
blah-blah-blah-blah-
blah-blah-blah-blah-
blah-blah-blah-blah-
blah-blah-blah-blah-
blah-blah-blah-blah-

(I was visiting my grandmother and I had found this machine in the
basement. It looked at first like nothing more than a wooden box.)

blah-blah-blah-blah-
blah-blah-blah-blah-
blah-blah-blah-blah-

THE SECRET HISTORY OF FANTASY

(More junk, more debris, I thought.)

blah-blah-blah-blah-
blah-blah-blah-blah-
blah-blah-blah-blah-
blah-blah-blah-blah-
blah-blah-blah-blah-
blah-blah-blah-blah-

(My grandmother, you see, clings to her possessions. She throws away nothing. Everything has value. As a young wife she lived through the Great Depression, and shortly after the war her husband died, leaving her alone to raise four children. She suffered through loss, loneliness, poverty, tough times. By dint of hard work, multiple jobs, careful investments and frugality, she managed to raise her children — with great success, in fact: she produced a journalist, a physician, a diplomat poet and a cloistered Benedictine nun. But she can't forget the price of every success along her difficult road. Having known the word "want" for too long, she cannot understand its antonym, "enough." She's like that gold prospector in the Jack London tale who, months after being rescued from starvation, still hoards nuts, biscuits, tinned food and dried fish in his pockets and in every nook and cranny of his room.)

blah-blah-blah-blah-
blah-blah-blah-blah-
carrying a tray with
cups and cookies.
And who should I see
standing squarely in
the living room — I can
still see him perfectly!
Standing so straight.
Looking out with his
kind face and beautiful

eyes. It was Doctor
"Searching for a Bride."
He smiled at me and
I at him. Father Bouillon
had invited the new
doctor in town, telling
him his house was full
of pretty girls. We spoke
a little that day, the
doctor and I, and some
more in the next two
weeks each time he came
by. He was so earnest
and attentive. Later he
told me that on that very
first day, as he was
leaving, he whispered to
Father Bouillon, "There's
my wife." I thought he
blah-blah-blah-blah-
blah-blah-blah-blah-

(I made to push the box aside. It wasn't what I was looking for. I was looking for my grandmother's snowshoe moccasins. I was on all fours in the
basement, buried in the cold closet where she keeps her coats. She wanted
to go snowshoeing. But the box was unexpectedly heavy, a good fifteen
pounds. And it was attractively made of burnished walnut wood.)

blah-blah-blah-blah-
blah-blah-blah-blah-
blah-blah-blah-blah-

(I was curious, so I pulled the box out. It was about fifteen inches wide,
twelve inches deep and eight inches high. And it was not a box: it did

not open. It was rather some sort of mechanical device. A half-inch slit ran the length of one of the long sides, near the bottom. It had lips of red velvet that revealed, when pulled back, a series of ten or so rollers. Clearly, some thing, some product, came in or out this way. Above this slit, towards the left and embedded in the wood, was a thermometer-like tube with two gradations marked in red, MAX near the top and MIN near the bottom. On the side of the device opposite these two features was a door with a tiny brass doorknob that opened horizontally. The words HIGH-GRADE WHITE SAND ONLY were inscribed on this door, and it opened with a click. It had rounded panels on each side. On one of these I could read the sentence DO NOT FILL OVER THIS LINE. I peered into the cavity that the open door revealed, but could see nothing. I closed the door. On the machine's top side were three holes and a plaque: a small hole near the edge, level with the thermometer-like tube, with the words HIGH-GRADE LIQUID SILVER ONLY inscribed around it; another hole in the opposite corner, this one surrounded by the words HIGH-GRADE OIL ONLY; and, finally, a third, larger, cork-stopped hole midway along one of the sides. The oblong plaque, neatly affixed with golden nails, was in the centre. THE VITA ÆTERNA MIRROR COMPANY, PORT HOPE, ONTARIO, it said. MIRRORS TO LAST TILL KINGDOM COME.)

blah-blah-blah-blah-
blah-blah-blah-blah-
blah-blah-blah-blah-
blah-blah-blah-blah-

("Have you found them? Must I come down?" came a voice of vexed curiosity from above.

"Not yet. A minute more," I replied. I entered the closet again. Among quantities of shoes, boots, slippers and sneakers, I found the snowshoe moccasins. And near where the machine had been, I came upon a grey felt bag with the Vita Æterna Mirror Company logo on it. I brought it out. Replacing disturbed footwear and displaced coat hangers with the care of an archaeologist, I closed the closet door, gathered up the results of my dig and made my way upstairs.)

blah-blah-blah-blah-
blah-blah-blah-blah-
blah-blah-blah-blah-
blah-blah-blah-blah-
blah-blah-blah-blah-

(She was waiting for me at the top of the stairs. She is a woman in her early eighties. Vain in a dignified way, she dresses well, invariably in one shade or another of purple, her favourite colour. Except for a few of the normal indignities of old age — cataracts (operated on), some arthritis, a certain physical sagging — she is in perfect health. Because she saves up all the conversation she can't have when she's alone and lonely, she talks nonstop. She listens, but sometimes not really; sometimes one's words are like a menu from which she'll choose a word or phrase that will set her off. Her beliefs are solid and well constructed, nearly impregnable, and her ways, though not intolerant, are nonetheless fixed. Great Questions do not disturb her any more; her questions now are well within the limits of the Great Answers that have brought her comfort throughout her life. She loves me, for sure, but with the bias of her age. My lack of religiousness saddens her, and my existential hesitations (as exemplified by the fact that I'm considerably closer to thirty than to twenty yet have never held down a real, steady job, bungled my university studies, have accomplished precious little in my life) make her impatient because she can't understand them. She thinks I'm lost. We are meant to stand firm like a house, she tells me, not to be tossed about like a ship. To her, the world is a place run by God where goodness and hard work are ultimately rewarded and evil and sloth are ultimately punished. She is a poor loser at cards — worse than I — and she cheats. My grandmother loves me and I love my grandmother — which doesn't mean that we always get along.)

blah-blah-blah-blah-

THE SECRET HISTORY OF FANTASY

blah-blah-blah-blah-
blah-blah-blah-blah-
blah-blah-blah-blah-
blah-blah-blah-blah-
blah-blah-blah-blah-
blah-blah-blah-blah-

("What's this?" she asked.

"That was my question," I said.

"Oh my," she exclaimed when she had a closer look. Her voice changed. "That old thing. I'd forgotten we still had it." She ran her fingers along it.)

blah-blah-blah-blah-
blah-blah-blah-blah-
blah-blah-blah-blah-
blah-blah-blah-blah-

(I looked about her lair. I will just mention that my grandmother's house is cluttered with furniture that clashes in style; that she owns no complete set of dishware or kitchenware or bedsheets or towels, only the surviving veterans of six decades of housekeeping; that she is well supplied in religious paraphernalia (the crucifix over the front door, the lithographs of the Virgin Mary and of Jesus on the walls, the tourist-shop foreign icons resting on the mantelpiece, the rosary of large wooden beads hanging from the back of a door, the framed colour photos of the Pope, etc.); that after her children moved out she embarked on organized world travels from which she brought home the bric-a-brac of the world (an ouzo-bottle lamp, pseudo-antique Greek vases, Easter Island-like sculptures, African masks, a Swiss cuckoo clock, a huge Pacific shell, a Tunisian birdcage, purple Russian dolls, Chinese china, etc.); that she likes fishing and gardening and owns all one might need to pursue those activities — and there is much, much more. Cubic metres. An ample etcetera of goods, chattels and knick-knacks. My grandmother has a sort of Midas touch: every object she touches becomes eternal. And did I mention that her house is tiny and she owns a piano?)

blah-blah-blah-blah-
blah-blah-blah-blah-
blah-blah-blah-blah-

(I brought the machine to the kitchen table and set the moccasins on the floor.

"So, what is it?" I asked.

"It's an old appliance. It's a mirror machine."

As she said this, she nodded towards the living room, at the large mirror above the fireplace. I looked at it.)

blah-blah-blah-blah-
blah-blah-blah-blah-

(In the reflected rectangle I could see the rounded shoulders and white mane of an old woman and the serious expression of a young man.)

blah-blah-blah-blah-
blah-blah-blah-blah-

("What's a mirror machine?"

"It's a machine that makes mirrors. That's how we used to make mirrors when I was a girl."

I had never heard of such a thing. "Does it still work?"

"I don't see why not. Let's see…"

She sat down and with her twisted fingers she opened the felt bag. I sat down beside her. She pulled out a grey plastic bottle. LIQUID SILVER, said the silver letters on it. She twisted the cap off, turned the bottle upside down, and placed the nozzle into the hole for silver atop the machine. But as she squeezed the bottle, the nozzle jumped and a heavy, round drop formed on the wood.)

blah-blah-blah-blah-
blah-blah-blah-blah-

("Here, I'll do it," I said.

The bottle, for its size, was remarkably heavy. I looked closely at the drop of silver. I teased its tense surface with the nozzle, squeezed the bottle, increasing the size of the drop, then let go, sucking it back into the bottle.)

blah-blah-blah-blah-
blah-blah-blah-blah-

("Good," said my grandmother. "Silver is expensive.")

blah-blah-blah-blah-
blah-blah-blah-blah-

(I fitted the nozzle into the hole and squeezed the bottle. A column of silver appeared at the bottom of the tube. I let it rise. When it was half-way between the MIN and MAX marks, my grandmother said, "That's enough." I squeezed a second longer and stopped.)

blah-blah-blah-blah-
blah-blah-blah-blah-

(Next she brought out of the bag a small bottle of oil and some sand. The sand was in a black, yellow and white cardboard carton. It had a drawing of a black man on a beach. He had a wide, colonized-and-happy-about-it grin on his face and wore a straw hat and clothes that were studiously tattered. NOVAK'S FINE JAMAICAN WHITE, announced the sky above him. In smaller, ornate letters around a barely decipherable coat of arms were the words "Purveyors of Fine White Sand to His Majesty's Household.")

blah-blah-blah-blah-

blah-blah-blah-blah-
blah-blah-blah-blah-
blah-blah-blah-blah-
blah-blah-blah-blah-

("Some people would use cheap sand, sand from around here," said my grandmother. "But it makes for smoky mirrors. The best sand comes from the Caribbean.")

blah-blah-blah-blah-
blah-blah-blah-blah-
blah-blah-blah-blah-
blah-blah-blah-blah-
blah-blah-blah-blah-
blah-blah-blah-blah-

(While she poured sand through the small door, I squirted oil into the machine.)

blah-blah-blah-blah-
blah-blah-blah-blah-
blah-blah-blah-blah-
blah-blah-blah-blah-

(My grandmother sighed. "It must be fifty years since I last used this machine. Even in my time it was old and out of fashion. Now it's so much easier. You just go to a hardware store and buy an industrially manufactured, clear mirror any size or shape you want."

She paused. She was staring into midair. Her lips trembled.

"Ohhhhh, your grandfather used to rage against this machine. He who was normally such a patient man. He would jump up and want to rush out and buy a mirror that very minute. 'But we can't afford it,' I would tell him. 'We don't have the money. And the machine was given to us. We might as well use it.' He would fume. But we really didn't have the money. What do you expect? He wasn't a money man. He would often treat his patients for nothing, would even buy them the pills he prescribed them when they couldn't afford them. 'Go, go for a walk, go rest, go read. I'll finish,' I'd tell him. 'Away you go!' But he would just look at me with his oh-so-beautiful eyes. Then he'd sit down beside me again and we would go on together."

She sighed tremulously.

"The long, patient hours we spent on this machine. I cannot count them." She swallowed. Her eyes were red.)

blah-blah-blah-blah-
blah-blah-blah-blah-

(On any other day I would have jostled her reminiscing aside and bluntly asked her how this contraption worked, but that day, for no particular reason, I let her come round in her slow, anecdotal way. I eyed the fireplace mirror again. I had noticed before that it wasn't perfect. None of her mirrors were perfect. They all had ridges that distorted the reflection, and various stains and marks. But I had ascribed these defects to age, not to handicraft origin.)

blah-blah-blah-blah-
blah-blah-blah-blah-

(She rubbed her face with her hands. She looked at the machine. "I wonder if it still works," she said quietly.)

blah-blah-blah-blah-
blah-blah-blah-blah-
blah-blah-blah-blah-

(She extracted from the bag the most amazing thing. It was a horn. Like for a gramophone, only smaller. The narrow end fitted into a short, shiny brass tube with screw threads. The other end curved and flared out, with the edges looking like the petals of a flower. In all decency it should have been made of plastic, but it was genuine, politically incorrect ivory, creamy white and cool and streaked with very fine black veins. It had intricate arabesque decorations on the outside, and lines that spiralled downwards on the inside. My grandmother pulled the cork from the third hole atop the machine and screwed in the horn. It could easily be rotated 360 degrees.)

blah-blah-blah-blah-
blah-blah-blah-blah-
blah-blah-blah-blah-

(The device was now fully assembled. It looked old-fashioned, peculiar and beautiful.)

blah-blah-blah-blah-
blah-blah-blah-blah-
blah-blah-blah-blah-

(Just before I could ask how it worked, she sighed.)

blah-blah-blah-blah-
blah-blah-blah-blah-
blah-blah-blah-blah-
blah-blah-blah-blah-

("Such a good man he was. I thank the Lord every day for having put that man in my way. He took him away from me after twenty-two years of bliss, but even if I had to go through that pain ten times over, those twenty-two years would still be worth it.")

blah-blah-blah-blah-
blah-blah-blah-blah-
blah-blah-blah-blah-

THE SECRET HISTORY OF FANTASY

blah-blah-blah-blah-
blah-blah-blah-blah-

(This was not the first time I was hearing about my grandfather. He had died of cancer of the pancreas long before I was born, and ever since I can remember he has been held up to me as the very font of goodness. He was a kind and considerate man, a devoted husband, a good father, an excellent doctor, a man of wit and culture, a lover of nature; he was wise, thoughtful, generous, sensible, decent, rational, discreet, judicious, level-headed, sober, modest, steady, virtuous; he was totally exempt from the common sins of envy, laziness, mendacity, fondness for the bottle, lechery, tardiness; he was never known to be evil-tempered, pompous, capricious, rude; and he was the possessor of magical blue eyes — they were a beacon of his goodness — of which mine were only washed-out, watered-down imitations.)

blah-blah-blah-blah-
blah-blah-blah-blah-

(For me, the man exists only in black-and-white photographs, so I cannot verify any of his attributes myself, not even the blueness of his eyes. He is a short, slightly plump man with a balding head and an oval face. He has a tiny moustache. He is neither handsome nor ugly. His other qualities are a mystery. I have often tried to extract a personality from these prints, to imagine the man beyond the frozen frames. He does look plausibly kind; perhaps a kind man of no great ambition, amply content to live his life out quietly with his family. Shy. A quiet voice, I'd think.)

blah-blah-blah-blah-
blah-blah-blah-blah-

("So how does it work?" I put in, taking advantage of a pause.
    "It runs on memories."
    "Sorry?"

"I said it runs on memories. On recollections, souvenirs, stories. The past."

She suffered a sudden fit of coquetry and started arranging her hair with her fingers. She cleared her throat.)

blah-blah-blah-blah-
blah-blah-blah-blah-

(Memories?)

blah-blah-blah-blah-
blah-blah-blah-blah-
blah-blah-blah-blah-
blah-blah-blah-blah-
blah-blah-blah-blah-
blah-blah-blah-blah-
blah-blah-blah-blah-

(She brought her mouth close to the horn. "I," she said clearly, "I remember…")

blah-blah-blah-blah-
blah-blah-blah-blah-
blah-blah-blah-blah-

(A sharp click sound. Followed by the strangest little noise, something like a tiny locomotive starting up. And unmistakably coming from within the machine.)

blah-blah-blah-blah-
blah-blah-blah-blah-
blah-blah-blah-blah-

("It still works!" she said, bringing her hands to her mouth. "Oh dear, oh dear.")

blah-blah-blah-blah-
blah-blah-blah-blah-

(That's when she started.)

blah-blah-blah-blah-
blah-blah-blah-blah-
blah-blah-blah-blah-
blah-blah-blah-blah-
blah-blah-blah-blah-
blah-blah-blah-blah-
blah-blah-blah-blah-
blah-blah-blah-blah-
blah-blah-blah-blah-

("I remember how I met my husband. My dear, sweet husband. It was
the summer of 1928. I was sixteen and I was dressed in white. I was also
wearing a straw hat, only it was too small and I was always losing it in
the wind. This was in…")

blah-blah-blah-blah-
blah-blah-blah-blah-
blah-blah-blah-blah-
on the day he returned
home to Levis, he asked
me if he could write to me
and would I answer back.
I've kept all his letters.
Thirty-seven in a little
over a month. In the
thirty-seventh he

informed me that he was
driving down to ask for
my hand. He bought a
brand new suit just for
the occasion, and he
washed and waxed the
car. He brought Father
Bouillon along for moral
support and as a
character witness for my
parents. It was a Saturday
in early September. We
agreed to meet by the
church. I saw the car
drive up. We were both
so nervous. While
Father Bouillon
wandered off for a few
minutes, my husband, a
man of thirty but as shy
as I was, asked for my hand
in marriage. He wanted to
kiss me — and I wouldn't
have stopped him — but
there were people
walking by. I ran all the
way home and, while a
suitable hour went by, I
sat on my bed, unable to
read a line in my book,
bursting with happiness,
that Yes! Yes! Yes!
ringing in my heart. He
came at exactly four, my

handsome knight, and
Father Bouillon, who
had already mentioned
several times in glowing
terms this doctor friend
of his in letters to my
parents, spoke far too
much for a priest and
all went well. The next
spring I was seventeen
and a doctor's wife, and
six months later I was a
woman. For six months
the good man did not
touch me. Such a caring,
respectful, tender man.
What luck I had, what
a blessing he was.
I could never have found
a better man. I thank
the Lord every day for
His gift. I've had many
men propose to me since
he passed away, but no
one could replace my
sweetheart, no one. Oh
Lord, I have su-su-
suffered so much!"

She's crying.

(Far from slowing down or stopping at this interruption, the machine,
with a click and a clack, kicked into even higher gear.)

"As he was dying, he told me,
'At least I die knowing that
our children have a good
mother.' I worked myself to
the bone to bring them up
so their father would be
proud of them. It wasn't
easy, God knows. In those
days, a widow with four
children. But I managed.
I did what I had to do.
And their father would be
proud of them! They are
good children. They made
their sacrifices, too.
His example was a
blah-blah-blah-blah-
blah-blah-blah-blah-
blah-blah-blah-blah-
blah-blah-blah-blah-
blah-blah-blah-blah-
blah-blah-blah-blah-
blah-blah-blah-blah-
blah-blah-blah-blah-
blah-blah-blah-blah-
blah-blah-blah-blah-   This woman.
blah-blah-blah-blah-
blah-blah-blah-blah-
blah-blah-blah-blah-
blah-blah-blah-blah-
blah-blah-blah-blah-   Soft, white, wrinkled
blah-blah-blah-blah-   face. Green eyes but red
blah-blah-blah-blah-   this moment. An
blah-blah-blah-blah-   exasperatingly familiar

blah-blah-blah-blah-
blah-blah-blah-blah-
blah-blah-blah-blah-
blah-blah-blah-blah-
blah-blah-blah-blah-
blah-blah-blah-blah-
blah-blah-blah-blah-
blah-blah-blah-blah-
blah-blah-blah-blah-
blah-blah-blah-blah-
blah-blah-blah-blah-
blah-blah-blah-blah-
blah-blah-blah-blah-
blah-blah-blah-blah-
blah-blah-blah-blah-
blah-blah-blah-blah-
blah-blah-blah-blah-
blah-blah-blah-blah-
blah-blah-blah-blah-
blah-blah-blah-blah-
blah-blah-blah-blah-
blah-blah-blah-blah-
blah-blah-blah-blah-
blah-blah-blah-blah-
will you, my child?"

"Are you deaf? I said,
Get me the photo
albums, please."

face I have known since I
can remember. With
pouts, stares and glares
that are beyond the
description of words but
that all of us in the
family know all too well.
A woman who has
always been in my life.

But not for much longer,
I suppose.

And what will be left of
her?

Her things. This mountain
of junk.
I hate all — eh?

"I'm sorry?"

"Yes, right away."

(They are in a bookshelf near the piano. Volume after volume. The oldest ones have wooden covers bound with string and pages of soft, heavy black paper; the others are the standard modern type, with adhesive pages and clear plastic jackets. I brought over five volumes.)

"Thank you. Let's see...
There he is! This is
blah-blah-blah-blah-
blah-blah-blah-blah-
blah-blah-blah-blah-

(Pictures of the mystery man. A medical-school graduation portrait.)

blah-blah-blah-blah-
blah-blah-blah-blah-   I hate all her junk. Gives
blah-blah-blah-blah-   me claustrophobia.
blah-blah-blah-blah-

(Sitting at the dining-room table in this house, looking at the camera.)

blah-blah-blah-blah-
blah-blah-blah-blah-   A crossed electrical wire
blah-blah-blah-blah-   would do it.
blah-blah-blah-blah-

(On a path in a wood, a cane in his right hand.)

blah-blah-blah-blah-
blah-blah-blah-blah-   Just a little fire to tidy
blah-blah-blah-blah-   things up while she's
blah-blah-blah-blah-   out.

(On the rocky shores of the St. Lawrence, his hair blown across his forehead by the wind.)

blah-blah-blah-blah-
blah-blah-blah-blah-   I won't lead my life this
blah-blah-blah-blah-   way, that's for sure.
blah-blah-blah-blah-
blah-blah-blah-blah-

(At the stern of a rowboat. A young woman, my grandmother, at the bow.)

blah-blah-blah-blah-
blah-blah-blah-blah-   Happiness doesn't come in dry
blah-blah-blah-blah-   in dry goods of varying
blah-blah-blah-blah-   sizes. Happiness isn't a
blah-blah-blah-blah-   product.

(Sitting in a garden chair, with his arms around two of his boys, one my father, a child of seven.)

blah-blah-blah-blah-
blah-blah-blah-blah-   I won't exist through
blah-blah-blah-blah-   objects. Objects leave
blah-blah-blah-blah-   me cold.

(With all his children, in front of a tent.)

blah-blah-blah-blah-
blah-blah-blah-blah-   Let beautiful things live
blah-blah-blah-blah-   in museums. Or in
blah-blah-blah-blah-   nature.

(Sitting in a sun-splashed landscape of snow, my grandmother with a radiant smile.)

blah-blah-blah-blah-
blah-blah-blah-blah-

blah-blah-blah-blah-
blah-blah-blah-blah-
blah-blah-blah-blah-
blah-blah-blah-blah-
blah-blah-blah-blah-
blah-blah-blah-blah-

I'm more preoccupied
with furnishing my head
than the place where I
live. The most beautiful
rooms I have entered
have been empty ones.

(A frontal portrait done some weeks before his death.)

blah-blah-blah-blah-
blah-blah-blah-blah-
blah-blah-blah-blah-
blah-blah-blah-blah-
blah-blah-blah-blah-
blah-blah-blah-blah-
blah-blah-blah-blah-
blah-blah-blah-blah-
blah-blah-blah-blah-

Warehouses full of light
and dust.
Empty attics with a view.
Coastlines.
Prairies.

(Reclining in an easy chair, covered with a blanket, asleep; the beginning of his illness?)

blah-blah-blah-blah-
blah-blah-blah-blah-
blah-blah-blah-blah-
blah-blah-blah-blah-
blah-blah-blah-blah-

All places where my
bare, fertile humanity
has been most evident
to me.

(Sitting on a bench, looking away.)

blah-blah-blah-blah-
blah-blah-blah-blah-
blah-blah-blah-blah-
blah-blah-blah-blah-

"Blessed are the poor in
spirit." Indeed. Blessed
in spirit are the

THE SECRET HISTORY OF FANTASY

blah-blah-blah-blah-   materially poor.

(Group photo. Second from left.)

blah-blah-blah-blah-
blah-blah-blah-blah-   I don't want the
blah-blah-blah-blah-   captivity of ownership.
blah-blah-blah-blah-   I want nothing but the
blah-blah-blah-blah-   human, nothing else.
blah-blah-blah-blah-
blah-blah-blah-blah-
blah-blah-blah-blah-
blah-blah-blah-blah-

(Full-length, standing, looking at the camera, background indistinct, hands in pockets of jacket except for thumbs.)

blah-blah-blah-blah-
blah-blah-blah-blah-
And then he died. Oh,
it breaks my heart!"

                                          She's crying again.

(Full throttle, actually trembling with activity.)

"Why, dear Lord? Of all
people on this earth, why
my sweetheart? I don't
doubt Your all-seeing
wisdom, but why my
sweetheart? I loved that
man with all my being.
I was happy with him

for twenty-two years. For
twenty-two years it was a
pleasure to go to bed at
night, it was a pleasure to
wake up in the morning, it
was a pleasure to go about
my day. And then, then, this
unimaginable ending?
How did I survive?
I didn't. A part of me
died that day that has
never come back to life.
To my dying day I will
blah-blah-blah-blah-
blah-blah-blah-blah-
blah-blah-blah-blah-
blah-blah-blah-blah-
blah-blah-blah-blah-
blah-blah-blah-blah-
blah-blah-blah-blah-
blah-blah-blah-blah-
blah-blah-blah-blah-
blah-blah-blah-blah-
blah-blah-blah-blah-
blah-blah-blah-blah-
blah-blah-blah-blah-
blah-blah-blah-blah-
blah-blah-blah-blah-
blah-blah-blah-blah-   I want nothing but the
blah-blah-blah-blah-   human, nothing else.
blah-blah-blah-blah-
blah-blah-blah-blah-
blah-blah-blah-blah-

blah-blah **THE END!"**   Eh?

(The ending was abrupt. She shouted her last two words. The machine stopped with a sharp click. A low blowing sound started.

"Is that it?" I asked.

"It should be long enough," she replied.

There was a high-pitched, grinding squeal. After a minute or so, it stopped. I heard a rolling metallic sound. Something was pushed through the machine's red velvet lips and plopped onto the table.

My eyes beheld a small elliptical mirror.

"There we go," said my grandmother. She held it up and looked at herself, satisfied. "Good. No blemishes. Sometimes, for larger mirrors, you get blemishes, especially near the corners. And you have to talk for such a long time and the pieces don't always fit together perfectly. But for pocket mirrors, it does a good job."

I took hold of the mirror. It was quite warm. The back was a grey, leaden colour. I looked at my reflection.

Something caught my eye. I looked closely, angling the mirror in the light.

"It'll go away," she said. "As soon as the mirror is perfectly dry."

She was referring to the lines of print. The silver surface of the mirror was made of layer upon layer of lines of print, neatly criss-crossing at right angles.)

(I'm something of an expert on the subject now. There are generally two places in old mirrors where it is possible, with the help of a magnifying glass, to detect the lines of print: on the very edges, where the silver is thinnest; and, especially, in the stains, where oxidation sometimes brings out the print. Twice I have even managed to decipher words. The first time was in a New York antique store. I was able to tell the storekeeper that a simple but pleasing hand-mirror was the work of a German-speaker. In the middle of a stain I had made out the words "ganz allein." The second time was on a subsequent visit to my grandmother. On the edge of her bedroom mirror I was able to read the syllables "ortneuf." I had no idea what word they came from until I asked her. "St-Raymond-de-Portneuf," she replied. This is how I found out where my grandfather was born.

Modern mirrors are of no interest. They are indeed industrially manufactured — and clear, totally clear. There's nothing to be seen in them.)

(A late twentieth-century animist, that's what she was. Every object in her house was infused with an indwelling psyche that spoke to her of somebody or something from her long life. Her possessions were inter-mediaries with the deceased eternal. My grandmother lived alone in her village on the south shore of the St. Lawrence, but in fact her small house was a bustling metropolis of spirits.)

(She gave me the mirror. I still have difficulty with ownership — the apartment where I live is bare, I have few clothes, I own very little — but this pocket mirror is a prized possession. I often take it out and look at it and try to imagine all the words I so stupidly ignored.)

THE SECRET HISTORY OF FANTASY

SLEIGHT OF HAND

PETER S. BEAGLE

SHE HAD NO idea where she was going. When she needed to sleep she stopped at the first motel; when the Buick's gas gauge dropped into the red zone she filled the tank, and sometimes bought a sandwich or orange juice at the attached convenience store. Now and then during one of these stops she spoke with someone who was neither a desk clerk nor a gas-station attendant, but she forgot all such conversations within minutes, as she forgot everything but the words of the young policeman who had come to her door on a pleasant Wednesday afternoon, weeks and worlds ago. Nothing had moved in her since that point except the memory of his shakily sympathetic voice, telling her that her husband and daughter were dead: ashes in a smoking, twisted, unrecognizable ruin, because, six blocks from their home, a drowsy adolescent had mistaken his accelerator for his brake pedal.

There had been a funeral — she was present, but not there — and more police, and some lawyer; and Alan's sister managing it all, as always, and for once she was truly grateful to the interfering bitch. But that was all far away too, both the gratitude and the old detestation, made nothing by the momentary droop of a boy's eyelids. The nothing got her snugly through the days after the funeral, dealing with each of the endless phone calls, sitting down to answer every condolence card and e-mail, informing Social Security and CREF of Alan's death, going with three of his graduate students to clean out his office, and attending the memorial on campus, which was very tasteful and genuinely moving, or so the nothing was told. She was glad to hear it.

The nothing served her well until the day Alan's daughter by his first marriage came to collect a few of his possessions as keepsakes. She was a perfectly nice girl, who had always been properly courteous in an interloper's presence, and her sympathy was undoubtedly as real as good manners could make it; but when she had gone, bearing a single brown paper grocery bag of photographs and books, the nothing stepped aside for the meltdown.

Her brother-in-law calmed her, spoke rationally, soothed her out of genuine kindness and concern. But that same night, speaking to no one, empty and methodical, she had watched herself pack a small suitcase and carry it out to Alan's big old Buick in the garage, then go back into the house to leave her cell phone and charger on Alan's desk, along with a four-word note for her sister-in-law that read *Out for a drive*. After that she had backed the Buick into the street and headed away without another look at the house where she used to live, once upon a time.

The only reason she went north was that the first freeway on-ramp she came to pointed her in that direction. After that she did not drive straight through, because there was no *through* to aim for. With no destination but away, without any conscious plan except to keep moving, she left and returned to the flat ribbon of the interstate at random intervals, sometimes wandering side roads and backroads for hours, detouring to nowhere. Aimless, mindless, not even much aware of pain — that too having become part of the nothing — she slogged onward. She fell asleep quickly when she stopped, but never for long, and was usually on her way in darkness, often with the moon still high. Now and then she whistled thinly between her teeth.

The weather was warm, though there was still snow in some of the higher passes she traversed. Although she had started near the coast, that was several states ago: now only the mountains were constant. The Buick fled lightly over them, gulping fuel with abandon but cornering like a deer, very nearly operating and guiding itself. This was necessary, since only a part of her was behind the wheel; the rest was away with Alan, watching their daughter building a sandcastle, prowling a bookshop with him, reaching for his hand on a strange street, knowing without turning her head that it would be there. At times she was so busy talking to him that she was slow to switch on the headlights, even long after sunset. But the car took care of her, as she knew it would. It was Alan's car, after all.

From time to time the Buick would show a disposition to wander toward the right shoulder of the road, or drift left into the oncoming lane, and she would observe the tendency with vague, detached interest. Once she asked aloud, "Is this what you want? I'm leaving it to you — are you taking me to Alan?" But somehow, whether under her guidance or its own, the old car always righted itself, and they went on together.

The latest road began to descend, and then to flatten out into farm and orchard country, passing the occasional township, most of them overgrown crossroads. She had driven for much of the previous night, and all of today, and knew with one distant part of herself that it would soon be necessary to stop. In early twilight, less than an hour later, she came to the next town. There was a river winding through it, gray and silver in the dusk, with bridges.

Parking and registering at the first motel with a *Vacancy* sign, she walked three blocks to the closest restaurant, which, from the street, looked like a bar with a 1950s-style diner attached. Inside, however, it proved larger than she had expected, with slightly less than half of the booths and tables occupied. Directly to the left of the *Please Wait To Be Served* sign hung a poster showing a photograph of a lean, hawk-nosed man in late middle age, with white hair and thick eyebrows, wearing evening dress: tailcoat, black bowtie, top hat. He was smiling slightly and fanning a deck of playing cards between long, neat fingers. There was no name under the picture; the caption read only *DINNER MAGIC.* She looked at it until the young waitress came to show her to her booth.

After ordering her meal — the first she had actually sat down to since leaving home — she asked the waitress about Dinner Magic. Her own voice sounded strange in her ears, and language itself came hard and hesitantly. The girl shrugged. "He's not full time — just comes in now and then, does a couple of nights and gone again. Started a couple of weeks ago. Haven't exchanged two words with him. Other than my boss, I don't know anybody who has."

Turning away toward the kitchen, she added over her shoulder, "He's good, though. Stay for the show, if you can."

In fact, the Dinner Magic performance began before most of the current customers had finished eating. There was no stage, no musical flourish or formal introduction: the man in evening dress simply walked out from the kitchen onto the floor, bowed briefly to the diners, then tossed a gauzy multicolored scarf into the air. He seized it again as it fluttered down, then held it up in front of himself, hiding him from silk hat to patent-leather shoes...

...and vanished, leaving his audience too stunned to respond. The applause began a moment later, when he strolled in through the restaurant's front door.

Facing the audience once more, the magician spoke for the first time. His voice was deep and clear, with a certain engaging roughness in the lower range. "Ladies, gentlemen, Dinner Magic means exactly what it sounds like. You are not required to pay attention to me for a moment, you are free to concentrate on your coffee and pie — which is excellent, by the way, especially the lemon meringue — or on your companion, which I recommend even more than the meringue. Think of me, if you will, as the old man next door who stays up all night practicing his silly magic tricks. Because that, under this low-rent monkey suit, is exactly what I am. Now then."

He was tall, and older than the photograph had suggested — how old, she could not tell, but there were lines on his cheeks and under his angled eyes that must have been removed from the picture; the sort of thing she had seen Alan do on the computer. From her booth, she watched, chin on her fist, never taking her eyes from the man as he ran through a succession of tricks that bordered on the miraculous even as his associated patter never transcended a lounge act. Without elephants or tigers, without a spangled, long-legged assistant, he worked the room. Using his slim black wand like a fishing rod he reeled laughing diners out of their seats. Holding it lightly between his fingertips, like a conductor's baton or a single knitting needle, he caused the napkins at every table to lift off in a whispering storm of thin cotton, whirl wildly around the room, and then settle docilely back where they belonged. He identified several members of his audience by name, address, profession, marital status, and, as an afterthought, by driver's license state and number. She was never one of these; indeed, the magician seemed to be consciously avoiding eye contact with her altogether. Nevertheless, she was more intrigued — more *awakened* — than she had meant to let herself be, and she ordered a second cup of coffee and sat quite still where she was.

Finishing at last with an offhanded gesture, a bit like an old-fashioned jump shot, which set all the silverware on all the tables chiming applause, the magician walked off without bowing, as abruptly as he had entered. The waitress brought her check, but she remained in her booth even after the busboy cleared away her dishes. Many of the other diners lingered as she did, chattering and marveling and calling for encores. But the man did not return.

The street was dark, and the restaurant no more than a quarter full, when she finally recollected both herself and her journey, and stepped out into the warm, humid night. For a moment she could not call to mind where she had parked her car; then she remembered the motel and started in that direction. She felt strangely refreshed, and was seriously considering the prospect of giving up her room and beginning to drive again. But after walking several blocks she decided that she must have somehow gone in the wrong direction, for there was no motel sign in sight, nor any landmark casually noted on her way to the restaurant. She turned and turned again, making tentative casts this way and that, even starting back the way she had come, but nothing looked at all familiar.

Puzzlement had given way to unease when she saw the magician ahead of her, under a corner streetlamp. There was no mistaking him, despite his having changed from evening clothes into ordinary dress. His lean-ness gave him the air of a shadow, rather than a man: a shadow with lined cheeks and long bright eyes. As she approached, he spoke her name. He said, "I have been waiting for you." He spoke more slowly than he had when performing, with a tinge of an accent that she had not noticed.

Anxiety fled on the instant, replaced by a curious stillness, as when Alan's car began to drift peacefully toward the guardrail or the shoulder and the trees. She said, "How do you know me? How did you know all about those other people?"

"I know nearly everything about nearly everyone. That's the curse of my position. But you I know better than most."

She stared at him. "I don't know you."

"Nevertheless, we have met before," the magician said. "Twice, actually, which I confess is somewhat unusual. The second time was long ago. You were quite small."

"That's ridiculous." She was surprised by the faint touch of scorn in her voice, barely there yet still sharp. "That doesn't make any sense."

"I suppose not. Since I know how the trick's done, and you don't, I'm afraid I have you at a disadvantage." He put one long finger to his lips and pursed them, considering, before he started again. "Let's try it as a riddle. I am not entirely what I appear, being old as time, vast as space, and endless as the future. My nature is known to all, but typically misunderstood. And I meet everyone and everything alive at least once. Indeed, the encounter is entirely unavoidable. Who am I?"

She felt a sudden twist in the nothing, and knew it for anger. "Show's over. I'm not eating dinner anymore."

The magician smiled and shook his head very slightly. "You are lost, yes?"

"My motel's lost, I'm not. I must have taken a wrong turn."

"I know the way," the magician said. "I will guide you."

Gracefully and courteously, he offered his arm, but she took a step backward. His smile widened as he let the arm fall to his side. "Come," he said, and turned without looking to see whether she followed. She caught up quickly, not touching the hand he left open, within easy reach.

"You say we've met before. Where?" she asked.

"The second time was in New York City. Central Park," the magician said. "There was a birthday party for your cousin Matthew."

She stopped walking. "Okay. I don't know who you are, or how you knew I grew up in New York City and have a cousin named Matthew. But you just blew it, Sherlock. When we were kids I *hated* stupid, nasty Matthew, and I absolutely never went to any of his birthday parties. My parents tried to make me, once, but I put up such a fuss they backed down. So you're wrong."

The magician reached out abruptly, and she felt a swift, cool whisper in her hair. He held up a small silver figure of a horse and asked with mock severity, "What are you doing, keeping a horse up in there? You shouldn't have a horse if you don't have a stable for it."

She froze for an instant, wide-eyed and open-mouthed, and then clutched at the silver horse as greedily as any child. "That's *mine!* Where did you get it?"

"I gave it to you." The magician's voice sounded as impossibly distant as her childhood, long gone on another coast.

And then came his command: *"Remember."*

At first she had enjoyed herself. Matthew was fat and awful as usual, but his birthday had been an excuse to bring together branches of the family that rarely saw one another, traveling in to Central Park from places as whispered and exotic as Rockaway and Philadelphia. She was excited to see her *whole* family, not just her parents and her very small baby brother, and Matthew's mother and father, but also uncles and aunts and cousins, and some very old relatives she had never met before in her life. They all gathered together in one corner of the Sheep Meadow, where they spread out picnic blankets, coverlets, beach towels, anything you could sit down on, and they brought out all kinds of old-country dishes: *piroshki, pelmeni, flanken, kasha, rugelach, kugel mit mandlen,* milk bottles full of *borscht* and *schav* — and hot dogs and hamburgers too, and baked beans and deviled eggs, and birthday cake and candy and cream soda. It was a hot blue day, full of food.

But a four-year-old girl can only eat and drink so much...and besides, after a while the uncles all began to fall asleep on the grass, one by one, much too full to pay attention to her...and all the aunts were sitting to-gether telling stories that didn't make any sense...and Matthew was fuss-ing about having a "stummyache," which she felt he certainly deserved. And her parents weren't worth talking to, since whenever she tried they were busy with her infant brother or the other adults, and not really listen-ing. So after a time she grew bored. Stuffed, but bored.

She decided that she would go and see the zoo.

She knew that Central Park had a zoo because she had been taken there once before. It was a long way from the picnic, but even so, every now and then she could hear the lions roaring, along with the distant sounds of busses and taxis and city traffic that drifted to her ears. She was sure that it would be easy to find her way if she listened for the lions.

But they eluded her, the lions and the zoo alike. Not that she was lost, no, not for a minute. She walked along enjoying herself, smiling in the sunlight, and petting all the dogs that came bouncing up to her. If their owners asked where her parents were, she pointed firmly in the direction she was going and said "right up there," then moved on, laughing, before they had time to think about it. At every branching of the path she would stop and listen, taking whatever turn sounded like it led toward the lions. She didn't seem to be getting any closer, though, which eventually grew frustrating. It was still an adventure, still more exciting than the birthday picnic, but now it was beginning to annoy her as well.

Then she came around a bend in the path, and saw a man sitting by himself on a little bench. To her eyes he was a *very* old man, almost as old as her great-uncle Wilhelm — you could tell that by his white hair, and the deep lines around his closed eyes, and the long red blanket that covered his legs stretched out in front of him. She had seen other old men sitting like that. His hands were shoved deep into his coat pockets, and his face lifted to the angle of the afternoon sun.

She thought he was asleep, so she started on past him, walking quietly, so as not to wake him. But without opening his eyes or changing his position, he said in a soft, deep voice, "An exceptional afternoon to you, young miss."

Exceptional was a new word to her, and she loved new words. She turned around and replied, trying to sound as grown up as she could, "I'm very exceptional, thank you."

"And glad I am to hear it," the old man said. "Where are you off to, if I may ask?"

"I'm going to see the lions," she told him. "And the draffs. Draffs are excellent animals."

"So they are," the old man agreed. His eyes, when he opened them, were the bluest she had ever seen, so young and bright that they made the rest of him look even older. He said, "I used to ride a draff, you know, in Africa. Whenever I went shopping."

She stared at him. "You can't ride a draff. There's no place to *sit*."

"I rode way up on the neck, on a little sort of platform." The old man hadn't beckoned to her, or shifted to make room for her on the bench, but she found herself moving closer all the same. He said, "It was like being in the crow's-nest on the mast of a ship, where the lookout sits. The draff would be swaying and flowing under me like the sea, and the sky would be swaying too, and I'd hang onto the draff's neck with one hand, and wave to all the people down below with the other. It was really quite nice."

He sighed, and smiled and shook his head. "But I had to give it up, because there's no place to put your groceries on a draff. All your bags and boxes just slide right down the neck, and then the draff steps on them. Draffs have very big feet, you know."

By that time she was standing right in front of him, staring into his lined old face. He had a big, proud nose, and his eyebrows over it were all tangly. To her they looked mad at each other. He said, "After that, I did all my shopping on a rhinoceros. One thing about a rhinoceros" — and for the first time he smiled at her — "when you come into a store, people are always remarkably nice. And you can sling all your packages around the rhino's horn and carry them home that way. *Much* handier than a draff, let me tell you."

He reached up while he was talking and took an egg out of her right ear. She didn't feel it happen — just the quick brush of his long fingers, and there was the egg in his hand. She grabbed for her other ear, to see if there might be an egg in there too, but he was already taking a quarter out of that one. He seemed just as surprised as she was, saying, "My goodness, now you'll be able to buy some toast to have with your egg. Extraordinary ears you have — my word, yes." And all the time he was carrying on about the egg, he was finding all kinds of other things in her ears: seashells and more coins, a couple of marbles (which upset him — "You should *never* put marbles in your ears, young lady!"), a tangerine, and even a flower, although it looked pretty mooshed-up, which he said was from being in her ear all that time.

She sat down beside him without knowing she was sitting down. "How do you *do* that?" she asked him. "Can *I* do that? Show me!"

"With ears like those, everything is possible," the old man answered. "Try it for yourself," and he guided her hand to a beautiful cowrie shell tucked just behind her left ear. Then he said, "I wonder...I just wonder..." And he ruffled her hair quickly and showed her a palm full of tiny silver stars. Not like the shining foil ones her preschool teacher gave out for good behavior, but glittering, sharp-pointed metal stars, as bright as anything in the sky.

"It seems your hair is talented, too. *That's* exceptional."

"More, please!" she begged him.

The old man looked at her curiously. He was still smiling, but his eyes seemed sad now, which confused her.

"I haven't given you anything that wasn't already yours," he said. "Much as I would otherwise. But *this* is a gift. From me to you. Here." He waved one hand over his open palm, and when it passed she saw a small silver figure of a horse.

She looked at it. It was more beautiful, she thought, than anything she had ever seen.

"I can keep it? Really?"

"Oh yes," he said. "I hope you will keep it always."

He put the exquisite figure in her cupped hands, and closed her fingers gently over it. She felt the curlicues of the mane, blowing in a frozen wind, against her fingertips.

"Put it in your pocket, for safekeeping, and look at it tonight before you go to bed." As she did what he told her, he said, "Now I must ask where your parents are."

She said nothing, suddenly aware how much time had passed since she had left the picnic.

"They will be looking everywhere for you," the old man said. "In fact, I think I can hear them calling you now." He cupped his hands to his mouth and called in a silly, quavering voice, "Elfrieda! *Elfrieda!* Where are you, Elfrieda?"

This made her giggle so much that it took her a while to tell him, "*That's* not my name." He laughed too, but he went on calling, "*Elfrieda! Elfrieda!*" until the silly voice became so sad and worried that she stood up and said, "Maybe I ought to go back and tell them I'm all right." The air was starting to grow a little chilly, and she was starting to be not quite sure that she knew the way back.

"Oh, I wouldn't do that," the old man advised her. "If I were you, I'd stay right here, and when they come along you could say to them, 'Why don't you sit down and rest your weary bones?' That's what *I'd* do."

The idea of saying something like that to grownups set her off giggling again, and she could hardly wait for her family to come find her. She sat down by the old man and talked with him, in the ordinary way, about school and friends and uncles, and all the ways her cousin Matthew made her mad, and about going shopping on rhinoceroses. He told her that it was always hard to find parking space for a rhino, and that they really didn't like shopping, but they would do it if they liked you. So after that they talked about how you get a rhinoceros to like you, until her father came for her on the motorcycle.

"I lost it back in college." She caressed the little object, holding it against her cheek. "I looked and looked, but I couldn't find it anywhere." She looked at him with a mix of wonder and suspicion. She fell silent then, frowning, touching her mouth. "Central Park...there was a zoo in Central Park."

The magician nodded. "There still is."

"Lions. Did they have lions?" She gave him no time to answer the question. "I do remember the lions. I heard them roaring." She spoke slowly, seeming to be addressing the silver horse more than him. "I wanted to see the lions."

"Yes," the magician said. "You were on your way there when we met."

"I remember now," she said. "How could I have forgotten?" She was speaking more rapidly as the memory took shape. "You were sitting with me on the bench, and then Daddy...Daddy came on a motorcycle. I mean, no, the *policeman* was on the motorcycle, and Daddy was in the...the side-car thing. I remember. He was so furious with me that I was glad the policeman was there."

The magician chuckled softly. "He was angry until he saw that you were safe and unharmed. Then he was so thankful that he offered me money."

"Did he? I didn't notice." Her face felt suddenly hot with embarrassment. "I'm sorry, I didn't know he wanted to give you money. You must have felt so insulted."

"Nonsense," the magician said briskly. "He loved you, and he offered what he had. Both of us dealt in the same currency, after all."

She paused, looking around them. "This isn't the right street either. I don't see the motel."

He patted her shoulder lightly. "You will, I assure you."

"I'm not certain I want to."

"Really?" His voice seemed to surround her in the night. "And why would that be? You have a journey to continue."

The bitterness rose so fast in her throat that it almost made her throw up. "If you know my name, if you know about my family, if you know things *I'd* forgotten about, then you already know why. Alan's dead, and Talley — my Mouse, oh God, *my little Mouse* — and so am I, do you understand? I'm dead too, and I'm just driving around and around until I rot." She started to double over, coughing and gagging on the rage. "I wish I were dead with them, that's what I wish!" She would have been desperately happy to vomit, but all she could make come out were words.

Strong old hands were steadying her shoulders, and she was able, in a little time, to raise her head and look into the magician's face, where she saw neither anger nor pity. She said very quietly, "No, I'll tell you what I really wish. I wish *I* had died in that crash, and that Alan and Talley were still alive. I'd make that deal like a shot, you think I wouldn't?"

The magician said gently, "It was not your fault."

"Yes it was. It's my fault that they were in my car. I asked Alan to take it in for an oil change, and Mouse...Talley wanted to go with him. She loved it, being just herself and Daddy — oh, she used to order him around so, pretending she was me." For a moment she came near losing control again, but the magician held on, and so did she. "If I hadn't asked him to do that for me, if I hadn't been so selfish and lazy and sure I had more important things to do, then it would have been me that died in that crash, and they'd have lived. They *would* have lived." She reached up and gripped the magician's wrists, as hard as she could, holding his eyes even more intently.

"You see?"

The magician nodded without answering, and they stood linked together in shadow for that moment. Then he took his hands from her shoulders and said, "So, then, you have offered to trade your life for the lives of your husband and daughter. Do you still hold to that bargain?"

She stared at him. She said, "That stupid riddle. You really *meant* that. What *are* you? Are you Death?"

"Not at all. But there are things I can do, with your consent."

"My consent." She stood back, straightening to her full height. "Alan and Talley...nobody needed *their* consent — or mine, either. I meant every word."

"Think," the magician said urgently. "I need you to know what you have asked, and the extent of what you think you mean." He raised his left hand, palm up, tapping on it with his right forefinger. "Be very careful, little girl in the park. There *are* lions."

"I know what I wished." She could feel the sidewalk coiling under her feet.

"Then know this. I can neither take life nor can I restore it, but I *can* grant your wish, exactly as it was made. You have only to say — and to be utterly certain in your soul that it *is* your true desire." He chuckled suddenly, startlingly; to her ear it sounded almost like a growl. "My, I cannot recall the last time I used that word, *soul*."

She bit her lip and wrapped her arms around herself, though the night continued warm. "What can you promise me?"

"A different reality — the exact one you prayed for just now. Do you understand me?"

"No," she said; and then, very slowly, "You mean, like running a movie backward? Back to...back to *before*?"

The old man shook his head. "No. Reality never runs backward; each thing is, and will be, as it always was. Choice is an uncommon commodity, and treasured by those few who actually have it. But there *is* magic, and magic can shuffle some possibilities like playing cards, done right. Such craft as I control will grant your wish, precisely as you spoke it. Take the horse I have returned to you back to the place where the accident happened.

The *exact* place. Hold it in your hand, or carry it on your person, and take a single step. One single step. If your commitment is firm, if your choice is truly and finally made, then things as they always were will *still* be as they always were — only now, the way they always were will be forever different. Your husband and your daughter will live, because they never drove that day, and they never died. *You* did. Do you understand now?"

"Yes," she whispered. "Oh, yes, *yes,* I do understand. Please, do it, I accept, it's the only wish I have. Please, *yes.*"

The magician took her hands between his own. "You are certain? You know what it will mean?"

"I can't live without them," she answered simply. "I told you. But... how —"

"Death, for all His other sterling qualities, is not terribly bright. Efficient and punctual, but not bright." The magician gave her the slightest of bows. "And I am very good with tricks. You might even say exceptional."

"Can't you just send me there, right this minute — transport me, or e-mail me or something, never mind the stupid driving. Couldn't you do that? I mean, if you can do — you know — *this?*"

He shook his head. "Even the simplest of tricks must be prepared...and this one is not simple. Drive, and I will meet you at the appointed time and place."

"Well, then." She put her hands on his arms, looking up at him as though at the sun through green leaves. "Since there are no words in the world for me to thank you with, I'm just going to go on back home. My family's waiting."

Yet she delayed, and so did he, as though both of them were foreigners fumbling through a language never truly comprehended: a language of memory and intimacy. The magician said, "You don't know why I am doing this." It was not a question.

"No. I don't." Her hesitant smile was a storm of anxious doubt. "Old times' sake?"

The magician shook his head. "It doesn't really matter. Go now."

The motel sign was as bright as the moon across the street, and she could see her car in the half-empty parking lot. She turned and walked away, without looking back, started the Buick and drove out of the lot. There was nothing else to collect. Let them wonder in the morning at her unruffled bed, and the dry towels never taken down from the bathroom rack.

The magician was plain in her rear-view mirror, looking after her, but she did not wave, or turn her head.

Free of detours, the road back seemed notably shorter than the way she had come, though she took it distinctly more slowly. The reason, to her mind, was that before she had been so completely without plans, without thought, without any destination, without any baggage but grief. Now, feeling almost pregnant with joy, swollen with eager visions — *they will live, they will, my Mouse will be a living person, not anyone's memory* — she felt a self that she had never considered or acknowledged conducting the old car, as surely as her foot on the accelerator and her hands on the wheel. A full day passed, more, and somehow she did not grow tired, which she decided must be something the magician had done, so she did not question it. Instead she sang nursery songs as she drove, and the sea chanteys and Gilbert and Sullivan that Alan had always loved. *No, not loved. Loves! Loves now, loves now and will go on loving, because I'm on my way. Alan, Talley, I'm on my way.*

For the last few hundred miles she abandoned the interstate and drove the coast road home, retracing the path she and Alan had taken at the beginning of their honeymoon. The ocean was constant on her right, the massed redwoods and hemlocks on her left, and the night air smelled both of salt and pinesap. There were deer in the brush, and scurrying foxes, and even a porcupine, shuffling and clicking across the road. Once she saw a mountain lion, or thought she had: a long-tailed shadow in a shadow, watching her shadow race past. *Darlings, on my way!*

It was near dawn when she reached the first suburbs of the city where she had gone to college, married, and settled without any control — or the desire for control — over very much of it. The city lay still as jewels before her, except when the infrequent police siren or fire-engine clamor set dogs barking in every quarter. She parked the Buick in her driveway, startled for a moment at her house's air of abandonment and desolation. *What did you expect, disappearing the way you did, and no way to contact you?* She did not try the door, but stood there for a little, listening absurdly for any sound of Alan or Talley moving in the house. Then she walked away as calmly as she had from the magician.

Six blocks, six blocks. She found the intersection where the crash had occurred. Standing on the corner angle of the sidewalk, she could see the exact smudge on the asphalt where her life had ended, and this shadowy leftover had begun. Across the way the light grew beyond the little community park, a glow as transparent as seawater. She drank it in, savoring the slow-rising smells of warming stone and suburban commuter breakfasts. *Never again...never again,* she thought. Up and down the street, cars were backing out of garages, and she found herself watching them with a strange new greed, thinking, *Alan and Mouse will see them come home again, see the geese settle in on the fake lake for the night. Not me, never again.*

The street was thickening with traffic, early as it was. She watched a bus go by, and then the same school van that always went first to the furthest developments, before circling back to pick up Talley and others who lived closer to school. *He's not here yet,* she thought, fingering the silver horse in her pocket. *I could take today. One day — one day only, just to taste it all, to go to all the places we were together, to carry that with me when I step across that pitiful splotch — tomorrow? My darlings will have all the other days, all their lives...couldn't I have just the one? I'd be right back here at dawn, all packed to leave — surely they wouldn't mind, if they knew? Just the one.*

Behind her, the magician said, "As much as you have grieved for them, so they will mourn you. You say your life ended here; they will say the same, for a time."

Without turning, she said, "You can't talk me out of this."

A dry chuckle. "Oh, I've suspected that from the beginning."

She did turn then, and saw him standing next to her: unchanged, but for a curious dusk, bordering on tenderness, in the old, old eyes. His face was neither pitying nor unkind, nor triumphant in its foreknowledge, but urgently attentive in the way of a blind person. "There she was, that child in Central Park, stumping along, so fierce, so determined, going off all alone to find the lions. There was I, half-asleep in the sun on my park bench..."

"I don't understand," she said. "Please. Before I go, tell me who you are."

"You know who I am."

"I don't!"

"You did. You will."

She did not answer him. In silence, they both turned their heads to follow a young black man walking on the other side of the street. He was carrying an infant — a boy, she thought — high in his arms, his round dark face brilliant with pride, as though no one had ever had a baby before. The man and child were laughing together: the baby's laughter a shrill gurgle, the father's almost a song. Another bus hid them for a moment, and when it passed they had turned a corner and disappeared.

The magician said, "Yet despite your certainty you were thinking, unless I am mistaken, of delaying your bargain's fulfillment."

"One day," she said softly. "Only to say goodbye. To remind myself of them and everything we had, before giving it all up. Would that…would it be possible? Or would it break the…the spell? The charm?"

The magician regarded her without replying immediately, and she found that she was holding her breath.

"It's neither of those. It's just a trick, and not one that can wait long on your convenience." His expression was inflexible.

"Oh," she said. "Well. It would have been nice, but there — can't have everything. Thank you, and goodbye again."

She waited until the sparse morning traffic was completely clear. Then deliberately, and without hesitation, she stepped forward into the street. She was about to move further when she heard the magician's voice behind her. "Sunset. That is the best I can do."

She wheeled, her face a child's face, alight with holiday. "*Thank* you! I'll be back in time, I promise! Oh, *thank* you!"

Before she could turn again the magician continued, in a different voice, "I have one request." His face was unchanged, but the voice was that of a much younger man, almost a boy. "I have no right to ask, no claim on you — but I would feel privileged to spend these hours in your company." He might have been a shy Victorian, awkwardly inviting a girl to tea.

She stared back at him, her face for once as unreadable as his. It was a long moment before she finally nodded and beckoned to him, saying, "Come on, then — there's so little time. Come on!"

In fact, whether or not it was due to his presence, there was time enough. She reclaimed the Buick and drove them first up into the hills, to watch the rest of dawn play itself out over the city as she told him stories of her life there. Then they joined an early morning crowd of parents and preschoolers in the local community playground. She introduced the magician to her too-solicitous friends as a visiting uncle from Alan's side of the family, and tried to maintain some illusion of the muted grief she knew they expected of her; an illusion which very nearly shattered with laughter when the magician took a ride with some children on a miniature train, his knees almost up to his ears. After that she brought them back down to the bald flatlands near the freeway, to the food bank where she had worked twice a week, and where she was greeted with cranky affection by old black Baptist women who hugged her and warned her that she needn't be coming round so soon, but if she was up to it, well, tomorrow was likely to be a particularly heavy day, and Lord knows they could use the extra hand. The magician saw the flash of guilt and sorrow in her eyes, but no one else did. She promised not to be late.

Time enough. They parked the car and took a ferry across the bay to the island where she had met Alan when they were both dragged along on a camping trip, and where she and Alan and Talley had picnicked often after Talley was born. Here she found herself chattering to the magician compulsively, telling him how Alan had cured their daughter of her terror of water by coaxing her to swim sitting up on his back, pretending she was riding a dolphin. "She's become a wonderful swimmer now, Mouse has, you should see her. I mean, I guess you *will* see her — anyway you *could* see her. I won't, but if you wanted to…" Her voice drifted away, and the magician touched her hand without replying.

"We have to watch the clock," she said. "I wouldn't want to miss my death." It was meant as a joke, but the magician did not laugh.

Time enough. Her vigilance had them back at the house well before sunset, after a stop at her family's favorite ice-cream shop for cones: coffee for herself — "Double scoop, what the hell?" — and strawberry, after much deliberation, for the magician. They were still nibbling them when they reached the front door.

"God, I'll miss coffee," she said, almost dreamily; then laughed. "Well, I guess I won't, will I? I mean, I won't know if I miss it or not, after all." She glanced critically up at the magician beside her. "You've never eaten an ice-cream cone before, have you?"

The magician shook his head solemnly. She took his cone from him and licked carefully around the edges, until the remaining ice-cream was more or less even; then handed it back to him, along with her own napkin. "We should finish before we go in. Come on." She devoted herself to devouring the entire cone, crunching it up with a voracity matching the sun's descent.

When she was done she used her key to open the door, and stepped inside. She was halfway down the front hall, almost to the living room, when she realized the magician had not followed.

"Hey," she called to him. "Aren't you coming?"

"I thank you for the day, but this moment should be yours alone. I will wait outside. You needn't hurry," he said, glancing at the sky. "But don't dawdle, either."

With that he closed the door, leaving her to the house and her memories.

Half an hour later, six blocks away, she stood slightly behind him on the sidewalk and studied the middle of the intersection. He did not offer his hand, but she lifted it in both of hers anyway. "You are very kind."

He shook his head ruefully. "Less than you imagine. Far less than I wish."

"Don't give me that." Her tone was dismissive, but moderated with a chuckle. "You were waiting for me. You said so. I would have bumped into you wherever I drove, wouldn't I? If I'd gone south to Mexico, or gotten on a plane to Honolulu or Europe, sooner or later, when I was ready to listen to what you had to say, when I was ready to make this deal, I'd have walked into a restaurant with a sign for Dinner Magic. Right?"

"Not quite. You could only have gone the way you went, and I could only have met you there. Each thing is, and will be, as it always was. I told you that."

"I don't care. I'm still grateful. I'm still saying thanks."

The magician said softly, "Stay."

She shook her head. "You know I can't."

"This trick…this misdirection…I can't promise you what it will buy. Your husband and daughter will live, but for how long cannot be known by anyone. They might be killed tomorrow by another stupid, sleepy driver — a virus, a plane crash, a madman with a gun. What you are giving up for them could be utterly useless, utterly pointless, by next sunrise. Stay — do not waste this moment of your own choice, your own power. *Stay.*"

He reached out for her, but she stepped away, backing into the street so suddenly that a driver honked angrily at her as he sped by. She said, "Everything you say is absolutely true, and none of it matters. If all I could give them was one single extra second, I would."

The old man's face grew gentle. "Ah. You are indeed as I remembered. Very well, then. I had to offer you a choice. You have chosen love, and I have no complaint, nor would it matter if I did. In this moment you are the magician, not I."

"All right, then. Let's do this."

The huge red sun was dancing on tiptoe on a green horizon, but she waited until the magician nodded before she started toward the intersection. Traffic had grown so heavy that there was no way for her to reach the stain that was Alan and Talley's fading memorial. The magician raised his free hand, as though waving to her, and the entire lane opened up, cars and drivers frozen in place, leaving her free passage to where she needed to be. Over her shoulder she said, "Thank you," and stepped forward.

The little girl shook her head and looked around herself. She was confused by what she saw, and if anyone in the park other than the old man had been watching, they would have wondered at the oddly adult way that she stood still and regarded her surroundings.

"Hello," the magician said to her.

"This...isn't what I expected."

"No. The audience sees a woman cut in half, while the two women folded carefully within separate sections of the magic box experience it quite differently. You're in the trick now, so of course things are different than you expected. It's hardly magic if you can guess in advance how it's done."

She looked at her small hands in amazement, then down the short length of her arms and legs. "I *really* don't understand. You said I would die."

"And so you will, on the given day and at the given time, when you think about asking your husband to take care of your oil change for you and then decide — in a flickering instant, quite without knowing why — that you should do this simple errand yourself, instead." He looked enormously sad as he spoke. "And you will die now, in a different way, because that one deeply buried flicker is the only hint of memory you may keep. You won't remember this day, or the gifts I will give you, or me. The trick won't work, otherwise. Death may not be bright, but he's not stupid, either — all the cards have to go back in the deck, or he *will* notice. But if you and I, between us, subtly mark one of the cards...that should slip by. Just."

He stopped speaking; and for a little it seemed to the woman in the girl, staring into the finality of his face as though into a dark wood, that he might never again utter a word. Then he sighed deeply. "I told you I wasn't kind."

She reached up to touch his cheek, her eyes shining. "No one could possibly be kinder. You've not only granted my wish, you're telling me I'll get to see them again. That I'll meet Alan again, and fall in love again, and hold my little Mouse in my arms, exactly as before. That *is* what you are saying, isn't it?"

He held both his hands wide, elegant fingers cupped to catch the sun. "You are that child in Central Park, off to see the lions. And I am an old man, half-asleep on a bench...from this point on the world proceeds just as it ever was, and only one thing, quite a bit ahead of today and really not worth talking about, will be any different. Please look in your pocket, child."

She reached into the front of her denim coverall, then, and smiled when she felt her four-year-old hand close around the silver horse. She took it out, and held it up to him as if she were offering a piece of candy.

"I don't know who you are, but I know what you are. You're something good."

"Nonsense," he said, but she could see he looked pleased. "And now..." The magician placed his vast, lined hands around hers, squeezed once, gently, and said, *"Forget."* When he took his hands away the silver horse was gone.

The little girl stood on the green grass, looking up at the old man with the closed eyes. He spoke to her. "Where are you off to, if I may ask?"

"I'm going to see the lions," she told him. "And the draffs. Draffs are excellent animals."

"So they are," the old man agreed, tilting his head down to look at her. His eyes, when he opened them, were the bluest she had ever seen.

Mythago Wood

Robert Holdstock

One

In May 1944 I received my call-up papers and went reluctantly away to war, training at first in the Lake District, then shipping over to France with the 7th Infantry.

On the eve of my final departure I felt so resentful of my father's apparent lack of concern for my safety that, when he was asleep, I went quietly to his desk and tore a page out of his notebook, the diary in which his silent, obsessive work was recorded. The fragment was dated simply "August 34," and I read it many times, dismayed by its incomprehensibility, but content that I had stolen at least a tiny part of his life with which to support myself through those painful, lonely times.

The entry began with a bitter comment on the distractions in his life — the running of Oak Lodge, our family home, the demands of his two sons, and the difficult relationship with his wife, Jennifer. (By then, I remember, my mother was desperately ill.) It closed with a passage quite memorable for its incoherence:

> A letter from Watkins — agrees with me that at certain times of the year the aura around the woodland could reach as far as the house. Must think through the implications of this. He is keen to know the power of the oak vortex that I have measured. What to tell him? Certainly not of the first mythago. Have noticed too that the enrichment of the pre-mythago zone is more persistent, but concomitant with this, am distinctly losing my sense of time.

I treasured this piece of paper for many reasons, but particularly for the moment or two of my father's passionate interest that it represented — and yet, it locked me out of its understanding, as he had locked me out at home. Everything he loved, everything I hated.

I was wounded in early 1945 and when the war finished I managed to stay in France, travelling south to convalesce in a village in the hills behind Marseilles, where I lived with old friends of my father. It was a hot, dry place, very still, very slow; I spent my time sitting in the village square and quickly became a part of the tiny community.

Letters from my brother Christian, who had returned to Oak Lodge after the war, arrived every month throughout the long year of 1946. They were chatty, informative letters, but there was an increasing note of tension in them, and it was clear that Christian's relationship with our father was deteriorating rapidly. I never heard a word from the old man himself, but then I never expected to; I had long since resigned myself to the fact that, even at best, he regarded me with total indifference. All his family had been an intrusion in his work, and his guilt at neglecting us, and especially at driving our mother to taking her own life, had blossomed rapidly, during the early years of the war, into a hysterical madness that could be truly frightening. Which is not to say that he was perpetually shouting; on the contrary, most of his life was spent in silent, absorbed contemplation of the oak woodland that bordered our home. At first infuriating, because of the distance it put between him and his family, soon those long periods of quiet became blessed, earnestly welcomed.

He died in November 1946, of an illness that had afflicted him for years. When I heard the news I was torn between my unwillingness to return to Oak Lodge, at the edge of the Ryhope estate in Herefordshire, and my awareness of Christian's obvious distress. He was alone now, in the house where we had lived through our childhood together. I could imagine him prowling the empty rooms, perhaps sitting in father's dank and unwholesome study and remembering the hours of denial, the smell of wood and compost that the old man had trudged in through the glass-panelled doors after his week-long sorties into the deep woodlands. The forest had spread into that room as if my father could not bear to be away from the rank undergrowth and the cool, moist oak glades, even when making token acknowledgement of his family. He made that acknowledgement in the only way he knew: by telling us — and mainly telling my brother — stories of the ancient forestlands beyond the house, the primary woodland of oak, ash, beech and the like, in whose dark interior (he once said) wild boar could still be heard, and smelled, and tracked by their spoor.

I doubt if he had ever seen such a creature, but that evening, as I sat in my room overlooking the tiny village in the hills (Christian's letter a crushed ball still held in my hand) I vividly recalled how I had listened to the muffled grunting of some woodland animal, and heard the heavy, unhurried crashing of something bulky moving inwards, towards the winding pathway that we called deep track, a route that led spirally towards the very heartwoods of the forest.

I knew I would have to go home, and yet I delayed my departure for nearly another year. During that time Christian's letters ceased abruptly. In his last letter, dated April 10th, he wrote of Guiwenneth, of his unusual marriage, and hinted that I would be surprised by the lovely girl to whom he had lost his "heart, mind, soul, reason, cooking ability and just about everything else, Steve." I wrote to congratulate him, of course, but there was no further communication between us for months.

Eventually I wrote to say I was coming home, that I would stay at Oak Lodge for a few weeks, and then find accommodation in one of the nearby towns. I said good-bye to France, and to the community that had become so much a part of my life. I travelled to England by bus and train, by ferry, and then by train again. On August 20th I arrived by pony and trap at the disused railway line that skirted the edge of the extensive estate. Oak Lodge lay on the far side of the grounds, four miles further round the road, but accessible via the right of way through the estate's fields and woodlands. I intended to take an intermediate route and so, lugging my single, crammed suitcase as best I could, I began to walk along the grass-covered railway track, peering on occasion over the high, red-brick wall that marked the limit of the estate, trying to see through the gloom of the pungent pinewoods.

Soon this woodland, and the wall, vanished, and the land opened into tight, tree-bordered fields, to which I gained access across a rickety wooden stile, almost lost beneath briar and full-fruited blackberry bushes. I had to trample my way out of the public domain and so on to the south trackway that wound, skirting patchy woodland and the stream called "sticklebrook," up to the ivy-covered house that was my home.

It was late morning, and very hot, as I came in distant sight of Oak Lodge. Somewhere off to my left I could hear the drone of a tractor. I thought of old Alphonse Jeffries, the estate's farm supervisor, and with the memory of his weather-tanned, smiling face came images of the mill-pond, and fishing for pike from his tiny rowing boat.

Memory of the tranquil mill-pond haunted me, and I moved away from the south track, through waist-high nettles and a tangle of ash and hawthorn scrub. I came out close to the bank of the wide, shadowy pool, its full extent hidden by the gloom of the dense stand of oak woodland that began on its far side. Almost hidden among the rushes that crowded the nearer edge of the pond was the shallow boat from which Chris and I had fished, years before; its white paint had flaked away almost entirely now, and although the craft looked watertight, I doubted if it would take the weight of a full grown man. I didn't disturb it but walked around the bank and sat down on the rough concrete steps of the crumbling boat-house; from here I watched the surface of the pool rippling with the darting motions of insects, and the occasional passage of a fish, just below.

"A couple of sticks and a bit of string...that's all it takes."

Christian's voice startled me. He must have walked along a beaten track from the Lodge, hidden from my view by the shed. Delighted, I jumped to my feet and turned to face him. The shock of his appearance was like a physical blow to me, and I think he noticed, even though I threw my arms about him and gave him a powerful brotherly bear-hug.

"I had to see this place again," I said.

"I know what you mean," he said, as we broke our embrace. "I often walk here myself." There was a moment's awkward silence as we stared at each other. I felt, distinctly, that he was not pleased to see me. "You're looking brown," he said. "And very drawn. Healthy and ill together..."

THE SECRET HISTORY OF FANTASY

"Mediterranean sun, grape-picking, and shrapnel. I'm still not one hundred percent fit." I smiled. "But it *is* good to be back, to see you again."

"Yes," he said dully. "I'm glad you've come, Steve. Very glad. I'm afraid the place...well, is a bit of a mess. I only got your letter yesterday and I haven't had a chance to do anything. Things have changed quite a bit, you'll find."

And he more than anything. I could hardly believe that this was the chipper, perky young man who had left with his army unit in 1942. He had aged incredibly, his hair quite streaked with grey, more noticeable for his having allowed it to grow long and untidy at the back and sides. He reminded me very much of Father: the same distant, distracted look, the same hollow cheeks and deeply wrinkled face. But it was his whole demeanor that had shocked me. He had always been a stocky muscular chap; now he was like the proverbial scarecrow, wiry, ungainly, on edge all the time. His gaze darted about, but never seemed to focus upon me. And he smelled. Of mothballs, as if the crisp white shirt and grey flannels that he wore had been dragged out of storage; and another smell beyond the naphtha...the hint of woodland and grass. There was dirt under his fingernails, and in his hair, and his teeth were yellowing.

He seemed to relax slightly as the minutes ticked by. We sparred a bit, laughed a bit, and walked around the pond, whacking at the rushes with sticks. I could not shake off the feeling that I had arrived home at a bad time.

"Was it difficult...with the old man, I mean? The last days."

He shook his head. "There was a nurse here for the final two weeks or so. I can't exactly say that he went peacefully, but she managed to stop him damaging himself...or me, for that matter."

"I was going to ask you about that. Your letters suggested hostility between the two of you."

Christian smiled quite grimly, and glanced at me with a curious expression, somewhere between agreement and suspicion. "More like open warfare. Soon after I got back from France, he went quite mad. You should have seen the place, Steve. You should have seen him. I don't think he'd washed for months. I wondered what he'd been eating...certainly nothing as simple as eggs and meat. In all honesty, for a few months I think he'd been eating wood and leaves. He was in a wretched state. Although he let me help him with his work, he quickly began to resent me. He tried to kill me on several occasions, Steve. And I mean that, really desperate attempts on my life. There was a reason for it, I suppose…"

I was astonished by what Christian was telling me. The image of my father had changed from that of a cold, resentful man into a crazed figure, ranting at Christian and beating at him with his fists.

"I always thought he had a touch of affection for you; he always told *you* the stories of the wood; I listened, but it was you who sat on his knee. Why would he try to kill you?"

"I became too involved," was all Christian said. He was keeping something back, something of critical importance. I could tell from his tone, from his sullen, almost resentful expression. Did I push the point or not? It was hard to make the decision. I had never before felt so distant from my own brother. I wondered if his behavior was having an effect on Guiwenneth, the girl he had married. I wondered what sort of atmosphere she was living in up at Oak Lodge.

Tentatively, I broached the subject of the girl.

Christian struck angrily at the rushes by the pond. "Guiwenneth's gone," he said simply, and I stopped, startled.

"What does that mean, Chris? Gone where?"

"She's just gone, Steve," he snapped, angry and cornered. "She was Father's girl, and she's gone, and that's all there is to it."

"I don't understand what you mean. Where's she gone *to?* In your letter you sounded so happy.…"

"I shouldn't have written about her. That was a mistake. Now let it drop, will you?"

After that outburst, my unease with Christian grew stronger by the minute. There was something very wrong with him indeed, and clearly Guiwenneth's leaving had contributed greatly to the terrible change I could see; but I sensed there was something more. Unless he spoke about it, however, there was no way through to him. I could find only the words, "I'm sorry."

"Don't be."

We walked on, almost to the woods, where the ground became marshy and unsafe for a few yards before vanishing into a musty deepness of stone and root and rotting wood. It was cool here, the sun being beyond the thickly foliaged trees. The dense stands of rush moved in the breeze and I watched the rotting boat as it shifted slightly on its mooring.

Christian followed my gaze, but he was not looking at the boat or the pond; he was lost, somewhere in his own thoughts. For a brief moment I experienced a jarring sadness at the sight of my brother so ruined in appearance and attitude. I wanted desperately to touch his arm, to hug him, and I could hardly bear the knowledge that I was afraid to do so.

Quite quietly I asked him, "What on earth has happened to you, Chris? Are you ill?"

He didn't answer for a moment, then said, "I'm not ill," and struck hard at a puffball, which shattered and spread on the breeze. He looked at me, something of resignation in his haunted face. "I've been going through a few changes, that's all. I've been picking up on the old man's work. Perhaps a bit of his reclusiveness is rubbing off on me, a bit of his detachment."

"If that's true, then perhaps you should give up for a while."

"Why?"

"Because the old man's obsession with the oak forest eventually killed him. And from the look of you, you're going the same way."

Christian smiled thinly and chucked his reedwhacker out into the pond, where it made a dull splash and floated in a patch of scummy green algae. "It might even be worth dying to achieve what he tried to achieve...and failed."

I didn't understand the dramatic overtone in Christian's statement. The work that had so obsessed our father had been concerned with mapping the woodland, and searching for evidence of old forest settlements. He had invented a whole new jargon for himself, and effectively isolated me from any deeper understanding of his work. I said this to Christian, and added, "Which is all very interesting, but hardly *that* interesting."

"He was doing much more than that, much more than just mapping. But do you remember those maps, Steve? Incredibly detailed..."

I could remember one quite clearly, the largest map, showing carefully marked trackways and easy routes through the tangle of trees and stony outcrops; it showed clearings drawn with almost obsessive precision, each glade numbered and identified, and the whole forest divided into zones, and given names. We had made a camp in one of the clearings close to the woodland edge. "We often tried to get deeper into the heartwoods, remember those expeditions, Chris? But the deep track just ends, and we always managed to get lost; and very scared."

"That's true," Christian said quietly, looking at me quizzically, and added, "What if I told you the forest had *stopped* us entering? Would you believe me?"

I peered into the tangle of brush, tree and gloom, to where a sunlit clearing was visible. "In a way I suppose it did," I said. "It stopped us penetrating very deeply because it made us scared, because there are few trackways through, and the ground is choked with stone and briar…very difficult walking. Is that what you meant? Or did you mean something a little more sinister?"

"Sinister isn't the word I'd use," said Christian, but added nothing more for a moment; he reached up to pluck a leaf from a small, immature oak, and rubbed it between thumb and forefinger before crushing it in his palm. All the time he stared into the deep woods. "This is primary oak woodland, Steve, untouched forest from a time when all of the country was covered with deciduous forests of oak and ash and elder and rowan and hawthorn…."

"And all the rest," I said with a smile. "I remember the old man listing them for us."

"That's right, he did. And there's more than three square miles of such forest stretching from here to well beyond Grimley. Three square miles of original, post-Ice Age forestland. Untouched, uninvaded for thousands of years." He broke off and looked at me hard, before adding, "Resistant to change."

I said, "He always thought there were boars alive in there. I remember hearing something one night, and he convinced me that it was a great big old bull boar, skirting the edge of the woods, looking for a mate."

Christian led the way back towards the boathouse. "He was probably right. If boars *had* survived from medieval times, this is just the sort of woodland they'd be found in."

With my mind opened to those events of years ago, memory inched back, images of childhood — the burning touch of sun on bramble-grazed skin; fishing trips to the mill-pond; tree camps, games, explorations…and instantly I recalled the Twigling.

As we walked back to the beaten pathway that led up to the Lodge, we discussed the sighting. I had been about nine or ten years old. On our way to the sticklebrook to fish we had decided to test out our stick and string rods on the mill-pond, in the vain hope of snaring one of the predatory fish that lived there. As we crouched by the water (we only ever dared to go out in the boat with Alphonse) we saw movement in the trees, across on the other bank. It was a bewildering vision that held us enthralled for the next few moments, and not a little terrified: standing watching us was a man in brown, leathery clothes, with a wide, gleaming belt around his waist, and a spiky, orange beard that reached to his chest: on his head he wore twigs, held to his crown by a leather band. He watched us for a moment only, before slipping back into the darkness. We heard nothing in all this time, no sound of approach, no sound of departure.

Running back to the house we had soon calmed down. Christian decided, eventually, that it must have been old Alphonse, playing tricks on us. But when I mentioned what we'd seen to my father he reacted almost angrily (although Christian recalls him as having been excited, and bellowing for that reason, and not because he was angry with our having been near the forbidden pool). It was Father who referred to the vision as "the Twigling," and soon after we had spoken to him he vanished into the woodland for nearly two weeks.

"That was when he came back hurt, remember?" We had reached the grounds of Oak Lodge, and Christian held the gate open for me as he spoke.

"The arrow wound. The gypsy arrow. My God, that was a bad day."

"The first of many."

I noticed that most of the ivy had been cleared from the walls of the house; it was a grey place now, small, curtainless windows set in the dark brick. The slate roof, with its three tall chimney stacks, was partially hidden behind the branches of a big old beech tree. The yard and gardens were untidy and unkempt, the empty chicken coops and animal shelters ramshackle and decaying. Christian had really let the place slip. But when I stepped across the threshold, it was as if I had never been away. The house smelled of stale food and chlorine, and I could almost see the thin figure of my mother, working away at the immense pinewood table in the kitchen, cats stretched out around her on the red-tiled floor.

Christian had grown tense again, staring at me in that fidgety way that marked his unease. I imagined he was still unsure whether to be glad or angry that I had come home like this. For a moment I felt like an intruder. He said, "Why don't you unpack and freshen up. You can use your old room. It's a bit stuffy, I expect, but it'll soon air. Then come down and we'll have some late lunch. We've got all the time in the world to chat, as long as we're finished by tea." He smiled, and I thought this was some slight attempt at humor. But he went on quickly, staring at me in a cold, hard way, "Because if you're going to stay at home for a while, then you'd better know what's going on here. I don't want you interfering with it, Steve, or with what I'm doing."

"I wouldn't interfere with your life, Chris —"

"Wouldn't you? We'll see. I'm not going to deny that I'm nervous of you being here. But since you are..." He trailed off, and for a second looked almost embarrassed. "Well, we'll have a chat later on."

Two

Intrigued by what Christian had said, and worried by his apprehension of me, I nonetheless restrained my curiosity and spent an hour exploring the house again from top to bottom, inside and out, everywhere save Father's study, the contemplation of which chilled me more than Christian's behavior had done. Nothing had changed, except that it was untidy, and untenanted. Christian had employed a part-time cleaner and cook, a woman from a nearby village who cycled to the Lodge every week and prepared a pie or stew that would last him three days. Christian did not go short of farm produce, so much so that he rarely bothered to use his ration book. He seemed to get all he needed, including sugar and tea, from the Ryhope estate, which had always been good to my family.

My old room was almost exactly as I remembered it. I opened the window wide and lay down on the bed for a few minutes, staring out and up into the hazy, late summer sky, past the waving branches of the gigantic beech that grew so close to the Lodge. Several times, in the years before my teens, I had climbed from window to tree, and made a secret camp among the thick branches; I had shivered by moonlight in my underpants, crouched in that private place, imagining the dark activities of night creatures below.

Lunch, in mid-afternoon, was a substantial feast of cold pork, chicken and hard-boiled eggs, in quantities that, after two years in France on strict rations, I had never thought to see again. We were, of course, eating his food supply for several days, but the fact seemed irrelevant to Christian, who in any case only picked at his meal.

Afterwards we talked for a couple of hours, and Christian relaxed quite noticeably, although he never referred to Guiwenneth, or to Father's work, and I never broached either subject.

We sprawled in the uncomfortable armchairs that had belonged to my grandparents, surrounded by the time-faded mementos of our family... photographs, a noisy rosewood clock, horrible pictures of exotic Spain, all framed in cracked mock-gilded wood, and all pressed hard against the same floral wallpaper that had hugged the walls of the sitting-room since a time before my birth. But it was home, and Christian was home, and the smell, and the faded surrounds, all were home to me. I knew, within two hours of arriving, that I would have to stay. It was not so much that I belonged here (although I certainly felt that) but simply that the place belonged to me — not in any mercenary sense of ownership, more in the way that the house and the land around the house shared a common life with me; we were part of the same evolution. Even in France, even in the village in the south, I had not been separated from that evolution, merely stretched to an extreme.

As the heavy old clock began to whirr and click, preceding its labored chiming of the hour of five, Christian abruptly rose from his chair and tossed his half-smoked cigarette into the empty fire grate.

"Let's go to the study," he said, and I rose without speaking and followed him through the house to the small room where our father had worked. "You're scared of this room, aren't you?" He opened the door and walked inside, crossing to the heavy oak desk and pulling out a large leather-bound book from one of the drawers.

I hesitated outside the study, watching Christian, almost unable to move my legs to carry myself into the room. I recognized the book he held, my father's notebook. I touched my back pocket, the wallet I carried there, and thought of the fragment of that notebook which was hidden inside the thin leather. I wondered if anyone, my father or Christian, had ever noticed that a page was missing. Christian was watching me, his eyes bright with excitement now, his hands trembling as he placed the book on the desk top.

"He's dead, Steve. He's gone from this room, from the house. There's no need to be afraid any more."

"Isn't there?"

But I found the sudden strength to move, and stepped across the threshold. The moment I entered the musty room I felt totally subdued, deeply affected by the coolness of the place, the stark, haunted atmosphere that hugged the walls and carpets and windows. It smelled slightly of leather, here, and dust too, with just a distant hint of polish, as if Christian made a token effort to keep this stifling room clean. It was not a crowded room, not a library as my father would perhaps have liked it to be. There were books on zoology and botany, on history and archaeology, but these were not rare editions, merely the cheapest copies he could find at the time. There were more paperbacks than hardcover books; the exquisite binding of his notes, and the deeply varnished desk, had an air of Victorian elegance about them that belied the otherwise shabby studio.

On the walls, between the cases of books, were his glass-framed specimens: pieces of wood, collections of leaves, crude sketches of animal and plant life made during the first years of his fascination with the forest.

THE SECRET HISTORY OF FANTASY

And almost hidden away among the cases and the shelves was the patterned shaft of the arrow that had struck him fifteen years before, its flights twisted and useless, the broken shaft glued together, the iron head dulled with corrosion, but a lethal-looking weapon nonetheless.

I stared at that arrow for several seconds, reliving the man's agony, and the tears that Christian and I had wept for him as we had helped him back from the woodlands, that cold autumn afternoon, convinced that he would die.

How quickly things had changed after that strange and never fully explained incident. If the arrow linked me with an earlier day, when some semblance of concern and love had remained in my father's mind, the rest of the study radiated only coldness.

I could still see the greying figure, bent over his desk writing furiously. I could hear the troubled breathing, the lung disorder that finally killed him; I could hear his caught breath, the vocalized sound of irritation as he grew aware of my presence, and waved me away with a half-irritated gesture, as if he begrudged even that split second of acknowledgment.

How like him Christian looked now, standing there behind the desk dishevelled and sickly, his hands in the pockets of his flannels, shoulders drooped, his whole body visibly shaking, and yet with the mark of absolute confidence about him.

He had waited quietly as I adjusted to the room, and let the memories and atmosphere play through me. As I stepped up to the desk, my mind back on the moment at hand, he said, "Steve, you should read the notes. They'll make a lot of things clear to you, and help you understand what it is I'm doing as well."

I turned the notebook towards me, scanning the sprawling, untidy handwriting, picking out words and phrases, reading through the years of my father's life in a few scant seconds. The words were as meaningless, on the whole, as those on my purloined sheet. To read them brought back a memory of anger, of danger, and of fear. The life in the notes had sustained me through nearly a year of war and had come to mean something outside of their proper context. I felt reluctant to dispel that powerful association with the past.

"I intend to read them, Chris. From beginning to end, and that's a promise. But not for the moment."

I closed the book, noticing as I did that my hands were clammy and trembling. I was not yet ready to be so close to my father again, and Christian saw this, and accepted it.

Conversation died quite early that night, as my energy expired, and the tensions of the long journey finally caught up with me. Christian came upstairs with me and stood in the doorway of my room, watching as I turned back the sheets and pottered about, picking up bits and pieces of my past life, laughing, shaking my head and trying to evoke a last moment's tired nostalgia. "Remember making camp out in the beech?" I asked, watching the grey of branch and leaf against the fading evening sky. "Yes," said Christian with a smile. "Yes, I remember very clearly."

But the conversation was as tired as that, and Christian took the hint and said, "Sleep well, old chap. I'll see you in the morning."

If I slept at all, it was for the first four or five hours after putting head to pillow. I woke sharply, and brightly, in the dead of night, one or two o'clock perhaps; the sky was very dark now, and it was quite windy outside. I lay and stared at the window, wondering how my body could feel so fresh, so alert. There was movement downstairs, and I guessed that Christian was doing some tidying, restlessly walking through the house, trying to adjust to the idea of my moving in.

The sheets smelled of mothballs and old cotton; the bed creaked in a metallic way when I shifted on it, and when I lay still the whole room clicked and shuffled, as if adapting itself to its first company in so many years. I lay awake for ages, but must have drifted to sleep again before first light, because suddenly Christian was bending over me, shaking my shoulder gently.

I started with surprise, awake at once, and propped up on my elbows, looking around. It was dawn. "What is it, Chris?"

"I've got to go. I'm sorry, but I have to."

I realized he was wearing a heavy oilskin cape, and had thick-soled walking boots on his feet. "Go? What d'you mean, go?"

"I'm sorry, Steve. There's nothing I can do about it." He spoke softly, as if there were someone else in the house who might be woken by raised voices. He looked more drawn than ever in this pale light, and his eyes were narrowed — I thought with pain, or anxiety. "I have to go away for a few days. You'll be all right. I've left a list of instructions downstairs, where to get bread, eggs, all that sort of thing. I'm sure you'll be able to use my ration book until yours comes. I shan't be long, just a few days. That's a promise..."

He rose from his crouch and walked out of the door. "For God's sake, Chris, where are you going?"

"Inwards," was all he said, before I heard him clump heavily down the stairs. I remained motionless for a moment or two, trying to clear my thoughts, then rose, put on my dressing-gown and followed him down to the kitchen. He had already left the house. I went back up to the landing window and saw him skirting the edge of the yard and walking swiftly down towards the south track. He was wearing a wide-brimmed hat and carrying a long, black staff; on his back he had a small rucksack, slung uncomfortably over one shoulder.

"Where's inwards, Chris?" I said to his vanishing figure, and watched long after he had disappeared from view.

"What's going on, Chris?" I asked of his empty bedroom as I wandered restlessly through the house; Guiwenneth, I decided in my wisdom, her loss, her leaving...how little one could interpret from the words "she's gone." And in all our chat of the evening before he had never alluded to his wife again. I had come home to England expecting to find a cheerful young couple, and instead had found a haunted, wasting brother living in the derelict shadow of our family home.

By the afternoon I had resigned myself to a period of solitary living, for wherever Christian had gone (and I had a fairly good idea) he had said clearly that he would be gone for some time. There was a lot to do about the house and the yard, and there seemed no better way to spend my time than in beginning to rebuild the personality of Oak Lodge. I made a list of essential repairs, and the following day walked into the nearest town to order what materials I could, mostly wood and paint, which I found in reasonable supply.

I renewed my acquaintance with the Ryhope family, and with many of the local families with whom I had once been friendly. I terminated the services of the part-time cook; I could look after myself quite well enough.

And at last I visited the cemetery; a single, brief visit, coldly accomplished.

The month of August turned to September, and I noticed a definite crispness in the air by evening, and early in the morning. It was a season I loved, the turn from summer to autumn, although it bore with it associations of return to school after the long holiday, a memory I didn't cherish.

I soon grew used to being on my own in the house, and although I took long walks around the deep woodlands, watching the road and the railway track for Christian's return, I had ceased to feel anxious about him by the end of my first week home, and had settled comfortably into a daily routine of building in the yard, painting the exterior woodwork of the house ready for the onslaught of winter, and digging over the large, untended garden.

It was during the evening of my eleventh day at home that this domestic routine was disturbed by a circumstance of such peculiarity that afterwards I could not sleep for thinking about it.

I had been in the town of Hobbhurst for most of the afternoon, and after a light evening meal was sitting reading the newspaper; towards nine o'clock, as I began to feel ready for an evening stroll, I thought I heard a dog, not so much barking as howling. My first thought was that Christian was coming back, my second that there were no dogs in this immediate area at all.

I went out into the yard; it was after dusk, but still quite bright, although the oakwoods were melded together into a grey-green blur. I called for Christian, but there was no response. I was about to return to my paper when a man stepped out of the distant woodland, and began to trot towards me. He was holding on a short, leather leash the most enormous hound I have ever seen.

At the gate to our private grounds he stopped, and the dog began to growl; it placed its forepaws on the fence, and in so doing rose almost to the height of its master. I felt nervous at once, keeping my attention balanced between the gaping, panting mouth of that dark beast, and the strange man who held it in check.

It was difficult to make him out clearly, for his face was painted with dark patterns and his moustaches drooped to well below his chin; his hair was plastered thickly about his scalp; he wore a dark woollen shirt, with a leather jerkin over the top, and tight, check-patterned breeches that reached to just below his knees. When he stepped cautiously through the gate I could see his rough and ready sandals. Across his shoulder he carried a crude-looking bow, and a bundle of arrows, held together with a simple thong and tied to his belt. Like Christian, he bore a staff.

Inside the gate he hesitated, watching me. The hound was restless beside him, licking its mouth and growling softly. I had never seen a dog such as this, shaggy and dark-furred, with the narrow pointed face of an Alsatian, but the body, it seemed to me, of a bear — except that its legs were long and thin, an animal made for chasing, for hunting.

The man spoke to me, and although I felt familiar with the words, they meant nothing. I didn't know what to do, so I shook my head and said that I didn't understand. The man hesitated just a moment before repeating what he had said, this time with a distinct edge of anger in his voice. And he started to walk towards me, tugging at the hound to prevent it straining at the leash. The light was draining from the sky, and he seemed to grow in stature in the greyness as he approached. The beast watched me, hungrily.

"What do you want?" I called, and tried to sound firm when I would rather have run inside the house. The man was ten paces away from me. He stopped, spoke again, and this time made eating motions with the hand that held his staff. *Now* I understood.

I nodded vigorously. "Wait here," I said, and went back to the house to fetch the cold joint of pork that was to last me four more days. It was not large, but it seemed a hospitable thing to do. I took the meat, half a granary loaf, and a jug of bottled beer out into the yard. The stranger was crouched now, the hound lying down beside him, rather reluctantly, it seemed to me. As I tried to approach them, the dog growled, then barked in a way that set my heart racing and nearly made me drop my gifts. The man shouted at the beast, and said something to me. I placed the food where I stood and backed away. The gruesome pair approached and again squatted down to eat.

As he picked up the joint I saw the scars on his arm, running down and across the bunched muscles. I also smelled him, a raw, rancid odor, sweat and urine mixed with the fetid aroma of rotting meat. I felt sick, but held my ground watching as the stranger tore at the pork with his teeth, swallowing hard and fast. The hound watched me.

After a few minutes the man stopped eating, looked at me, and with his gaze fixed on mine, almost challenging me to react, passed the rest of the meat to the dog, which growled loudly and snapped at the joint. The hound chewed, cracked and gulped the entire piece of pork in less than four minutes, while the stranger cautiously — and without much apparent pleasure — drank beer and chewed on a large mouthful of bread.

Finally this bizarre feast was over. The man rose to his feet and jerked the hound away from where it was licking the ground noisily. He said a word I intuitively recognized as "thank you." He was about to turn when the hound scented something; it uttered first a high-pitched keen, and then a raucous bark, and snatched itself away from its master's restraining grip, racing across the yard to a spot between the ramshackle chicken houses. Here it sniffed and scratched until the man reached it, grabbed the leather leash, and shouted angrily and lengthily at his charge. The hound moved with him, padding silently and monstrously into the gloom beyond the yard. They ran at full speed around the edge of the woodland, towards the farmlands around the village of Grimley, and that was the last I saw of them.

In the morning the place where the man and beast had rested *still* smelled rank. I skirted the area quickly as I walked to the woods and found the place where my strange visitors had emerged from the trees; it was trampled and broken, and I followed the line of their passage for some yards into the shade before stopping and turning back.

Where on earth had they come from? Had the war had such an effect on men in England that some had returned to the wild, using bow and arrow and hunting dog for survival?

Not until midday did I think to look between the chicken huts, at the ground so deeply scored by that brief moment's digging. What had the beast scented, I wondered, and a sudden chill clawed at my heart. I left the place at a run, unwilling, for the moment, to confirm my worst fears.

How I knew I cannot say: intuition, or perhaps something that my subconscious had detected in Christian's words and mannerisms the week or so before, during our brief encounter. In any event, late in the afternoon that same day I took a spade to the chicken huts, and within a few minutes of digging had proved my instinct right.

It took me half an hour of sitting on the back doorstep of the house, staring across the yard at the grave, to find the courage to uncover the woman's body totally. I was dizzy, slightly sick, but most of all I was shaking; an uncontrollable, unwelcome shaking of arms and legs, so pronounced that I could hardly pull on a pair of gloves. But eventually I knelt by the hole and brushed the rest of the dirt from the corpse.

Christian had buried her three feet deep, face down; her hair was long and red; her body was still clad in a strange green garment, a patterned tunic that was laced at the sides and, though it was crushed up almost to her waist now, would have reached to her calves. A staff was buried with her. I turned the head, holding my breath against the almost intolerable smell of putrefaction, and with a little effort could gaze upon the withering face. I saw then how she had died, for the head and stump of the arrow were still embedded in her eye. Had Christian tried to withdraw the weapon and succeeded only in breaking it? There was enough of the shaft left for me to notice that it had the same carved markings as the arrow in my father's study.

Poor Guiwenneth, I thought, and let the corpse drop back to its resting place. I filled in the dirt again. When I reached the house I was cold with sweat, and in no doubt that I was about to be violently sick.

THREE

Two days later, when I came down in the morning, I found the kitchen littered with Christian's clothes and effects, the floor covered with mud and leaf litter. I crept upstairs to his room and stared at his semi-naked body: he was belly down on the bed, face turned towards me, sleeping soundly and noisily, and I imagined that he was sleeping enough for a week. The state of his body, though, gave me cause for concern. He was scratched and scarred from neck to ankle, filthy, and malodorous to an extreme. His hair was matted. And yet, about him there was something hardened and strong, a tangible physical change from the hollow-faced, rather skeletal young man who had greeted me nearly two weeks before.

He slept for most of the day, emerging at six in the evening wearing a loose-fitting grey shirt and flannels, torn off just above the knee. He had half-heartedly washed his face, but still reeked of sweat and vegetation, as if he had spent the days away buried in compost.

I fed him, and he drank the entire contents of a pot of tea as I sat watching him; he kept darting glances at me, suspicious little looks as if he were nervous of some sudden move or surprise attack upon him. The muscles of his arms and wrists were pronounced. This was almost a different man.

"'Where have you been, Chris?" I asked after a while, and was not at all surprised when he answered, "In the woods. Deep in the woods." He stuffed more meat into his mouth and chewed noisily. As he swallowed he found a moment to say, "I'm quite fit. Bruised and scratched by the damned brambles, but quite fit."

In the woods. Deep in the woods. What in heaven's name could he have been doing there? As I watched him wolf down his food I saw again the stranger, crouching like an animal in my yard, chewing on meat as if he were some wild beast. Christian reminded me of that man. There was the same air of the primitive about him.

"You need a bath rather badly," I said, and he grinned and made a sound of affirmation. I went on, "What have you been doing? In the woods. Have you been camping?"

He swallowed noisily, and drank half a cup of tea before shaking his head. "I have a camp there, but I've been searching, walking as deep as I could get. But I still can't get beyond..." He broke off and glanced at me, a questioning look in his eyes. "Did you read the old man's notebook?"

I said that I hadn't. In truth, I had been so surprised by his abrupt departure, and so committed to getting the house back into some sort of shape, that I had forgotten all about Father's notes on his work. And even as I said this I wondered if the truth of the matter was that I had put Father, his work and his notes, as far from my mind as possible, as if they were specters whose haunting would reduce my resolve to go forward.

Christian wiped his hand across his mouth and stared at his empty plate. He suddenly sniffed at himself and laughed.

"By God, I do stink. You'd better boil me up some water, Steve. I'll wash right now."

But I didn't move. Instead I stared across the wooden table at him; he caught my gaze and frowned. "What is it? What's on your mind?"

"I found her, Chris. I found her body. Guiwenneth. I found where you buried her."

I don't know what reaction I expected from Christian. Anger, perhaps, or panic, or a sudden babbling burst of explanation. I half hoped he would react with puzzlement, that the corpse in the yard would turn out not to be the remains of his wife, and that he had no involvement with its burial. But Christian knew about the body. He stared at me blankly, and a heavy, sweaty silence made me grow uncomfortable.

Suddenly I realized that Christian was crying, his gaze not wavering from my own, but moistened now by the tears that coursed through the remaining grime on his face. And yet he made no sound, and his face never changed its expression from that of bland, almost blind contemplation.

"Who shot her, Chris?" I asked quietly. "Did you?"

"Not me," he said, and with the words his tears stopped, and his gaze dropped to the table. "She was shot by a mythago. There was nothing I could do about it."

Mythago? The meaning was alien to me, although I recognized the word from the scrap of my father's notebook that I carried. I queried it and Chris rose from the table, but rested his hands upon it as he watched me. "A mythago," he repeated. "It's still in the woods...they all are. That's where I've been, seeking among them. I tried to save her, Steve. She was alive when I found her, and she might have stayed alive, but I brought her out of the woods...in a way, I did kill her. I took her away from the vortex, and she died quite quickly. I panicked, then. I didn't know what to do. I buried her because it seemed the easiest way out...."

"Did you tell the police? Did you report her death?"

Christian smiled, but it was not with any morbid humor. It was a knowing smile, a response to some secret that he had not so far shared; and yet the gesture was merely a defense, for it faded rapidly. "Not necessary, Steve...the police would not have been interested."

I rose angrily from the table. It seemed to me that Christian was behaving, and had behaved, with appalling irresponsibility. "Her family, Chris...her parents! They have a right to know."

And Christian laughed.

I felt the blood rise in my face. "I don't see anything to laugh at."

He sobered instantly, looked at me almost abashed. "You're right. I'm sorry. You don't understand, and it's time you did. Steve, she had no parents because she had no life, no real life. She's lived a thousand times, and she's never lived at all. But I still fell in love with her...and I shall find her again in the woods; she's in there somewhere...."

Had he gone mad? His words were the unreasoned babblings of one insane, and yet something about his eyes, something about his demeanor, told me that it was not so much insanity as obsession. But obsession with what?

"You *must* read the old man's notes, Steve. Don't put it off any longer. They will tell you about the wood, about what's going on in there. I mean it. I'm neither mad nor callous. I'm just trapped, and before I go away again, I'd like you to know why, and how, and where I'm going. Perhaps you'll be able to help me. Who knows? Read the book. And then we'll talk. And when you know what our dear departed father managed to do, then I'm afraid I shall have to take my leave of you again."

Four

There is one entry in my father's notebook that seems to mark a turning point in his research, and his life. It is longer than the other notes of that particular time, and follows an absence of seven months from the pages. While his entries are often detailed, he could not be described as having been a dedicated diarist, and the style varies from clipped notes to fluent description. (I discovered, too, that he himself had torn many pages from the thick book, thus concealing my minor crime quite effectively. Christian had never noticed the missing page.) On the whole, he seems to have used the notebook, and the quiet hours of recording, as a way of conversing with himself — a means of clarification of his own thoughts.

The entry in question is dated September 1935, and was written shortly after our encounter with the Twigling. After reading the entry for the first time I thought back to that year and realized I had been just eight years old.

Wynne-Jones arrived after dawn. Walked together along the south track, checking the flux-drains for signs of mythago activity. Back to the house quite shortly after — no one about, which suited my mood. A crisp, dry autumn day. Like last year, images of the Urscumug are strongest as the season changes. Perhaps he senses autumn, the dying of the green. He comes forward, and the oak-woods whisper to him. He must be close to genesis. Wynne-Jones thinks a further time of isolation needed, and it must be done. Jennifer already concerned and distraught by my absences. I feel helpless — can't speak to her. Must do what is needed.

Yesterday the boys glimpsed the Twigling. I had thought him resorbed — clearly the resonance is stronger than we had believed. He seems to frequent the woodland edge, which is to be expected. I have seen him along the track several times, but not for a year or so. The persistence is worrying. Both boys clearly disturbed by the sighting; Christian less emotional. I suspect it meant little to him, a poacher perhaps, or local man taking a short cut to Grimley. Wynne-Jones suggests we go back into woods and call the Twigling deep, perhaps to the hogback glade where he might remain in the strong oak vortex and eventually fade. But I know that penetrating into deep woodland will involve more than a week's absence, and poor Jennifer is already deeply depressed by my behavior. Cannot explain it to her, though I dearly want to. Do not want the children involved in this, and it worries me that they have now twice seen a mythago. I have invented magic forest creatures — stories for them. Hope they will associate what they see with products of their own imaginations. But must be careful.

Until it is resolved, until the Urscumug mythago forms from the woodland, must not let any but Wynne-Jones know of what I have discovered. The completeness of the resurrection essential. The Urscumug is the most powerful because he is the primary. I know for certain that the oakwoods will contain him, but others might be frightened of the power they would certainly be able to feel, and end it for everyone. Dread to think what would happen if these forests were destroyed, and yet they cannot survive forever.

Thursday: Today's training with Wynne-Jones: test pattern 26: iii, shallow hypnosis, green light environment. As the frontal bridge reached sixty volts, despite the pain, the flow across my skull was the most powerful I have ever known. Am now totally convinced that each half of the brain functions in a slightly different way, and that the hidden awareness is located on the right-hand side. It has been lost for so long! The Wynne-Jones bridge enables a superficial communion between the fields around each hemisphere, and the zone of the pre-mythago is excited accordingly. If only there were some way of exploring the living brain to find exactly where the site of this occult presence lies.

Monday: The forms of the mythagos cluster in my peripheral vision, still. Why never in fore-vision? These unreal images are mere reflections, after all. The form of Hood was subtly different — more brown than green, the face less friendly, more haunted, drawn. This is certainly because earlier images (even the Hood mythago that actually formed in the woodland, two years ago) were affected by my own confused childhood images of the greenwood, and the merry band. But now, evocation of the pre-mythago is more powerful, reaches to the basic form, without interference. The Arthur form was more real as well, and I glimpsed the various marshland forms from the latter part of the first millennium A.D. Also, a hint of the haunting presence of what I believe is a Bronze Age necromantic figure. A terrifying moment. The guardian of the Horse Shrine has gone, the shrine destroyed. I wonder why? The huntsman has been back to the "Wolf Glen"; his fire was quite fresh. I also found evidence of the neolithic shaman, the hunter-artist who leaves the strange red ochre patterns on tree and rock. Wynne-Jones would love me to explore these folk heroes, unrecorded and unknown, but I am anxious to find the primary image.

The Urscumug has formed in my mind in the clearest form I have ever seen him. Hints of the Twigling in shape, but he is much more ancient, far bigger. Decks himself with wood and leaves, on top of animal hides. Face seems smeared with white clay, forming a mask upon the exaggerated features below; but it is hard to see the face clearly. A mask upon a mask? The hair a mass of stiff and spiky points; gnarled hawthorn branches are driven up through the matted hair, giving a most bizarre appearance. I believe he carries a spear, with a wide, stone blade...an angry-looking weapon, but again, hard to see, always just out of focus. He is so old, this primary image, that he is fading from the human mind. He is also touched with confusion. The overlaying of later cultural interpretation of how his appearance would have been...a hint of bronze particularly, mostly about the arms (torques). I suspect that the legend of the Urscumug was powerful enough to carry through all the neolithic and on into the second millennium B.C., perhaps even later. Wynne-Jones thinks the Urscumug may pre-date even the neolithic.

Essential, now, to spend time in the forest, to allow the vortex to interact with me and form the mythago. I intend to leave the house within the next week.

Without commenting on the strange, confusing passages I had read, I turned the pages of the diary and read entries here and there. I could clearly recall that autumn in 1933, the time when my father had packed a large rucksack and wandered into the woods, walking swiftly away from my mother's hysterical shouting, flanked by his diminutive scientist friend (a sour-faced man who never acknowledged anyone but my father, and who seemed embarrassed to be in the house when he came to visit). Mother had not spoken for the rest of the day, and she did nothing but sit in her bedroom and occasionally weep. Christian and I had become so distraught at her behavior that in the later afternoon we had penetrated the oakwoods as deeply as we dared, calling for our father and finally panicking at the gloomy silence, and the loud, sudden sounds that disturbed it. He had returned weeks later, dishevelled and stinking like a tramp. The entry in his notebook, a few days subsequently, is a short and bitter account of failure. Nothing had happened. A single, rather rambling paragraph caught my attention.

> The mythogenetic process is not only complex, it is reluctant. I am too old! The equipment helps, but a younger mind could accomplish the task unaided, I'm sure. I dread the thought! Also, my mind is not at rest and as Wynne-Jones has explained, it is likely that my human consideration, my worries, form an effective barrier between the two mythopoetic energy flows in my cortex — the *form* from the right brain, the *reality* from the left. The premythago zone is not sufficiently enriched by my own life force for it to interact in the oak vortex.
>
> I fear too that the natural disappearance of so much life from the forest is affecting the interface. The boars are there, I'm sure. But perhaps the life number is critical. I estimate no more than forty, moving within the spiral vortex bounded by the ashwood intrusions into the oak circle. There are few deer, few wolves, although the most important animal, the hare, frequents the woodland edge in profusion. But perhaps the absence of so much that once lived here has thrown the balance of the formula. And yet, throughout the primary existence of these woods, life was changing. By the thirteenth century there was *much* botanical life that was alien to the *ley matrix* in places where the mythagos still formed. The form

THE SECRET HISTORY OF FANTASY

of the myth men changes, adapts, and it is the later forms that generate most easily.

Hood is back — like all the Jack-in-the-Greens, is a nuisance, and several times moved into the ridge-zone around the hogback glade. He shot at me, and this is becoming a cause of great concern! But I cannot enrich the oak vortex sufficiently with the pre-mythago of the Urscumug. What is the answer? To try to enter more deeply, to find the *wildwoods*? Perhaps the memory is too far gone, too deep in the silent zones of the brain, now, to touch the trees.

Christian saw me frown as I read through this tumble of words and images. Hood? Robin Hood? And someone — this Hood — shooting at my father in the woods? I glanced around the study and saw the iron-tipped arrow in its long, narrow glass case, mounted above the display of woodland butterflies. Christian was turning the pages of the notebook, having watched me read in silence for the better part of an hour. He was perched on the desk; I sat in father's chair.

"What's all this about, Chris? It reads as if he were actually trying to create copies of storybook heroes."

"Not copies, Steve. The real thing. There. Last bit of reading for the moment, then I'll go through it with you in layman's terms."

It was an earlier entry, not dated by year, only by day and month, although it was clearly from some years before the 1933 recording.

I call those particular times "cultural interfaces"; they form zones, bounded in space, of course, by the limits of the country, but bounded also in time, a few years, a decade or so, when the two cultures — that of the invaded and the invader — are in a highly anguished state. The mythagos grow from the power of hate, and fear, and form in the natural woodlands from which they can either emerge — such as the Arthur, or Artorius form, the bearlike man with his charismatic leadership — or remain in the natural landscape, establishing a hidden focus of hope — the Robin Hood form, perhaps Hereward, and of course the hero-form I call the

Twigling, harassing the Romans in so many parts of the country. I imagine that it is the combined emotion of the two races that draws out the mythago, but it clearly sides with that culture whose roots are longest established in what I agree could be a sort of *ley matrix*; thus, Arthur forms and helps the Britons against the Saxons, but later Hood is created to help the Saxons against the Norman invader.

I drew back from the book, shaking my head. The expressions were confusing, bemusing. Christian grinned as he took the notebook, and weighed it in his hands. "Years of his life, Steve, but his concern with keeping detailed records was not everything it might have been. He records nothing for years, then writes every day for a month. *And* he has removed and hidden several pages." He frowned slightly as he said this.

"I need a drink of something. And a few definitions."

We walked from the study, Christian carrying the notebook. As we passed the framed arrow I peered closely at it. "Is he saying that the real Robin Hood shot that into him? And killed Guiwenneth too?"

"It depends," said Christian thoughtfully, "on what you mean by real. Hood came to that oak forest, and may still be there. I think he is. As you have obviously noticed, he was there four months ago when he shot Guiwenneth. But there were many Robin Hoods, and all were as real or unreal as each other, created by the Saxon peasants during their time of repression by the Norman invader."

"I don't comprehend this at all, Chris — but what's a 'ley matrix'? What's an 'oak vortex'? Does it mean anything?"

As we sipped scotch and water in the sitting-room, watching the dusk draw closer, the yard beyond the window greying into a place of featureless shapes, Christian explained how a man called Alfred Watkins had visited our father on several occasions and shown him on a map of the country how straight lines connected places of spiritual or ancient power — the barrows, stones and churches of three different cultures. These lines he called leys, and believed that they existed as a form of earth energy running below the ground, but influencing that which stood upon it.

My father had thought about leys, and apparently tried to measure the energy in the ground below the forest, but without success. And yet he had measured *something* in the oakwoods — an energy associated with all the life that grew there. He had found a spiral vortex around each tree, a sort of aura, and those spirals bounded not just trees, but whole stands of trees, and glades.

Over the years he had mapped the forest. Christian brought out that map of the woodland area, and I looked at it again, but from a different point of view, beginning to understand the marks made upon it by the man who had spent so much time within the territories it depicted. Circles within circles were marked, crossed and skirted by straight lines, some of which were associated with the two pathways we called south and deep track. The letters HB in the middle of the vast acreage of forest were clearly meant to refer to the "hogback" glade that existed there, a clearing that neither Christian nor I had ever been able to find. There were zones marked out as "spiral oak," "dead ash zone" and "oscillating traverse."

"The old man believed that all life is surrounded by an energetic aura — you can see the human aura as a faint glow in certain light. In these ancient woodlands, *primary woodlands,* the combined aura forms something far more powerful, a sort of creative field that can interact with our unconscious. And it's in the unconscious that we carry what he calls the pre-mythago — that's *myth imago,* the image of the idealized form of a myth creature. The image takes on substance in a natural environment, solid flesh, blood, clothing, and — as you saw — weaponry. The form of the idealized myth, the hero figure, alters with cultural changes, assuming the identity and technology of the time. When one culture invades another — according to Father's theory — the heroes are made manifest, and not just in one location! Historians and legend-seekers argue about where Arthur of the Britons and Robin Hood *really* lived and fought, and don't realize that they lived in *many* sites. And another important fact to remember is that when the mind image of the mythago forms it forms in the *whole* population…and when it is no longer needed, it remains in our collective unconscious, and is transmitted through the generations."

"And the changing form of the mythago," I said, to see if I had understood my sketchy reading of Father's notes, "is based on an archetype, an archaic primary image which Father called the Urscumug, and from which all later forms come. And he tried to raise the Urscumug from his own unconscious mind...."

"And failed to do so," said Christian, "although not for want of trying. The effort killed him. It weakened him so much that his body couldn't take the pace. But he certainly seems to have created several of the more recent adaptations of the Urscumug."

There were so many questions, so many areas that begged for clarification. One above all: "But a thousand years ago, if I understand the notes correctly, there was a country-wide *need* of the hero, the legendary figure, acting for the side of Right. How can one man capture such a passionate mood? How did he *power* the interaction? Surely not from the simple family anguish he caused among us, and in his own head. As he said, that created an unsettled mind and he couldn't function properly."

"If there's an answer," said Christian calmly, "it's to be found in the woodland area, perhaps in the hogback glade. The old man wrote in his notes of the need for a period of solitary existence, a period of meditation. For a year now I've been following his example directly. He invented a sort of electrical bridge which seems to *fuse* elements from each half of the brain. I've used his equipment a great deal, with and without him. But I already find images — the pre-mythagos — forming in my peripheral vision *without* the complicated programme that he used. He was the pioneer; his own interaction with the wood has made it easier for those who come after. Also, I'm younger. He felt that would be important. He achieved a certain success; I intend to complete his work, eventually. I shall raise the Urscumug, this hero of the first men."

"To what end, Chris?" I asked quietly, and in all truth could not see a reason for so tampering with the ancient forces that inhabited both woodland and human spirit. Christian was clearly obsessed with the idea of raising these dead forms, of finishing something the old man had begun. But in my reading of his notebook, and in my conversation with Christian, I had not heard a single word that explained *why* so bizarre a state of nature should be so important to the ones who studied it.

Christian had an answer. And as he spoke to me his voice was hollow, the mark of his uncertainty, the stigma of his lack of conviction in the truth of what he said. "Why, to study the earliest times of man, Steve. From these mythagos we can learn so much of how it was, and how it was hoped to be. The aspirations, the visions, the cultural identity of a time so far gone that even its stone monuments are incomprehensible to us. To learn. To communicate through those persistent images of our past that are locked in each and every one of us."

He stopped speaking, and there was the briefest of silences, interrupted only by the heavy rhythmic sound of the clock. I said, "I'm not convinced, Chris." For a moment I thought he would shout his anger; his face flushed, his whole body tensed up, furious with my calm dismissal of his script. But the fire softened, and he frowned, staring at me almost helplessly. "What does that mean?"

"Nice-sounding words; no conviction."

After a second he seemed to acknowledge some truth in what I said. "Perhaps my conviction has gone, then, buried beneath…beneath the other thing. Guiwenneth. She's become my main reason for going back now."

I remembered his callous words of a while ago, about how she had no life yet a thousand lives. I understood instantly, and wondered how so obvious a fact could have remained so doggedly elusive to me. "She was a mythago herself," I said. "I understand now."

"She was my father's mythago, a girl from Roman times, a manifestation of the Earth Goddess, the young warrior princess who, through her own suffering, can unite the tribes."

"Like Queen Boadicea," I said.

"Boudicca," Christian corrected, then shook his head. "Boudicca was historically real, although much of her legend was inspired by the myths and tales of the girl Guiwenneth. There are no recorded legends about Guiwenneth. In her own time, and her own culture, the oral tradition held sway. Nothing was written; but no Roman observer, or later Christian chronicler, refers to her either, although the old man thought that early tales of Queen Guenevere might have drawn partly from the forgotten legends. She's lost from popular memory —"

"But not from hidden memory!"

Christian nodded. "That's exactly right. Her story is very old, very familiar. Legends of Guiwenneth rose out of stories from previous cultures, perhaps right back to the post-glacial period, or to the time of the Urscumug itself!"

"And each of those earlier forms of the girl will be in the wood too?"

Christian shrugged. "The old man saw none, and nor have I. But they *must* be there."

"And what *is* her story, Chris?"

He looked at me peculiarly. "That's hard to say. Our dear father tore the pages about Guiwenneth from his diary. I have no idea why, or where he hid them. I only know what he told me. Oral tradition again." He smiled. "She was the child to the younger of two sisters, by a young warrior banished to a secret camp in the wildwoods. The elder sister was the wife of one of the invaders, and she was both barren and jealous, and stole the girl child. The child was rescued by nine hawks, or some such, sent by her father. She was brought up in the forest communities all around the country, under the guardianship of the Lord of Animals. When she was old enough, and strong enough, she returned, raised the ghost of her warlord father, and drove the invaders out."

"Not much to go on," I said.

"A fragment only," Christian agreed. "There is something about a bright stone, in a valley that breathes. Whatever else the old man learned about her, or from her, he has destroyed."

"Why, I wonder?"

Christian said nothing for a moment, then added, "Anyway, legends of Guiwenneth inspired many tribes to take offensive action against the invader, whether they were Wessex Chieftain, which is to say, Bronze Age, Stonehenge and all that; Belgic Celts, which is to say Iron Age; or Romans." His gaze became distant for a moment. "And then she was formed in this wood, and I found her and came to love her. She was not violent, perhaps because the old man himself could not think of a woman being violent.

He imposed a structure on her, disarming her, leaving her quite helpless in the forest."

"How long did you know her?" I asked, and he shrugged.

"I can't tell, Steve. How long have I been away?"

"Twelve days or so."

"As short as that?" He seemed surprised. "I thought more than three weeks. Perhaps I knew her for no time at all, then, but it seems like months. I lived in the forest with her, trying to understand her language, trying to teach her mine, speaking with signs and yet always able to talk quite deeply. But the old man pursued us right to the heartwoods, right to the end. He wouldn't let up — she was *his* girl, and he had been as struck by her as had I. I found him, one day, exhausted and terrified, half buried by leaves at the forest edge. I took him home and he was dead within the month. That's what I meant by his having had a reason for attacking me. I took Guiwenneth from him."

"And then she was taken from you. Shot dead."

"A few months later, yes. I became a little too happy, a little too content. I wrote to you because I had to tell *someone* about her...clearly that was too much for fate. Two days later I found her in a glade, dying. She might have lived if I could have got help to her in the forest, and left her there. I carried her out of the wood, though, and she died." He stared at me and the expression of sadness hardened to one of resolve. "But when I'm back in the wood, her myth image from my own subconscious has a chance of being formed... she might be a little tougher than my father's version, but I can find her again, Steve, if I look hard, if I can find that energy you asked about, if I can get into the deepest part of the wood, to that central vortex...."

I looked at the map again, at the spiral field around the hogback glade. "What's the problem? Can't you find it?"

"It's well defended. I get near it, but I can't ever get beyond the field that's about two hundred yards around it. I find myself walking in elaborate circles even though I'm convinced I've walked straight. I can't get in, and whatever's in there can't get out. All the mythagos are tied to their genesis zones, although the Twigling, and Guiwenneth too, could get to the very edge of the forest, down by the pool."

But that wasn't true! And I'd spent a shaky night to prove it. I said, "One of the mythagos has come out of the wood...a tall man with the most un-believably terrifying hound. He came into the yard and ate a leg of pork."

Christian looked stunned. "A mythago? Are you sure?"

"Well, no. I had no idea at all what he was until now. But he stank, was filthy, had obviously lived in the woods for months, spoke a strange language, carried a bow and arrows..."

"And ran with a hunting dog. Yes, of course. It's a late Bronze Age, early Iron Age image, very widespread. The Irish have taken him to their own with Cuchulainn, made a big hero out of him, but he's one of the most powerful of the myth images, recognizable all across Europe." Christian frowned, then. "I don't understand...a year ago I saw him, and avoided him, but he was fading fast, decaying...it happens to them after a while. Something must have fed the mythago, strengthened it...."

"Some *one,* Chris."

"But who?" It dawned on him, then, and his eyes widened slightly. "My God. Me. From my own mind. It took the old man years, and I thought it would take me a lot longer, many more months in the woodlands, much more isolation. But it's started already, my own interaction with the vortex...."

He had gone quite pale, and he walked to where his staff was propped against the wall, picked it up and weighed it in his hands. He stared at it, touched the markings upon it.

"You know what this means," he said quietly, and before I could answer went on, "She'll form. She'll come back; *my* Guiwenneth. She may be back already."

"Don't go rushing off again, Chris. Wait a while; rest."

He placed his staff against the wall again. "I don't dare. If she has formed by now, she's in danger. I have to go back." He looked at me and smiled thinly, apologetically. "Sorry, brother. Not much of a homecoming for you."

FIVE

As quickly as this, after the briefest of reunions, I had lost Christian again. He was in no mood to talk, too distracted by the thought of Guiwenneth alone and trapped in the forest to allow me much of an insight into his plans, and into his hopes and fears for some resolution to their impossible love affair.

I wandered through the kitchen and the rest of the house as he gathered his provisions together. Again and again he assured me that he would be gone for no more than a week, perhaps two. If she was in the wood he would have found her by that time; if not, then he would return and wait a while before going back to the deep zones and trying to form her mythago. In a year, he said, many of the more hostile mythagos would have faded into non-existence, and she would be safer. His thoughts were confused, his plan that he would strengthen her to allow her the same freedom as the man and the hound did not seem supportable on the evidence from our father's notes; but Christian was a determined man.

If one mythago could escape, then so could the one he loved.

One idea that appealed to him was that I should come with him as far as the glade where we had made camp as children, and pitch a tent there. This could be a regular rendezvous for us, he said, and it would keep his time sense on the right track. And if I spent time in the forest I might encounter other mythagos, and could report on their state. The glade he had in mind was at the edge of the wood, and quite safe.

When I expressed concern that my own mind would begin to produce mythagos, he assured me that it would take months for the first pre-mythago activity to show up as a haunting presence at the edge of my vision. He was equally blunt in saying that, if I stayed in the area for too long, I would certainly start to relate to the woodland, whose aura — he thought — had spread more towards the house in the last few years.

Late the following morning we set off along the south track. A pale yellow sun hung high above the forest. It was a cool, bright day, the air full of the scent of smoke, drifting from the distant farm where the stubbly remains of the summer harvest were being burned. We walked in silence until we came to the mill-pond; I had assumed Christian would enter the oak woodland here, but wisely he decided against it, not so much because of the strange movements we had seen there as children, but because of the marshy conditions. Instead, we walked on until the woodland bordering the track thinned. Here Christian turned off the path.

I followed him inwards, seeking the easiest route between tangles of bracken and nettles, enjoying the heavy stillness. The trees were small, here at the edge, but within a hundred yards they began to show their real age, great gnarled oak trunks, hollow and half-dead, twisting up from the ground, almost groaning beneath the weight of their branches. The ground rose slightly, and the tangled undergrowth was broken by weathered, lichen-covered stubs of grey limestone. We passed over the crest and the earth dipped sharply down, and a subtle change came over the woodland. It seemed darker, somehow, more alive, and I noticed that the shrill September bird-sound of the forest edge was replaced, here, by a more sporadic, mournful song.

Christian beat his way through bramble thickets, and I trudged wearily after, and we soon came to the large glade where, years before, we had made our camp. One particularly large oak tree dominated the surrounds, and we laughed as we traced the faded initials we had once carved there. In its branches we had made our lookout tower, but we had seen very little from that leafy vantage point.

"Do I look the part?" asked Christian, holding his arms out, and I grinned as I surveyed his caped figure, the rune-inscribed staff looking less odd, now, more functional.

"You look like something. Quite what I don't know."

He glanced around the clearing. "I'll do my best to get back here as often as I can. If anything goes wrong, I'll try and leave a message if I can't find you, some mark to let you know…"

"Nothing's going to go wrong," I said with a smile. It was clear that he didn't wish me to accompany him beyond this glade, and that suited me. I felt a chill, an odd tingle, a sense of being watched. Christian noticed my discomfort and admitted that he felt it too, the presence of the wood, the gentle breathing of the trees.

We shook hands, then embraced awkwardly, and he turned on his heels and paced off into the gloom. I watched him go, then listened, and

THE SECRET HISTORY OF FANTASY

only when all sound had gone did I set about pitching the small tent.

For most of September the weather remained cool and dry, a dull sort of month that enabled me to drift through the days in a very low-key state. I worked on the house, read some more of Father's notebook (but quickly tired of the repetitive images and thoughts) and with decreasing frequency walked into the woodlands and sat near, or in, the tent, listening for Christian, cursing the midges that haunted the place, and watching for any hint of movement.

With October came rain and the abrupt, almost startling realization that Christian had been gone for nearly a month. The time had slipped by, and instead of feeling concerned for him I had merely assumed that he knew what he was doing, and would return when he was quite ready. But he had been absent for weeks without even the slightest sign. He could surely have come back to the glade once, and left some mark of his passing.

Now I began to feel more concern for his safety than perhaps was warranted. As soon as the rain stopped I trudged back through the forest and waited out the rest of the day in the miserable, leaking canvas shelter. I saw hares, and a wood owl, and heard distant movements that did not respond to my cries of "Christian? Is that you?"

It got colder. I spent more time in the tent, creating a sleeping bag out of blankets and some tattered oilskins I found in the cellar of Oak Lodge. I repaired the splits in the tent, and stocked it with food and beer, and dry wood for fires. By the middle of October I noticed that I could not spend more than an hour at the house before becoming restless, an unease that could only be dispelled by returning to the glade and taking up my watching post, seated cross-legged just inside the tent, watching the gloom a few yards away. On several occasions I took long, rather nervous sorties further into the forest, but I disliked the sensation of stillness and the tingling of my skin which seemed to say repeatedly that I was being watched. All this was imagination, of course, or an extremely sensitive response to woodland animals, for on one occasion, when I ran screaming and yelling at the thicket wherein I imagined the voyeur was crouched, I saw nothing but a red squirrel go scampering in panic up into the crossed and confused branches of its home oak.

Where *was* Christian? I tacked paper messages as deep in the wood, and in as many locations, as I could. But I found that wherever I walked too far into the great dip that seemed to be swallowing the forest down, I would, at some point within the span of a few hours, find myself approaching the glade and the tent again. Uncanny, yes, and infuriating too; but I began to get an idea of Christian's own frustration at not being able to maintain a straight line in the dense oakwood. Perhaps, after all, there *was* some sort of field of force, complex and convoluted, that channelled intruders back on to an outward track.

And November came, and it was very cold indeed. The rain was sporadic and icy, but the wind reached down through the dense, browning foliage of the forest and seemed to find its way through clothes and oilskin and flesh to the cooling bones beneath. I was miserable, and my searches for Christian grew more angry, more frustrated. My voice was often hoarse with shouting, my skin blistered and scratched from climbing trees. I lost track of time, realizing on more than one occasion, and with some shock, that I had been two, or perhaps three days in the forest without returning to the house. Oak Lodge grew stale and deserted. I used it to wash, to feed, to rest, but as soon as the worst ravages of my body were corrected, thoughts of Christian, anxiety about him, grew in my mind and pulled me back to the glade, as surely as if I were a metal filing tugged to a magnet.

I began to suspect that something terrible had happened to him; or perhaps not terrible, just natural: if there really were boars in the wood, he might have been gored by one, and be either dead or dragging himself from the heartwoods to the edge, unable to cry for help. Or perhaps he had fallen from a tree, or quite simply gone to sleep in the cold and wet and failed to revive in the morning.

I searched for any sign of his body, or of his having passed by, and I found absolutely nothing, although I discovered the spoor of some large beast, and marks on the lower trunks of several oaks that looked like nothing other than the scratchings of a tusked animal.

But my mood of depression passed, and by mid-November I was quite confident again that Christian was alive. My feelings, now, were that he had somehow become trapped in this autumnal forest.

For the first time in two weeks I went into the village, and after obtaining food supplies, I picked up the papers that had been accumulating at the tiny newsagent's. Skimming the front pages of the weekly local, I noticed an item concerning the decaying bodies of a man and an Irish wolfhound, discovered in a ditch on farmland near Grimley. Foul play was not suspected. I felt no emotion, apart from a curious coldness, a sense of sympathy for Christian, whose dream of freedom for Guiwenneth was surely no more than that: a fervent hope, a desire doomed to frustration.

As for mythagos, I had only two encounters, neither of them of much note. The first was with a shadowy man-form that skirted the clearing, watching me, and finally ran into the darkness, striking at the trunks of trees with a short, wooden stick. The second meeting was with the Twigling, whose shape I followed stealthily as he walked to the mill-pond and stood in the trees, staring across at the boathouse. I felt no real fear of these manifestations, merely a slight apprehension. But it was only after the second meeting that I began to realize how alien the wood was to the mythagos, and how alien the mythagos were to the wood. These creatures, created far away from their natural age, echoes of a past given substance, were equipped with a life, a language and a certain ferocity that was quite inappropriate to the war-scarred world of 1947. No wonder the aura of the woodland was so charged with a sense of solitude, an infectious loneliness that had come to inhabit the body of my father, and then Christian, and which was even now crawling through my own tissues, and would trap me if I allowed it.

It was at this time, too, that I began to hallucinate. Notably at dusk, as I stared into the woodlands, I saw movement at the edge of my vision. At first I put this down to tiredness, or imagination, but I remembered clearly the passage from my father's notebook in which he described how the pre-mythagos, the initial images, always appeared at his peripheral vision. I was frightened at first, unwilling to acknowledge that such creatures could be resident in my own mind, and that my own interaction with the woodland had begun far earlier than Christian had thought; but after a while I sat and tried to see details of them. I failed to do so. I could sense movement, and the occasional manlike shape, but whatever field was inducing their appearance was not yet strong enough to pull them into full view; either that, or my mind could not yet control their emergence.

On the 24th of November I went back to the house and spent a few hours resting and listening to the wireless. A thunderstorm passed overhead and I watched the rain and the darkness, feeling wretched and cold. But as soon as the air cleared, and the clouds brightened, I draped my oilskin about my shoulders and headed back to the glade. I had not expected to find anything different, and so what should have been a surprise was more of a shock.

The tent had been demolished, its contents strewn and trampled into the sodden turf of the clearing. Part of the guy rope dangled from the higher branches of the large oak, and the ground hereabouts was churned as if there had been a fight. As I walked into the space I noticed that the ground was pitted by strange footprints, round and cleft, like hooves, I thought. Whatever the beast had been it had quite effectively torn the canvas shelter to tatters.

I noticed then how silent the forest was, as if holding its breath and watching. Every hair on my body stood on end, and my heartbeat was so powerful that I thought my chest would burst. I stood by the ruined tent for just a second or two and the panic hit me, making my head spin and the forest seem to lean towards me. I fled from the glade, crashing into the sopping undergrowth between two thick oak trunks. I ran through the gloom for several yards before realizing I was running *away* from the woodland edge. I think I cried out, and turned and began to run back.

A spear thudded heavily into the tree beside me and I had run into the black wood shaft before I could stop; a hand gripped my shoulder and flung me against the tree. I shouted out in fear, staring into the mud-smeared, gnarled face of my attacker. He shouted back at me.

"Shut up, Steve! For God's sake, shut up!"

My panic quietened, my voice dropped to a whimper and I peered hard at the angry man who held me. It was Christian, I realized, and my relief was so intense that I laughed, and for long moments failed to notice what a total change had come about him.

He was looking back towards the glade. "You've got to get out of here," he said, and before I could respond he had wrenched me into a run, and was practically dragging me back to the tent.

In the clearing he hesitated and looked at me. There was no smile from behind the mask of mud and browning leaves. His eyes shone, but they were narrowed and lined. His hair was slick and spiky. He was naked but for a breechclout and a ragged skin jacket that could not have supplied much warmth. He carried three viciously pointed spears. Gone was the skeletal thinness of summer. He was muscular and hard, deep-chested and heavy-limbed. He was a man made for fighting.

"You've got to get out of the wood, Steve; and for God's sake don't come back."

"What's happened to you, Chris...?" I stuttered, but he shook his head and pulled me across the clearing and into the woods again, towards the south track.

Immediately he stopped, staring into gloom, holding me back. "What is it, Chris?"

And then I heard it too, a heavy crashing sound, something picking its way through the bracken and the trees towards us. Following Christian's gaze I saw a monstrous shape, twice as high as a man, but man-shaped and stooped, black as night save for the great white splash of its face, still indistinct in the distance and greyness.

"God, it's broken out!" said Christian. "It's got between us and the edge."

"What is it? A mythago?"

"*The* mythago," said Christian quickly, and turned and fled back across the clearing. I followed, all tiredness suddenly gone from my body.

"The Urscumug? That's *it?* But it's not human...it's animal. No human was ever that tall."

Looking back as I ran, I saw it enter the glade and move across the open space so fast I thought I was watching a speeded-up film. It plunged into the wood behind us and was lost in darkness again, but it was running now, weaving between trees as it pursued us, closing the distance with incredible speed.

Quite suddenly the ground went out from under me. I fell heavily into a depression in the ground, to be steadied, as I tumbled, by Christian, who moved a bramble covering across us and put a finger to his lips. I could barely make him out in this dark hidey hole, but I heard the sound of the Urscumug die away, and queried what was happening.

"Has it moved off?"

"Almost certainly not," said Christian. "It's waiting, listening. It's been pursuing me for two days, out of the deep zones of the forest. It won't let up until I'm gone."

"But why, Chris? Why is it trying to kill you?"

"It's the old man's mythago," he said. "He brought it into being in the heartwoods, but it was weak and trapped until I came along and gave it more power to draw on. But it was the old man's mythago, and he shaped it slightly from his own mind, his own ego. Oh God, Steve, how he must have hated, and hated *us*, to have imposed such terror on to the thing."

"And Guiwenneth…" I said.

"Yes…Guiwenneth…" Christian echoed, speaking softly now. "He'll revenge himself on me for that. If I give him half a chance."

He stretched up to peer through the bramble covering. I could hear a distant, restless movement, and thought I caught the sound of some animal grumbling deep in its throat.

"I thought he'd failed to create the primary mythago."

Christian said, "He died believing that. What would he have done, I wonder, if he'd seen how successful he'd been." He crouched back down in the ditch. "It's like a boar. Part boar, part man, elements of other beasts from the wildwood. It walks upright, but can run like the wind. It paints its face white in the semblance of a human face. Whatever age it lived in, one thing's for sure, it lived a long time before man as *we* understand 'man' existed; this thing comes from a time when man and nature were so close that they were indistinguishable."

He touched me, then, on the arm; a hesitant touch, as if he were half afraid to make this contact with one from whom he had grown so distant.

THE SECRET HISTORY OF FANTASY

"When you run," he said, "run for the edge. Don't stop. And when you get out of the wood, don't come back. There is no way out for me, now I'm trapped in this wood by something in my own mind as surely as if I were a mythago myself. Don't come back here, Steve. Not for a long, long time."

"Chris —" I began, but too late. He had thrown back the covering of the hole and was running from me. Moments later the most enormous shape passed overhead, one huge, black foot landing just inches from my frozen body. It passed by in a split second. But as I scrambled from the hole and began to run I glanced back and the creature, hearing me, glanced back too; and for that instant of mutual contemplation, as we both moved apart in the forest, I saw the face that had been painted across the blackened features of the boar.

The Urscumug opened its mouth to roar, and my father seemed to leer at me.

26 Monkeys, Also the Abyss

Kij Johnson

1

AIMEE'S BIG TRICK is that she makes 26 monkeys vanish onstage.

2

She pushes out a claw-foot bathtub and asks audience members to come up and inspect it. The people climb in and look underneath, touch the white enamel, run their hands along the little lion's feet. When they're done, four chains are lowered from the proscenium stage's fly space. Aimee secures them to holes drilled along the tub's lip, gives a signal, and the bathtub is hoisted ten feet into the air.

She sets a stepladder next to it. She claps her hands and the 26 monkeys onstage run up the ladder one after the other and jump into the bathtub. The bathtub shakes as each monkey thuds in among the others. The audience can see heads, legs, tails; but eventually every monkey settles and the bathtub is still again. Zeb is always the last monkey up the ladder. As he climbs into the bathtub, he makes a humming boom deep in his chest. It fills the stage.

And then there's a flash of light, two of the chains fall off, and the bathtub swings down to expose its interior.

Empty.

3

They turn up later, back at the tour bus. There's a smallish dog door, and in the hours before morning, the monkeys let themselves in, alone or in small groups, and get themselves glasses of water from the tap. If more than one returns at the same time, they murmur a bit among themselves, like college students meeting in the dorm halls after bar time. A few sleep on the sofa, and at least one likes to be on the bed, but most of them wander back to their cages. There's a little grunting as they rearrange their blankets and soft toys, and then sighs and snoring. Aimee doesn't really sleep until she hears them all come in.

Aimee has no idea what happens to them in the bathtub, or where they go, or what they do before the soft click of the dog door opening. This bothers her a lot.

4

Aimee has had the act for three years now. She was living in a month-by-month furnished apartment under a flight path for the Salt Lake City airport. She was hollow, as if something had chewed a hole in her body and the hole had grown infected.

There was a monkey act at the Utah State Fair. She felt a sudden and totally out-of-character urge to see it, and afterward, with no idea why, she walked up to the owner and said, "I have to buy this."

He nodded. He sold it to her for a dollar, which he told her was the price he had paid four years before.

Later, when the paperwork was filled out, she asked him, "How can you leave them? Won't they miss you?"

"You'll see, they're pretty autonomous," he said. "Yeah, they'll miss me and I'll miss them. But it's time, they know that."

He smiled at his new wife, a small woman with laugh lines and a vervet hanging from one hand. "We're ready to have a garden," she said.

He was right. The monkeys missed him. But they also welcomed her, each monkey politely shaking her hand as she walked into what was now her bus.

5

Aimee has: a nineteen-year-old tour bus packed with cages that range in size from parrot-sized (for the vervets) to something about the size of a pickup bed (for all the macaques); a stack of books on monkeys ranging from *All about Monkeys!* to *Evolution and Ecology of Baboon Societies*; some sequined show costumes, a sewing machine, and a bunch of Carhartts and tees; a stack of show posters from a few years back that say 24 MONKEYS! FACE THE ABYSS; a battered sofa in a virulent green plaid; and a boyfriend who helps with the monkeys.

She cannot tell you why she has any of these, not even the boyfriend, whose name is Geof, whom she met in Billings seven months ago. Aimee has no idea where anything comes from any more: she no longer believes that anything makes sense, even though she can't stop hoping.

The bus smells about as you'd expect a bus full of monkeys to smell; though after a show, after the bathtub trick but before the monkeys all return, it also smells of cinnamon, which is the tea Aimee sometimes drinks.

6

For the act, the monkeys do tricks, or dress up in outfits and act out hit movies — *The Matrix* is very popular, as is anything where the monkeys dress up like little orcs. The maned monkeys, the lion-tails and the colobuses, have a lion-tamer act, with the old capuchin female, Pango, dressed in a red jacket and carrying a whip and a small chair. The chimpanzee (whose name is Mimi, and no, she is not a monkey) can do actual sleight-of-hand; she's not very good, but she's the best Chimp Pulling A Coin From Someone's Ear in the world.

The monkeys also can build a suspension bridge out of wood chairs and rope, make a four-tier champagne fountain, and write their names on a whiteboard.

The monkey show is very popular, with a schedule of 127 shows this year at fairs and festivals across the Midwest and Great Plains. Aimee could do more, but she likes to let everyone have a couple months off at Christmas.

7

This is the bathtub act:

Aimee wears a glittering purple-black dress designed to look like a scanty magician's robe. She stands in front of a scrim lit deep blue and scattered with stars. The monkeys are ranged in front of her. As she speaks they undress and fold their clothes into neat piles. Zeb sits on his stool to one side, a white spotlight shining straight down to give him a shadowed look.

She raises her hands.

"These monkeys have made you laugh, and made you gasp. They have created wonders for you and performed mysteries. But there is a final mystery they offer you — the strangest, the greatest of all."

She parts her hands suddenly, and the scrim goes transparent and is lifted away, revealing the bathtub on a raised dais. She walks around it, running her hand along the tub's curves.

"It's a simple thing, this bathtub. Ordinary in every way, mundane as breakfast. In a moment I will invite members of the audience up to let you prove this for yourselves.

"But for the monkeys it is also a magical object. It allows them to travel — no one can say where. Not even I —" she pauses; "— can tell you this. Only the monkeys know, and they share no secrets.

"Where do they go? Into heaven, foreign lands, other worlds — or some dark abyss? We cannot follow. They will vanish before our eyes, vanish from this most ordinary of things."

And after the bathtub is inspected and she has told the audience that there will be no final spectacle in the show — "It will be hours before they return from their secret travels" — and called for applause for them, she gives the cue.

8

Aimee's monkeys:

2 siamangs, a mated couple

2 squirrel monkeys, though they're so active they might as well be twice as many

2 vervets

a guenon, who is probably pregnant, though it's still too early to tell for sure. Aimee has no idea how this happened

3 rhesus monkeys. They juggle a little

an older capuchin female named Pango

a crested macaque, 3 Japanese snow monkeys (one quite young), and a Java macaque. Despite the differences, they have formed a small troop and like to sleep together

a chimpanzee, who is not actually a monkey

a surly gibbon

2 marmosets

a golden tamarin; a cotton-top tamarin

a proboscis monkey

red and black colobuses

Zeb

9

Aimee thinks Zeb might be a de Brazza's guenon, except that he's so old that he has lost almost all his hair. She worries about his health but he insists on staying in the act. By now all he's really up for is the final rush to the bathtub, and for him it is more of a stroll. The rest of the time, he sits on a stool that is painted orange and silver and watches the other monkeys, looking like an aging impresario watching his *Swan Lake* from the wings. Sometimes she gives him things to hold, such as a silver hoop through which the squirrel monkeys jump.

10

No one seems to know how the monkeys vanish or where they go. Sometimes they return holding foreign coins or durian fruit, or wearing pointed Moroccan slippers. Every so often one returns pregnant, or leading an unfamiliar monkey by the hand. The number of monkeys is not constant.

"I just don't get it," Aimee keeps asking Geof, as if he has any idea. Aimee never knows anything any more. She's been living without any certainties, and this one thing — well, the whole thing, the fact the monkeys get along so well and know how to do card tricks and just turned up in her life and vanish from the bathtub; *everything* — she coasts with that most of the time, but every so often, when she feels her life is wheeling without brakes down a long hill, she starts poking at this again.

Geof trusts the universe a lot more than Aimee does, trusts that things make sense and that people can love, and therefore he doesn't need the same proofs. "You could ask them," he says.

II

Aimee's boyfriend:

Geof is not at all what Aimee expected from a boyfriend. For one thing, he's fifteen years younger than Aimee, twenty-eight to her forty-three. For another, he's sort of quiet. For a third, he's gorgeous, silky thick hair pulled into a shoulder-length ponytail, shaved sides showing off his strong jaw line. He smiles a lot, but he doesn't laugh very often.

Geof has a degree in history, which means that he was working in a bike-repair shop when she met him at the Montana Fair. Aimee never has much to do right after the show, so when he offered to buy her a beer she said yes. And then it was 4 A.M. and they were kissing in the bus, monkeys letting themselves in and getting ready for bed; and Aimee and Geof made love.

In the morning over breakfast, the monkeys came up one by one and shook his hand solemnly, and then he was with the band, so to speak. She helped him pick up his cameras and clothes and the surfboard his sister had painted for him one year as a Christmas present. There's no room for the surfboard so it's suspended from the ceiling. Sometimes the squirrel monkeys hang out there and peek over the side.

Aimee and Geof never talk about love.

Geof has a class-C driver's license, but this is just lagniappe.

12

Zeb is dying.

Generally speaking, the monkeys are remarkably healthy and Aimee can handle their occasional sinus infections and gastrointestinal ailments. For anything more difficult, she's found a couple of communities online and some helpful specialists.

But Zeb's coughing some, and the last of his fur is falling out. He moves very slowly and sometimes has trouble remembering simple tasks.

When the show was up in St. Paul six months ago, a Como Zoo biologist came to visit the monkeys, complimented her on their general health and well-being, and at her request looked Zeb over.

"How old is he?" the biologist, Gina, asked.

"I don't know," Aimee said. The man she bought the show from hadn't known either.

"*I'll* tell you then," Gina said. "He's old. I mean, seriously old."

Senile dementia, arthritis, a heart murmur. No telling when, Gina said. "He's a happy monkey," she said. "He'll go when he goes."

13

Aimee thinks a lot about this. What happens to the act when Zeb's dead? Through each show he sits calm and poised on his bright stool. She feels he is somehow at the heart of the monkeys' amiability and cleverness. She keeps thinking that he is somehow the reason the monkeys all vanish and return.

Because there's always a reason for everything, isn't there? Because if there isn't a reason for even *one* thing, like how you can get sick, or your husband stop loving you, or people you love die — then there's no reason for anything. So there must be reasons. Zeb's as good a guess as any.

14

What Aimee likes about this life:

It doesn't mean anything. She doesn't live anywhere. Her world is 38 feet and 127 shows long and currently 26 monkeys deep. This is manageable.

Fairs don't mean anything, either. Her tiny world travels within a slightly larger world, the identical, interchangeable fairs. Sometimes the only things that cue Aimee to the town she's in are the nighttime temperatures and the shape of the horizon: badlands, mountains, plains, or skyline.

Fairs are as artificial as titanium knees: the carnival, the animal barns, the stock-car races, the concerts, the smell of burnt sugar and funnel cakes and animal bedding. Everything is an overly bright symbol for something real, food or pets or hanging out with friends. None of this has anything to do with the world Aimee used to live in, the world from which these people visit.

She has decided that Geof is like the rest of it: temporary, meaningless. Not for loving.

15

These are some ways Aimee's life might have come apart:

a. She might have broken her ankle a few years ago, and gotten a bone infection that left her on crutches for ten months, and in pain for longer.

b. Her husband might have fallen in love with his admin and left her.

c. She might have been fired from her job in the same week she found out her sister had colon cancer.

d. She might have gone insane for a time and made a series of questionable choices that left her alone in a furnished apartment in a city she picked out of the atlas.

Nothing is certain. You can lose everything. Eventually, even at your luckiest, you will die and then you will lose it all. When you are a certain age or when you have lost certain things and people, Aimee's crippling grief will make a terrible poisoned dark sense.

16

Aimee has read up a lot, so she knows how strange all this is.

There aren't any locks on the cages. The monkeys use them as bedrooms, places to store their special possessions and get away from the others when they want some privacy. Much of the time, however, they are loose in the bus or poking around in the worn grass around it.

Right now, three monkeys are sitting on the bed playing a game where they match colored balls. Others are playing with skeins of wool yarn, or rolling around on the floor, or poking at a piece of wood with a screwdriver, or climbing on Aimee and Geof and the battered sofa. Some of the monkeys are crowded around the computer watching kitten videos on YouTube.

The black colobus is stacking children's wooden blocks on the kitchenette table. He brought them back one night a couple of weeks ago, and since then he's been trying to make an arch. After two weeks and Aimee showing him repeatedly how a keystone works, he still hasn't figured it out, but he's still patiently trying.

Geof's reading a novel out loud to the capuchin, Pango, who watches the pages as if she's reading along. Sometimes she points to a word and looks up at him with her bright eyes, and he repeats it to her, smiling, and then spells it out.

Zeb is sleeping in his cage: he crept in there at dusk, fluffed up his toys and his blanket, and pulled the door closed behind him. He does this a lot lately.

17

Aimee's going to lose Zeb, and then what? What happens to the other monkeys? 26 monkeys is a lot of monkeys, but they all like each other. No one except maybe a zoo or a circus can keep that many, and she doesn't think anyone else will let them sleep wherever they like or watch kitten videos. And if Zeb's not there, where will they go, those nights when they can no longer drop through the bathtub and into their mystery? And she doesn't even know whether it *is* Zeb, whether he is the cause of this, or that's just her flailing for reasons again.

And Aimee? She'll lose her safe artificial world: the bus, the identical fairs, the meaningless boyfriend. The monkeys. And then what?

18

Just a few months after she bought the act, when she didn't care much about whether she lived or died, she followed the monkeys up the ladder in the closing act. Zeb raced up the ladder, stepped into the bathtub and stood, lungs filling for his great call. And she ran up after him. She glimpsed the bathtub's interior, the monkeys tidily sardined in, scrambling to get out of her way as they realized what she was doing. She hopped into the hole they made for her, curled up tight.

This only took an instant. Zeb finished his breath, boomed it out.

There was a flash of light, she heard the chains release, and felt the bathtub swing down, monkeys shifting around her.

She fell the ten feet alone. Her ankle twisted when she hit the stage but she managed to stay upright. The monkeys were gone again.

There was an awkward silence. It wasn't one of her more successful performances.

19

Aimee and Geof walk through the midway at the Salina Fair. She's hungry and doesn't want to cook, so they're looking for somewhere that sells $4.50 hotdogs and $3.25 Cokes, and suddenly Geof turns to Aimee and says, "This is bullshit. Why don't we go into town? Have real food. Act like normal people."

So they do: pasta and wine at a place called Irina's Villa. "You're always asking why they go," Geof says, a bottle and a half in. His eyes are an indeterminate blue-gray, but in this light they look black and very warm. "See, I don't think we're ever going to find out what happens. But I don't think that's the real question, anyway. Maybe the question is, why do they come back?"

Aimee thinks of the foreign coins, the wood blocks, the wonderful things they bring back. "I don't know," she says. "Why *do* they come back?"

Later that night, back at the bus, Geof says, "Wherever they go, yeah, it's cool. But see, here's my theory." He gestures to the crowded bus with its clutter of toys and tools. The two tamarins have just come in, and they're sitting on the kitchenette table, heads close as they examine some new small thing. "They like visiting wherever it is, sure. But this is their home. Everyone likes to come home sooner or later."

"If they have a home," Aimee says.

"Everyone has a home, even if they don't believe in it," Geof says.

20

That night, when Geof's asleep curled up around one of the macaques, Aimee kneels by Zeb's cage. "Can you at least show me?" she asks. "Please? Before you go?"

Zeb is an indeterminate lump under his baby-blue blanket, but he gives a little sigh and climbs slowly out of his cage. He takes her hand with his own hot leathery paw, and they walk out the door into the night.

The back lot where all the trailers and buses are parked is quiet, only a few voices still audible from behind curtained windows. The sky is blue-black and scattered with stars. The moon shines straight down on them, leaving Zeb's face shadowed. His eyes when he looks up seem bottomless.

The bathtub is backstage, already on its wheeled dais waiting for the next show. The space is nearly pitch-dark, lit by some red EXIT signs, and a single sodium-vapor away off to one side. Zeb walks her up to the tub, lets her run her hands along its cold curves and the lion's paws, and shows her the dimly lit interior.

And then he heaves himself onto the dais and over the tub lip. She stands beside him, looking down. He lifts himself upright and gives his great boom. And then he drops flat and the bathtub is empty.

She saw it, him vanishing. He was there and then he was gone. But there was nothing to see, no gate, no flickering reality or soft pop as air snapped in to fill the vacated space. It still doesn't make sense, but it's the answer that Zeb has.

He's already back at the bus when she gets there, already buried under his blanket and wheezing in his sleep.

21

Then one day:

Everyone is backstage. Aimee is finishing her makeup, and Geof is double-checking everything. The monkeys are sitting neatly in a circle in the dressing room, as if trying to keep their bright vests and skirts from creasing. Zeb sits in the middle, beside Pango in her little green sequined outfit. They grunt a bit, then lean back. One after the other, the rest of the monkeys crawl forward and shake his hand, and then hers. She nods, like a small queen at a flower show.

That night, Zeb doesn't run up the ladder. He stays on his stool and it's Pango who is the last monkey up the ladder, who climbs into the bathtub and gives a screech. Aimee has been wrong that it is Zeb who is still the heart of what is happening with the monkeys, but she was so sure of it that she missed all the cues. But Geof didn't miss a thing, so when Pango screeches, he hits the flash powder. The flash, the empty bathtub.

Zeb stands on his stool, bowing like an impresario called onstage for the curtain call. When the curtain drops for the last time, he reaches up to be lifted. Aimee cuddles him as they walk back to the bus, Geof's arm around them both.

Zeb falls asleep with them that night, between them in the bed. When she wakes up in the morning, he's back in his cage with his favorite toy. The monkeys cluster at the bars peeking in. He doesn't wake up.

Aimee cries all day. "It's okay," Geof says.

"It's not about Zeb," she sobs.

"I know," he says. "Come home, Aimee."

22

Here's the trick to the bathtub trick. There is no trick. The monkeys pour across the stage and up the ladder and into the bathtub and they settle in and then they vanish. The world is full of strange things, things that make no sense, and maybe this is one of them. Maybe the monkeys choose not to share, that's cool, who can blame them.

Maybe this is the monkeys' mystery, how they found other monkeys that ask questions and try things, and figured out a way to all be together to share it. Maybe Aimee and Geof are really just houseguests in the monkeys' world: they are there for a while and then they leave.

23

Six weeks later, a man walks up to Aimee as she and Geof kiss after a show. He's short, pale, balding. He has the shell-shocked look of a man eaten hollow from the inside. She knows the look.

"I need to buy this," he says.

Aimee nods. "I know you do."

She sells it to him for a dollar.

THE SECRET HISTORY OF FANTASY

24

Three months later, Aimee and Geof get their first houseguest in their apartment in Bellingham. They hear the refrigerator close and come out to the kitchen to find Pango pouring orange juice from a carton. They send her home with a pinochle deck.

THE CRITICS, THE MONSTERS, AND THE FANTASISTS

URSULA K. LE GUIN

THERE WAS A while when people kept telling me, you must read this wonderful book about a school for wizards, it's so original, there's never been anything like it!

The first time this happened, I confess I thought they were telling me to read my own *A Wizard of Earthsea*, which involves a school for wizards, and has been in print since 1969. No such luck! I had to hear all about Harry, and it was hard, at first. I felt ignoble envy. But I soon felt a growing and less ignoble astonishment. Reviewers and critics were talking about Rowling's book as if it were a unique, unprecedented phenomenon.

The true phenomenon was the huge, genuine popularity the book earned before the best-seller machinery took over. It was a charmer, in the wizardly sense of the word: it cast the narrative spell. Word-of-mouth led adults to read it who had not read anything remotely like it since they were ten, if then; and finding it new to their experience, they thought it original.

But people who write about books are supposed to have some experience in reading. Those who praised *Harry Potter* for its originality were demonstrating blank ignorance of the traditions to which it belongs — not only a British subgenre, the "school story," but also a major world tradition, the literature of fantasy. How could so many reviewers and literary critics know so little about a major field of fiction, have so little background, so few standards of comparison, that they believed a book that was typical of a tradition, indeed quite conventional, even derivative, to be a unique achievement?

The modernists are largely to blame. Edmund Wilson and his generation left a tradition of criticism that is, in its way, quite a little monster.

In this school for anti-wizards, no fiction is to be taken seriously except various forms of realism, labeled "serious." The rest of narrative fiction is labeled "genre" and is dismissed unread.

Following this rule, the universities taught generations of students to shun all "genres," including fantasy (unless it was written before 1900, wasn't written in English, and/or can be labeled magical realism). Students in English departments were also taught to flee most children's books, or books that appeal to both children and adults, as if they were ripe buboes. And in many universities this still holds. Academic professionalism is at stake — possibly tenure. To touch genre is to be defiled. Reviewers in the popular journals, most of whom come out of the universities, mostly still obey the rule. If the reality of what people read forces a periodical to review mysteries or science fiction, they keep the reviews separate, in purdah, under a coy title.

Nobody can rightly judge a novel without some knowledge of the standards, expectations, devices, tropes, and history of its genre (or genres, for increasingly they mix and interbreed). The knowledge and craft a writer brings to writing fantasy, the expectations and skills a reader brings to reading it, differ significantly from those they bring to realistic fiction — or to science fiction, or the thriller, or the mystery, or the western, or the romance, or the picture book, or the chapter-book for kids, or the novel for young adults.

There are of course broad standards of competence in narrative. It would be interesting to identify writers whose narrative gift transcends genre, to find out what it is that Jane Austen, Rudyard Kipling, and Patrick O'Brian have in common (arguably a great deal). But distinction is essential to criticism, and the critic should know when a standard is inappropriate to a genre.

It might be an entertaining and educative exercise in fiction courses to make students discover inappropriate standards by using them. For example: Judge *The Lord of the Rings* as if it were a late-twentieth-century realistic novel. (Deficient in self-evident relevance, in sexual and erotic components, in individual psychological complexity, in explicit social references... Exercise too easy, has been done a thousand times.)

Judge *Moby-Dick* as science fiction. (Strong on technological information and on motivation, and when the story moves, it moves; but crippled by the author's foot-dragging and endless self-indulgence in pompous abstractions, fancy language, and rant.)

Judge *Pride and Prejudice* as a western. (A pretty poor show all round. Women talking. Darcy is a good man and could be a first-rate rancher, even if he does use those fool little pancake saddles, but with a first name like Fitzwilliam, he'll never make it in Wyoming.)

And to reverse the whole misbegotten procedure: Judge modern realist fiction by the standards of fantasy. (A narrow focus on daily details of contemporary human affairs; trapped in representationalism, suffocatingly unimaginative, frequently trivial, and ominously anthropocentric.)

The mandarins of modernism and some of the pundits of postmodernism were shocked to be told that a fantasy trilogy by a professor of philology is the best-loved English novel of the twentieth century. Why were they surprised?

Until the eighteenth century in Europe, imaginative fiction *was* fiction. Realism in fiction is a recent literary invention, not much older than the steam engine and probably related to it. Whence the improbable claim that it is the only form of fiction deserving to be admired and loved?

The particular way we make distinctions between factual and fictional narrative is also quite recent, and though useful, inevitably unreliable. As soon as you tell a story, it turns into fiction (or, as Borges put it, all narrative is fiction). It appears that in trying to resist this ineluctable process, or deny it, we of the Scientific West have come to place inordinate value on fiction that pretends to be, or looks awfully like, fact.

But in doing so, we've forgotten how to read the fiction that most fully exploits fictionality.

I'm not saying people don't read fantasy; a whole lot of us *people* do; but our scholars and critics for the most part don't read it and don't know how to read it. I feel shame for them. Sometimes I feel rage. I want to say to the literature teacher who remains wilfully, even boastfully ignorant of a major element of contemporary fiction: you are incompetent to teach or judge your subject. Readers and students who do know the field, meanwhile, have every right to challenge your ignorant prejudice. Rise, undergraduates of the English departments! You have nothing to lose but your A on the midterm!

And to the reviewers, I want to say, O critic, if you should come upon a fantasy, and it should awaken an atrophied sense of wonder in you, calling with siren voice to your dear little Inner Child, and you should desire to praise its incomparable originality, it would be well to have read in the literature of fantasy, so that you can make some comparisons and bring some critical intelligence to bear. Otherwise you're going to look like a Patent Office employee rushing out into the streets of Washington crying, "A discovery, amazing, unheard of! A miraculous invention, which is a circular disc, pierced with an axle, upon which vehicles may roll with incredible ease across the earth!"

I often wish I could indicate to such people that there are pleasant and easy ways to remedy their ignorance. I would like to ask them to read *The Lord of the Rings,* because to me the book is in itself a sufficient demonstration of the value of fantasy literature. But if they don't know how to read it, it will do more harm than good. They'll come away snarling *childish, primitive, escapist, simplistic,* and other mantras of the school for anti-wizards, having learned nothing.

The author of *The Lord of the Rings* was himself a scholar, and while wearing his professorial hat he wrote essays about the kind of fiction he wrote. Anybody who wants to be able to think about fantasy literature would do well to begin with them. The best introductory guide I know to the domain of fantasy is the essay in his book *The Monsters and the Critics* called — unfortunately — "On Fairy Stories."[1] (Why Tolkien, who came to have a murderous hatred of sweet little fairies of the Tinker Bell breed, used that phrase instead of the already acceptable words *fantasy* or *fantastic* literature, I don't know; but he did. All professors have a streak of madness.) At any rate, it is perfectly possible to disagree with Tolkien's explanation and justification of the nature of fantasy, but it is really not admissible to talk seriously about fantasy without knowing what he said. Critics and academics who refuse to recognise fantasy as literature must at the very

THE SECRET HISTORY OF FANTASY

least have read Tolkien, both as critic and as novelist, and be able to justify their opinion against both his opinion and his accomplishment.

Alas, many of them read Todorov instead. Todorov said many interesting things in his book on fantasy, but few of them have anything to do with fantasy. Anyone familiar with the literature he should have read can only admire his perverse ingenuity in getting off the subject.

But then, I wonder how many of the teachers and critics who so stoutly refuse to consider fantasy as literature have read Bakhtin or Borges? Or Kroeber or Attebery, to name two of the most informed and thoughtful contemporary writers about the field?

I wonder how many of them have actually read a fantasy novel since they were nine or ten years old?

This essay designedly began by talking about a children's book, for in talking about fantasy, one can't exclude children's literature (something that evidently never occurred to Todorov).

The capacity of much fantasy literature to override age-boundaries, to me a most admirable power, is to the anti-wizards a degrading weakness. That a novel can be read by a ten-year-old implies to them that it must be faulty as an adult novel: out comes the mantra, *primitive escapist simplistic* — in a word, *childish*. "Oh, those awful orcs," Wilson squeals cutely, believing himself to be imitating a reader of fantasy. The modernists wanted so badly to be perceived as grown-ups that they left a legacy of contempt for children's literature, which is still rarely questioned. Scholars of kiddilit are relegated to a drab kindergarten annex to the canonical structure of Literature, an embarrassment to the architects of Importance.

To throw a book out of serious consideration because it was written for children, or because it is read by children, is in fact a monstrous act of anti-intellectualism. But it happens daily in academia.

The prejudice is by no means only against fantasies; any novel accessible to children is suspect. The principal reason Kipling's *Kim* has very seldom been given its rightful place in the curriculum or the canon of English novels is probably the notion that, since it can give immense delight to a twelve-year-old, it cannot possibly reward an adult reader. That this is a mistaken assumption can be proved by reading *Kim;* but prejudice is easier and safer. Respectability lies in never raising one's eyes from the texts of Flaubert or James, which can at least be guaranteed to bore most children almost as quickly as *The Swiss Family Robinson*.

Lewis Carroll is one of the few writers for children who escapes defenestration — partly, perhaps, because of his mathematical games in the Alice books, which daunt most literary people, and the hoopla about his sexuality, which allows them to speak of him, if not his texts, in adult terms, signaling and sniggering over the children's heads. So much foolishness has been written about Carroll, indeed, that I wonder if I am wise in wanting the critics and professors to talk seriously about children's books. Will they insist on burrowing after sexual perversion in the author as the only way of making the book respectable?

I have been asking for thirty years why most critics are afraid of dragons while most children, and many adults, are not. It is a question that really, by now, deserves some answer other than the repetition of mantras; for the restriction of literary fiction to a "mainstream" of realism becomes daily less tenable, more, dare I say, fantastic. It is not only the incursion from South America that must be dealt with, but the frequency of treason and defection in the ranks of contemporary literary fiction in English. What is the critic to do when he sees one of A. S. Byatt's impeccably adult, dourly sophisticated heroines turning slowly and elaborately into a troll? He (the pronoun has been considered and accepted) is being asked to deal with a fantasy: with, as Kroeber puts it, "an artistic experience of confronting as real what one knows cannot be real, the arousal of belief in the unbelievable."[2]

What does it mean, that a woman turns into a troll?

It may mean as much, and have as many meanings, as a girl's turning into Emma Bovary. It may indeed mean more, to more people. Incompleteness and suggestion are very powerful tools for the artist of our time; the impossible, the incredible, the fantastic all suggest the limitations and the falsity of ordinary perception. In the useful words quoted by Kroeber, *Madame Bovary* has "the imposing completeness of a delusion" — but we may prefer, in this age, "the broken fragment of truth."

The untrained critic, unable to perceive the rules a fantasy works by, may perceive it as meaningless. To excuse or hide failure of comprehension, labels may be stuck onto the story — surrealist, dada, etc. But while surrealism is a subversion of meaning, fantasy is a construction of meaning, perhaps purely linguistic, perhaps more than that. Successful fantasy narrative is notable particularly for its strong inner coherence; its rules are not those of the ordinary world, but it never flouts them. Surrealism subverts in order to destroy, fantasy subverts in order to rebuild.[3]

The untrained mind trying to deal with fantasy is most likely to try to rationalise it — to "explain" it as reflecting an order outside the order of the story, whether a theological order, or psychological, or political, anything so long as it's familiar. But true fantasy is not allegory. Allegory and fantasy may overlap, as with Spenser, who obeys the rational convention of allegory yet keeps considerable freedom of invention; but Spenser is rather the exception than the model.

Rational inexplicability and avoidance of point-to-point symbolism do not automatically imply moral irresponsibility or social irrelevance. You might think critics would know that from having read the poetry of the last two hundred years; but the lesson seems not to be taken. The tendency to explain fantasy by extracting the fantastic from it and replacing it with the comprehensible reduces the radically unreal to the secondhand commonplace. Thus we have attempts to explain *The Lord of the Rings* as an apologia for Tolkien's Catholicism, or a kind of private mental asylum from his experiences in the First World War, etc. Such rationalisations may be earnestly perceived as a defense of fantasy, but are in fact refusals of it, attempts to explain it away. Only by approaching it on its own terms can a reader begin to apprehend the moral stance and the social relevance of a fantasy.

The purpose of a fantasy may be as inexplicable, in social or political terms, as the purpose (to paraphrase Maxwell) of a baby. To expect to explain or understand a fantasy as disguised ethics or politics is to fall into the reductionist trap. The purposive, utilitarian approach to fantasy and folktale of a Bettelheim or Bly, and in general the "psychological" approach to fantasy, explaining each element of the story in terms of its archetype or unconscious source or educative use, is deeply regressive; it perceives literature as magic, it is a verbomancy. To such interpreters the spell is a spell only if it works immediately to heal or reveal.

Most critics of fiction now eschew such reductive readings; even those who admit that reading a novel may have a profound and lasting effect on the mind and feelings of the reader, possibly including healing and enlightenment, are aware that the effect is not to be prescribed and often may not even be defined. If literary criticism doesn't demand purposive "meaning" of realism, why does it demand it of fantasy?

Probably because critics still equate fantasy with kiddilit. Children's books are particularly defenseless against utilitarian interpretations and judgments. I have been appalled to see my fantasies discussed in journals and columns of children's literature as if they were tracts. That there could be more to a child's book than a brisk story and an explicit ethical lesson — that children need active imagination more than closed moralities, that they respond to beauty in imagery and language, that they read to learn how to ask questions more than to be told answers — this seems to be news to those who judge children's books. But then, how much can you ask of critics and reviewers who are routinely despised and ignored by their peers and inferiors in academia and journalism?

The habit of reducing text to political-economic terms has prevented many Marxian and neo-Marxian critics from reading fantasy at all. If they can't read it as utopian, dystopian, or of clear social relevance, they're likely to dismiss it as frivolous. They see kings, and assume reactionary politics; they see wizards, and assume superstition; they see dragons, and assume nonsense. A literal mind is a great asset to reading fantasy, and so is a liberal mind, but not when either has been programmed too rigidly. Still, I welcome any socially conscious reading of fantasy, so long as it isn't ideologically puristic, for too many modern fantasies are intolerably trivial and complacent in their half-baked feudalism.

The charge that the whole enterprise of fantasy is "escapist" has been discussed by Tolkien and others, and only the ignorant continue to repeat it. It is a fact, however, that much fantasy, especially of the "heroic" kind, seems on the face of it socially and historically regressive: withdrawing from the Industrial Revolution and Modern Times, the fantasy story is often set in a green, underpopulated world of towns and small cities surrounded by wilderness, beyond which the exact and intricate map in the frontispiece does not go. This certainly appears to be a return to the world of the folktale. So it is; and to the world of Homer, Vergil, Shakespeare, Cervantes, Swift, Wordsworth, Dickens — the world of literature and human experience until a hundred and fifty years ago or so. This world is lost now to city folk, but still inhabited by many others, and still accessible to most of us in memories of childhood, hours or days in the woods or the fields, vacations in the mountains or by the shore — the country: the world we call, since it is no longer natural to us, "nature."

Fantasy's green country is one that most of us enter with ease and pleasure, and it seems to be perfectly familiar to most children even if they've never been out of the city streets. It partakes of the Golden Age, whether mythic or personal, though it may also partake of the darkness that ends the golden ages.

Nostalgia is probably essential to it. Nostalgia is a suspect emotion these days, and I will not attempt to defend it, aside from saying that I think it fuels more great poetry, perhaps, than any other emotion. But I will defend fantasy's green country.

Tolkien's Middle Earth is not just pre-industrial. It is also pre-human and non-human. It can be seen as a late and tragic European parallel to the American myth-world where Coyote and Raven and the rest of them are getting things ready for "the people who are coming" — human beings. At the end of *The Lord of the Rings,* we know that the non-human beings of Middle Earth are "dwindling" away or passing into the West, leaving the world to mankind alone. The feeling-tone indeed is less nostalgia than bereavement, the grief of those exiled from dear community, tears by the waters of Babylon.

My Earthsea and the familiar forests and towns of much fantasy are not informed by that great vision: but I think they too imply that modern humanity is in exile, shut out from a community, an intimacy, it once knew. They do not so much lament, perhaps, as remind.

The fields and forests, the villages and byroads, once did belong to us, when we belonged to them. That is the truth of the non-industrial setting of so much fantasy. It reminds us of what we have denied, what we have exiled ourselves from.

Animals were once more to us than meat, pests, or pets: they were fellow-creatures, colleagues, dangerous equals. We might eat them; but then, they might eat us. That is at least part of the truth of my dragons. They remind us that the human is not the universal.

What fantasy often does that the realistic novel generally cannot do is include the non-human as essential.

The fantasy element of *Moby-Dick* is Moby-Dick. To include an animal as a protagonist equal with the human is — in modern terms — to write a fantasy. To include *anything* on equal footing with the human, as equal in importance, is to abandon realism.

Realistic fiction is relentlessly focused on human behavior and psychology. "The proper study of mankind is Man." When fiction disobeys Pope and begins to include the Other, it begins to shade into the ghost story, the horror story, the animal story, or science fiction, or fantasy; it begins the movement outward to the not-entirely-human. Even "regional" fiction, always looked at disparagingly by the modernists, is part of this movement, sliding from human psychology into that which contains it, the landscape.

We need better definitions of terms than the ones we have. Hardy's Egdon Heath is in itself entirely realistic, but its centrality to *The Return of the Native* decentralises the human characters in a way quite similar to that of fantasy and even science fiction. Melville's white whale isn't a real whale, he's a beast of the imagination, like dragons or unicorns; hence *Moby-Dick* is not an animal story, but it is a fantasy. Woolf's *Flush* is an animal story, because Flush is (and actually was) a real spaniel; but of course it is also a novel about the Brownings; it is also definable as a fantasy, since the dog is a central character, and we know what he is thinking; but then we know what the dog is thinking in the hunting scene in *War and Peace*, too, which does not make *War and Peace* a fantasy… The clean, sharp definition of what realism is and what fantasy is recedes ever further, along with any justification for despising genre.

I venture a non-defining statement: realistic fiction is drawn towards anthropocentrism, fantasy away from it. Although the green country of fantasy seems to be entirely the invention of human imaginations, it verges on and partakes of actual realms in which humanity is not lord and master, is not central, is not even important. In this, fantasy may come much closer to the immense overview of the exact sciences than does science fiction, which is very largely obsessed by a kind of imperialism of human knowledge and control, a colonial attitude towards the universe.

The only world we know of, now, that isn't shaped and dominated by human beings, is "long ago." "Far away" won't do any more, unless we leap to a literally other world, another planet, or into an imagined future — and these options will be labeled science fiction, even though they may well be fantasies grasping at the specious plausibility, the pseudo-rationalism, provided by popular concepts of "Science" and "the Future."

It is a fact that we as a species have lived for most of our time on earth as animals among animals, as tribes in the wilderness, as farmers, villagers, and citizens in a closely known region of farmlands and forests. Beyond the exact and intricately detailed map of local knowledge, beyond the homelands, in the blank parts of the map, lived the others, the dangerous strangers, those not in the family, those not (yet) known. Even before they learn (if they are taught) about this small world of the long human past, most children seem to feel at home in it; and many keep an affinity for it, are drawn to it. They make maps of bits of it — islands, valleys among the mountains, dream-towns with wonderful names, dream-roads that do not lead to Rome — with blank spaces all around.

The monstrous homogenization of our world has now almost destroyed the map, any map, by making every place on it exactly like every other place, and leaving no blanks. No unknown lands. A hamburger joint and a coffee shop in every block, repeated forever. No Others; nothing unfamiliar. As in the Mandelbrot fractal set, the enormously large and the infinitesimally small are exactly the same, and the same leads always to the same again; there is no other; there is no escape, because there is nowhere else.

In reinventing the world of intense, unreproducible, local knowledge, seemingly by a denial or evasion of current reality, fantasists are perhaps trying to assert and explore a larger reality than we now allow ourselves. They are trying to restore the sense — to regain the knowledge — that there is somewhere else, anywhere else, where other people may live another kind of life.

The literature of imagination, even when tragic, is reassuring, not necessarily in the sense of offering nostalgic comfort, but because it offers a world large enough to contain alternatives and therefore offers hope.

The fractal world of endless repetition is appallingly fragile. There is no illusion, even, of safety in it; a human construct, it can be entirely destroyed at any moment by human agency. It is the world of the neutron bomb, the terrorist, and the next plague. It is Man studying Man alone. It is the reality trap. Is it any wonder that people want to look somewhere else? But there is no somewhere else, except in what is not human — and in our imagination.

If we want to get out of the Mandelbrot set world, that's where the roadmap is. Exact, intricate, inexplicable, and indispensable.

ENDNOTES

1   Tolkien, John Ronald Reuel: *The Monsters and the Critics and Other Essays*, ed. C. Tolkien, Houghton Mifflin, 1984.

2   Kroeber, Karl: *Romantic Fantasy and Science Fiction*, Yale, 1988, p. 48.

3   Ibid. p. 48.

The Making of the American Fantasy Genre

David G. Hartwell

I. Fantasy Fiction Leaves the Mainstream of Literature

Tales of wonder and the fantastic are integral to all world literature and are as old as recorded human imaginative thought. Fantasy fiction has been a significant part of literature in the English language at least since the first translations of fairy tales from the French. From 1699 to 1750, Mme. d'Aulnoy's tales were translated and published, apparently successfully, for adult women readers. Ironically, Robert Samber's 1729 translation of Charles Perrault's tales for child readers did not sell well, so the impact of fairy tales as children's literature came into being only in the second half of the eighteenth century and the nineteenth. At about the same time, the translations of the oriental tales of *The Arabian Nights* (1704, 1714 and following) had a significant impact and influence. By the middle and later eighteenth century, the early Gothic novels (such as Horace Walpole's *The Castle of Otranto* and William Beckford's *Vathek*) and stage plays were extremely important and, though often rationalized, were often rich in fantasy content. As the literary form of the short story developed in the late eighteenth and early nineteenth century, the earliest short stories were often fantasy stories.

But as far as most serious readers of recent decades are concerned — really ever since the mid-nineteenth century, when English culture demoted fantasy to children's literature — fantasy fiction in English is for kids, even the works widely read by adults (for instance, the stories of the Brothers Grimm or of Hans Christian Andersen). Famous works — from *Alice's Adventures in Wonderland* by Lewis Carroll and George MacDonald's *Phantastes*, through *The Book of the Three Dragons* by

Kenneth Morris to *A Wizard of Earthsea* by Ursula K. Le Guin — have tended to emerge from, or quickly be demoted to, children's or young adult publishing. Works for mature readers such as William Morris's *The Wood Beyond the World*, Lord Dunsany's *The Sword of Welleran*, or William Hope Hodgson's *The Night Land* are unusual and do not form a particular tradition — the fiction of each of these writers seems to come almost from nowhere, to be unique.

Fantasy for adults has been in large part an unfashionable pleasure for nearly a century, until very recent decades. The American Modernists progressively marginalized that strain of the fantastic in literature that evolved into what we now consider genre fantasy (while they generally approved of sexual fantasies and non-supernatural horror). Their high art/low art distinction categorized the fantastic and the supernatural with the merely popular and the low — and the religious. This view dominated literary fashion in the twentieth century to the extent that, for instance, James Branch Cabell's whole body of ornate mandarin fiction, once embraced by H. L. Mencken and others as the cutting edge of contemporary American fiction, was nearly lost from sight and is now no more seriously considered than Edgar Rice Burroughs's *Tarzan of the Apes* (always a popular and non-literary phenomenon, pulp art), though both were read very widely by adults for at least a generation. Cabell formerly ranked very high in American literary circles. Late in this process of marginalization, I recall that in an English Literature course at Williams College in 1961, when I was assigned E. M. Forster's *Aspects of the Novel*, the chapter on fantasy was the only one skipped. (I read it anyway and was introduced to such delights as *Flecker's Magic* by Norman Matson.) Realism was good art; the novel of the inner life of character was good; the fantastic was not.

So unfashionable did fantastic works for adults become during the early decades of the twentieth century — at the same time that fantasy and fairy tales for children underwent a relative renaissance — that fantasy fiction was taken in during the 1930s and '40s under the umbrella of the growing American science fiction field, where it has remained to a significant extent. While it is now possible for many publishers to publish and market a fantasy novel for adults (one thinks of such examples as Susanna Clarke's *Jonathan Strange & Mr Norrell*), it is usual for fantasy fiction to be brought to market by publishers specializing in science fiction and fantasy. Fantasy is acquired for publication by sf and fantasy editors, and, still, by the editors of children's literature. The link between the genres remains very strong.

II. THE FIRST ATTEMPTS AT GENREFICATION OF FANTASY FOR ADULTS

By the beginning of the 1940s, such pulp magazines as *Unknown Worlds* and *Famous Fantastic Mysteries* became the center of publication for adult fantasy in America. *Famous Fantastic Mysteries* was devoted to reprinting stories and complete novels from the earlier history of fantasy publishing, drawing both from books and from pulp adventure magazines of the late nineteenth century through the 1930s. Early issues featured novellas by A. Merritt, Austin Hall, George Allan England, Francis Stevens, Ray Cummings, and Ralph Milne Farley; but also stories by G. K. Chesterton, Irvin S. Cobb, Jack London, E. F. Benson, C. S. Forester, Algernon Blackwood, Lord Dunsany, and Fitz-James O'Brien. *FFM* was, in fact, one of the early attempts to draw the disparate instances of fantasy fiction from the previous decades into a genre tradition.

Unknown Worlds, on the other hand, was the brainchild of the great sf editor, John W. Campbell, Jr., and his stated project was to revolutionize fantasy, just as he was doing with sf in *Astounding*. Campbell specifically wanted fantasy writers to use the same rational approaches and urban settings that were being used in the science fiction he was publishing. He accepted all the furniture of fantasy, from witches and fairies and elves to magic and ghosts, but he encouraged their appearance in urban, even contemporary settings, as opposed to exclusively in historical, pastoral settings or gardens. Among the most famous stories were psychological horror fantasies such as "Fear" and "He Didn't Like Cats" by L. Ron Hubbard, the "mathematics of magic" (Harold Shea) stories by L. Sprague de Camp and Fletcher Pratt, and significant early stories by Theodore Sturgeon, Fritz Leiber, and Robert A. Heinlein.

This urban fantasy tradition persisted as a minority taste after *Unknown Worlds* ceased publication (in 1943, under pressure of the wartime paper shortage), in the short fiction of Leiber, Ray Bradbury, Richard Matheson in the 1940s, 1950s, and 1960s. This tradition underpinned, for instance, the creation of *The Twilight Zone* in the 1960s. Urban fantasy appeared to readers in the 1940s, '50s, and '60s as the true center of fantasy fiction, and was generally called the *Unknown* tradition. It was understood to have replaced or overthrown the earlier *Weird Tales* tradition, though that venerable magazine persisted into the 1950s and has been periodically revived. This newer tradition was centered in the short story and not the novel form. It had a predominantly male audience from its inception. Charles de Lint reinvigorated the urban fantasy tradition in the early 1980s, and that strain has evolved in the 1980s and 1990s. Urban fantasy has enjoyed an especially rapid growth since the turn of the millennium in novel form, especially in the subcategory of the paranormal romance. It is a major part of contemporary fantasy publishing today, incorporated into the genre with a mass audience — though the paranormal romances are most often produced by romance genre editors and houses, not fantasy or sf editors, while most of the current form of urban fantasy is published within f/sf lines. But despite this history, urban fantasy did not form the center of genrefied fantasy. It had to be overcome, or brushed aside, for the mass genre to form.

There were many other fantasy magazines, particularly the aforementioned *Weird Tales*, where the adventures of Conan the Barbarian by Robert E. Howard, the gorgeous fantasy stories of Clark Ashton Smith, and the fiction of H. P. Lovecraft all appeared. The still-publishing *Magazine of Fantasy & Science Fiction* has a distinguished history of supporting short fantasy fiction for adults for sixty years now. (It is notable that *F&SF*, especially in its first decade, made a notable attempt to develop women writers.) Between its first issue in 1949 and the late 1960s, *F&SF* pursued a strategy of reprinting fiction, along with its original fiction, to broaden the literary scope of its remit. It should be obvious by this point in the discussion that the incorporation of reprints (and translations) is a continuing leitmotif in the early attempts to gather together and form a fantasy genre tradition.

Though the great days of *Black Mask*, *The Shadow*, *The Saturday Evening Post*, and *Argosy*, the era of mass commercial fiction magazines, are long gone in the twenty-first century, several of the surviving small commercial magazines that publish science fiction also publish fantasy. The predominantly short-form fantasy subgenre of the mid-twentieth century still exists, but not with an audience significant enough to attract the attention of mass-marketers. Ironically, when I joined a committee to found the first World Fantasy Convention in 1975, we all had grown up reading fantasy as primarily a short-fiction form and viewed it as a minority taste within the larger and vigorous sf genre.

III. The Roots of Successful Genrefication

Let us return to the 1950s and see what was not evident until later. The roots of mass-market genrefication are there.

The major events in commercial fantasy in the 1950s were the publication of *The Lord of the Rings* trilogy by J. R. R. Tolkien and of *The Once and Future King* by T. H. White. Both were successful, but the White was an immediate bestseller, while the Tolkien took time to build popularity (though it did win a significant award in the sf field, The International Fantasy Award, in 1957).

It is notable that, though the White remained popular for decades, it was originally published as a work of general fiction. It was not published as a fantasy genre work until the late 1970s, after the creation of the commercial fantasy genre. The Tolkien, on the other hand, was released in mass-market paperback for the first time in 1965 as a fantasy work. The trilogy was released from Ace Books, a prominent sf publisher in the US, because of a technical error in copyright that made it (arguably) a public domain work in the States. It was quickly revised cosmetically and published later the same year by Ballantine Books. (This was an echo of the pattern established in 1963 when Ballantine published the authorized editions of Edgar Rice Burroughs's novels after Ace began to publish out-of-copyright titles in 1962.) Ace agreed to stop its own editions of Tolkien, and thereafter was widely known as the "pirate" publisher. In

Ballantine editions, *The Lord of the Rings* remained on the bestseller lists for a decade, and beyond, an impressive publishing phenomenon, massively profitable beyond the ordinary dreams of genre publishing.

Genrefication of fantasy as it exists today was motivated in earnest by the 1965 mass-market editions of *The Lord of the Rings*. This unique masterpiece of contemporary literature, praised by W. H. Auden and many others in the 1950s and subject of Tom Shippey's bestseller of literary criticism in this new century, sold well in hardcover but not in bestseller numbers. But it became a cult classic and a mass-market bestseller of millions of copies in its first year in paperback, which shocked and motivated publishers.

Tolkien's sales paid the light bills for its second publisher, Ballantine Books, for nearly a decade. Being smart publishers, Ian and Betty Ballantine cast about, looking for ways to repeat that phenomenon — as did Donald A. Wollheim, that other publisher of Tolkien, at Ace Books. They spent years of work trying.

Wollheim tried a variety of fantasy at Ace Books with some notable commercial successes, but generally in the barbarian hero vein, somewhere in the territory of Edgar Rice Burroughs or Robert E. Howard, the subgenre called "sword & sorcery" in those days, later renamed "heroic fantasy." By the end of the decade, sword & sorcery was the most successful segment of the marketing effort, and Frank Frazetta the artist who set the tone for fantasy illustration.

The Ballantines tried reprinting in paper other uniquely individual and powerfully original works excluded from the Modernist canon: Mervyn Peake's *Gormenghast* trilogy, E. R. Eddison's *The Worm Ouroboros* and his Zimiamvian Trilogy, and a few others. Then, in 1969, they founded the Ballantine Adult Fantasy series, under the guest editorship of the knowledgeable fantasy fan Lin Carter, reprinting a book a month from the past century, bringing into mass editions nearly all the adult fantasy stories and novels worth reading — from William Morris's medievalism to Evangeline Walton's literate retellings of Welsh mythology, Clark Ashton Smith's poetic visions, George MacDonald's moral allegories, and H. P. Lovecraft's magnificent darkness. And, of course, the novels of James Branch Cabell.

However, to the consternation of most marketers, critics, and discerning readers, only the Lancer Books edition of Robert E. Howard's Conan the Barbarian stories really caught on and stuck. These editions, with now-famous Frank Frazetta covers, and sequels, expansions, and interpolations by L. Sprague de Camp, Lin Carter, and others, were a major success: at the start of the 1970s, the Conan line was the bestselling fantasy material other than Tolkien. Similar series, such as Fritz Leiber's Fafhrd and the Grey Mouser and Michael Moorcock's Elric, rode the crest too. Barbarian fantasy sold, and it was the conventional wisdom that it sold to young male readers — teenaged and early twenties — not to the wider Tolkien audience. Nothing but Tolkien sold like that.

The United States is the largest fiction market in the English language world. Mass-market publishers in the 1960s had established the woman's Gothic romance genre as a bestselling phenomenon. They did it a short while later with the immensely profitable contemporary romance genre. The mass-market industry tried it with science fiction as well in the 1970s with initial success. I was a part of that effort at several publishers in that decade. But sf didn't remain as successful in later years (though at one time sf was nearly ten percent of the fiction market), because sf couldn't capture and hold enough female readers. All the polls show that the huge majority of readers of mass-market fiction in the US are women. Besides, the sf writers kept coming up with new ideas (inherently a part of that genre) and new ideas are hard to market to an audience larger than confirmed genre converts.

Fantasy, like the truly successful marketing genres before it, had to be made predictable, had to be able to be sold as product to achieve large-scale success. After all, one doesn't expect one Chevrolet or one can of tuna fish to stand above the others. Mass-market product success is based on the promise of comfortable familiarity, of more of the same. And in the 1970s it was accomplished, after decades of work and false starts, with fantasy.

Fantasy promises escape from reality. It is characteristic of fantasy stories that they take the readers out of the real worlds of hard facts, hard objects, and hard decisions into a world of wonders and enchantments, a world that need not be either frivolous or inherently juvenile. But adult fantasy didn't sell well enough in its classic forms as the 1970s progressed for Ballantine Books to continue to be able to support it, and the Adult Fantasy series was discontinued in 1974, leaving in print only a few contemporary monuments, such as Peter S. Beagle's lively and sentimental classic, *The Last Unicorn*. Yet the Ballantines knew that some kind of breakthrough had been made, that there was a market out there of adult men and women, as well as teenaged boys, who read and were still reading Tolkien in the millions and who could be sold fantasy if only the right way could be found. They lost control of the company before they found the way, but it was Ballantine Books that succeeded.

IV. Success

"Dear Reader," said the letter reproduced on the front cover of a glossy white advance copy addressed to reviewers and booksellers:

> "Every so often, a book appears which is so outstanding that its publication becomes an event.
>
> You've no doubt seen that claim more than once before. But rarely — very rarely — has it proved to be true. In the field of fantasy fiction, such an event occurred more than twenty years ago when J. R. R. Tolkien's marvelous *The Lord of the Rings* appeared and re-established the tale of wonder in the world of literature. Since then, however, no novel of true epic fantasy has appeared to satisfy the millions of readers who are eager for other such secondary-universe journeys.
>
> Now, I believe, there is such a novel — *The Sword of Shannara*, by a new and highly gifted writer, Terry Brooks."

Lester del Rey was born Leonard Knapp; his public identity was a decades-old construction, apparently following the death of his first wife in an automobile accident in 1935, of a fictitious persona that he maintained until his true identity was discovered after his death in 1993. He was a Ballantine Books consulting editor who found the way to genrefication in the form of a manuscript by Terry Brooks entitled *The Sword of Shannara*. He went to Ron Busch, then the publisher of Ballantine Books (now a division of Random House) and mapped out a strategy. They would take this slavish imitation by an unknown writer, reputedly originally written as an unauthorized sequel to Tolkien, and create a bestseller using mass-marketing techniques and so satisfy the hunger in the marketplace for more Tolkien. It was their simple and inspired marketing insight into what the audience wanted: not more *fantasy* but more *Tolkien*, and it would accept imitations while waiting for the eventual completion of *The Silmarillion*. As an experienced pulp editor and writer (he had edited *Fantasy Magazine* in 1953), del Rey knew what he was about — even to the inclusion of color illustrations by The Brothers Hildebrandt, who were famous for producing the Tolkien calendars in the mid-1970s — and it worked, much to the amazement and admiration of all the other marketers in publishing. *The Sword of Shannara* was a major bestseller in 1977.

I worked for Mr. Busch after he moved to Pocket Books, from 1978 to 1983, and he was wont to tell stories about the planning and execution of the marketing campaign for Brooks's book. My favorite one from Busch was that Ian Ballantine, while still employed at the company that he formerly owned, would sometimes loiter outside Busch's office door muttering, "The barbarians are at the gates."

Shortly thereafter, the Del Rey fantasy imprint was founded, with its criteria set up by Lester del Rey. The books would be original novels set in invented worlds in which magic works. Each would have a male central character who triumphed over evil — usually associated with technical knowledge of some variety — by innate virtue, with the help of an elder tutor or tutelary spirit. He had codified a children's literature that could be sold as adult. It was nostalgic, conservative, pastoral, and optimistic. That was what was to be genre fantasy. I sometimes had lunch in later years with Judy Lynn del Rey, Lester's wife, and the full-time head of sf at her own imprint, Del Rey Books, after 1978. We would shake our heads and agree that we would never have suspected that genre fantasy would outsell sf.

Kathryn Cramer, seeking an explanation for why an American audience would adopt and support such a body of fiction, and create an essentially worldwide popular genre, has remarked that it was essentially a revival of the form of the utopian novel of the old South, the Plantation Novel, in which life is rich and good, the lower classes are happy in their place and sing a lot, and evil resides in the technological North. The fantasy plot is the Civil War run backward: the South wins. That pattern seems to fit a majority of early genre fantasy works well.

The Del Rey fantasy covers were rich, detailed illustrations of a colorful scene. Since unknown writers, or children's book writers unknown to the adult market, would usually be used, the cover art and production were often more costly than the advance paid to the writer. Through this process, Lester del Rey quickly discovered another unknown writer, Stephen R. Donaldson. His *The Chronicles of Thomas Covenant the Unbeliever*, which focuses on an ordinary man with leprosy transported into a fantasy Land where he is forced to be a hero, is a work of great psychological power. (Joanna Russ has published a delicious parody, "Dragons and Dimwits," whose hero, Thomas, points out the conspicuous and unrealistic absence of meals or agriculture: "By St. Marx, and St. Engels," said Thomas, "and by St. Common Sense, I declare that neither thou nor thy people eatest or drinkest in the least (for I have never seen them do it) but subsistest upon fancies and fooleries imagined out of thin air.") The series made Donaldson an enormous bestseller, thus proving the repeatability of Del Rey Books' experiment on the largest scale in publishing. And Del Rey acquired the paperback rights to a distinguished young adult series, the *Riddle-Master of Hed* trilogy, by Patricia A. McKillip, also a major commercial success. Del Rey fantasy quickly became a monthly publishing staple.

By 1980, the success of the Del Rey formula was so confirmed that many other publishers had begun to publish in imitation. Dragons and unicorns began to appear all over the mass-market racks, and packaging codes with the proper subliminal and overt signals developed. A whole new mass-market genre had been established. One can understand it best perhaps in comparison to the toy market's discovery in the 1970s — after decades of trying — that you could sell dolls to boys if you call them action figures and make them hypermasculine. Writers such as Piers Anthony, a moderately successful and respected science fiction author who switched to fantasy, and Anne McCaffrey, a science fiction writer whose novels of a world of dragons could be marketed as fantasy, became Del Rey bestsellers. Then everyone in publishing wanted in.

In the '80s, most mass-market publishers did get in. Trilogies were the order of the day. Some writers complained that publishers often requested revisions to the endings of their fantasy works so that a single novel, if popular, might be extended by two more volumes. Lou Aronica, then a Bantam Books vice-president responsible for his company's fantasy publishing program, was interviewed in *SF Eye* magazine on his program's long-term success in publishing some works of high quality and low sales. "One of the reasons I have been able to do it for longer," he said, "is that I've been a little bit more willing to sell out for my list. I've published books that I don't like editorially, that I understand will sell a lot of copies." The implications of that attitude are manifest on book racks everywhere.

We today as readers are the inheritors of this phenomenon. Unquestionably, it created an enormous wave of trash writing to fill the neurotic hungers of an established audience trained in the '70s and later to accept tiny nuances and gestures overlaying mediocrity and repetition as true originality. Mr. Aronica commented that negative remarks from readers and critics:

> ...are actually being echoed in the responses we've seen in the marketplace. A lot of epic fantasy doesn't sell nearly as well as it used to sell, probably because there aren't too many new avenues being taken in epic fantasy, and readers are saying, "Hey, I've read this book already — in fact I've read this book about fourteen times."
>
> It is enough to make a serious reader distrust all multivolume category works and any book with a unicorn or a dragon depicted on the cover.

The notion that literate adults not oriented to genre reading might read fantasy for pleasure did take hold again in recent years, but it is still a dubious proposition for most literary readers, given the amount of obvious silliness, junk, and fiction for the immature on the fantasy bookshelves. Yet the fantasy tradition in literature remains, at its peaks, a distinguished one. Authentic works of the literary imagination have emerged in recent decades and should not be ignored by association with humble (category) origins.

The various kinds of fashionable literary fiction in America have progressively, since the '30s, become obsessed with technique and with the nuances and gestures of ordinary characters in ordinary situations. They have exhausted in particular every avenue in illuminating the inner life of characters. Genre fantasy, on the other hand, characteristically manifests and dramatizes internal and psychological states, images, and struggles as external and concrete, and it focuses on the external actions of its characters. Fantasy fiction takes the reader clearly out of the world of reality. Sometimes the story begins in the "real" world, but it quickly becomes evident that behind the veil of real things and people, perhaps through a portal, another world exists, rich and strange and magical. The genre fantasy generally takes place in a world in which moral coordinates are clear and distinct, in a landscape in which moral qualities are most often embodied in major characters other than the central character (who is usually at first portrayed as an Everyman, a fairly ordinary person of no particular consequence in the world). But the central character becomes a crucial figure in a struggle between good and evil. This pattern has rich artistic possibilities when properly executed, especially when in the hands of the finest writers working in fantasy today.

There is a body of work, much of it published originally in paperback in the last two decades, which has not generally received adequate recognition for its literary excellence because of its origins in genre publishing. Samuel R. Delany has written a four-volume set in an imaginary world, Nevèrÿon, that is a masterpiece of imagination and stylistic innovation. John Crowley's *Little, Big* is a dense, literate novel that is a standard against which others are now measured. Gene Wolfe's novels and stories, particularly his *Soldier of the Mist* and sequels, and his massive *The Wizard Knight*, are a significant contribution to American literature, and his fiction is perhaps the most important body of work in the fantasy field from the 1980s to the present.

The biggest genre fantasy name from the 1990s to 2000 was Robert Jordan, whose *Wheel of Time* series, in the tradition of Tolkien, was the biggest commercial success since Tolkien's trilogy, an impressive achievement. It is also a marker in the transition from fantasy trilogies to fantasy books in series as the dominant form of popular publication. This is, of course, a great advantage for marketers. The series maintained its popularity until Jordan's death in 2007, and will now be continued and completed posthumously by another writer, Brandon Sanderson.

(The greatest fantasy success of the new century was, of course, J. K. Rowling's *Harry Potter* series, the most successful novels yet published. However, these were marketed outside of the fantasy genre; they were initially marketed as young adult novels, especially by their American publisher, Scholastic Books. An explosion of fantasy targeted at young adult readers followed Rowling's success; the degree to which it persists and reshapes the fantasy genre will be interesting to watch over the next few years.)

While genre fantasy may still dominate the market, the fantastic in literature is healthy and growing in America. There are signs that the dominance of the genre by the bestselling, intensively marketed books, while it prevails, does provide a publishing home and a supportive audience for writers and for unusual works of quality, otherwise unsupported by fashion. As a mass-market phenomenon, the fantasy field can perhaps be understood as protectively covering a small body of work that is experimenting successfully with unfashionable techniques and subject matter that is ignored or rejected by the general literary culture of our time. And now it seems is a bad time for serious adult readers to reject, wholesale, the tale of wonder and the illumination of the human condition that fantasy has brought us throughout history.

David G. Hartwell lives in Pleasantville, New York. This essay is revised and expanded from "Dollars and Dragons: The Truth about Fantasy" in his Age of Wonders, *second edition, 1995.*

SECRET

THE HISTORY

OF FANTASY